Love always,
WILD

A.M. JOHNSON

Cover Design: E. James Designs
Editing: Elaine York, Allusion Publishing
www.allusionpublishing.com
Proofreading: Kathleen, Payne Proofing

Love always,
WILD

TO THOSE AFRAID TO COME OUT, TO SPEAK UP,
TO SIMPLY BE IN YOUR OWN SKIN, THERE'S AN ENTIRE COMMUNITY
AND FAMILY WAITING FOR YOU WITH OPEN ARMS.
YOU WILL BE LOVED. YOU ARE WORTHY OF IT.

For

Gwen, you're an inspiration,
and Braxton, for teaching me
about the world of dragons...

"There's some good in this world,
Mr. Frodo. And it's worth fighting for."
—Sam Wise

The Two Towers
By J.R.R Tolkien

Prologue

WILDER

Then

"*Oh God,*" *he muttered breathless against my mouth. His teeth digging into my bottom lip as his fingers wrapped into my hair. The sticky heat of his release coated my stomach, the decadent weight of his body hovering over mine, the taut line of his jaw, the deep crease in his brow, he was trembling. Nothing had ever been this perfect.*

"Loser."

The word tore me from my private memory. Just another daily dose from the homophobic pricks who wished they could change me, fit me into some box that didn't challenge their own masculinity. That sound. Their laughter. The joy. It was a deep darkness and it filled all the fucking space between me and them. I couldn't connect with these assholes. I couldn't feel that sunshine, that full-blown, goddamn light that poured in from the hallway windows. I tried to catch it with my fingers, but it was translucent as if I didn't exist. Maybe to them I shouldn't exist.

I was a ghost.

I hated that they'd made me feel like this. Like I was worthless, and as the marching band played down the hall, practicing for tomorrow's game, I found myself alone. A silent laugh trapped itself inside my throat as I thought about what I'd done. What we'd done this morning. How maybe I'd gone and screwed up everything. I lowered my eyes to the yellowed pages of my book, Tolkien's *Fellowship of the Ring.* I'd read it a thousand times, and it was usually a distraction, but as my eyes scanned the familiar words, my nervous fingers toyed with the shreds of denim surrounding my right knee. The cold of the concrete hallway floor seeped through to my spine, the hard wall pressing through my thin cotton t-shirt. The sentences blurred and curled as the passersby, the sheep, whispered about me, as I thought about him. You'd think being in college the high school dynamic would've faded, but when you're the outcast, the openly gay kid at Eastchester University, even the simple act of reading in a hallway drew attention.

The corners of my lips tipped into a frown as I thought about what he'd said this morning. On his way out of my dorm room, blond hair disheveled with sex, cheeks blotched with pink, his green eyes pooled with confusion and clouded with his recent orgasm. I thought about how he'd be running across the basketball court about now. His smile wide, his full, broad shoulders tan, exposed in his uniform. He'd be gorgeous as always, and he'd have the taste of me still on his lips.

"No one can know, Wild. No one."

I was a secret, an illusion, but he was in my bones, every slight, every snicker, and every trace of his fingertips on my skin. I'd let him take me and discard me. It wasn't ideal, but I'd let him in knowing the consequences. The hazards of falling for the wrong guy. For Jaxon Stettler. All-American Jock. Closeted and unavailable. The same guy I'd crushed on since freshman year, tutored chemistry to all of our sophomore year, and finally, after those two years of longing, I'd gotten what I'd always wanted. Him. I closed my eyes and my thoughts drifted back to this morning.

The tang of his citrus body wash tickled my nose as I lowered my eyes back to the book in front of me. His scent was a punishment. A way the universe had found to torture me for my thoughts. He was straight, and I wanted him.

I'd studied him more tonight than the books I'd brought to tutor him. I'd noticed when he was frustrated or confused, he'd suck on his bottom lip. God, it was a beautiful lip. Soft and kissable. And the way his forehead turned into angry creases when I'd tell him he had the answer wrong. Even when he was in full-blown, self-doubt, crisis mode, he was stunning. It's how he looked when he played basketball. Stern and focused and slightly ready to stab you. Call me twisted, but it was sexy. My favorite thing, though, was the way the left corner of his mouth lifted when he got the answer right. It was like a ton of bricks had fallen off his shoulders and his hard lines melted into this spectacular sideway smirk just for me. His crystal green eyes would light up, and I'd see something special I was sure he never allowed most people to see.

That thought brought my gaze to the thick mop of blond hair that fell into his eyes. He chewed his bottom lip as he poured over the notes I'd written along the side of his chem homework. The semester was halfway over, and I couldn't believe my luck, or maybe it was a curse, that Jaxon Stettler was bent over a textbook in my dorm after midnight. He was oblivious to my watching eyes, but I wondered if he'd ever noticed my ogling before. If he'd ever wondered what I was thinking, like I wondered about him.

He groaned and let his face fall into his hands. "It's late, I should go."

"Or you could stay?"

Jax lifted his head, his green eyes dark in the dim light of the desk lamp. "You up for an all-nighter?"

"Will it help you pass?" I asked, my smile more for me. Having Jax in my room all night was a fantasy I'd love to live through. I was one of the lucky ones who'd scored a single this year.

The air in the room thickened as his eyes flicked to my mouth for the briefest of seconds.

He nodded. "I sure as hell hope so."

When I'd asked him to stay, I never could have dreamt up what would happen the next morning. Part of me was glad for it, but the more sensible, less masochist side of me knew this would never work. I wanted him.

I exhaled a shaky breath and whispered to myself, "Yeah, but at what cost?"

The gym doors opened at precisely the time they did every Tuesday, and when the hall filled with booming bravado I stood and closed my book. A couple of guys from the team stared at me as they passed, their eyes wide and wondering. Their expression twisted like they smelled something funny. I ran my fingers through my loose, jet-black waves, let it flop over my forehead, and ·obscure my eyes, my fear. I wasn't afraid of them, more of what they'd see when I looked at Jax. Because even though he ran out on me this morning, we'd shared something. And maybe he wasn't ready to broadcast it, but that didn't have to mean he didn't care.

"I'll be ready in twenty," Jax said, his green eyes igniting me, making all the empty space in my stomach, the hollow, disappear.

One of his friends shoved his shoulder from behind. "Look, it's your boyfriend."

Jaxon's eyes narrowed enough I noticed, his Adam's apple working as he swallowed. Anyone else would've missed his anxious glance in my direction. But I hadn't, and the warmth from this morning's memory spoiled in my throat.

"Fuck you, Carson," I crooned with a staged smirk.

"You wish fa—"

"Wilder." Jax blurted my name, interrupting the bigoted asshat he called a friend, and my heart tripped. "You got those notes from Professor Stark like I asked?"

"Amino acids? Sure did." I licked my lips and his eyes fell to my mouth. I ignored it. Leaning over, I grabbed my book bag. "I'll be at the carrel when you're ready?"

Carson eyed me, the hate turning his brown eyes black before he turned and headed toward the locker room. Jax lingered behind, his team long gone.

"Can we study at your place today?" he whispered, and the husky vibration of his voice rattled my resolve.

I was a glutton, and all I wanted to do was gorge myself on him. On the way he made the hair on the back of my neck rise. How without even touching me, I ached for him.

I shrugged my shoulders, holding onto my pride. I needed to hear him say it. "If that's what you want, Jax."

He took a step closer, his head turning once to the right and then left. Once he surmised we had some privacy, he leaned in and his breath dusted my lips. My mouth watered as he whispered, "It's what I want."

When he walked away, his scent, a musky citrus, surrounded me. I closed my eyes and forgot how vacant I'd felt when he'd practically ran out on me this morning, and chose to only remember his sated smile, his real words. *"I've never allowed myself to feel this good."* I remembered, even if sometimes I was treated like a ghost, I was somebody... somebody to him.

A little over thirty minutes later, Jax met me at my dorm, and was now treating me to the usual incessant tap-tap-tap of his foot. He was keyed up. Our hookup this morning, a silent weight between us. His chemistry midterm, a perfect deflection. I didn't want to be that guy, though. The guy who took any chance to sit as close as possible to him. Close enough I could smell his sporty-smelling deodorant and the chocolate on his breath. There were about seven balled-up silver foils on my desk. Hershey's Kisses. Jax's drug of choice. I had to admit I loved how he always smelled like chocolate... tasted like it too.

"I don't fucking get it." He stood, only to drop his six-foot-four frame dramatically onto my full-size mattress.

"Are you even paying attention?" I raised my eyebrows when he growled.

The sound sent a stampede of goosebumps across my neck and arms.

"Who gives a shit about bio-chem?"

I chuckled. "I'm pretty sure every pharmacy program you're going to apply to."

His breathing deepened into the silence. His chest sinking and then rising in slow beats that made my heart sprint.

"It's not going to happen," he whispered, and my stomach fell. "Shit... I give up. I'll never be him, Wild..." He exhaled and raised his muscled arm to cover his eyes. "I'll never be him." He spoke so quiet, I didn't think the words were meant for me.

I stood from the chair I'd been perched on for an hour and a half and sat on the bed. The mattress joggled his big body and he lowered his arm. Sea green eyes met mine and I almost forgot to breathe.

"Then, be you, Jax."

His expression darkened. "My dad has certain expectations."

"Yeah, so did mine. And I told him to fuck off. I'm gay and he hates it, but he deals. And yours will too. It just takes time. I know my parents love me, it's fear that makes them say stupid shit."

He laughed without humor. "My dad's gonna kick my ass when I tell him I'm failing bio-chem, there's no way in hell I'm telling him my life has been a total lie, that I'm..."

"Gay, Jax. Just say it."

His defiant eyes softened when he heard the crack in my voice. He lifted his fingers and trailed them over the thin muscles of my forearm.

"I don't want to think about this shit right now." I shivered as his finger curled into the fabric of my shirt. "Come here."

I should've said no. Of course, I should have. But I could feel my pulse in my fingertips, hear my heart in my ears as he leaned up onto his elbow. His gray t-shirt stretched tight across his broad shoulders. His biceps etched into triceps I wanted to touch. His skin was smooth and tan, and when he wet his lips, something in my brain misfired. I knew better, but Jaxon Stettler made me stupid.

Inching closer, he smiled, and the dimple I craved popped in his right cheek. "Fucking kiss me already, Wild. Make everything good like you do."

His words stabbed me, made my ribs feel small as the butterflies fought their way from my stomach to the gaping hole. I wanted to be more than an easy distraction. I made him feel good. Feel something other than fear and self-doubt. Hell yeah, I'd kiss him. I'd do everything I could to make that smile permanent.

Our mouths met in a crash of lips, teeth, and tongue. Jax didn't do soft. He was rough on the basketball court, rough with everyone who knew him, and his kisses were just as brutal. But my favorite part was when he'd slow the burn of his kiss. He'd take and take and take, and then soothe with soft brushes of lips and fingertips. I liked to think those gentle lips, and touches, his sweet tastes, were only for me.

My eyes flashed to the bulge in his jeans as I leaned back to catch a breath. My right palm skimmed the denim. He let me unbutton him, unzip him until he was heavy in my hand.

"Fuck," he moaned as he raised his hips, pushing his dick into my fist.

His head fell back as I applied more pressure. I admired the long expanse of his neck, the strain in his muscles as I stroked once and then again before leaning down and licking the crown of his cock. Salty and masculine. My left hand combed through the soft golden hairs at his shaft, and my hard-on pushed against the denim of my jeans. The way he shivered, how he fell back onto the bed, offering himself to me, my need for release, the throbbing pain was almost unbearable. I took his thick length all the way to the back of my throat as strong hands cradled my head, his fingers twisting into the short strands of hair at the nape of my neck. He pumped his hips, fucking my mouth, and I groaned around the head. The muscle in his jaw clenched with every suck, every slow lick, but I let him control the pace.

His fierce eyes found mine as I came up for air. Jaxon sat up and grabbed my waist with a powerful grip, rolling my lean body with ease until he was on top of me. He took off his shirt and helped me pull mine over my head. Just like this morning, his hands shook as he unbuttoned my jeans. I folded my fingers into his hair, pulling him to me. Skin to skin, I pressed my lips to his as he grasped our dicks with his hand. He worked us both at the same time until our hips found a hard rhythm, and our tongues pulsed and danced to it as well.

Jaxon's sweet tongue was on my lips, my jaw. His teeth dragging across my ear lobe. He grunted, deep and low, as he brought us closer. Everything bottomed out when our eyes opened, and he spilled his secrets onto my chest and stomach. His hips twitched and he kissed me as I came just a few seconds later. He smiled, lazy, and his body spent, fell heavily onto mine. I drowned in the feel of him, the heaviness and how it pinned me, grounded me, in the perfect mess we'd made.

The heat of his breath on my neck, his mouth sneaking tastes of my skin, he said, "Every day..." He braced himself with his hands on either side of my head. "I'm hiding from something, someone, and with you... even if it's only for an afternoon, I get to just... be me." Something big bloomed in his eyes, the pupils eclipsing the green. "I'm not ready to face some shit, but I know one thing."

I held his face between my hands, and his jaw ticked against my palm.

"What's that?" I asked.

"I don't want to lose you."

Chapter 1

WILDER

Present Day

It didn't matter how many times I saw the number. I couldn't believe it. Number three. I stared at the screen, read the headline over and over. *Atlanta's Own Wilder Welles Soars Straight to the Top with His Debut Release.* Busy chatter and the whir of a coffee grinder blended into white noise. The familiar sounds offered me no rope to hold. I was lifted, and my heart, the smile on my face, couldn't be contained.

"I told you, Wilder. I knew it the minute you let me read your story. I knew you would be a hit." Anders knocked his knuckles on the table. "Are you listening to me?"

"Don't make this about you," I said, sipping the last dredges of my latte as I closed my laptop.

"I'm not. I'm simply saying—"

"That you're the one who got me the deal. Therefore, you deserve some credit. Yeah, I think I know you pretty well by now, Andi."

He cringed, setting his Americano down on the table. "Ugh, don't call me that in public."

A content grin settled across my lips. "Only in bed, then?"

"We *should* celebrate. It's not every day a debut author makes it to number three on *The New York Times* best seller list."

I leaned across the table. "Are we still playing games, then?"

"Only if you want to." Anders' smug smile faded as a flash of vulnerability crossed his pale blue eyes. "It's been awhile."

"It's unprofessional to sleep with your client," I reminded him.

Anders and I had an on-again, off-again relationship. I'd met him while working as a copy editor at Bartley Press a few years ago. He was smart, cocky, and sexy as hell in a suit. One thing led to another, and by another, I meant dinner, movie, and blow jobs. We've been friends with benefits ever since. Lately, our relationship had become more for him, he'd become too invested in me and in my writing career. But I couldn't give him what he wanted. Trust was something I struggled with, something I didn't give to men who I was involved with sexually. Sex was a release. A need to fill. Anders Lowe was a top literary agent, and I was a means to an end for him. An author who needed representation. Not that I'd slept my way into a contract. It wasn't until after I'd published a few pieces in *The New Yorker* that I'd signed with him. He'd said I had a big future in publishing. I hadn't believed a word of it. Turns out I was wrong.

He lowered his voice, serious he said, "You mean more to me than that."

My reply stuck in my throat. Anders ran his fingers through his blond hair, the light catching the golden strands in a way that reminded me of *him*. Of Jax. The only guy I'd ever loved. The only guy I'd ever hated. Jax was the perpetual ghost that haunted me.

"Don't."

"Don't what? Wilder... get another agent." He reached across the table and rested his hand on mine. "I'm serious about you. About us."

"You only say that because I'm a *New York Times* bestselling author now," I joked and pulled my hand out from under his. "I'm money in your pocket."

He didn't laugh. The vein in his forehead pulsed. I'd pissed him off. "You always push me away."

"I'm..."

"Fucked up, I know. I read your story. Remember? I pitched the damn thing. He's dead, Wilder. It's been nine years. When are you going to let him go?" He didn't know the truth. When I didn't answer, he sighed and reached into his bag. Anders handed me a book. My book. "Open it."

Looking at my name on the dust jacket of a book was surreal. The cover was deep red, the font slightly raised. This was my book. My story. My words painted across paper, my heart splattered out for the whole damn world to see. To judge, to own in their personal interpretation. The title, always a knife to the chest, taunted me.

Love Always, Wild.

This was my true story with a fictionalized twist. That's how I'd sold it. A world inspired by true events.

Where I was wanted and loved but left behind by death. I'd changed Jax's name, and instead of it being an autobiography, I'd turned a huge chunk of my life into fiction. The lie worked for me. I'd told myself he'd died because it was better than the alternative. The truth? In our junior year at Eastchester University, he'd left for winter break after we'd gotten into a fight about him coming out to his parents without me. I'd wanted to be there as a support, but he'd said his father would probably kill us both, that he didn't want me to get hurt.

Hurt.

In the end, Jax's dad hadn't been the one to wound me, it'd been Jax himself. He'd left and never came back to campus. Never answered one of my calls or texts. I'd worried myself sick. So sick I'd almost failed out of school. What had happened? Where had he gone? Jax Stettler had disappeared. None of his shithead friends had known anything, and it'd made it worse that Jax had deleted the two social media accounts he'd barely used anyway. The only information I'd gotten was from the registration office. He'd withdrawn. He'd never told me the address to his parents' house in Florida, and the school wouldn't give it to me either. The darkest days of my life were locked inside my dorm room walls back in North Carolina. I'd tried to write the truth, that I hadn't mattered to him, that I almost lost myself once, but this part of me, morbid and cold, wondered if he might've died. Or maybe I wished for it. I had no closure. Nine years later, and I still couldn't stomach the taste of chocolate.

"Don't just stare at it, open it, for Christ's sake." Anders opened the book for me, and I smiled when I saw all the signatures. "Everyone at Bartley signed it."

I ran my thumb over one of the signatures. The letter B curled brazen and big on the page. I looked up at Anders in surprise.

He chuckled, and I let the sound of it erase the memories of Jax, at least for now. "Even Mr. Bartley himself."

"I thought he was in the Hamptons until August?" I asked.

"I have my ways."

I shut the book, and Anders's smile warmed the lingering cold of my past. "This is amazing."

"Very true. I am pretty amazing." He stood and grabbed his bag. "I have to meet with a client." He hesitated and squared his shoulders. "Look, I'm asking you as your agent... Have dinner with me tonight?"

"To celebrate our success."

"Your success. To celebrate you, Wilder."

"Want to try that new place we've been eyeing near Piedmont? I'll bring June."

He lowered his eyes, focusing on anything but me. He was disappointed.

"She's my best friend."

He raised his arm and looked at his watch. "I better get going. Eight o'clock work for you?"

"I'll have to text June, but I think that should work." I stood, picking up my laptop and shoved it into its case. "I'll walk you to your car. I don't think I'll be able to get any writing done today anyway."

The summer air hit us like a brick as we left the coffee shop. It was ninety degrees today. The clouds hovered like large castles above the city, their gray linings threatening rain and filling the air with a wet heaviness that I despised and irrationally adored. I reached for Anders's hand and he let me hold it with a small shake of his head.

"You are the most confusing guy I've ever known. You know that?"

I tugged on his arm and he pulled me into his side. He was taller than me only by a few inches, and I liked how easy this was, how easy I fit alongside him. I never really seemed to fit anywhere else, not in a long time.

"Thank you," I said. "I couldn't have done any of this without you."

Anders slowed his pace as his car came into view. He released me, only to grip his hands on my waist. He was silent for two, three long seconds before he kissed my forehead. His lips had always been too soft.

"Yes, you could have. You're brilliant. I'm just a salesman."

He let go of me, pulling his keys from his pants pocket. His BMW chirped twice. "See you at eight."

I wished I could get in his car, tell him to cancel his appointment, and come home with me. I wished I could give him my hands, my skin—my mouth. I wanted to be capable of loving him more than I loved what could have been. I thought about the story I wrote, the book about the boys who fell in love with each other despite the odds, only to be ripped apart by the permanence of dirt and worms. I wished for a tombstone to visit. Maybe then I could see beyond the wall built by nine years of what ifs.

A loud clap of thunder warned me I was too late, and the sky opened with fat, cool drops that soaked the sidewalk. I held my bag to my chest and ran under the nearest awning. My hair dripped down my cheeks and I laughed as I noticed one of those old metal newspaper boxes by the front door of the shop. A local arts magazine sat on top of it with a face on the cover. My face. Flat brown eyes stared back at me from the page. Another headline. *Love Always, Wild Debuts at Number Three.* I could try to wish him away, but the fact remained, that without him, without the pain of Jax, this success, this story might have never been.

I pulled my phone from my pocket and opened my contacts list.

The phone rang three times before he answered. "Miss me already?"

"June can't make it," I lied.

"Oh…" I heard his intake of breath. "Do you want to reschedule?"

The rainwater poured off the awning in reverberant sheets. A car horn honked somewhere in the distance, and the outline of the book he'd given me pressed against my hip through my satchel. I had to leave Jax there, leave him in Eastchester, leave him as ink and paper and pen. Time wouldn't stand still, not for me, not for Anders, and not for Jax.

"No."

"Just me and you, then?" he asked.

"Yeah… I guess it is."

Chapter 2

JAX

"Come on, Jason, we have to go," I said, picking up the beach towel and shaking out the sand.

The small, salty grains stuck to my bare chest as the wind chilled the air. The thunderheads above had moved in about ten minutes ago, and if we didn't start packing up, we'd get stuck in the storm.

"Aw, Jax. Can I have a few more minutes?" Jason shielded his eyes from the dimming summer sun as he looked at me. "It's almost exactly how I want it."

"I don't think Mother Nature is gonna wait, buddy."

My little brother let the heavy clumps of sand drip through his fingers as he got back to work on his sandcastle. I had to admit he was pretty good at this shit. The lady who'd been eye-fucking me all day stared at our interaction. She looked confused, and it pissed me off even though I was used to it. But if I were in her shoes, I might've stared too. People in Bell River already knew my story. Jason's story. The disrespectful glances that led to full-on gawking only happened when we ventured outside the safety of our small town.

A flash of lightning lit up the sky, and my brother jumped to his feet. He slammed his hands over his ears and started hollering. I swore under my breath and grabbed the buckets, leaving the shovels to fend for themselves.

"It's just lightning, Jay."

I tried to talk to him like the adult that he was. I always tried to give him that much. But when your brain was stuck at a fifth-grade level, I supposed lightning was one of the scariest things in the world. It didn't help matters much it'd been storming the night everything in our lives imploded. Another crack of thunder, and Jason ran for the car. Maybe nine years ago I would've laughed at him, called him a pussy or something equally offensive. But things had changed the day my dad decided to drive drunk.

"Hold up," I called as I ran after him.

The car was unlocked, and he practically threw himself into the passenger seat. Laughing, I opened the driver-side door. "You're lucky this car is a piece of shit, Jay. You got sand everywhere."

"Mom says it's unchristian to swear." He blinked his big blue eyes as the rain started to pummel the windshield.

I shoved the key into the ignition and turned it. Nothing happened. "Goddamn it." Slamming my hand onto the dashboard, I swore again, instantly regretting my behavior as Jason curled in on himself. "I'm sorry... I didn't mean to scare you." He wouldn't look at me. "I'm sorry, okay." Taking a deep breath, I held up my hands. "See... calm as a cucumber."

He chuckled, and I knew I'd fixed it. "Cucumbers are gross."

"I guess that means I'm gross too."

"Why *do* you swear so much?" he asked, clipping his seatbelt into place.

I turned the key again and the engine clicked a few times. "Just start already," I grumbled to myself, ignoring his question. After a few more tries I exhaled and shoved an angry hand through my hair. "Because... Jay," I finally answered. "Sometimes... people got all kinds of bad stuff inside them, and it's hard to hide it. Sometimes people are mean and sometimes they swear."

"But you're not mean or bad."

"You're just saying that 'cause you're my kid brother."

His innocence was probably the only good thing his accident had left behind. He didn't know the bad things inside of me. No one did. I closed my eyes as *his* name flooded my brain. *Wilder.* I've never loved something more dangerous than Wild. And I never would again. That chapter in my life was a history I couldn't ever bring to light. The feelings I had for him were wrong, no matter how much I wanted to deny it. What we'd done, even if it was out of love, was wrong. My father's death, the accident, taught me that. I'd been told my whole life that sinners would be judged. That punishment was a grace of God showing you the way of the Lord when you strayed too far from His path. I never used to believe, and maybe I still didn't, but it was the only thing I had left to hold on to. My junior year of college I'd fallen in love with a guy. A guy who saw sides of me I'd learned to lock up tight. Wilder was everything to me. Everything. Hell, I'd almost brought him home with me over that winter break. I'd wanted my parents to see how happy I was, and maybe then they wouldn't hate the idea of having a gay son. I'd wanted to come out to them the day before Christmas because I figured you couldn't hate anyone on Christ's birthday. But that chance had been stolen by a six pack of beer and a late afternoon storm.

Dad and Jason had gone fishing, and like always, my dad drank too much. Jason had just gotten his license that year, but there was no way in hell Dad would have let him drive his precious Cadillac. He took a corner too fast, crashed the car down the embankment into Bell River. They'd said my dad died on impact because he wasn't wearing a seatbelt. Jason had been submerged under water for at least five minutes. They'd had to bring him back to life. When Mom and I got to the hospital, they wouldn't let us see him at first. To this day, I could feel the ache of the hard, cold hospital floor on my knees, and on some days, hear the Christmas songs that had played softly over the hospital intercom speakers. Mom and I had prayed that night. I'd asked God to bring my brother home. I promised I'd be better. If He'd just give me Jason, I could let go of Wilder. The course of our lives had been irrevocably altered that night. Jason had what they'd called an anoxic brain injury. Because he'd been without air for so long in the water, his brain had started to die. He used to be better than me at playing basketball, got good grades too, had his sights set on Duke University. Now he was a twenty-five-year-old who made sandcastles, and I couldn't get my fucking car to start.

"Stay here, I'll be back in a second," I said as I leaned down and pulled the handle under the dash to pop open the hood of the car.

The rain had dissipated a little, but I was soaked by the time I rounded the front end of my well-used Hyundai. The battery was coated with an orange-tinged crust that I tried to pick off with my thumb and finger.

"Jax? That you?"

I startled and almost hit my head on the damn hood. Ethan Calloway rolled down his passenger-side window and smiled at me like I was the best thing he'd seen all day. Guy was weird if you asked me. He was always too nice to me. People usually avoided me. For one, I was kind of a dick. And two, what were people supposed to say to a guy who was almost thirty, living at home with his mom, working a shit construction job, and dated a girl who only stuck around out of charity. My life had stalled at twenty when I dropped out of college to help my mom. People can sense it, that hopelessness, it sticks to you like shit on a shoe.

"Hey, Ethan."

"Need some help?" he asked, pulling his car closer.

"You don't happen to have any jumper cables in there, do you?"

His nose crinkled as he bit his bottom lip. "I don't, but I can give you and Jason a ride back to town?"

I stared at him, unsure. I didn't know him all that well. He worked at Harley's, the hardware store that neighbored my dad's old pharmacy. When I first started at JW Construction he hadn't worked there, they'd only hired him a year ago. The guys at work didn't like him. Said he was too much of a pansy to work at Harley's. I'd never noticed. It was a habit I had when dealing with men. I never looked too closely. And to be fair, the guys I worked with called everyone a pansy for one reason or another.

"I promise I'm not a serial killer." He smiled, and his cheeks pinked when I laughed.

"Even if you were, it's better than standing in the rain waiting for a tow truck. Let me grab a few things?"

"Sure."

He rolled up the window as I shut the hood. When I opened the door, Jason asked, "Is he gonna give us a ride?"

"He is, buddy."

"That's lucky," he said, and I saw a glimmer of the sixteen-year-old I used to know.

I had to clear my throat to speak. "Grab a few towels from the back, alright? I don't want to ruin his seats."

Jason grabbed two extra towels and handed them to me. He reached for his sand buckets, but I stopped him. "Let's leave those. I'll come back later with Mom when it stops raining, see if I can jump the car, if not, I promise to get your buckets."

"Don't forget."

"I promise and when I promise..."

"You mean it." His smile swelled.

"That's right, Jay. You ready now?"

We both made a run for Ethan's car. I opened the back door for Jason, laying the slightly damp towel over the cloth seats.

"Don't worry about that. Get in before you get struck by lightning." Ethan took the towel I'd tried to lay on the front seat from my hand and threw it toward the back. Jason caught it with a chuckle, wrapping it around his bare shoulders. "This is a Toyota, not a Porsche."

"Thanks," I said and shut the passenger-side door. "For giving us a ride."

"I was headed home, it's not even a big deal, and if you want, I think I might have a shirt back there somewhere, but it's probably too small for you."

Jason reached over my shoulder and handed me a green t-shirt. "That's okay, I'm—"

"It's fine, Jax. I don't mind." Ethan lifted his gaze.

I allowed myself to notice his brown eyes. They were a coppery sort of brown, light and warm. The type of eyes I would have loved to get lost in. My breath caught in my throat at the thought. I clenched my jaw and turned toward the windshield to pull on the shirt. It smelled like beach and salt, with a hint of men's soap. My Adam's apple bobbed uncomfortably in my throat.

"Fit okay?" he asked as he drove out of the parking lot.

It was too tight. I was taller and had way more muscle than Ethan, but I lied and nodded my head. "It works," I said and snapped my seatbelt in place.

The storm had gotten worse by the time we'd hit the highway. I could feel Jason's knee bouncing against the back of my seat. Music usually helped him during weather like this. The stereo was on, but the volume was too low. If I hadn't been paying attention, I would have missed what was playing. "Is this 'Group Love'?"

Ethan hit a button on his steering wheel, and the familiar song spilled through the speakers. "I love this song," he said.

The scratchy vocals, the pop beat, I couldn't stop my fingers from tapping on my knee. "I forgot how much I liked this song."

"Turn it up," Jason called from the back, and Ethan obliged.

The lyrics filled the car, the sound of it pushing my heart into an unsteady rhythm. When Ethan started to sing along, I almost did too. He drummed his hands on the steering wheel, looking over at me with a wide grin. I gave him a smile of my own and my cheeks ached with it. I couldn't remember the last time I'd felt like this, unworried and light, but as the song came to an end, the feeling faded with it.

Ethan lowered the volume as a song I didn't recognize began to play. "I knew you weren't always so grumpy," he teased.

"You don't know me all that well," I said, more annoyed than I'd meant to sound.

I hated that I was such an asshole. I hated that I couldn't be happy, singing in a car, with a friend and my brother. I'd paid my price, hadn't I? When would it be my turn at happiness? I caught a glimpse of Jason in the rearview mirror and regretted the selfish thoughts.

"I'd like to." Ethan kept his eyes on the road as he turned right onto Bell River Road. "Get to know you better."

"Me and the guys from work shoot hoops sometimes over at the park. You're always welcome to join us." The words tumbled out of my mouth before I thought better of it. The guys hated him, and I didn't need or want any friends. My girlfriend Mary was enough to contend with. I shouldn't have invited him.

"I'm not much of a ball player," he said, and Jason laughed.

"Nope. You were always the worst."

"Jason," I admonished. "That's not a nice thing to say."

Ethan's laugh was as warm as his eyes. "It's okay, he's right." He glanced into his rearview. "Though I'm surprised he remembers that..." Ethan's smile paled. "With the accident and everything."

No one ever brought up the accident. Everyone dribbled around it like Michael Jordan against a defensive line.

"I'm sorry," he said so only I could hear. "I shouldn't have—"

"No, you shouldn't... but it's kind of... I don't know... refreshing? Maybe that's not the right word... Everyone treats him like glass. He's stronger than that."

"You know Jason and I were in class together?"

I looked at Ethan again, but this time I assessed him in a way I normally would have given myself shit for. He was young but easily could've been around Jason's age. His face was not familiar to me, not beyond Harley's, at least. And why would it be? I was in college when he was a freshman in high school.

"I didn't."

"If I may..." He paused. "I think it's awful what happened... But I think what you did... was pretty selfless.

To stay home like you did. Not too many people would've done that. I think you're brave."

His regard irritated me. I wasn't selfless. I was the most selfish person in this fucking car. The things I'd done, the things I still wanted had brought a wrathful misery to my family. At least that's what I'd thought for so long. Lately, though, I'd begun to wonder if there was really even a god at all, and if there was, why would He hurt me like that. Being with a man was a sin, but love... how was that a sin? I had to push the thought away. It didn't make a difference anymore.

"I did what I had to do to help my family, it's not about bravery."

The old oak trees by my house came into view. They stood out against the gray of the storm, the leaves were a canopy over our roof, bleeding green down the shingles and white siding. Ethan's Toyota rolled to a stop at the end of our long, gravel driveway.

"Thanks Ethan," Jason said as he burst from the back seat, laughing and running through the rain toward the front door.

"I really appreciate it. It would've sucked to be stuck out in this shit waiting for a jump." I gripped the door handle and Ethan touched my shoulder.

"I think I might've said something I shouldn't. I do that. It's a bad habit when I'm nervous. And your..." He pressed his lips together, hiding a smile. "I ramble and I.... I just... I'm sorry I said anything, about..."

"No need for an apology." When I stepped out of the car, I forced a smile. Leaning down, I said, "I'll get this shirt back to you on Monday when I come by Harley's for supplies."

"Keep it." He waved me off with an anxious laugh. "It looks better on you anyway."

"It's almost a full size too small."

He smirked. "Exactly."

I didn't know what he was playing at, but I didn't need his shirt or his charitable smiles. I took it off, and the cold drops of rain lifted the bare skin on my chest into a thousand goosebumps. I shivered as I reached in and handed him the shirt.

"Thanks again for the ride."

I shut the door before he could say anything else and walked toward the house. I slowed, stopping before I went inside, and let the rain wash away the rest of his scent. I didn't need his damn shirt or his smell on my skin.

Chapter 3

JAX

With sweat dripping down my back from a long day of framing in the Florida summer sun, I pushed off my work boots by the back door. Mom and Jay sat at the small, four-seat table in the corner by the stove, snapping green beans, my mother's favorite honky-tonk station playing from the old radio she kept on the kitchen counter. Like most houses in the South, blessed with enough money for an air conditioner, ours was like a freezer compared to the sweltering, humid heat outside. My damp shirt stuck to my skin, and I shivered like the ugly, white lace curtains that hung over the kitchen window under the vent.

"You just gonna stand there all day? I got potatoes that need peeling."

I shook my head and chuckled. "Hey, Momma." I leaned down and kissed her cheek before messing up Jason's hair.

"Don't," he whined, his usual humor trapped behind a scowl. "I'm not a little kid."

Guilt expelled from my lungs with a sigh. "I know, I was just playing." I noticed the green beans were almost overflowing from the bowl. "What's all this for?" I asked, picking up a bean and popping it into my mouth.

Mom swatted my leg. "You're a filthy mess, Jaxon Stettler. Go wash up and come help with dinner."

"Dinner?" A large bag of potatoes was cut open, laying on the counter. That's when I noticed the oven light was on. "I told you this morning, Momma. I'm going out with Mary tonight."

"I remember," she said, raising her eyebrow, giving a pointed stare to my little brother as he snickered. "I just think... and hear me out, Jax, before you get all... dramatic." She snapped the last green bean, wiped her hands on her apron, and stood. My mother wasn't necessarily a small woman. She was on the taller side, but she was thin as a rail. Even so, she scared me sometimes. "I think it's high time I met the girl my boy has been out messing around with. You know, Mrs. Sinclair said she saw y'all kissing over at the park last Monday when you were supposed to be playing basketball with those boys you work with."

"Jesus Christ, Mom, last time I checked, I was a grown man. You don't need to be keeping tabs on me."

"*Jaxon,*" she gasped, like I was Satan himself coming to take her to Hell. "You do *not* use the Lord's name in vain in this house. I taught you better than that."

"Yes, ma'am, you did." Next week was my thirtieth birthday, but today I was that small boy standing in the kitchen with my head down, wishing I wasn't such a disappointment. "I'm sorry."

She exhaled a long breath and sat down at the table. Her blue eyes seemed tired. "I don't want you wasting your time, thinking you need to be taking care of me or Jason. You gotta start living your life. This girl Mary... I hear she's a good girl, and God knows there aren't enough of them around here that haven't already been married or got themselves pregnant. Now, go get yourself cleaned up and call that girlfriend of yours." She waved me off. "Just tell her plans changed and invite her to meet your momma like the good son I raised you to be." The smile she gave me was like a wood gavel in the courtroom. Case closed.

I wasn't serious about Mary. I wasn't serious about anyone. I hated lying to my family, to myself, but it was easier to fake it. To pretend that kissing Mary was it for me, that when we were alone and naked in a way that should mean something, that I actually wanted to be there, that it was more than just fucking around. But it wasn't. This was me, keeping my end of the bargain with God, and I was bone tired of it.

When I looked at my little brother, tapping his foot to the music, I told myself it wasn't about me. "What time should I tell Mary I'll pick her up?"

"Six seems reasonable." She smiled and winked at Jason.

I left the room to get cleaned up, stripping my sawdust-covered clothes into the laundry hamper by the linen closet in the bathroom. I turned on the shower, and before getting in, I thought about the text I needed to send to Mary. This dinner needed to sound as casual as possible. This was not some come-meet-the-parents-let's-bring-our-relationship-to-the-next-level   bullshit.

We'd met at a bar last year. I'd gone home with her that night because I'd gotten shit-faced with Chuck and Hudson after work. I didn't usually drink that often because of what happened with my dad. The night I'd met Mary, I'd been feeling in some sort of way. Isolated and alone. Chuck had given me a ration of shit about how I'd never had a girl coming around that he could remember, made some homophobic remark, and of course I'd had to prove to him he was wrong about me. Or maybe I'd been trying to prove it to myself. Mary had been the closest target. She was small, blonde, big tits, and curvy hips. The absolute opposite of what I liked. An image of Wild, long with lean, cut muscle stretched under pale skin against his gray sheets assaulted me. I closed my eyes and let the blood pump through me as I thought about our last night together. The last chance I'd had to be me. I didn't think about the fight we'd gotten in, or how angry he'd been when I left. Right now, as I gripped the edge of the counter with one hand, and my dick with the other, all I wanted to think about was Wild and how good he always made me feel.

"Can we talk about it later?" I asked, pulling my shirt over my head, and throwing it onto the floor. Tomorrow I left for winter break. Four weeks without Wild. I didn't think I'd be able to handle it. Standing in just my underwear, I reached under the elastic and stroked myself with a groan. "I need this. Need you."

He inched his naked body backward onto his mattress and rested on his elbows. It was all the invitation I needed. I pushed down my briefs and crawled over his body, pinning him to the bed with my weight. Dragging the length of my shaft along the soft skin of his hip, I swallowed his small, quiet gasp, and dipped my tongue into his mouth. Wild's fingers ran through my hair, twisting, pulling me closer. He lifted his hips, hungry for friction. I held his face in my hands, our lips fighting with each other for more. More teeth. More tongue, until he was sitting up, until I was straddled around his waist. His hands trailed down my ribs and I shuddered. He grasped my hips, tugging me until we were almost chest to chest.

I reached down, desperate to touch him, wanting the satisfaction that I made him feel crazy too, but he stopped me. Smiling against my lips he said, "Wait."

He placed my hand on his chest, and I could feel his heart beating under the muscle. Smoothing my palm over his soft skin, my thumb circled his nipple. He moaned into my mouth as his skin raised with goosebumps and his fingers dug into my hips. Wild's touch was hard like I needed. He could kiss me with gentle lips all fucking day, but I needed his hands. Strong and firm. His arms cut and lean, long enough to wrap around me and hold me steady.

Wild was breathless when he reached over and opened the bedside table drawer. I took advantage of his position and leaned down to lick the head of his cock.

"You're going to make me come if you keep doing that."

But he didn't protest as I took his entire length into my mouth. He fell back onto the mattress, propping

33

himself on one elbow to watch me. Dropping a small bottle of lube onto the bed, he dragged the fingers of his right hand through my hair.

"Jax," he pleaded, his eyes dark and wanting. "Wait," he said again, and I almost didn't stop.

I loved watching the tension in his jaw, his neck, Wild gave me power I never thought I had. But I wasn't ready for this to be over yet either. I wasn't ready for the four weeks I'd have without him. Or the loneliness that would set in the minute I stepped foot in my parents' house. Drawing tonight out was the only thing we had left. I heard the cap of the bottle click shut and I brought my mouth to his hip, leaving wet kisses on his skin. He slid his slippery hand, slow and deliberate, down the length of my dick as we both sat up. Straddling him again, he kissed me, stroking us both at the same time. Our kiss had become nothing more than moans and gasping lips pressed against each other. I stilled his hand, needing more time, and he rested his forehead in the crook of my neck to catch his breath. His skin was hot and damp and perfect. I grabbed the bottle off the bed and opened it. Taking Wilder's hand in mine, he met my eyes as I poured more liquid over his fingers.

We moved our bodies into position like we'd known each other, like this, open and vulnerable, for the entirety of our lives. Wilder knew what I wanted without even asking, and as I lay down, he lifted my knee, his fingers marking a path to something only he could give me. My eyes closed as his fingers slid inside me, my face instantly flushing with heat. Wild's long fingers moved slowly,

finding that spot, that spot only he could find, and I was
fucking lost in it. The heat of his mouth covered me, the
flat, smooth curve of his tongue around the head of my
dick and I was gone.

"Oh shit," I whispered through clenched teeth,
staring at myself in the mirror as I came into my hand.

I slammed my eyes shut, breathing through the
memory, the orgasm, trying to push down the nausea.
The shame. All the years between us, and I'd never been
able to suppress the need I had for him. I opened my
eyes, avoiding my reflection, and washed my hands in
the sink. It wasn't like I hadn't been attracted to other
men. I'd been struggling with my burden of truth since
I was twelve. And after my dad died, and I withdrew
from school, it wasn't like I could just flip a switch and
go back to pretending right away. This time I had to be
more careful. I was gay, but I'd never acted on it before
Wild. He was my first and my last. After everything that
happened, I promised myself, God, and whoever else
was listening that night, I would be the man my father
raised, and the son my mother needed. It hadn't been
easy, trying to erase a part of myself like that. It was a
day-to-day fight, and lately I was losing the battle. Like
jacking off to a memory of something I should've never
wanted in the first place. This was the exact reason I had
to cut things off with Mary. I didn't want her like that,
and it wasn't fair to her, all this lying I'd been doing. She
was a pretty girl, smart as hell, she could get a good guy,
not some sick asshole like me.

The steam from the shower started to fill the room,
but I picked up my phone and sent her a text.

Me: My mom made dinner, wanted me to invite you, can I come pick you up at six?

She didn't wait too long to respond.

Mary: I'd love to. Should I bring anything?
Me: That's alright. I think my mom probably thought of everything. See you at six.

I set my phone on the counter and finally got into the shower. The hot water levelled the ache of my twelve-hour day. And by the time I was dressed and ready, I'd decided I'd end things with Mary tonight. As much of an asshole as that made me, in the end, I'd be doing that girl a favor.

❦   ❦   ❦

"Don't be a stranger." My mom pulled Mary into a hug.

She gave me a thumbs up before letting Mary go, and I wished for the millionth time in my life that this was what I wanted. This girl. This life.

"Thanks again, Mrs. Stettler."

"Call me Barb."

Shit. She liked her. Of course, she did.

"Alright, Momma. If we don't hurry, the ice cream shop's gonna close." I took Mary's hand and laced our fingers together.

"Thanks again." Mary waved goodbye before we stepped off the porch.

I opened the passenger door, and letting go of her hand, I helped her get into the car. I curled my fingers into a fist as I walked around to the driver's side. This was going to be a shit show.

"Jaxon, your momma is just the sweetest thing."

"Don't let her fool you. The woman you met tonight was not my momma. I don't know who that was, some weird showroom model. Mom two-point-oh."

Her laugh filled the car as she pulled her long blonde waves over her right shoulder. She turned to look at me. "I think she's sweet, and your brother too."

"Sweet..." I smiled and started the car, grateful for the new battery I'd installed last week. "You haven't seen her at seven in the morning."

Mary cringed. "Not a morning person?"

"Not even a little bit."

Her smile widened. "Guess the apple doesn't fall far from the tree."

"I won't argue." I smiled, and she placed her hand on my knee.

"You're welcome to stay over tonight. Despite your surly disposition in the morning, I like having you in my bed."

My grip on the steering wheel tightened as we made our way down Bell River Road to the highway. When I didn't answer, she lifted her hand from my leg and placed it in her lap.

Staring at me, she said, "Got something on your mind, Jax?" I let a few more seconds pass than I should have, but I was a coward, and all the things I'd wanted to say seemed stupid to me now. "It's okay, you know. If you think what we got going isn't working out. I kind of had a feeling... that this..." She waved her hand between us. "Wasn't going to last."

"You did?" I asked, glancing at her. Her eyes were glassy, and I had to be the biggest douche bag in all of Okaloosa County. "Shit, I'm sorry, Mary. Please don't cry. Not over me. I'm not worth it."

She wiped at her eyes. "That's the problem, Jaxon. You are and you don't see it. How can anyone love you right and proper if you don't make an effort to love you first?"

"Mary... I—"

"I mean, there were times," she said, whispering like she was talking to herself. "Where I could feel it. That distance you put up. It was like you weren't really ever there. And then I hear you talk about Jason, and your whole face lights up, and I know you love your family, I do, but..."

"Mary..."

"No... let me finish what I want to say."

I pulled into the parking lot of the small strip mall. The windows of the ice cream shop were the only ones illuminated.

"Okay." I put the car in park and picked at the cracked vinyl covering the center console.

"What good will it do you, living there in that house? You're young, Jax, you got so much living to do. And maybe it's not with me, and it's with someone else, that's fine." She took a breath and toyed with the hem of her skirt, straightening her shoulders. "I mean, is there someone else?"

"No." I lied, but I didn't know if keeping memories was the same as cheating.

She nodded. "Okay, then."

"Are you mad?" I asked, feeling like a little kid for the second time in one day.

"I'm sad." She reached over and squeezed my knee. "For you, I mean."

"Don't be sad for me."

We sat, for three, maybe five long minutes, in a tight, pressured silence.

Where do we go from here?

"Friends?" I finally asked.

"The jury is still out. A year is a long time to string a girl along, even if you didn't mean to." She gave me a sad smile.

"That's fair." I exhaled and nodded toward the shop. "Still want some ice cream?"

She shook her head, the tears welling in her eyes again, spilled down her cheek. If I hadn't already hated myself, this whole thing, me, and Mary, would've been the thing to tip the scale.

"Can you just take me home?"

"Yeah, I can do that." I grabbed my wallet from the dashboard. "Can I run in and get something to go for Jason. I'll only be a minute."

She sniffled, her laugh a little wet as she said, "I'd never forgive myself if that boy was deprived of anything."

Tell me about it.

"I'll only be a second."

The ice cream shop was empty when I stepped in, the cold air sinking into my skin, I hit the bell on the counter with the palm of my hand. While I waited, I wandered to the small shelf of books they had on the back wall. The owner of the shop also owned Birdie's Book Sellers down the street. Nothing caught my eye at first. I wasn't much of a reader. At least, I wasn't until I met Wilder. He'd always had that raggedy-ass copy of *The Fellowship of the Ring* with him wherever he went. I'd noticed it our freshmen year when he'd started to tutor me. When I worked on the problems he'd given me, he'd sit tucked in a chair, knees up so he could rest his chin while he read. I smiled, so immersed in the thought, I almost didn't see it.

On the shelf of new releases, there were two copies. It was the bold red cover that had caught my attention. But it was the title that had my heart racing, thundering hard and stealing my breath. I picked it up, tracing the curve of the font with the tips of my fingers, and spoke the title out loud in a slow whisper, *Love Always, Wild*.

A semester's worth of emails opened themselves all at once in my head. When we were together, every email, every letter he'd ever written me, ended with Love always, Wild. The author's name was scrolled at the bottom, and in this moment, there was nothing but this book in my hands, heavy and terrible.

Wilder Welles.

Without any care for the years I'd placed between myself and what had happened between us, I opened that book like my fucking life depended on it, like it was that last breath you took before diving into the ocean, praying the rip tide didn't sweep you away. I opened it, reading the words but not seeing them. I turned the page, and then another, looking at all the letters, until a few, well-placed sentences stood out, and I almost dropped it to the floor.

The rose of his cheeks bled down his neck to his chest as I pushed inside him. My life ended in the heat of his body, he was mine and I his, and all the barriers we had to overcome, to climb, meant nothing. We moved slow with a purposeful longing, his eyes, those ocean green eyes, told me everything, every secret he kept, tight and bound were mine in this second, this breath. Jake granted me his body and his heart as he reached for my face and kissed me with violent lips before whispering, "I love you."

Jake.

He'd changed my name, but not the moment. I read it again, without regard for the girl waiting for me to drive her home, my chest squeezing against the pressure of my lungs. I read it again and remembered. Every touch, every fucking feeling of that night, how at peace I'd been with myself, with him, that I'd let him have me like that. I'd pushed it all down, thrown it away into some dark place where memories went to drown.

"Can I help you with something?" the girl said from behind the counter.

I shut the book and stared at the cover.

No. She couldn't help me. No one could. Not anymore.

Chapter 4

WILDER

Restless, I sat up in bed and looked at the time on my phone. It was a little after ten. Anders was next to me, snoring lightly. His body generating too much heat, I pulled down the blanket. I admired his profile, his long lashes, his perfectly sculpted jawline. Looking at him, I could picture all the possible Sunday mornings, sleepy-eyed and mussed, reading the newspaper over coffee. A future with him could be book tours and shared spaces. Sleeping in on Mondays and fucking until we were boneless every night. He was young and handsome and rich, and I was an up-and-coming author. We could have the dream. Two rings and maybe one day a house in Brookhaven. I could frame it all into this photograph inside my head, like the outline of another book. Another fiction I could try to believe belonged to me. But this disquiet, this unease under my skin. I didn't love him and never would.

He was too selfish, and I was too self-deprecating. His habits and my delicate idiosyncrasies. I hated that he chewed the tops of pens. He despised it when I wore eyeliner. He was a terrible tipper, and I whined too much about everything. It was inside these tiny details

I realized we could never be more than friends who indulged in each other every now and then. He was solid in a way I would never be, and I was too precious in a way he'd never understand. Our relationship was something for us both to hide behind. It was unhealthy, but how did I untangle myself from him, from an us I never wanted in the first place? This was why you shouldn't sleep with your agent.

With all the thoughts racing in my head, sleep eluded me, and instead of sitting here staring at the ceiling, I should've been writing. As soundless as possible, I stood, grabbing my laptop from the bedside table. In the doorway of my bedroom, I paused when he rolled to his right side, not wanting to wake him. I counted to twenty in my head, and when he snored softly, I shut the door behind me as I left the room. The second bedroom, which I'd converted into an office, was down the stairs. With blackout curtains on the window, I would lock myself in there for days and write until my fingertips hurt. Or until my best friend, June, stopped by to make sure I was alive and forced me to shower or dragged me to our favorite coffee shop. Writing was personal, everyone had their own process. Mine just happened to err on the side of insomnia.

I switched on the desk lamp and sat my laptop down onto the wood surface. The desk was shaped like an L and fit nicely in the corner of the room. I had a small couch that sat under the window and two large, floor-to-ceiling shelving units, thank you Ikea, bursting with journals, books, and *Lord of the Rings* memorabilia.

Instead of pining for the one that got away, Tolkien was an addiction I could be proud of. The left side of the desk housed my PC and a large, flat-screen monitor. I fired it up, the reassuring purr of the processor soothed some of my unwanted anxiety. I'd get like this often. Wired and awake. The only cure I'd ever found was to write until I was tired. Sometimes it was a couple of hours, sometimes it was several days.

I opened my laptop and clicked on the email icon. This was the most daunting part of being an author. *Love Always, Wild* had finally topped out at number two on *The New York Times* best seller list and sat there for a few weeks without budging. Though this was fabulous for my career and my ego, success and notoriety came at a cost. Insecurity, the inevitability of the end, started to pick away at all of my weak spots. How long would this last? What if I never finished another book? Did all the people pulling me in every direction really give a shit about me as a person, or was I just an accessory, a new toy? How long would it take before they all realized I wasn't as talented as they thought? These hundred or so emails, all from people I didn't know, made my success feel more precarious. A month ago, I had maybe ten emails, all from June or Anders. The closest I'd ever gotten to one hundred emails was in my spam folder. But now, I had an email address set up by my publisher with the specific intention of interacting with my *fans.* I hated that word, it was pretentious. I wasn't a fucking pop singer. All these people had flooded into my life like a ditch collected rainwater after a storm. But the sun always came out, didn't it? How fast would all these people disappear under someone else's heat?

Ignoring the emails for now, I pulled up my work in progress on the PC. I reread the first twenty pages, hating every last word. At one point I deleted it all, then panicked, hitting that blessed undo button. I rearranged and rewrote the first paragraph of chapter one about a thousand times before I growled and threw my pen at the wall. It was almost eleven-thirty, and I was about to give up, take some Benadryl, and call it a night, when an email notification alerted from my laptop speaker. I moved the tip of my finger over the touchpad, curious who'd email me this late. The message was from the Bartley Press account, the one for my *fans*. Usually, I had Anders look through these for me, but the email address and its obvious nod to Tolkien, piqued my curiosity.

FROM: fool0fatook54@bellinx.mail.com
TO: wildwelleslit@bartpress.com
Date: Jul 13 11:28 PM
SUBJECT: It's my birthday so why not?

I'm not even sure you're going to get this. And I'm not a great writer, not like you. But today is my birthday and I figured what the hell? Worst case, I don't get a response, but at least I got to say what I wanted to say to you. First, let me apologize for the lack of greeting. I didn't know whether I was supposed to address this to Wilder, Wild, or Mr. Welles, those all sounded a bit wrong to me, seeing how you're a stranger, so I figured screw it, I'll just get right to the point.

I've been thinking about writing to you for a few days, I finished your book, and it was... I don't even know a word for it. A revelation, maybe? I've known I was gay since I was a little kid. Even had a boyfriend once, but I've been in the closet for my entire life, for reasons I won't get into because I'm sure you have better things to do with your day. I just wanted to thank you, I guess, for writing Jake. I can relate to him in more ways than one. Reading him, I saw so many things reflected in myself.

Your book got me thinking. I don't know if you've ever seen the movie Shawshank Redemption, but there's this phrase, it's a pretty popular quote from the movie, "Get busy living or get busy dying." I don't want to be like your Jake. I don't want to die living a half-life. I'm tired of hiding. But I'm not ready to come out yet, again for reasons I shouldn't dump on a stranger. I know your book is fiction, inspired by your life, and I wanted to say how much I admire what you've done. I'm jealous of your courage. Who knows, maybe one day I'll find some courage of my own.

Wishing you well, Jordan.

P.S. I agree with what you said about Sam and Frodo in your book.

The last sentence made me laugh out loud, the smile on my face growing as I immediately started to reread the email. There was something about this letter that was familiar, his words striking some chord inside me. I wanted to respond to him but wasn't sure if I should. The Internet was a minefield and he was a complete stranger. I drummed my fingers over the keys, debating with myself. I decided to open a few of the other emails I'd gotten from readers to see if they were all this complimentary and personal. The first few I'd opened were simple, mostly consisting of "thank you for writing this book" while others I'd wished I would have never opened in my lifetime. After I'd opened a message that had a naked picture of what looked like a teenage boy, I closed out of the email program entirely.

"What the fuck is wrong with people?" I whispered to myself, completely horrified by what I'd seen.

I figured it was best if I didn't respond to Jordan's email. His letter was sweet, and my heart ached for him, ached for the fact he thought he had to hide who he was in his life. One thing I'd learned from writing this book, thinking about Jax and how he'd been scared all the time, was how lucky I was. Never once had I ever given a damn about what others thought of me. And when I'd decided to publish the book, after my parents said I shouldn't, and then disowned me for going through with it anyway, I realized I was better for it. I didn't need people like that. I'd never been close to my parents anyway. I'd built my own family, with people who cared about me as I was. I have always been Wilder, and I'd never apologize for it, for being me.

I thought about how Jordan had said I was courageous for writing the book, and here I was afraid to write him back. It didn't have to be elaborate. I could just send him a quick thank you for his kind words. After all, it was the guy's birthday.

FROM: wildwelleslit@bartpress.com
TO: fool0fatook54@bellinx.mail.com
Date: Jul 13 11:55 PM
SUBJECT: RE: It's my birthday so why not?

Thank you for reaching out. It's always nice to hear from my readers. That sounded narcissistic, didn't it? I should probably erase this and start over, but it's late, and to be honest, I usually don't open my emails. My agent does. God, that sounds terrible too. I swear I'm not a conceited, pompous asshole. I'm new to this published-author thing and the navigation of it all seems overwhelming at times. For example, after reading your message, I figured maybe I should read a few more. Bad idea. There are some things a man will never unsee.

But on a more serious note, I wanted to tell you, I admired your candid words. I'm humbled, actually. It's easy for me to forget how lucky I am to be able to live out and proud, and I wish, for you, that one day you will be able to as well. Life is too short to live in bubbles. I hope you get to break yours soon.

And, to answer your question, I have seen that movie. The scene in the sewer always makes me gag. I don't think there's anything I'd ever want bad enough that I would crawl through miles of shit and piss for it. Also, please, call me Wilder, as Mr. Welles makes me think of my father and his overgrown mustache... and something personal for you since you were so open with me, "Jake" is the only person who's ever been allowed to call me Wild.

Anyway, I think it's easier sometimes, talking to a stranger. There's no history or judgment to deal with, is there? So, thank you for thinking my book is a revelation, and for trusting me with your own story. Hopefully one day you'll find your own happily ever after.

Happy Birthday, Jordan
Wilder~

P.S. I think, if Tolkien were alive today, I'd ask him why he didn't allow for an openly gay hobbit relationship. It's obvious to anyone the feelings these two halflings share for each other.

⬧ ⬧ ⬧

"Did he email you back?" June was way too excited about my late-night correspondence.

I tore my croissant in half and placed it on June's plate. "No, why would he?"

"How did you end the letter?" she asked, peeling back the wrapper on a packet of jelly.

"I told him thank you and happy birthday."

She paused. Her plastic knife, covered with strawberry preserves, hovered over her pastry. "You never told me it was his birthday."

"Does it matter?" I asked, annoyed with all of her questions. She was making this a bigger deal than it needed to be. "This isn't a big deal."

June shrugged. "A complete stranger emails you to say thanks for writing a character he can relate to. Jake being the said character, aka Jax, the guy who obliterated your heart, turned you into the unfeeling manslayer that you are, a stranger who, I might also add, is admittedly in the closet as well, and you don't feel the least bit triggered by that?"

"Not at all," I lied, sipping from my coffee cup to hide my facial expression. June was a walking lie detector. "And I am *not* a manslayer."

She wiped her hands on a napkin and narrowed her eyes. "What did Anders say?"

Shit. She was like a bloodhound.

"I didn't tell him about it."

"Really." She smiled. "That's interesting."

"June, you're exhausting." Exhaling, I asked, "Why would I tell Anders I answered some fan mail? It's not a big deal, so cut the shit. Don't you have to get to work? Aren't there some babies that need to be born today?"

"My shift doesn't start for another half an hour." She played with the string dangling from her cup of tea.

"Great." I gave her a wide, fake smile, and she threw a packet of sugar at me. "Jesus, are we twelve now?"

"Wilder, I've known you for five years. And I know when something is off."

"I should have never befriended you. I should have walked right out of the Cup and Quill and never looked back." I playfully kicked her foot under the table. "You've been nothing but a pain in my ass since that day."

She snorted. "I was your favorite barista, don't lie."

"My point exactly. I should have never helped you study during nursing school. I could be drinking my favorite latte right now. You know it always helped me with writer's block?"

"You can't distract me with flattery. Tell me what's going on with you and Anders?" Her humor faded.

I could try to deflect all day, but June was too smart for that. It's why I loved her. She worked her way through nursing school without asking for any handouts. Her parents, like mine, had decided that they'd rather have no child than a gay one. Sure, I'd helped her with chemistry, but she'd graduated with honors because she'd busted her ass. Now she worked in labor and delivery, and if I could have a baby, I wouldn't let anyone else in the room but her. She was more than my best friend. She was like a sister to me, and it's why I knew I could always trust her, even with things I didn't trust myself with.

"I don't think I should be with him anymore," I admitted.

"As an agent or a boyfriend?"

"He's never been my boyfriend." She pinned me with an impatient glare. "As a guy I sleep with. I always feel like such an awful person when we're on again. He wants a white picket fence and I'm not…"

"Over Jax, oh, I know."

It was my turn to glare. "I'm not *ready*. I'm not fit for that big of a commitment. Everything is finally happening for me. I want to enjoy it and not have to worry whose feelings might get hurt or about anything else right now."

"Anders isn't right for you anyway."

There was this hollow spot underneath my breastbone that longed to be filled by something other than regret. "What if I never find it again, what I had with Jax before it all fell to shit?"

"You will. It might never be the same as Jax, but who says it has to be. Love who you want, just give yourself a chance to feel it." She reached across the small table and gave my hand a short squeeze.

"Sorry I treat you like my surrogate parent sometimes."

"We make our own families, you know that." June's expression darkened.

"Are Gwen's parents still giving you a hard time?"

"I honestly don't know what bothers them more. That I'm black, or that their daughter is a lesbian." She pulled her wallet out of her bag and opened it.

She threw a twenty onto the table as I asked, "What does Gwen say?"

June laughed. "She said fuck 'em."

"Amen." I raised my cup and she did the same, tapping them together in solidarity.

"I better get going." June pulled her bag over her shoulder as she stood. "You better tell me if that guy emails you back."

"He's not going to email me back."

"But you want him to?"

"Go to work."

She hummed. "Mm-hmm."

"You really are a pain in the ass..."

"I knew you wanted him to," she said as she turned to leave. "I'm always right, Wilder." June waved over her shoulder as she opened the front door of the coffee shop and stepped into the hot, humid Atlanta morning.

She was *always* right. I did want him to email me back. Even if it meant I might have to resurrect some of my old ghosts.

Chapter 5

JAX

I worried if Chuck had any sense at all. He'd rounded the corner faster than anyone in their right mind would have, causing the tools in the bed of the work truck to rattle. Hudson rolled down the passenger-side window and spit, the brown liquid coating the back window where I sat.

"You're disgusting," I hollered over the radio.

With Chuck in the driver seat, there was usually a washed-up rock band from the eighties spewing from the speakers. Today was no different. Hudson laughed and pulled a wad of chewing tobacco from his cheek, turning in his seat, he said, "Want some?"

"Throw that garbage out the window." I refused to play into his bullshit.

Ignoring his antics, I focused on the green blur of scenery outside. Eventually, he turned around and stuffed the chew back into his mouth. Working with these guys everyday had started to wear on me. The stench of B.O. was overwhelming. It didn't help that whatever Chuck had eaten for lunch smelled like rotten eggs. Add to that, all the sharp turns he'd been dealing out, it was no wonder my stomach was sick. At least that's what I told myself. I didn't want to think about the emails from last night. How I lied through my damn teeth just to get a glimpse of him, a taste of Wild again. That book he'd written. It had turned me inside out. Seeing us, through his eyes, seeing how I'd hurt him, it tore something open inside of me. Reaching out to him was stupid... but lying to him was unforgivable.

Wild had changed our story. His ending, more dramatic. Instead of me leaving, cutting him off like the coward I was, he'd created a hero. He'd renamed me, formed me into this brave and tragic character. Jake. A guy who'd finally come out to his abusive father. Jake chose Wild when I couldn't. But in the end, after everything Jake had fought for, he'd died. Traveling to see him for winter break, Jake had been hit by a car while crossing some street in Atlanta. Reading Wild's words, with every fiber, I wished the story was true. That I could somehow reverse time. I'd die on that corner if it meant I'd done right by him. Wild had always deserved better than me, but I was selfish, writing to him, lying, and choosing my own self-preservation over the truth. I was still in love with the boy who'd given me peace, even if it was in death. I was dead to him—both figuratively and literally—and maybe that's how I should stay.

Chuck ran over a pothole and I almost hit my head against the window. "Jim's gonna kick your ass if you fuck up his truck," Hudson said, holding on to the dashboard.

"Jim ain't gonna care as long as we get that house painted before Friday. I'm just trying to buy us some time." Chuck smirked. "Besides, Jim Walker owns ten of these trucks."

"Doesn't mean he wants you to wreck this one. Just drive the speed limit," I said, irritated at his blatant disregard for our boss and a paycheck. "You never know, he may dock your salary if you end up messing up an axle."

Chuck's face paled. "Shit, I didn't think about that."

The truck slowed and I laughed under my breath, pulling my phone from my pocket. I should've deleted the emails after I'd read Wild's response, but I'd read his email about twenty times before I'd fallen asleep last night. Would it hurt to read it one more time? I knew the answer but ignored it anyhow. I opened up the email app on my phone, tapped the edge of my thumb on Wild's message, and got caught up in his words a few more times before we pulled into the parking lot for Harley's. Chuck and Hudson jumped out of the truck, and I followed behind, slipping my phone into my back pocket.

Ethan was behind the register and offered us a hello as we walked in. The guys didn't acknowledge him, feeling bad for the guy, I gave him a smile.

"Hey, Jax." His eyes were a light caramel today, his cheeks turning pink as I approached. He sure was a nervous guy. "Happy birthday... I'm a little late."

Embarrassed by the attention, I rubbed the back of my neck. "Uh... thanks."

"Your mom told me. I saw her at the bakery yesterday when she was buying your cake." Ethan fidgeted, his long fingers tapping the side of the register.

"Did you make a wish when you blew out the candles, Jackie?" Chuck snickered, lifting a five-gallon bucket of primer onto the counter.

"I did... I wished for a co-worker who didn't run his damn mouth so much." I shook my head and left to grab a few more buckets of paint.

Being around Hudson and Chuck made me regret dropping out of school. I should have listened to my mom and transferred my credits to an online program. But I never would have made it into pharmacy school, and once my dad died, it no longer mattered. That had been *his* dream for me. I had no idea what I could do with a degree, but it sure as hell would be better than working with these jackasses in the blazing sun every day.

I grabbed two more five-gallon buckets and hauled them to the register. Ethan's eyes trailed over my chest and arms, and I looked down to see if I had something on my shirt.

"Could you be more obvious, faggot?" Hudson's deep voice curdled in the air.

"What the hell did you say?" I asked, that word like a hammer, as I dropped the weight of the buckets to the ground.

"He's always checking you out, it's fucking disgusting."

Ethan's cheeks flamed a tomato red, his expression more horrified than angered. The muscle in his jaw flexed and his eyes plummeted to the floor. A fury burned inside me, scorching my lungs, and awakening memories of the times when Wild had been harassed and mocked. It had cut him and hurt me too. He'd always stuck up for himself though, and I'd stayed silent. Silence was hate packaged in privilege.

"Don't be a dick, Hudson." I couldn't stand up for Wild, or myself, but I wouldn't be quiet anymore. I was sick and tired of the silence.

"What'd he do now?" Chuck asked, throwing a couple of paint rollers on the countertop.

"Not a damn thing." Hudson squared his shoulders. "Just calling it like I see it."

"What're you talking about?" Chuck asked as we continued to ignore him.

I fixed my eyes on Hudson, taking a step toward him, I lowered my voice. "That shit you just said. It's hateful. Shut your fucking mouth or I'll shut it for you."

He smiled like he'd figured something out, and the heaviness in my chest was almost unbearable. My pulse raced as he spoke. "Maybe you like him looking at you?" He glanced at Ethan. "Did you hear that, Ethan, I think Jax has a thing for pansies."

Chuck laughed and pulled out his wallet. "Wouldn't surprise me, giving up a sweet piece like Mary."

"You need to mind your business." I planted my hand hard into Chuck's chest and he almost fumbled his wallet.

Eyes wide and fists clenched, he darted toward me. Hudson stopped him, laughing at the shit he'd stirred up. "As entertaining as all of this is, we have a house to paint... That is, if y'all still wanna get paid."

Chuck glared at me, and when he didn't make another attempt to confront me, I turned and headed out of the shop. I slammed the truck door as I got in, my heart pounding when I realized I probably should've stayed inside and made sure they didn't harass Ethan anymore. How did Wild live so open? How did he make it through every day without punching some asshole in the face? Maybe it was just Bell River. Small town, small-minded. But that didn't explain why all the guys on my basketball team back in Eastchester had been so mean. My church would tell me I was a sinner for thinking about men like I did, for all the things I'd done with Wild. The hate I'd seen in Hudson's eyes was just as much of a sin, if you asked me. Worse even. He didn't even know if Ethan was gay, and that bullshit about him checking me out, Hudson had lost his mind. Guys like Hudson built themselves up by breaking everyone else down.

The truck shifted as Hudson and Chuck loaded the primer into the back. Trying not to stir up any more trouble, I grabbed my earbuds from my backpack on the floor and plugged them into my phone. I scrolled through my playlist until I found something loud enough to get me through this day.

* * *

FROM: fool0fatook54@bellinx.mail.com
TO: wildwelleslit@bartpress.com
Date: Jul 14 10:12 PM
SUBJECT: Openly gay hobbits

Wilder,

I can think of a few things worth crawling through shit and piss for. Freedom being at the top of that list. I'm already stuck inside a cell in some ways, and if there was a way to escape, sewer swimming and all, I'd do it. But I shouldn't take up any more of your time. Thank you for responding to my message. I sure am glad your agent didn't because I think I really needed to hear what you had to say. Best birthday ever.

P.S. I don't think the world is ready for openly gay hobbits.

Take care,
Jordan

I read the message, making sure I didn't sound like a total idiot. It seemed alright to me. I should've left well enough alone, but I'd wanted to say thank you for his response. Asking for anything more from him wasn't right, and if he didn't reply back, that was okay. I'd said my goodbyes to Wild a long time ago. I pressed send and set my phone on the bedside table.

Jason's light was on in his room as I walked by. I knocked on the door frame twice before walking in. He was in bed facing the wall. "It's getting late," I said but he didn't answer. "Jason," I called his name a little louder and he jumped.

"Geez, Jax." He exhaled, rolling onto his back. "I was sleeping."

I huffed out a laugh. "You left your light on."

He rubbed his eyes and reached to turn off his lamp. "Thanks."

The room darkened and I waited until his breathing evened out before closing the door. I didn't take long in the bathroom getting ready for bed, and when I finally fell back into my mattress, the exhaustion of my day pulled me under. Half asleep, I reached for my phone to set my alarm and nearly jumped out of my skin as I sat up. Wild had sent me another email. Something fluttered inside my stomach as I opened it.

FROM: wildwelleslit@bartpress.com
TO: fool0fatook54@bellinx.mail.com
Date: Jul 14 10:25 PM
SUBJECT: The world is totally ready for gay hobbits

Jordan,

Sewer swimming aside, freedom is something you can find inside yourself. When you're ready. It's hard to say because I don't know you or your situation. And though you didn't ask for my advice, I have some for you. I know it's presumptuous of me, but maybe it will help you find the keys to that cell you're living in.

Fear is what kept me from coming out to my parents until I was almost eighteen. My friends at school knew. The bullies knew, but I wasn't scared of them. I was terrified of losing permanence. It sounds weird, right? But my home life, though fake as hell, was stable. All the unknown variables made it difficult for me to unlock myself from the lie I was living. Once I knew what I was afraid of, I did what I had to do to protect myself. I got a job, made sure I worked hard on my grades to earn a scholarship. I became self-sufficient. I had an insurance plan, so to speak. I made sure that if my parents turned me away, I'd have the ability to create a new life and family, one that would give me what I truly wanted. Unconditional love.

So, I'm going to ask you. As a stranger with no right to do so. What are you afraid of, Jordan?

P.S. I think queer theory could be applied to many works of fiction. Especially fantasy. I think it's important to challenge the heteronormative nature of the world we live in. Sam and Frodo alike. One does not simply walk across Mordor (like what I did there?) for just anyone. Sam's love for Frodo is infinite. Also, you're not taking up my time. It's kind of nice talking about something other than word count.

Wilder~

FROM: fool0fatook54@bellinx.mail.com
TO: wildwelleslit@bartpress.com
Date: Jul 14 10:45 PM
SUBJECT: What the hell is queer theory?

I don't think fear is what keeps me holed up in the closet. It's complicated. I have this sense of obligation, got people relying on me. If I tell them about... this thing inside me, I'm not sure they'll want me around anymore. Now you got me thinking... maybe it is fear holding me back. You asked me what I'm afraid of. I'm afraid that without me, my family will fall apart. My father passed a while ago. It was an accident, and my brother got hurt too. He was only sixteen at the time. He's disabled pretty much now. His brain isn't like it used to be and functions like a little kid. He's capable enough, I suppose, but he's basically a man trapped in a young boy's mind. And it's hard on my mom. She stays home with him, and I work to help supplement the insurance money she got from the accident. I have to be there for my mom and brother, even if that means I have to sacrifice a little. I feel funny dumping all of this on you, but I guess after you read this, we aren't really strangers anymore.

P.S. You lost me at queer theory. But I think I read somewhere that Sam and Frodo were based on J. R. R. and a war buddy. And I like writing to you, too. I'm not open to anyone in my life, not anymore. So yeah, it's nice having someone to listen, I guess.

Jordan~

FROM: wildwelleslit@bartpress.com
TO: fool0fatook54@bellinx.mail.com
Date: Jul 14 11:15 PM
SUBJECT: RE: What the hell is queer theory?

I'm so sorry about your dad. My parents disowned me last year, and I couldn't care less. But at the same time, if one of them died... I'd be pretty fucked up about it. See, I have my own issues to work through too. Speaking of issues, what about this "thing" inside of you do you think is so hard for your family to understand? That sounds a bit like self-loathing to me. Could you be projecting? Pushing your own stuff onto your mom? Sounds like you and your family have gone through a lot together. And that sucks about your brother. It's all so sad, really. I can see why you'd be afraid to shake things up. It sounds like you're afraid of losing permanence too, but more for your brother and mom than yourself. You give them stability. Holding together a family is no easy task. But why do you think the burden of that should only fall on you? I might be overstepping when I say this, but it's more than just a little sacrifice to fake your way through life.

I can't tell you what to do, but I hope, if anything, this conversation has helped a little. And don't worry, you're not dumping. Honestly, I know this sounds odd, but I like how familiar this all feels, it's like you weren't a stranger to me in the first place.

P.S. Do an internet search of queer theory. You can thank me later. I've heard that about Tolkien as well. But I wonder if his publisher made that up to hide the fact that Frodo and Sam were indeed in love. The war buddy was his beard. There, I said it.

Wilder~

Chapter 6

WILDER

FROM: fool0fatook54@bellinx.mail.com
TO: wildwelleslit@bartpress.com
Date: Jul 14 11:45 PM
SUBJECT: He was definitely a beard

Wilder,

Your parents disowned you! This kind of makes me want to kick someone's ass. My dad was a homophobic asshole. Said shit to me all the time about pussies and pansies and how a man ought to be. How marriage was between a man and a woman and how homosexuals were not created by God. My mom never argued, but she never said nothing to contradict him either. If your parents could do that to you, and you're amazing, if they could just throw you away like that, how can you think my mom wouldn't do the same? Or any parent?

I don't doubt that my dad is why I'm twisted up inside. And why I have so much hatred for who I want to be versus who I am. There's a big chance my mom won't be accepting of my attraction to men either. She's a good person, but she loved my dad. She still goes to the same church they both attended every Sunday. He's been gone for almost a decade, but sometimes it feels like he's still there, sitting in his recliner, judging everything I do. I almost came out to him and my mom, but that feels like another lifetime.

By the way, I did like you said and looked up queer theory. What a rabbit hole. I don't think I'm smart enough to be your friend. I'm a college dropout. Some of that stuff I tried to read was like another language. The most I got out of it was the idea that queer theory can be applied to everything. I had a good laugh when I found an article about queering up Cinderella. I think my mom would have a heart attack. It's one of her favorite movies.

I should probably let you get to sleep, not sure if you're in Atlanta still like your book said, but it's almost midnight here. When I reached out, I didn't think we'd be sharing such heavy shit, but I'm glad we are.

Thanks for listening,
Jordan

P.S. I had to look up the definition of beard. For someone who is in the closet, a beard is basically like a person or relationship to hide behind? I've had a few of those, unfortunately. Wouldn't Rosie be a beard for Sam? That really sucks that he had to marry her. I hope I don't end up like him.

FROM: wildwelleslit@bartpress.com
TO: fool0fatook54@bellinx.mail.com
Date: Jul 15 12:05 AM
SUBJECT: So, you think I'm amazing?

Jordan,

Since we're friends now, by your admission, I'd like to say something, and I hope it doesn't ruin our open dialogue. I know it's not respectful to talk ill about the dead, but your dad is exactly the reason you're still snuggled up nice and cozy in the closet. Well, him and the church he went to. And if we're keeping it real, for you and all of gay kind, I kind of hate him. I haven't given up hope yet on your mom. I mean, sure, you and I just "met," and I don't know her at all, but isn't she the wild card in all of this? If your dad was that much of a dick about people being queer, then think about his views on women. I would bet all of my Lord of the Rings Funko Pops that he thrived in the patriarchal role, and that what he said was the law of the land. Your mom might've been afraid of him too. Give her a chance to prove you wrong. You said you had a boyfriend once? And they had no idea? You'd be surprised, a lot of parents already know their kids are gay.

And thank you for the offer to kick my parents' ass (or is it asses?), but you'll have to get in line. Most of my friends have already sworn their fealty to me. I know I should be more fucked up over it, and I'm probably repressing some very needed emotional breakdown that will inevitably bite me in the ass later, but right now I truly don't give a damn about them. Their loss. I don't need them, never have and never will.

Another thing, I'm not that smart. There's this book, called "Gender Trouble" by Judith Butler. She's like the mother of queer theory, and I swear to God, I don't understand a word of it. Oh, and I'm going to need a link to this version of Cinderella. My friend June would die to read this.

Don't worry about the time, I was finishing up some writing. You know something? I just realized we've skipped over all the small details and jumped right into the deep end. My book gives a lot of details about me, most of which are true. I am indeed still a resident of Atlanta. What about you? Seems as though we are in the same time zone, at least. Green is my favorite color. Lord of the Rings is my religion and Aragorn is my Christ. I'm twenty-nine, but my birthday is August sixteenth. And yes, I'm a stubborn Leo to the core. I know you just had a birthday, and I almost, on purpose, forgot to tell you that you share a birthday with "Jake." But that's not your fault. You can't help the day you were born. I think this is probably enough information for now. After all, this isn't a dating app profile. I'm not sure you're ready to know if I'm a top or bottom yet. I almost inserted a wink emoji. It's definitely getting late.

Sleep well,
Wilder

P.S. I do concede that Rosie could have very well been a beard. But what if Sam was bi-sexual?

A stream of sunlight poured through the window and across my bed. I tossed and turned a few times before settling on my back and flopping my arm over my eyes. I didn't dare look at my phone to see what time it was. I was too afraid and too hopeful that Jordan had written me back. If it wasn't for the sour taste in my mouth, I'd probably avoid getting out of bed for at least another thirty minutes. But I had a meeting with my publisher at eleven, and no matter how long I lay here, I couldn't unsend that last email.

The sheet pooled around my waist as I sat up and lifted my phone from the other side of my mattress. He hadn't responded yet. I told myself he was probably at work like the rest of the day walkers and dragged my ass out of bed. I hadn't said anything too crazy in the email, had I? On my way to the bathroom, I reread it. I mean, I probably shouldn't have mentioned that bit about topping and bottoming. This was what happened when I drank too much caffeine. I was notoriously flirty when sleep deprived. I had no idea about this guy. He could be catfishing me for all I knew. But Jordan seemed genuine.

"That's exactly the point of catfishing, Wilder," I said out loud to no one as I turned on the shower.

After my meeting, I'd ask June what she thought when I met her at Cup and Quill. I'd let her read through all of the emails and let her decide if she thought Jordan was the real deal, or some homophobic closet case pulling my chain. It wasn't a total breach of Jordan's trust showing her his emails. I'd never meet the guy in real life, and she was my best friend. She wouldn't share my deepest secrets for all the money in the world. Jordan's secrets were as good as my own. Deciding it was futile to worry, I opened the shower door and stepped under the hot water. I closed my eyes and let the heat cover me. Too deep in my head, I hadn't heard the bathroom or the shower door open.

"I got here just in time," Anders said, and I jumped.

"Shit! You scared me." I lightly elbowed him in the ribs as he pressed himself against my ass. He was hard already. "How did you get in here?" I whispered as he kissed my neck.

"I have a key, remember?"

Anders skated his hand over my stomach, running his fingernails over my skin. He smelled like sandalwood, his scent heavy in the steam surrounding me.

"I forgot," I mumbled as he took me in his hand, stroking me until I was hard.

I turned my head and let his lips find mine as I pressed a hand to the tile.

Anders released me, and I turned to face him. His pupils were dilated, transfixed as he lowered himself onto his knees. My fingers curled into his wet hair as the heat of his mouth consumed me. He cupped my ass with his hands, pulling me deeper, until he gagged.

"Christ."

I raked my other hand through his hair. Holding his head, I fucked his mouth, knowing that I should stop, knowing that the conversation I had to have with him would be that much more hurtful after this. The complicated web I'd sewn tangled itself even more as I came in his mouth.

After I'd returned the favor, we'd both cleaned up and gotten dressed. Anders was running some pomade through his hair when he said, "So, I wanted to talk to you about something."

"That sounds ominous," I teased, putting the finishing touches on my eyeliner. When I opened the drawer to put it away, I saw the extra key I'd given him. I picked it up. "Are you giving this back to me?"

Anders dried his hands on the towel and set it on the sink. He clenched his jaw, swallowing, he looked at me.

"I hate it when you wear eyeliner," he said, grazing his thumb over my cheek.

"I know."

He dropped his hand and shoved it into his pocket. "I can feel it, Wilder. I've known you long enough. You're pretty good at distancing yourself, even when you're coming in my mouth."

"Anders, I—"

He shook his head, his lips spreading into a soft smile. "I can't be mad about it. You're not over him, and I don't know if you'll ever be, at least not anytime soon. Some hurts are never healed."

I nodded—my throat too tight to talk.

He brought his hand to the back of my neck and kissed my forehead. "It's my fault too, I should've known better. You warned me." He took a step back, his arm falling to his side. "I didn't want to listen. I wanted you too much."

"I wanted you, too," I said, finding my voice.

"But..."

"I'm not ready for the commitment you want. And I can't ask you to wait around for me to get my head on straight either."

"What do we do now?" he asked.

"That's up to you. Do you think you can still work with me?"

"Now I'm offended." He laughed. "Jesus, Wilder, of course, I can. We were friends before we were anything else. I may have to go home and lick my wounds for a bit, but I'll get over it." He took my hand in his, threading his fingers through mine. "Eventually."

"I'm sorry," I said, knowing those two words did nothing to help the situation. But I meant it.

He pulled me into a hug, his strong arms offering me a closure I shouldn't expect from him. "I know."

* * *

My breakup with Anders, if I could even call it that, was messing up my mojo. I'd only written about five-hundred words since I'd gotten to the coffee shop. As much as I needed to end things with him, it didn't feel great to lose yet another relationship. Yes, our friendship and professional relationship had remained intact, but I was exhausted with myself. I shut my laptop and checked my watch. June was late, not a new concept for her. My coffee was gone, and my mood was less reasonable by the minute. I thought about packing up and leaving, but in true form, June walked in right in the nick of time.

"Sorry I'm late." She kissed my cheek before she sat down. She waved at the barista with a smile. "The usual, Joyce," she hollered over the music and chatter of the room.

"I broke up with Anders," I blurted, and her eyes widened. "Well, he sort of broke up with me."

"Good for him."

I gave her a withering glare. "Excuse me. You're supposed to be my support system, not his."

"You'll live," she said, just as Joyce set her coffee onto the table. "Thank you."

"Let me know if you need another." Joyce smiled before leaving to help another customer.

June sipped from the cup with a little moan. "Thank God for caffeine, I wouldn't make it tonight without it."

"I don't know how you work three twelve-hour night shifts in a row and not kill anyone."

"Sometimes I wonder the same thing." She grinned. "Now give me what I came here for."

"You don't want to talk about Anders?" I asked.

"God, no. I want those emails. Anders is old news."

I opened up the messages on my phone, shaking my head. "Your disregard for my emotional wellbeing is shocking."

"Did you cry?" she asked, and I shook my head. "I didn't think so. Can we move on now?"

I handed her my phone but didn't let go when she tried to take it. "I'm betraying Jordan's trust by letting you read these."

"I'll be sure not to tell him." She tugged on the phone and I reluctantly let go.

I waited for an eternity as she read, tortured by every passing minute. June's facial expressions were my only saving grace, and I swore at one point I thought her eyes were glassy.

"This is so sad," she said, setting my phone on the table.

"Do you think I'm being catfished?"

"I mean, I can't be sure, but wow. His story, it's sad. It reminds me of Jax's."

"Unfortunately, shit like this happens for a lot of people. You know that as well as I do. It's not like Jax is the only closet case to ever live."

"I think this guy is for real, Wilder, and that makes me worry for you."

"For me?" My brows pinched together. "Why?"

"He's not Jax."

My face heated with anger. "No shit, June."

"Calm down, I'm just saying. You can't fix everyone."

"I never wanted to fix Jax," I argued, knowing I wasn't being honest with myself. She raised a brow and I folded. "Okay, maybe I tried to help him. I loved him, June. I wanted him to be able to live an open life. To be himself."

"And how did that turn out?"

"I hate you sometimes," I said, picking up my laptop and shoving it into my bag.

She sighed and leaned back in her chair. "I just want you to be careful."

"I will be." I stood, pulling my bag over my shoulder.

"Alright, then. Sit down. I just got here. Stop throwing a tantrum and tell me about this breakup."

June's concern was not unwarranted. I had a pattern, and she was simply reminding me to break the cycle.

"There's not much to tell. We had sex, and then he… we broke it off."

"Was the sex good, at least?" she asked and took another big gulp of her coffee.

Laughing, I shrugged. "Sex with Anders is always good."

"Was…"

"Yes, thank you for the past-tense reminder."

"No problem." She looked at my phone. "What do you think he looks like?"

"I don't know."

"He sounds southern... I mean, the tone he uses when he writes."

"Maybe like a young Matthew McConaughey?"

"See... I was thinking more like... Scott Eastwood."

"I could be down with that," I said.

"I bet you could." She laughed and the tension between us dissolved.

Between my morning with Anders and the mystery of Jordan, a powerful weight had attached itself to my shoulders. I thought about what I'd told Jordan. My need for stability. June had become my gravity. I didn't like it when we argued.

"I needed this," I said.

She knocked my knee with hers. "I know, it's why I'm here."

"Should we read the emails again, just in case you missed something important?"

"I thought you'd never ask."

Chapter 7

JAX

Heavy rain fell onto the metal roof of my house, the tin sound of it comforting, as I poured myself a glass of iced tea. Mom and Jason were in the living room watching *Goonies*. Whenever the weather got bad, my mom would put it on. It was his favorite movie and it helped keep his mind off the gusts of wind and lightning. I'd seen that damn movie too many times to enjoy it anymore, and with my workday getting cut short, I was restless. I'd asked my boss, Jim, if I could stick around and work on the trim inside the house, but he'd told me to take off. It was comical. You'd think people who lived through hurricanes wouldn't freak out over a tropical depression, but the guys, including Jim, had everything packed up and were gone by one.

I'd taken a drive to the beach, enjoying the emptiness that surrounded me. Without a soul in the parking lot, from the front seat of my car, the gray ocean waves beat at the shoreline. My feelings on religion had always been mixed with confusion and fear. But that angry sky, all that wind bending the palm trees like they were made of rubber, it had me thinking about how small I was in the grand scheme of it all, and how God had much bigger things to worry about than who I was or wasn't attracted to.

"Come watch the movie, Jax," Jason said, grabbing a glass from the cupboard. He poured himself some tea, took a huge gulp, and then filled his glass again. "We're not even to the best part yet."

"In a minute, Jay, I'm gonna send a message to my friend, and then I'll be right in."

His smile was a punch to the chest. He was such a handsome kid. He'd had his future stolen from him, and here I was whining about my sexuality. Once he left the kitchen, I pulled out my phone and opened up my email from Wild, debating on how much I could tell him, or should tell him. It would be smart to just thank him for his time and end this back and forth we'd started. Especially since it seemed he wanted to make things more personal. I was such an asshole, because I already knew everything about Wild, or I used to. He'd told me once that his favorite color was green because that was the color of my eyes. I already knew the date of his birthday, and that he hated cake. I knew that he wore eyeliner when he was feeling moody, and I loved the way it'd made his light brown eyes dark and smokey. And that when it came to us and those stolen moments we'd had, hands and fingers, top or bottom, it didn't matter to him. Sex had been something we'd shared together, on equal ground. I knew how soft his skin was under my fingers, and how his mouth tasted. I knew all of these things, and it made what I'd done, emailing him like this, seem cruel.

I typed out a message, erased it, and started it again. I did this about five times, staring at the screen of my phone. I tried to figure out a way to politely cut him off, thank him for all of his advice. But every time I tried to put all that shit into words, my hands would start to shake. Wild had only been back in my life for a couple of days, and I'd already fallen in too deep to let him go again. I sat down at the kitchen table, my head and stomach a mess of nerves. I knew what I needed to do, but I'd never been good at doing the right thing.

FROM: fool0fatook54@bellinx.mail.com
TO: wildwelleslit@bartpress.com
Date: Jul 15 3:30 PM
SUBJECT: RE: So, you think I'm amazing?

Wilder,

I've been thinking a lot about what you said, and maybe my mom would be more accepting than I've given her credit for. My dad was very controlling with me and my brother. It was probably the same way for her, but I didn't see it because I was too involved in my own shit. And yeah, I had a boyfriend. He was everything to me, but I fucked it up. My parents had no idea. I'm a pretty closed book. And I'm not sure what a Funko Pop is, but you can keep them. I'm not about to come out to my mom yet, or anytime soon. Maybe I could say something to my brother, but he'd probably tell my mom not even meaning to. What you said, about setting yourself up, just in case everything goes to hell, I want that. I need to find my own footing, my own stability, and then maybe coming out won't be as hard. At least not with my family. At work? That might never happen.

These homophobic idiots I work with started picking on this guy at the hardware store yesterday. They think he's into me or whatever, called him something I'd rather not say. Sorry. I hate that word, even typing it, I'm angry all over again. One of the guys accused him of checking me out, which is ludicrous.

How do you do it? Are people assholes all the time? I admire how much you don't give a shit. You're strong, and yes, amazing. You're talented, Wilder, and I don't care who that Judith, gender lady, is, you're smart as hell. Your book alone proves that.

As for the details, there isn't much to tell. I don't really have a favorite color. Today it's gray. It's raining, and I like how the sky makes the ocean change colors. I live in a small town near the Florida coast, Gulf side, not Atlantic, which made it easier for me to relate to Jake while I was reading. I think if I lived in Orlando, or Tampa, it might've been easier for me. Bigger the town, more open the mind. I don't have a favorite book, but I do love LOTR. In my opinion, Peregrin is the best hobbit, if you couldn't tell by my email address. Like me, he's constantly messing stuff up. My least favorite movie is Goonies because it's the only damn thing my brother will watch, and is currently playing again, in the other room, for the millionth time. I work in construction and hope one day to be a contractor. It'd be nice to be my own boss. Can't think of anything else at the moment, but the idea of putting all of this on a dating app makes me laugh. I always thought those things were filled with dick pics and abs. Which isn't a bad thing. But I'm not on the displaying-my-junk-for-the-world-to-see level of my gay experience yet.

I've attached a copy of that Cinderella story for your friend June. Let me know what she thinks.

Jordan~

P.S. I never thought about Sam being bi. Which kind of makes sense. Maybe he didn't realize it until his trip across Middle Earth. That's one hell of a wake-up call.

P.P.S. You can send wink emojis. I won't judge you… that much.

FROM: wildwelleslit@bartpress.com
TO: fool0fatook54@bellinx.mail.com
Date: Jul 15 4:02 PM
SUBJECT: RE: So, you think I'm amazing?

Jordan,

Full disclosure. I might've shown June our messages. This is quite the invasion of your privacy, and I'm sorry for that. I hope you will keep reading so I can explain. Most importantly, you should know that I have enjoyed these conversations, and I appreciate how you have trusted me with your honesty. It's why I wanted to tell you about June. I've been hurt in the past, and it's very hard for me to have faith in others. I asked June to look at our emails because I didn't have confidence in myself as a true judge of character. And perhaps, if I told you the real story about "Jake," you'd understand my hesitancy and need for confirmation from my dear friend June.

Love Always, Wild is true up until the end. The real truth of it is much less dramatic but cut me just as deeply. If not deeper. "Jake" didn't die. He left. He went home for winter break and never came back. My first and only love, vanished from my life without an explanation. I mean, like full-on ghosted me. As you know, he was in the closet, so everything we'd shared together had felt so important. At least for me it had. Without getting into too much of the melodrama of my real life, his leaving was a very dark time for me. I wanted you to know my reasoning for not fully trusting that you were real and not some weird fifty-year-old with a sex dungeon. If you happen to have a sex dungeon, that's your business, but I'm not into older men.

I'm happy to report you've passed the June test. She said, "He's the real deal."

I hope you will forgive me for sharing with her, but I promise, from here on out, what we talk about is just between us. Oh, and she says thanks for the Cinderella story.

In regard to your email, I think setting up a plan and a foundation for you to stand on is a great idea. Maybe then you'll feel less vulnerable when you decide to come out. I hope it didn't sound like I was pushing you. I tend to stick my nose where it doesn't belong. I hope since your last email you have searched the Internet for Funko Pops. If not, do it now. I'll wait…

FROM: fool0fatook54@bellinx.mail.com
TO: wildwelleslit@bartpress.com
Date: Jul 15 4:19 PM
SUBJECT: RE: So, you think I'm amazing?

I do NOT have a sex dungeon.

The Funko Pops look like bobble heads. You collect toys?

And please don't apologize to me, of all people, about anything. I understand completely why you'd ask your friend for her opinion. And I'm sorry about what Jake did to you. Though I'm sure he had his reasons, it doesn't make what he did any less terrible or right. I can only imagine how hard that was for you.

Jordan~

FROM: wildwelleslit@bartpress.com
TO: fool0fatook54@bellinx.mail.com
Date: Jul 15 4:26 PM
SUBJECT: Don't knock it until you try it

I think sex dungeons have their merit for those inclined to kinkery. Don't knock it until you try it. And I have NOT.

Why shouldn't I apologize to you "of all people?"

And yes, I do collect toys, but not like you're thinking. Funko Pops are small, adorable collectibles. Toys (not the dungeon variety) are for the bedroom, not the bookshelf. ;) I owed you a wink.

By the way, your co-workers are toxic. You should report them. Unless your boss is a homophobe too? Is the guy who works at the hardware store hot? And I'm totally jealous that you live by the beach. I love Atlanta, but sometimes the city can be oppressive.

I hope the weather isn't getting too bad.

Wilder ~

P.S. I could be down with a Peregrin fan. He's a nosey little hobbit, isn't he? About the dating app, it can be tedious shuffling through all the pornographic imagery, but it's great for hookups in a pinch.

Great for hookups? I read the last line again, sick to my stomach. Wild was out living his life, like he should. I had no right to feel jealous. But the feeling choked me all the same. I deserved it. I'd hurt him, in his own words, deeply. I'd left him like a coward, and it didn't matter if I had my reasons for leaving. All the pain I'd caused him, I'd never be able to take it away. He shouldn't thank me for my honesty, I'd only been dealing in half-truths and lies by omission. He'd told his best friend about Jordan, the fact that he even thought of me outside of these emails had my guilt spiraling. Wild had put his faith in me again, and this time, I had to figure out a way not to break him.

FROM: fool0fatook54@bellinx.mail.com
TO: wildwelleslit@bartpress.com
Date: Jul 15 4:39 PM
SUBJECT: RE: Don't knock it until you try it

"Me of all people" have made some serious mistakes, some might say they were unforgivable. So, I don't feel like I need any apologies from anyone. It's like God, or whoever, deals me what I deserve, and I take it in stride. Getting to talk to you, that's a gift in and of itself. You could have told me to fuck off, but you didn't. Thanks for that. I'm a work in progress. But I think we all are. I'll have to take your word for it about the toys. My experience with "adorable collectibles" and dungeons and sex toys are limited. As in, none. I'm pathetic, right?

As for Ethan, that's the guy at the hardware store, I haven't paid much attention. It's a habit, ignoring my basic instincts. He's got pretty eyes.

And he's always nice to me. A little too nice sometimes. He's like that with everyone.

The weather isn't too bad, but I'm used to it. We're safe.

Jordan~

P.S. What dating app do you use? Or is that too nosey?

FROM: wildwelleslit@bartpress.com
TO: fool0fatook54@bellinx.mail.com
Date: Jul 15 10:34 PM
SUBJECT: RE: Don't knock it until you try it

Jordan,

Mistakes happen. I mean, you're not a murderer or anything, right? You're an overall good human being? Don't be too hard on yourself. I am of the belief that most of the mistakes we make in life are forgivable. You just have to give people time to process. We are all, indeed, works in progress. And by the sound of it, this Ethan guy might be into you. Remember, you're a self-proclaimed self-loather. You might not notice all the signs he's sending. I have an assignment for you, well, a couple, actually. First, next time you see this Ethan of yours, take the time to notice him. I guarantee you, if he's into you, you'll know it. Second, I need you to research as many sex toys as possible and report back. This is kind of exciting, you're like a tiny little baby gay, spreading his adult wings. Can I call you my precious?

Wilder~

P.S. It's a little nosey, but I wouldn't expect anything less from a fool of a Took.

P.P.S. It's called Pegasus.

Chapter 8

JAX

FROM: fool0fatook54@bellinx.mail.com
TO: wildwelleslit@bartpress.com
Date: Jul 16 6:47 AM
SUBJECT: Too early for pet names

Wilder,

Sorry I fell asleep and didn't get your message until this morning. Don't have a lot of time before I have to leave for work but wanted to say thanks. I hope that's true, what you said about forgiveness. I feel like I've got a lot of fixing to do, but what you said... It gives me hope.

Talk to you soon,
Jordan (not a murderer)

P.S. It's a little early in the morning for sex toys and pet names.

FROM: wildwelleslit@bartpress.com
TO: fool0fatook54@bellinx.mail.com
Date: Jul 16 10:33 AM
SUBJECT: RE: Too early for pet names

My Precious,

How in the hell are you able to get up at six in the morning? I don't think there are enough dollars in the world that would get me out of bed that early. Though... I do think I could be persuaded if there were donuts involved. Maple glazed only. Everything else is garbage, in my opinion.

Also, don't think I didn't notice the whole lack of acknowledgement of the "Ethan situation." Will you see him today?

Wilder~

P.S. It is NEVER too early in the morning for sex toys.

My laugh was muted by the loud clap of thunder outside. The kitchen window rattled with the wind as I finished reading Wilder's message. I was at home, sitting at the kitchen table, with a dumbass grin on my face. I was glad my mom had gone next door to help Ms. Arlene with something, or she'd have about a thousand questions for me if she'd seen my expression. She hadn't forgiven me yet for breaking things off with Mary. I should've been at work, but when I'd gotten there, I'd shown up to an empty house and sat in my car for a good thirty minutes before I'd called Jim. He'd forgotten to call me this morning to tell me the project had been put on hold until this weather system that was parked over us moved north, most likely Monday. The humidity was shit for painting, so I didn't blame him, but it would've been nice to know before I'd woken up at the ass crack of dawn.

I reread Wild's message, loving how much he was the same, but different. He'd definitely come into his own, and I envied him that. I wondered what he'd be like in person, and if the pictures he had on his website were real or photoshopped. Wild had grown into his jaw line, the boyishness of his cheeks had chiseled with time. Not all things had changed, though. He still had those long, graceful limbs, and full lips. Thinking about his mouth heated my skin, and I had to stand up to shake off the flow of blood to my crotch.

Music played loudly from Jason's room as I walked by. He was situated and curled across his bed, reading one of his favorite wizard books. I knocked on the frame of the door.

"Jay, you mind if I borrow the laptop for a little bit?"

He sat up, letting the book fall into his lap. He yawned and brushed his hair from his eyes. "Sure, it's on the desk."

"Thanks."

His desk was covered in drawings and books about tornadoes. For a guy who hated the weather, he sure loved to read about it.

"If it stops raining, can we go to the beach later?" he asked, falling back against his pillows.

"I don't think the weather is gonna let up for a couple days."

He sighed and brought his attention back to his book.

"We could always go and watch the waves from the car. If you want?"

"But it's raining," he said, licking his finger and flipping a page.

I smiled and his tension eased. "I'll let you pick all the songs."

"Deal."

I tucked the laptop under my arm.

"We'll head out when mom gets home, alright?"

When he nodded, I figured that was all the answer I was going to get, and I headed to my room. With the door locked behind me, I settled on my bed. My back against the headboard, I set the laptop on my thighs and opened it. The browser window stared back at me, waiting for my next move. Anxiety rooted itself inside my gut. After a minute, I gave in and searched for the dating app Wilder had told me about. I read through the terms and conditions, typed in my email address, and date of birth, and just like that, I had a profile. It was blank, but it was there. I chose my username, mjordanfan0713, but left the picture blank. I skipped over the bio and went straight to the search feature.

I tried several different versions of Wilder's name and found nothing. Frustrated, I shut the laptop. Why the hell was I even looking for him in the first place. I was like a teenager with a crush, and I was a grown ass man. I opened the laptop again and typed in Ethan's name and almost choked when a picture of him, lying shirtless in the sand, popped up. *Ethan was gay.* I said the words out loud a few times to wrap my head around the idea, and then clicked on his profile. According to his bio, he lived in Florida, no city specified, and was into soccer, fishing, and bottoming. My face flushed. I closed my eyes and rubbed my forehead trying to ease away my growing headache.

As the seconds passed, I became more irrationally angry. My stomach revolted as I thought about all the times Ethan had smiled at me, looked at me longer than most would consider polite. That day when he'd given us a ride home, the smell of him on my skin from his shirt, I never wanted to like it. But I did. Resentment boiled up inside of me and I opened my eyes. I flipped through all of his pictures, all of his smiles. Those warm, coppery eyes. Did he know? Could he see through my lies? Would he expose them? I clicked out of his profile and then deleted my own.

Ethan's sexuality scared the shit out of me. Everything about my life in Bell River was about being straight and Christian and worthy. And Ethan's open, flirty smile threatened that. It rattled the doors I'd been hiding behind because, damn it, as much as I tried not to, maybe I'd noticed him too. My palms were damp as I closed the search browser and opened up my emails.

FROM: fool0fatook54@bellinx.mail.com
TO: wildwelleslit@bartpress.com
Date: Jul 16 11:17 AM
SUBJECT: RE: Too early for pet names

How is it that you knew Ethan was gay before I did, and you don't even know him? How am I that stupid?

FROM: wildwelleslit@bartpress.com
TO: fool0fatook54@bellinx.mail.com
Date: Jul 16 11:25 AM
SUBJECT: RE: Too early for pet names

You are not stupid. Denial is a powerful drug. Listen, we all have some level of internalized homophobia, right? The world tells us it's Male/ Female, all day every day. In the shit we read, the media, the history books, the churches... I could go on, but I'm more interested in how you came around to the revelation about our Ethan. You're not stupid, you're programmed.

FROM: fool0fatook54@bellinx.mail.com
TO: wildwelleslit@bartpress.com
Date: Jul 16 11:40 AM
SUBJECT: RE: Too early for pet names

I looked him up on that dating app and he was there, all out and proud.

Internalized homophobia.

Another thing I will add to the list of research you've given me. AKA Reprogramming.

FROM: wildwelleslit@bartpress.com
TO: fool0fatook54@bellinx.mail.com
Date: Jul 16 12:03 PM
SUBJECT: RE: Too early for pet names

He's on Pegasus?! More importantly, so are you! I'm more than happy to supplement your gay awakening with a little education and reprogramming, but eventually you must fly on your own, my precious.

Also, I need Ethan's last name… you know… for research.

P.S. Did you look up the sex toys?

FROM: fool0fatook54@bellinx.mail.com
TO: wildwelleslit@bartpress.com
Date: Jul 16 12:15 PM
SUBJECT: RE: Too early for pet names

I deleted my profile after I found Ethan. I guess it freaked me out a little. It's totally self-centered, but I worried that the attention he gave me might make people think I was like him. Which I am. But I'm not ready to admit that to anyone around here.

His last name is Calloway.

P.S. Not yet, still mind fucked over the whole "Ethan situation."

FROM: wildwelleslit@bartpress.com
TO: fool0fatook54@bellinx.mail.com
Date: Jul 16 12:43 PM
SUBJECT: The Ethan Situation

It's a bit self-centered if you want the truth, but I think it's human to feel that way. His attention is something you're not ready to deal with and that's fine. It's too bad, though, because Ethan is very easy on the eyes. Speaking of eyes, WOW. What color is that? It's like caramel. Those arms too. I like how matter of fact his bio is. Who doesn't like an assertive power bottom?

FROM: fool0fatook54@bellinx.mail.com
TO: wildwelleslit@bartpress.com
Date: Jul 16 12:59 PM
SUBJECT: RE: The Ethan Situation

I had to look up the definition of power bottom.

FROM: wildwelleslit@bartpress.com
TO: fool0fatook54@bellinx.mail.com
Date: Jul 16 1:05 PM
SUBJECT: RE: The Ethan Situation

Of course, you did, Precious.

We messaged like that, back and forth, on and off, for a while, looking up shit Wilder had said, and eventually, sex toys, to my own detriment. Who knew they made dildos shaped like dragons and fists? I flinched as I flipped through the images.

FROM: fool0fatook54@bellinx.mail.com
TO: wildwelleslit@bartpress.com
Date: Jul 16 2:30 PM
SUBJECT: Education?

Dragons? I feel so overwhelmed by all of this, to be honest. Or maybe shocked is a better word? I don't think I'd ever be into any of this stuff.

FROM: wildwelleslit@bartpress.com
TO: fool0fatook54@bellinx.mail.com
Date: Jul 16 2:35 PM
SUBJECT: RE: Education?

And you don't have to be. But it's healthy to explore, I think. Maybe we should have started you off with something simple, like cock rings and flavored lube?

FROM: fool0fatook54@bellinx.mail.com
TO: wildwelleslit@bartpress.com
Date: Jul 16 2:39 PM
SUBJECT: RE: Education?

Are you into this stuff? Or maybe I shouldn't even be asking?

FROM: wildwelleslit@bartpress.com
TO: fool0fatook54@bellinx.mail.com
Date: Jul 16 2:42 PM
SUBJECT: RE: Education?

It might be too soon in our "relationship" to reveal all my bedroom quirks. But you can rest at ease, the dragons and fists are not my type of fun. I'm too vanilla for all of that.

Jason knocked on my door and I jumped. "Mom's home. Are we still going to the beach?"

Shit.

"Yeah, buddy. I'll be right out."

I typed out a quick email to Wild.

FROM: fool0fatook54@bellinx.mail.com
TO: wildwelleslit@bartpress.com
Date: Jul 16 2:46 PM
SUBJECT: RE: Education?

This educational experience has been…
Terrifying? Eye opening?
I have to run though, taking my little brother to the beach.

Talk to you later,
Jordan

P.S. Thank you for today.

I closed out of everything and cleared the browser history before I stood and stretched, my limbs feeling stiff. I couldn't believe how long we'd let the conversation go or the path it had taken. My head was still trying to process everything when I opened my bedroom door.

"Can we stop and get fries on the way?" Jason asked, slipping into his raincoat.

I stepped into the hall with a chuckle. "Sure thing."

His smile was bigger than the world, and as we walked to the kitchen to tell Mom the plan for the afternoon, I couldn't help but feel lighter somehow. Talking to Wild again, he made me laugh, made me feel something other than that constant anger and fear I carried around all the time, even if it was all confusing as hell.

"Jax? I don't think I've seen you smile like that... ever. It's like you stole all the sunshine right out of the sky."

I swallowed the lump in my throat and rubbed the back of my neck. "I don't know what you're going on about, Momma. It's just a smile. I'm not a hard ass all the time."

"Please don't swear in my house." She pulled me into a hug and whispered, "I just want to see you happy. So, whatever it is that's got you smiling. Keep it up."

If she knew that I'd been looking up prostate massagers and other paraphernalia all afternoon, I don't think she'd so willingly approve. I wasn't even sure I approved.

She wiped at her eyes as she pulled away. "Where you boys headed?"

"Figured we'd watch the waves for a while, get some fries. Want to come?" I asked and she stared out the kitchen window.

The smokey gray sky lit up with lightning. "No, I think I'll stay here." She squeezed my arm with a smile before pulling Jason into a hug. "Don't be too long, you know how I worry."

"I have my phone," I reminded her.

"We could take some pictures," Jason offered, and she gave him a soft smile.

"I'd like that."

◆ ◆ ◆

Grease and salt stuck to my fingers as I grabbed the last fry from the bag. The waves had died down, and the old Foo Fighters album Jason chose to listen to had neared to its end.

"I wish we got waves like Daytona," Jason said, tracing the rain drops on his window.

I chuckled. "Why? Then you'd never get in the water."

"I would," he argued, and I knew better not to irritate him.

Jason's emotions were all over the place. One second, he was happy, chilling and listening to music, and then for no reason at all, he'd throw a fit that would challenge any eight-year-old. The older he got, the less he got angry. "A small blessing," my mom once said.

"Maybe you would," I said and messed up his hair with my hand.

He swatted my arm away, laughing too hard to be mad. "You know..." Jason caught his breath. "I don't remember what Dad's voice sounded like."

Struck silent, I turned to look at him. He never talked about Dad.

"I remember he was loud, but not what he sounded like," he said. "When I hear him talk in my head, he sounds like you, but louder."

I didn't want to say anything. I wanted Jason to keep talking. Talking like the man he should've been if he hadn't drowned. He hadn't seemed so grown up in over nine years.

"Was he loud?" he asked, and I nodded. "I should've driven."

It was hard to breathe, my chest and eyes burning as I tried, and failed, to hold everything in. I wiped the flat of my palm over my wet cheeks.

"He would have never let you drive, Jay." Jason looked at me with wet lashes of his own. "It's not your fault."

His throat worked as he swallowed. "You don't think so?"

"Not at all. Not for one second." I reached for him and he rested his head on my shoulder.

With the rain pouring down around us, I thought about the day my dad had died and how it had changed our lives. How each of us had accepted some type of blame. Mom thought she should have stopped him from fishing that day. I thought God had taken my dad as payment for what I'd had with Wild. And Jason, to think all this time, he'd thought it was his fault. We'd wasted all those years on a man who'd been too fucking prideful to let his son drive his drunk ass home. We had to let the past go. There was nothing to be done about it all anyway.

"You might not remember a whole lot about Dad. But I do." Jason lifted his head from my shoulder and rubbed his fists over his eyes. "He didn't listen to reason, Jay. Ever. Don't you blame yourself. He's at fault... for all of it, okay?"

"Yeah... okay." He buckled his seatbelt, his mood shifting again as quick as the wind whipped outside. "Can we go home now?"

I shifted the car into reverse and backed out of the parking spot. "When we get home, want to watch *Goonies* again?"

Jason's face lit up with that bright as hell smile I loved. "You hate that movie."

"It's not too bad, once you've seen it a thousand times or so."

He chuckled, and the sound of it cleared the air. "A thousand times?"

"At least." I laughed.

"No way. That's impossible."

"When it comes to your love for that movie, Jay... Nothing is impossible."

Chapter 9

WILDER

People were herded together like cattle, waiting behind the velvet rope. I peeked through the black curtain and saw that the entire bookstore lobby was packed. The smell of sugary coffee and caramel hung in the air, and on any other day, I would have breathed it in like the gleeful caffeine junkie that I was, but today it suffocated me. All those people had come here to see me, and for what? A signature and a smile? The idea of it, of an author scrawling their name like they were something to be remembered, across the title page of the book they'd written, seemed beyond narcissistic. I supposed, as a reader myself, I would no doubt forever cherish meeting someone I admired. But what happened when the reader died or if the book got misplaced? The signature lost in a sea of shelves, pages, and ink. The book and autograph would wither in some dusty, old, used bookstore where, inevitably, someone would buy it for a dollar and ninety-nine cents. No one caring how it got there, or about the life of work behind the simple curl of the blue penned signature, not giving a shit that the author had signed it in the first place because no one remembered who the hell the author was anymore anyway. That once upon a time, the author had stood behind a black curtain, sweating, worried he wasn't what everyone expected, and predicted that one day his legacy would end up being worth less than two dollars.

I inhaled a deep breath, shaking my hands at my sides to get rid of all the nervous energy bunching in my muscles. I wanted to email Jordan, ramble to him about my self-centered, first-world problems. He'd probably stroke my ego, tell me how much he loved my book, and how he wished he could be one of these people waiting to meet me. It should've been unusual, how fast our friendship had grown, and how quickly we'd opened up to each other. Three weeks... and there wasn't a day that had gone by that we didn't have some sort of correspondence. Sometimes we'd message back and forth for hours until he fell asleep, talking about our day-to-day nonsense. I liked that he'd let me talk about books, and how he'd let me push his boundaries when we'd discussed his sexuality. He'd fire back with question after question. He was like a sponge soaking me up, word by word, and I couldn't help but love the attention. Of course, there were warning bells ringing in my ears. I had no idea what he looked like, or how I shouldn't allow myself to get too close—feel so drawn to him. But I was. Drawn to him. There was something about his innocence, his freely given vulnerability that I craved. Jordan trusted me, and it made me feel needed, relevant in a way I hadn't felt in a long time.

"Ready?" Andrew asked, and I almost jumped out of my skin.

"Jesus, way to make a guy shit himself. You're like a stealthy ninja on the sneak attack."

He laughed and ran a fast hand through his dark curls. "Sorry, I didn't mean to scare you."

"Why do people say that? Of course you didn't purposely scare me," I said, waving my hands like a maniac. *This signing, all the people, I'd finally become the lunatic diva I'd always feared I'd turn out to be.*

Andrew handed me a bottle of water, his lips, which in that moment I realized were very nice to look at, twitched. "Nervous?" he asked, and I nodded. "First signing?"

"Am I that obvious?"

He shrugged, his grin widening. "Maybe a little bit. But I'm well versed in the jitters of a debut author."

"Anders told me you used to be a PA for authors at Random House," I said, trying to rein in my anxiety.

"And Penguin. I actually worked for an author who threw up five minutes before every signing."

"Every signing?" I asked, feeling more overwhelmed by the fact this fear might never go away.

"Like clockwork."

"I haven't puked yet."

"See, already above the curve."

"There's still time."

His laugh calmed me a little. "I think you'll do just fine."

"Thanks," I said, appreciating his dimples.

Andrew had been assigned to me by Bartley Press for PR. I didn't want a personal assistant, preferring to do things on my own, and my own way, but Anders had insisted. Andrew was way too good looking to be my assistant. Leaning against the wall with long, thick legs, wrapped in perfectly tailored slacks, I could already picture him starring in some of my more imaginative sex dreams. He was a distraction I didn't need. He was probably straight, and Anders had handpicked him to torture me.

He looked at his watch as he approached me. "So, you don't have to make a speech or anything. But maybe say something like, thanks for coming out, or whatever, and then we can start the line." He placed his hand at the small of my back, the light touch making me even more nervous as he guided me to the curtain. "You can do this, Wilder."

It wasn't a comfortable feeling, having him so close, but as he pulled back the curtain, and the room erupted in applause, I was grateful for his steady hand. Andrew followed me to the table they'd set up for me, leaning in, he said, "Wave, and don't forget to smile."

I did as he said, feeling ridiculous, but as I raised my hand the room quieted. This was where I was supposed to say something, but my fear had taken over in the silence. I offered the crowd a shaky smile, my cheeks on fire, I finally managed a few words.

"Fuck, I'm nervous."

Everyone laughed, and I thought I might actually puke.

"I was worried I would say something I shouldn't, now that I've checked that box, should we sign some books?"

There was a chorus of cheers, and as I got a closer look at the large crowd, my nerves subsided. Everyone had a smile on their face, the excitement in the room palpable, like I could reach out and grab it and save some for when I couldn't remember if this had been a dream or my reality.

A young man, maybe in his early twenties, was the first to walk up to the table. He handed me his book with a quiet grin. I opened it to the title page where a yellow Post-it had the name Griffin written across it.

"Nice to meet you, Griffin," I said, glancing up at him before scribbling a short note and my signature on the page. He didn't say anything, just stared at me with wide eyes. I closed the book and handed it to him. "Thanks for coming out today."

"Thank you," he said, almost too softly for me to hear, and walked toward the exit.

"You're a natural. Told you, you'd be fine," Andrew said, with a gentle tap of his foot against mine under the table.

"Is it part of your job to flatter me all the time?"

"It can be," he said with a mischievous glint in his silver eyes that had me thinking maybe I needed a personal assistant after all.

FROM: wildwelleslit@bartpress.com
TO: fool0fatook54@bellinx.mail.com
Date: Aug 7 8:08 PM
SUBJECT: Best Worst Day EVER

Jordan,

How was your brother's appointment? Did it go well?

The signing was weird, and great, and I'm still a little drunk, but... WOW. Have you ever felt so alone, but at the same time enveloped by a love you don't deserve? Today was that day, and I wish I could talk to you about it. Face to face. Like over dinner, or here in my condo with wine and... I'm drunk. I'm going to stop before I train wreck even further.

Wilder~

FROM: fool0fatook54@bellinx.mail.com
TO: wildwelleslit@bartpress.com
Date: Aug 7 8:19 PM
SUBJECT: RE: Best Worst Day EVER

Wilder,

How much have you had to drink?

I'm glad the signing was weird but great, but only if that's a good thing. I know you've been worried about it. Were there a lot of people? Why was it weird?

To answer your question, the appointment was as I expected. It's normal for people who've had brain injuries to have seizures sometimes. We are used to it by now. They gave us a new medication to try. But overall, my brother is fine. Thanks for asking.

Jordan~

P.S. I wish it was easier to talk to you. Maybe one day we can talk face to face.

FROM: wildwelleslit@bartpress.com
TO: fool0fatook54@bellinx.mail.com
Date: Aug 7 8:38 PM
SUBJECT: RE: Best Worst Day EVER

Text me
470-555-5784

FROM: fool0fatook54@bellinx.mail.com
TO: wildwelleslit@bartpress.com
Date: Aug 7 8:50 PM
SUBJECT: RE: Best Worst Day EVER

Are you sure that's a good idea? You've been drinking.

FROM: wildwelleslit@bartpress.com
TO: fool0fatook54@bellinx.mail.com
Date: Aug 7 8:52 PM
SUBJECT: RE: Best Worst Day EVER

And... I want you to text me. I don't see a problem. Do you?

FROM: fool0fatook54@bellinx.mail.com
TO: wildwelleslit@bartpress.com
Date: Aug 7 8:56 PM
SUBJECT: RE: Best Worst Day EVER

No... I mean, maybe. If you were sober you wouldn't have given me your number. That's kind of personal information. Three weeks ago, you thought I might be a serial killer.

FROM: wildwelleslit@bartpress.com
TO: fool0fatook54@bellinx.mail.com
Date: Aug 7 8:58 PM
SUBJECT: RE: Best Worst Day EVER

I'm feeling a touch offended, Jordan (not a serial killer).

Three weeks ago, I didn't know you. And I might not know you, know you, but I know I like you, like talking to you. I look forward to it every day. Of course, it's personal.

Wild~

I reread the message after I sent it, apprehension filling my lungs as I sank back against my pillows. I'd signed off as Wild, which I'd *never* done for anyone other than Jax. Goddamn it, alcohol made me stupid. My email sounded needy and dramatic, which, in this second was true, but I blamed my incredibly long day and the two-ish, three-ish bottles of wine I'd shared with June and Gwen after I'd left the bookstore. I typed out a damage control message and erased it, hating myself for being sappy with a guy I'd never actually met in "real life." I was about to send a simple, ignore me, I'm feeling sentimental, it's a full moon, and Mercury is in retrograde email, when my phone buzzed next to me on the bed.

Unknown Number: I look forward to talking to you every day too.

My heart had no business getting this excited over a text message. I shut my laptop and set it on the bedside table. My thumbs moved fast over the touch screen of my phone, adding Jordan to my contacts.

Me: See, that wasn't so scary.
Jordan: Hope you won't hate me for this.
Me: I gave you my number, why would I hate you?
Jordan: You've been drinking.
Me: I'm not that drunk. Figured this is easier than emails.
Me: Who knows? Maybe in a few weeks we can FaceTime. Oh, the possibilities.
Jordan: What did you mean when you said the signing was weird?

I smirked at his quick change of subject.

Me: No FaceTime, then?

Three-bubbles popped up and disappeared three times before his next text came through.

Jordan: Not ready to burst our bubble.

I could understand that. What we had was easy. FaceTime was like the pen-pal version of sex. It would only complicate things.

Me: That makes sense.
Jordan: I'm not saying no, just not yet.
Me: Did I make it weird?
Jordan: Nah, I think that was me.
Me: It was definitely you ;)

I pulled at my bottom lip with my teeth, grinning at my phone.

Me: About the signing...
Me: It was weird, having all these strangers stare at me like I was something shiny. Everyone was nice and said really complimentary things.
Jordan: But...
Me: I was alone, even though there were over a hundred people there. Everyone wanted to say hi, and get my signature, and asked great questions, but it felt shallow because I'm not that important or interesting.
Jordan: You're important to them. You talk about books all the time. How you feel about those books is how they feel about yours. Why is that bad?
Me: The usual self-deprecating bullshit. I don't deserve it. I should be better. Blah blah blah. You know. The creative mindset

Me: One bonus, my new PA is hot.

Jordan: PA?

Me: Personal Assistant. Andrew has a completely fuckable mouth, by the way.

Jordan: I shouldn't have taken a drink of water when I read that. I might've inhaled it.

Me: TMI?

Jordan: Does that mean you...

Me: ....

Jordan: Never mind.

Me: If you're inquiring as to whether or not I indeed fucked his mouth, unfortunately the answer is no.

Me: And most likely never will because I already fucked my agent. I should probably keep my dick out of the office from now on.

Jordan: You had sex with your agent?

Me: I thought I told you about Anders. Why? Are you jealous?

Jordan: I don't know how to answer that.

I hadn't expected that response. This thing we had together was different. I was flirty and he usually danced around it. There hadn't been a threat of intimacy beyond sharing our thoughts and ideas. After Jax, I struggled to trust anyone. Anders had been the closest thing I'd had to a real relationship in nine years. The physical distance between Jordan and me made it easier for me to be myself. I didn't even know his last name or the exact city he lived in and I wanted to keep it that way. Regardless, I couldn't stop myself from wanting to know his answer.

Me: How about with the truth?

It took him two full minutes to respond.

Jordan: It shouldn't make me jealous, but it does. But I'm used to wanting things I shouldn't.

Chapter 10

JAX

I leaned against my headboard and stared at my phone, worried I'd messed everything up with one text. Before he could respond, I sent another text. A total cop-out.

> *Me: I mean, I wish I could be with someone like that.*

My stomach rioted. The idea of him having sex with some random guy he'd just met made me feel nauseous. Jealous. Angry. I couldn't pick one. I was a wreck of all three. But he didn't need to know that. It didn't help that I had my own memories of us. Me on my knees for him. A firsthand account of what it was like to watch him lose control. The memories of him vivid enough I could feel the painful tug of his fingers in my hair.

"Christ," I whispered under my breath, annoyed with my overactive brain and the hard-on I had growing in my gym shorts.

> **Wilder: You can be.**

A sigh of relief exited my lungs in a long rush. It didn't seem as though he'd thought my previous text had been about him. This whole night had me twisted up on the inside. I should have never texted him. But I kept pushing boundaries. He'd signed off as Wild in that last email, and it'd been easy to pretend that he knew I was Jax, that the ties we'd shared weren't pulling me deeper into this mess I'd created.

> **Wilder: Do something you want for once.**
> **Me: It's not that easy.**
> **Wilder: Isn't it, though? What about Ethan?**
> **Me: Not this again.**
> **Wilder: Come on, tell me you haven't thought about some sort of behind the counter tryst.**
> **Wilder: Let's do a visualization exercise, shall we?**

A slow grin spread across my face.

> **Me: You're drunk.**
> **Wilder: I'm not drunk.**
> **Wilder: Anymore.**
> **Wilder: Fiiiiine, I'm buzzed.**

I laughed out loud as I typed.

> **Me: And out of your mind.**

A picture of Ethan popped up on my screen. He was standing on the beach, his light brown hair a mess in the wind. His smile was wide enough that it caused wrinkles to appear at the outer edges of his eyes. His hand rested on his toned stomach, and okay, the guy was sexy. The way his swim trunks hung low on his hips made it irritatingly impossible not to wonder what was going on underneath the white ties and blue fabric. I was a guy, who was into guys, being in the closet didn't mean I couldn't appreciate a beautiful body. But he wasn't Wild. And right now, all I fucking wanted was Wild. I couldn't tell him that, though. I couldn't tell him how much I hated that his ex-boyfriend was actually his agent. How jealous it made me that Anders got to see him every day. The guy's name even pissed me off. And now this personal assistant asshole. None of these things were relevant because I was a liar and a glutton for his punishment.

Me: Jesus, where did you get that?

Wilder: His Pegasus account. *shrugs*

Me: I was joking earlier when I said you were crazy, but now...

Wilder: Picture this. You're in the hardware store, all alone with Ethan.

Me: Stop.

Wilder: And, wouldn't you know, the power goes out.

Me: Wilder...

Wilder: What?

Me: I can promise you if I was in the hardware store and the power went out, the last thing I'd be thinking about is having sex with Ethan.

Wilder: Why are you so boring?

I tried to bite back my smile, a chuckle reverberating in my chest as I sat up.

Me: Ha. Ha.
Wilder: You're a total cock block.
Me: What the hell? How?
Wilder: Poor Ethan. All he wanted was a sloppy blow job from the hot, moody construction worker who ignores him on a daily basis.

My stomach ached from laughing so hard. If my mom or Jason hadn't already been asleep, they'd probably think I'd finally lost it.

Me: I'm not that cute.
Wilder: I figured as much. It's why I added the word moody for a little realism ;)
Me: Thanks for that.
Wilder: I wonder, though.
Me: About?
Wilder: What you look like.

My mouth went dry, reminding me how all of this, the emails and these text messages weren't real. Nothing said under a veil of bullshit could ever be real. When I didn't answer right away, he sent another text.

Wilder: But I think it's nice, not knowing. That way I get to choose how you look. I've been

picturing you as the actor who played Pippin in LOTR.
Me: I'm not hobbit-sized.

I thought about telling him what I looked like. The truth drummed inside my ribcage. Part of me wanted him to figure out who I was. That way I'd never have to tell him myself. He'd hate me and we could both move on.

Me: I'm actually pretty tall.
Wilder: Maybe I'll picture you as Legolas, but only when I'm practicing self-care.
Me: On that note...
Wilder: Did I scare you?
Me: Nah. But I should probably go to bed.
Wilder: Early day?
Me: Every day is an early day.
Wilder: I'll just be here thinking about poor Ethan and all the kinky storeroom sex he's not having.
Me: Good night, Wilder.
Wilder: Night, Precious.

I set my alarm, a dumb grin on my face, and tossed my phone onto my nightstand. The house was dark and quiet as I made my way to the bathroom, my head filled with Wild and all the over-the-top shit he'd said. I switched on the light and grabbed my toothbrush. When I was finished, I wiped my mouth with a towel and left the light on like I did every night in case Mom or Jay needed to get up and use the bathroom. Once I was back in bed, I closed my eyes, resting my hand just above the elastic of my underwear. I let myself drift off into a dream state. Half asleep, half awake, it started off with an image of Wild next to me, his fingertips tracing circles on my stomach, inching down, his thumb teasing me. I imagined my hand was his. But with my eyes shut tight, the image turned. It was Ethan's mouth on my skin, his wet heat on the head of my dick, and I gripped my shaft harder. A quiet curse ripped past my lips as I worked my hand, his hand, up and down, chasing my climax until I came fast and hard onto my stomach.

Feeling disoriented with shame, I reached with shaking hands for the shirt I'd taken off earlier and wiped myself clean. How long could I live like this? Alone, in my mother's house, hiding behind a bedroom door like a teenager. Sending secrets to a man who, if he knew my real identity, would hate me as sure as I hated myself.

"This isn't a life," I said, and threw the shirt into the hamper at the foot of my bed.

*   *   *

Ethan carried the fifty-pound bag of potting soil, slung over his shoulder, to my work truck like it weighed nothing. I followed behind him with a bag of my own, trying not to think about how I'd jerked off to the image of him blowing me last night. Jim waved at us from the front seat, cell phone to his ear. He'd been on the phone all damn day, making me drive him around like his personal errand boy when I'd rather be working on site, purposely ignoring Chuck and Hudson.

"You guys almost finished at the Hornsby place?" Ethan asked as he opened the gate to the bed of the truck.

"Just have a few touch-ups left and the front yard before we can call it good."

"That Mrs. Hornsby is something else."

Laughing, I set my bag into the truck and closed the gate. "I swear to God, if she makes us change the paint again, I'll quit."

"I hope not. I kind of like seeing you around the shop."

I was met with a crooked grin as I turned to face him. My neck hot with embarrassment as I thought about how fast I'd gotten off thinking about him. I'd told myself this morning it was Wilder's fault for putting ideas in my head.

Ethan didn't shy away from eye contact as I gave him a nervous smile. "I'm not going nowhere," I said, pushing my hands into the pockets of my jeans.

Ethan rubbed the back of his neck, his t-shirt riding up, exposing a sliver of tan skin, my eyes snagging on the dark line of hair that disappeared underneath the waistband of his shorts. All I could think about was Ethan's mouth, the cut muscle of his stomach. I cursed Wilder for sending me that fucking picture.

"Glad to hear it," he said with a laugh that made me think he'd caught me checking him out. "I was wondering, maybe sometime ..."

"Let's go, Jax, time is money," Jim called from the passenger-side window.

"Gotta go," I said, grateful for Jim's interruption. "Thanks for the help."

"No problem." The disappointment was visible behind his smile. "See you around."

My heart in my throat, I wondered what would've happened if I'd let him finish whatever it was he wanted to say. Was he about to ask me out? Maybe it had nothing to do with dating at all. Standing there, I hesitated longer than I should have, thinking about what it would be like to kiss Ethan Calloway, to run my fingertips through the hair on his stomach, to have the heavy weight of his body over mine. What would it be like to openly date the guy who graduated when my brother should have? The latter thought sobered me.

"Later," I said a beat or two too late, and walked around to the driver-side door.

Jim lowered his phone from his ear. "Run me to the bank, would ya?"

"Sure."

When he was finished with his call, he set his phone into the center console. "That was a buddy of mine from Marietta. He's got some work he wants me to help with."

"In Georgia?" I asked, pulling into the bank parking lot.

"He found this historic home he thinks he can flip. But it needs a full overhaul. Rewiring, plumbing, an entire renovation."

"That sounds like a huge project."

"Bigger than he can handle with his guys alone. Listen. Chuck's a great worker, but he's got his wife and that new baby. I know you take care of your momma and your brother. But I could really use you and Hudson on this."

Marietta wasn't too far from Atlanta. Being that close to Wild had me wanting something I wasn't sure was mine to have.

"How long would we be there?' I asked.

Jim keyed into my excitement and smiled like he'd caught the biggest bass in the Bell River.

"Two months, maybe three."

"I'd have to talk to my mom, make sure she could handle being on her own that long. When would we leave?"

"I was planning on driving up there this weekend, just a quick visit to see what we're dealing with first. But I'm thinking... September. That gives us enough time to fix anything we need to at the Hornsby place and get the final payout." Jim grabbed his phone as the truck rolled to a stop in front of the bank.

September would give me enough time to prepare Jason for my absence. And it wasn't like I'd be gone forever. I had to tell Wilder the truth, and this way I could do it in person. Maybe he'd forgive me and maybe he wouldn't, but I had to see him. Even if it meant it was my only chance to do so. He needed to know how much he'd always meant to me, how he'd always be my Wild, no matter what, how these past few weeks had changed me, had me thinking maybe one day I could be happy in my own skin.

Jim hadn't quite made it to the bank door when I rolled down the window and called out, "Mind if I tag along this weekend?"

"Not at all. You know how much I hate driving."

Several thoughts tangled inside my head at once. I should probably talk to my mom before saying anything to Wild, but at the same time, what if Wild didn't want to meet Jordan? If he said no, there'd be no point in going besides a paycheck, and there was plenty of work right here. My choice made, I pulled my phone from my pocket and opened my text messages.

Me: What are your plans this weekend?

Chapter 11

WILDER

I had to blink a few times to make sure I'd read Jordan's message correctly. June and Gwen were rambling at me about some cat they'd found slinking around their backyard, and I couldn't concentrate.

"Are you even listening to us?" Gwen asked, flipping her long, copper bangs from her eyes.

I ignored her.

What are your plans this weekend? His question stirred the butterflies in my stomach. Maybe it was just a hypothetical. Like hey, what's going on, or what are you up to? But he wasn't that casual of a guy. His question was too specific. Did he want to meet? Maybe he'd decided to FaceTime after all? Why was I freaking out about six simple words?

"Wilder?" June snapped and I raised my eyes from the screen. "What the hell?"

"Sorry." I held up my phone, signaling I'd gotten some type of important message. "I have to take care of this," I said, feeling shaky as I stood.

Gwen's smile faltered. "Everything okay?"

"You look paler than usual," June teased, but the concern in her voice was evident.

"I'm fine." I smiled, but June followed me out of my living room into the hallway. I waved my hand at her and added a few extra watts to my grin. "Go sit down. I'm fine. Just need a clear head when I respond to this." She didn't budge. With a sigh, I said, "It's Jordan, alright. Can I have three minutes of privacy in my own home?"

She raised her brows, an irritated glint in her dark eyes. "Don't be a bitch about it. I was worried. You looked—"

"I'm fine. Give me five minutes and I'll be ready to go."

"You know how I get when I'm hungry."

"I know, believe me." I smirked, and she punched me in the arm.

"Why am I friends with you?" she asked, and I leaned in and kissed her cheek.

"Because I'm brilliant."

"And humble," she hummed before heading back to the living room.

Once in my office, I swiped my thumb across the screen of my phone and typed out a quick message I hoped seemed nonchalant.

Me: This weekend?

Me: Oh, you know, the usual.

Me: Banging my head against my desk wondering how on Earth I ever got published in the first place and if I'll ever be able to write again...

Jordan: Are we feeling dramatic today?

Me: I'm always feeling dramatic, Jordan.
Me: Always.
Jordan: Maybe my news will help?
Jordan: Or make it worse?
Me: You have my full attention.

And he did. I pulled at the corner of my lip with my teeth, my fingers tapping the back of my phone. I was amped up and curious as hell.

Jordan: My boss is headed up to Marietta to check out a project he might take on, and I guess I'm driving him.

Marietta was less than twenty miles from where I lived in Ansley Park.

"Twenty miles," I whispered.

I paced back and forth a few times in my small office. The butterflies in my stomach threatened a full-on uprising. FaceTime was one thing. It was safe. Mutual, easy ground. A place where we could decide if this weird friendship we'd developed through letters and snippets of time was real and not some cooked-up scheme by a serial killer. My theatrics knew no bounds. But what if? I'd received quite a few hateful emails and messages on my social media since my book had gained popularity. Things I'd had June delete for me because I hadn't been able to bear reading them again. People whom I'd never met, telling me I'd brought disgrace to the state of Georgia, that I was sick and that I should die. That my book wasn't a love story, but a depraved work of the devil. The south really knew how to make a guy feel special. I wanted to believe Jordan wasn't like that.

"You know he's not." I spoke out loud, feeling unsure of myself.

Last night I did something I never permitted myself to do. I trusted my gut. I wanted to blame the wine for giving Jordan my number. Attribute my behavior to the surreal day I'd had. I'd wanted to feel grounded, and Jordan was the peg. I exhaled a tremulous breath knowing I liked Jordan more than I should. The miles between us had suddenly dwindled to less than twenty, and that scared the hell out of me. I'd invested more of myself in him than I'd ever meant to allow.

Me: This is big news.

I heard June and Gwen talking in the other room and remembered I didn't have all day to dwell on this. I figured my text was neutral enough. I didn't want him to think I assumed a meeting was inevitable. But as I sat, staring at my phone, watching those three dots dance, I realized I wanted to meet him. I wanted to meet this guy who I couldn't wait to hear from every day. This guy who'd given all of himself to help his mom and disabled brother. A guy who understood sacrifice and unconditional love, but never expected it in return.

Jordan: What do you think?
Jordan: Would you want to meet in person?

Me: Last night you said FaceTime would burst our bubble.
Me: Meeting in person is...
Jordan: Big.
Jordan: I get it if you think it's a bad idea.

It could be a bad idea. Or it could be the best. Either way, my heart was beating a million miles an hour, my chest rising and falling as I tried to calm my breathing and type.

Me: I don't think it's a bad idea.
Jordan: You don't?
Me: Can I be candid?
Jordan: Sure.
Me: I'm nervous.
Jordan: That I'm a serial killer?
Me: Maybe.
Me: And maybe I've grown quite fond of our bubble.
Me: But I think we'd have to rip the Band-Aid off eventually. Right?

He didn't answer right away, and I worried I'd said the wrong thing.

Jordan: I'm nervous too.
Jordan: Nervous you'll take one look at me and leave.
Me: You can't be that hideous. A guy as hot as Ethan wouldn't be into you otherwise ;)

"Wilder Welles. If you don't get your skinny ass out here, we're leaving without you," June hollered.

"And we'll take your Sauron Funko Pop with us." Gwen tried to sound angry, but her laughter sifted through the closed office door.

"Almost done," I yelled. "And if you touch my shit, I swear to God..."

Me: I have to go. June and her girlfriend are planning a mutiny if I don't take them for sushi this very second.
Me: When June's hungry the world must stop and bow at her feet.
Jordan: She sounds scary.
Me: She's harmless, but I'll spare you and not invite her to our meeting.
Me: There's this coffee shop called the Cup and Quill. Easy to find if you have GPS. Does Saturday work for you?
Jordan: I'll have to see what my schedule looks like while we're there and let you know. But a coffee shop sounds good.
Me: It's a date.
Me: A non-dragon dildo type of date.
Jordan: I'll make sure to leave mine in the hotel room, then.

I snorted.

Me: Oh my God!!

Me: Did you just make a joke about a sex toy?

Me: My work here is done.

Jordan: Bye, Wilder.

Me: Bye, Precious.

I slipped my phone into the pocket of my jeans and headed to the living room. The grin on my face matched the bubbled excitement bouncing inside my chest.

"Well?" June asked.

"Well, what?" I responded, the gleeful tone earning me a suspicious glare.

"Do I want to know?" she asked as Gwen took her hand.

"I think you might. But I'll tell you all the sordid details over a plate of sushi."

"Several plates," Gwen added.

I was about to agree with her assessment of June's voracious appetite when I heard a faint meow come from the kitchen.

"What the hell was that?" I asked.

Gwen gave June a pointed look.

"Knew you weren't listening," June accused.

Her tone was overly aggressive in my opinion, seeing that there was a small, yet fluffy-looking gray cat sitting on my kitchen floor with a bowl of what looked like tuna under its nose.

"Why is there a cat in my kitchen, June?"

"Happy... birthday?" Gwen shrugged, her burgeoning smile more repentant than celebratory.

"It's not my birthday for another eight days," I reminded her, as the pint-sized ball of fur's tail swished back and forth.

"As I was saying earlier, we found this little guy on the back patio chasing lizards. He looked malnourished so I brought him to an animal shelter. They said if no one claimed him or adopted him they'd euthanize him." June's eyes glimmered with unshed tears as she looked down at the fluff ball. "It's barbaric, Wilder."

"That's all very sad, truly, but why is it in *my* kitchen, June? Tell me you didn't get me a cat for my birthday."

"Surprise," she sang, wiggling her fingers in the air like a cheerleader.

On cue, the cat stood and circled himself around and through my legs until I bent down to pick him up. He had to weigh less than five pounds. His meow was more like a squeak, and though I refused to admit it, the little cotton ball was kind of fucking adorable.

"I hate you," I said and kissed it on the nose.

The cat snuggled against my chest, looking up at me with big bluish-silver eyes.

June and Gwen were grinning like idiots. "Don't even look at me like that. What the hell am I going to do with a cat? I'm going to be traveling all over the south for the book tour this fall. I won't have time to be attached to anything."

"We'll watch him while you're away," Gwen promised.

The damn thing started purring, the vibration shooting right through my chest to my heart. Goddamn it. I nuzzled my nose on the top of his head.

"I hate that you know me better than I know myself," I said, my angry tone more for show.

"Aw. Love you too." June and Gwen both hugged me at the same time. When they finally pulled away, June asked, "What are you going to name him?"

"Gandalf the Grey," I said proudly and they both rolled their eyes.

"You're a man-child," June said, taking the cat from my arms. She kissed it on the nose. "Well, Gandalf, welcome home."

Chapter 12

JAX

Jason walked into my room as I zipped up my duffel bag. He leaned in the doorway, silent, with his arms crossed. The thick slashes of his brow line furrowed. Jason wasn't your average twenty-five-year-old. He didn't really give a shit about his appearance. When he wasn't living in basketball shorts, his jeans were always torn or grass stained. He was lanky in a way he should've grown out of, but unlike his friends from high school, the gym and basketball didn't exist for him anymore. It's why my guilt soared the longer he stared at me. This house. Me. Our mom. His world, tiny as it was, it's all he wanted or knew.

"Aw, don't look at me like that, Jay." I sat on the foot of my bed and rested my elbows on my knees. "It's only for the weekend."

"I heard you talking to Momma. I'm not stupid."

Anger rolled off his shoulders, crashing against me. I scrubbed a palm over my face with a sigh. "You're not stupid."

"Then why are you leaving?" His voice broke, and I struggled to push down the wave of feeling about to drown me.

"Come in here." He shook his head. "Come on, Jay."

He gave in and sat down next to me on the bed. His weight pressed against me, I draped my arm over his shoulder, pulling him close.

"I'm not leaving 'cause I think you're stupid, Jay. It's a work thing, and I'll be back Sunday night."

"You told Mom you might have to stay for two or three months." He shrugged out of my hold and wiped at his eyes.

Goddamn it, he was crying. *Was I really this selfish?* If it wasn't for Wild, I would have never volunteered to go. I hated lying to Jason. But I needed this. I needed the closure. I needed to fix at least one fucked-up thing in my life. Wilder deserved that.

"I'm gonna miss you, too," I said. "But it's important that I go. And if I do end up going back for a couple of months, I'm not that far away. I could drive home on the weekends."

"Who's gonna take me to the beach, or to the river?"

A sad smile spread across my face. "Mom can take you, or Ms. Arlene."

Jason's expression twisted. "They don't know how to fish."

"That's true..." I mussed up his hair with my palm, and he shoved me. I almost fell off the bed, and he laughed. "You think that's funny?" I asked with humor and attempted to wrestle him into a headlock.

"Stop." He laughed, breathless. "You win."

I let go, but instead of pulling away, he grabbed me, wrapped his arms around my ribcage, his cheek against my chest, and hugged me so hard I started to cry. I fucking cried as I turned my body enough that he could give me a real hug. Jason rested his chin on my shoulder, and I held him like that until I got a hold of myself. I was a bastard for putting him through this. Again, my choices had caused my family, my brother, harm.

"When you get back I wanna go fishing," he said.

Jason stood, shoved his hands into the pockets of his basketball shorts. His eyes red and puffy, but I imagined mine looked about the same.

"Why don't we go right now?" I asked.

"Yeah? I thought you had to leave."

The relief in his voice made it easier to breathe.

"Not for a couple of hours." I stood and slipped my feet into a pair of worn flip flops. "Go grab your stuff."

He didn't hesitate, and I laughed as I heard my mom yell after him, *"Hey, slow down, don't come barging in here like a tornado."*

She was in the kitchen looking through a pile of mail when I walked in. "What's gotten into him?" she asked, engrossed with the letter in her hand.

"I told him I'd take him fishing before I headed out for Marietta."

She raised her eyebrows, finally giving me her attention. "Don't you and Jim have a six-hour drive."

"Five, if I'm driving."

"Jaxon Stettler, you will arrive alive, you hear me. Don't you dare be reckless. You know better than to say something like that to me."

"Yes, ma'am." I swallowed, feeling like an asshole. "I didn't think."

She pinched her lips together and nodded. "No, you didn't." She held out her hands and waved me over, pulling me in for a quick hug. "You promise me now. Promise you'll be careful. Wear a seatbelt, and if you get tired..."

"I promise, Momma."

"And put your damn phone on silent. Driving distracted is just as bad as driving dru—"

She stopped mid-word as Jason bounded into the kitchen through the back door, panting. "I... got... everything... ready."

I chuckled and gave my mom a squeeze. "We'll be back in an hour or so."

"Have fun, boys," she hollered as we shut the back door.

The drive to the river wasn't long. It'd only taken us five minutes before we were parked under a canopy of old oak trees. The Spanish moss hanging from the branches swayed in the sea breeze coming off the west coast. It creeped me out the way the moss moved, hovering over you like it was trying to reach out and touch you. Jason jogged down to the riverbank, leaving me to carry the gear, as usual. I set the cooler and bait box on the ground, and as I reached into the backseat, I heard the crunch of tires on gravel. Ethan smiled at me as his car rolled to a stop.

Shit.

I waved like an idiot and attempted to grab the bait box and the cooler in one hand without success.

"Let me help you with that," Ethan said, slamming his car door.

I noticed he held a fishing pole of his own and remembered that his profile said he liked to fish.

And bottom.

Jesus.

"Um, thanks," I stammered and handed him the bait box. "Don't you have your own shit to carry?"

"Don't worry about it, I'll grab it in a second."

His whole face lit up like a hundred fireflies when he smiled at me.

"Alright," I said and headed toward the riverbank.

Ethan walked beside me, too quiet. I could hear my heart racing inside my chest.

"Hey, Ethan." Jason waved. "You like to fish?"

"I do."

Among other things, I thought to myself and wished I hadn't. A flash of heat covered my neck and face. I bent down, setting the cooler on the grass, feeling out of sorts.

Ethan set our bait box on the top of the cooler and rested his fishing pole against the trunk of a tree. "Is it okay if I join you guys? I can hike down river if—"

"Stay," Jason blurted.

"I'd like that... it'd be nice to have company for a change."

"Of course. You should stay," I said. "We have to go in an hour anyway, no sense in us hogging the best spot."

"Jax is leaving town," Jason said, picking up his pole. "But he said we can go fishing again when he gets back."

"That's right, I might've heard someone saying something about y'all's trip yesterday at the store."

"Small town, news gets around fast." I laughed.

"Too fast," he agreed. "I'll be right back, gotta grab my bait from the car.

"Just use ours," I offered.

"Thanks." He gave me another one of those bright as hell smiles and I had to stop myself from staring.

Jason opened the box and started to bait his hook. The nightcrawler wiggled in his fingers and he laughed. I reached to grab my own, at the same time as Ethan, and his finger brushed against mine.

"Go ahead," I said, watching as his Adam's apple moved under the smooth skin of his throat.

My jaw ached as I grit my teeth. Ethan ran his hand through his light brown hair, his bicep tensing, and I forced my gaze away toward the river. My pulse increased, and I had to recite the name of every NCAA division one basketball team to stop myself from getting hard. I blamed my sex deprivation. I usually had this shit under control, especially when my brother was sitting right here.

"Want me to bait your hook?" Ethan asked.

It made me think of Wild, and how he'd probably turn that question into some weird sexual innuendo. I suppressed my laugh and nodded. "If you want. Thanks."

It had taken at least twenty minutes for the silence to become comfortable as all three of us stood at the river's edge. The mid-morning heat surrounded us as the stifling humidity covered my skin in sweat. I reeled in my line, not interested in standing in the sun and boiling to death. The fish weren't biting anyway. Jay had scared them away by splashing his feet in the water. I grabbed a soda from the cooler and sat down in the grass with my back against the tree. Jason waded out into the water, not really fishing anymore either. Ethan, however, stretched his arm and re-cast his line. He set his pole into the stand he'd propped up earlier, and I almost swallowed my tongue when he reached behind his head and pulled off his shirt. His back was sculpted with the type of muscle you got from real work, not a weight machine. Before I could stop the thought, I pictured my hands on his narrow hips, my mouth on his neck, his ass pressed against me, and swore under my breath.

Dropping my eyes, I rearranged my shorts as covertly as possible to hide the evidence of my wayward thoughts. Ethan showing up here had to be another form of punishment. I couldn't help that I was attracted to him. That Wilder had made me look at Ethan in a way I'd never intended. I was in love with a past I'd never be able to relive, and a future that was built on a lie. Ethan was a reality. A reality I had no idea what to do with. In a little over twenty-four hours, Wilder would be within an arm's reach. Everything I'd ever wanted. I could almost feel his skin under the palm of my hand. The anxiety that'd plagued me all week sank into my hollow stomach. I'd hardly eaten anything these past few days. I'd thought about backing out of this meeting with Wild about a thousand times. But every time the thought crossed my mind, I'd text him, reminding myself that I owed him this. Owed him the truth.

I pulled my phone from my pocket and opened up our string of texts.

Me: I'm leaving in an hour or so.

Wilder: You'll be here tonight?

Me: Yeah. We're gonna drive by the property before checking into the hotel.

Wilder: Saturday still works?

Me: It should. Jim has some paperwork he needs to do after we look over the house on Saturday morning. I should be free by five.

Wilder: Holy shit

Me: I know. This is crazy.

Wilder: Oh, sorry. I was talking about this damn cat.

Me: What did Gandalf do now?

Wilder: He was hiding in my sock drawer. Scared the crap out of me.

A picture came through of a small gray cat, more fur than actual cat, sleeping in a pile of socks, with *#CurrentView* typed below.

Me: Cute.

Wilder: If you're a good boy, maybe I'll introduce you to him on Saturday.

As much as I wanted that, the likelihood of that happening, on a scale of zero to ten, was negative two. Once Wilder found out that I was Jax, this thing we had going would be over. But at least he'd know why I'd done what I had nine years ago. And his hurt would be replaced by hate. Anger was easier to manage. After a while, the flame died out.

Me: That's if I'm not a serial killer?
Wilder: Duh.

I shook my head and huffed out another laugh.

Me: See you at six tomorrow.
Wilder: Weird.
Me: I know.
Wilder: How will I know it's you?
Me: I'll say hi.
Wilder: Six...
Wilder: Drive safe.
Me: I will.

When I glanced up from my phone, I caught Ethan staring at me. His hand hovered over the bait box, like he was about to reach in, but something grabbed his attention. Apparently that something was me.

"Taking a break?" he asked, reaching in, and grabbing a worm.

I stood, wiping the grass off the back of my shorts and pointed up at the sky. "It's too hot. And I'm not big on fishing if you want the truth."

Ethan flicked his gaze to my brother for a brief second. "But Jason is?"

I nodded as I approached him, his scent catching me off guard. He smelled like sunscreen and men's soap mixed with sweat. I inhaled deeper before I spoke. "Yeah. He used to fish all the time with my dad."

"You never did?"

"My father and I weren't as close," I admitted, and it surprised me. I didn't usually talk to people about my life. Well, besides Wild.

"Sorry, I didn't mean to pry."

"You're not. It's not much of a secret. Jay was my dad's basketball prodigy. I just played because I enjoyed it, not because I was that good at it."

"I always thought you were great," he said.

His comment caught me off guard.

"You did?"

"Yeah. I used to go to your games."

"When?" I pressed, liking how he blushed all the way to the tips of his ears.

"Junior High." His laugh was husky. "You were a senior. Me and my friends, we went to every home game. I remember Jason used to sit in the front row and scream at the refs with your dad."

I could see the memory as if it was played out on a screen before me. "That feels like another lifetime."

"You might've been my first crush," he said, looking over his shoulder at the river like he hadn't just come out to me in the flirtiest, most easygoing way possible. His smile was shy when his eyes met mine. "Thanks... for sticking up for me the other day. Those guys you work with..."

"Are assholes," I said. "They shouldn't say shit like that."

"I've got thick skin." He shrugged, and I admired his self-assurance. Nodding toward the river, he changed the subject. "Want to try again? It's not as hot now that the breeze has kicked up some."

146

I made sure I didn't stare at his chest, or his mouth, or the trickle of sweat dripping down his throat. I did what I did best. I nodded, repressing any sign of desire, any hope that I could end up with someone like Ethan, or Wild, or the thought that I might actually have a chance one day at something good.

* * *

"You sure you don't want to grab something to eat?" Jim asked as we pulled into the hotel parking lot.

"I need to catch some sleep."

"Thanks for driving yesterday. And today." He laughed as I switched off the ignition.

It was four-thirty and I still had to shower and drive thirty minutes into Ansley Park. I wasn't in the mood for small talk. This day had been the longest fucking day of my life. My stomach, empty, twisted in knots. I couldn't even think about eating anything.

"Not a problem," I said and opened the truck door.

The hotel lobby was busy as we walked in. Jim smiled and waved at a girl behind the counter.

"She's cute," he whispered, hitting the elevator button. "You should ask her to have dinner with you."

"Doubtful..." I hesitated. "But I might take the truck to get some food later, if that's alright?"

"Sure thing, kid."

We rode the elevator together to the third floor. When the doors opened, we stepped out. "If you do go out, don't be too late, we have to meet with the owners by eight-thirty tomorrow."

"I'll be ready."

"See you in the morning," he said, and headed down the hall.

Once I was in my room, I exhaled the tension I'd been holding in all day. I stripped out of my jeans and sweaty t-shirt and took the longest shower I could with the time I had. I shaved my face, brushed my teeth, trying the entire time to keep my mind numb. I went through the motions like it was any other day. The only difference was I actually tried to do something with my blond mop of hair. I'd purchased some type of styling stuff last night from the small convenience store across the street. I ran a little through the wet strands, and let it air dry like the instructions had suggested. I pulled on the nicest pair of jeans I'd packed and a fitted, light blue t-shirt. I stared at my reflection in the mirror and began to second-guess myself. What the hell do you wear to meet the guy you'd been in love with for the past nine years, and had lied to for the past month? I didn't get a chance to dwell on it because the alarm on my phone went off.

"Shit. I gotta get out of here."

I slipped on my watch, pulled on my ratty Converse, and grabbed my wallet, keys, and phone from the night table. I ignored the rush of fear in my pulse. I didn't think about how this all could blow up in my face. How I might destroy Wild all over again. I didn't allow my mind to travel beyond each individual second that ticked by. Until I was in the truck. Until I was on the interstate. Until I was parked outside the Cup and Quill.

Until I saw him.

Wild walked down the crowded sidewalk toward my truck, preoccupied by the city buzzing around him. His dark hair longer on top, the soft curls fell lazy over his forehead. He was taller than I remembered, in black skinny jeans with holes in the knees. His white t-shirt, hung off wide shoulders, slightly tucked in the front under his belt. His skin pale like cream, against dark brown eyes framed by heavy black lashes and eyeliner. The soft jaw line I used to kiss was angled and sharp. His fingers delicate as he pulled a phone from his back pocket. These past nine years had transformed him into something beyond what I'd imagined, or what a picture could have prepared me for. He was exactly as I remembered and everything I'd never know, but God I fucking wanted to. All those seconds that I'd managed to get through to get to this point, the years, the regret, the shame, added up to this one time stamp.

Five fifty-eight.

Wilder: I'm here.

Chapter 13

WILDER

The coffee shop was busy tonight. Every Saturday they had live music, and tonight was no different. A woman with long, dark hair and almond-shaped eyes sat behind a guitar that was too big for her, plucking at the strings, singing something about a war. I picked a spot in the back of the room, avoiding the crowd of people. Folk music wasn't really my thing, and I figured Jordan would appreciate the privacy. I flipped to the evening menu, perusing their spiked coffee selection, deciding on a Sambuca Café Ole. I didn't feel like my usual, my nerves were too raw, I needed something stronger than a latte. Only two people were working the floor tonight, and since the line at the counter was short, I opted not to wait. Besides, it gave me something to do while I internally freaked the fuck out about meeting Jordan. A complete stranger, June had reminded me before I'd left to come here tonight. I forgave her when she said my eyeliner looked fierce. Of course, it did.

I weaved my way through the over-filled room and got behind a couple who apparently couldn't wait until they were home to eat each other's faces. I pulled my phone out as a distraction and saw I'd missed a text from Jordan a few minutes ago.

Jordan: Running late. Finally found a parking spot.

God. He was parking. Was he already in here somewhere? I took a cursory glance around the room. There was a tall guy standing by himself, leaning against the wall with his hand in his pocket. I swallowed, trying to get a better look, when a girl slid in next to him. He leaned down and kissed her. Definitely not Jordan.

"What can I get for you?" the barista asked, drawing my attention away from the room.

"Can I get a Sambuca Café Ole?"

"Did you want the Sambuca mixed in or as a shot?"

Tough choice. As appealing as shots sounded right now, I needed to be sober. At least for a little while. The night was young.

"Mixed."

After I paid, I tried to focus on the light music. Anxious, I waited for my drink near the pick-up counter. Nodding my head to the slow beat of the song, I scanned the room again. Jordan could be anyone of these guys standing by themselves. There was a cute blond lingering by the front door, but he didn't seem like the construction-worker type. Not that I even knew what the hell that was. But I assumed tall and delicate wasn't quite right. This whole thing had me feeling self-conscious. Something I wasn't used to. Was he watching me? What if he never showed up? A suit with salt and pepper hair smiled at me and I cringed, looking away as fast as possible.

"Wilder," a man's voice called, and I turned a little too fast and ran into the girl standing beside me.

"Oh my God, I'm sorry," I said, grabbing her hands to help steady her drink. Coffee spilled onto my knuckles.

"It's okay." Her tone was curt, and I realized I was still holding her hands.

I immediately let go, apologizing again. This time her smile was genuine, and she handed me her napkin. "Don't worry about it," she said and walked away.

The barista called my name again as he set my coffee on the counter. I wiped my hands and threw the napkin away in the trash. I was such a mess. The ceramic mug was filled to the brim. Practically overflowing, I picked it up. With purposeful and careful hands, I brought it to my lips, taking a big enough sip to one, calm myself, and two, to prevent me from spilling it on this overly priced designer t-shirt. I licked the taste of licorice and cream from my lips and made it half-way back to the table without incident when I heard him say my name.

"Wild?"

Like a question. Deep and rough. The hairs on the back of my neck stood as a wash of goosebumps erupted down my spine.

Wild.

That unmistakable southern drawl.

For a split second, I thought I'd imagined it. Imagined the sudden pull inside my stomach. And in the crowded room, like a thread had connected us all this time, he reeled me in. My eyes found his and I lost my grip on the coffee mug. My fingers, too weak, my hold as hollow as the white noise roaring in my ears. Stilled with shock, my mind was unable to process that Jax Stettler was standing no more than ten feet away from me as the ceramic crashed onto the concrete floor. The music had chosen that very moment to end, and maybe I'd sworn, or maybe Jax had, but he stepped forward and reached toward me. I backed away, looking around the room at a sea of faces, wishing away his.

He bent down to pick up the broken mug when a staff member showed up with a broom and pail. "I got it from here." She gave Jax a reassuring smile. "Y'all can grab a table if you want. I'll send someone over to take your order."

Standing, he said, "Thanks."

Jax took a slow step, watching me with tired green eyes. "Hi."

How will I know it's you?

I'll say hi.

No.

I couldn't be that stupid.

"What are you doing here," I asked, my throat bone dry and my hands trembling. I balled them into fists at my sides. My usual confidence withered under the weight of his stare. "I can't believe you're here."

"Do you want to sit down?" he asked.

The muscle in his jaw pulsed when I didn't answer right away.

"I don't know…" I said.

I was scrambling. All the words and questions I'd been holding onto these past nine years wanted to fly past my lips at the same time. *Why are you here? What happened? Are you okay? Do you know how much you meant to me? How long I waited for you? How fucking broken I am?*

He was right here. Standing in front of me. Taller and bigger, his shoulders pulling his light blue shirt tight against his chest, revealing defined muscles underneath. His hair was longer too, blond and beach blown. Christ, he looked good. He had no right to show up here like this, looking like the years, the distance he'd forced between us, hadn't touched him at all.

"Let's sit down, alright?" He leaned in, and I could smell his soap.

That hadn't changed. The crisp, clean scent opened up a memory bank I thought I'd permanently deleted.

His head on my chest. His hair dusting the bottom of my chin. The tip of my nose on his thigh. His hands on my hips. His lips on my neck. The weight of his body on my back. The feel of his ribs under my fingers. His breath on my cheek. His parted lips hovering over mine.

I couldn't breathe.

"I... I can't." My skin was hot, my eyes burning with embarrassing and unwanted tears. "Shit..." I muttered, and my eyes shuttered closed. I clenched my jaw and opened my eyes. "I'm waiting for someone."

"I know," he said, but it sounded like I'm sorry.

"You know?"

Horrified, everything became crystal clear.

Jordan.

For Michael Jordan. Jax's favorite player.

This all started on his birthday. Jax's birthday.

"You're... Jordan," I said, backing away farther.

"Give me a chance to explain."

I'm sorry about what Jake did to you. Though I'm sure he had his reasons, it doesn't make what he did any less terrible or right.

The edges of the room were fuzzy, my head swimming. This couldn't be real. This wasn't happening. Everything we'd talked about. I'd trusted him. Anger replaced confusion with the realization that this past month had been nothing more than a lie. A cruel prank. I should've known. I should've seen right through it all. Why would he do this? I didn't think Jax had the power to hurt me any more than he already had. I guess I was wrong.

Humiliation soured in my stomach. "I think I'm going to be sick."

I pushed past him, my shoulder clipping his arm, as I moved across the room. I didn't hear or see anything. Everything was a colorful blur as I made my way to the bathroom. Thank God it was empty. Turning on the faucet, I caught my reflection in the mirror. My eyes were red and wide. Alone, I allowed myself to break down. I hung my head, unable to look at my face and let the tears fall. I braced myself on the edge of the sink, letting the anger boil over as I yelled hard enough my throat ached. The music was too loud for anyone to hear me. Tipping my head back, I glared at the ceiling. I wanted to punch something. Did his dad really die? And what about his brother... I knew Jax's home life was shit, but would he really make all of that up? And for what, to hurt me? I'd bled enough for the both of us.

I lowered my eyes to the mirror as he walked through the bathroom door. We stared at each other through the glass as he rested his back against the wall, his cheeks as wet as mine.

"Was any of it true?" I asked and turned off the faucet.

"All of it," he said, his tone low and pained. I turned to face him. "Everything I told you... it's all true. Everything except my name."

"Your dad died?"

He nodded. "I was gonna tell him about us over break. Figured if he was pissed, he'd at least wait until after Christmas to throw me out, and then maybe by then he would've had a chance to cool down. Change his mind." More tears streamed down his face and it gutted me. But his betrayal was a knife in my back. I stayed silent and listened. "He'd taken Jason fishing, but he'd had too much to drink, and with the rain that night..." He wiped at his eyes. "He drove them both into the river. He died and my brother drowned. Jason is lucky to be alive." His laugh bitter, he whispered, "At least that's what the doctors said."

"I'm sorry."

I hated apologies. The word sorry meant nothing without an action to prove it. I'm sorry was an excuse, a consolation for guilt. It didn't matter if I was sorry for him or not. It didn't change anything. It didn't pull the car out of the river. It didn't take a drink out of his father's hand. It didn't break the silence Jax had imprisoned me in for almost a decade.

"And the worst part of it…" he said, bowing his head. "Is that I can't shake the thought it was my fault." He raised his bloodshot eyes. "I thought everything that happened was a punishment for what we'd done. Me and you being together. Our love. It was a sin, and I had to pay for that."

His words were a sharp slap across my face.

"Is that why you're here?" I accused him and he flinched. "To blame me for what happened? To shove your bible bullshit down my throat?"

"What?" Confusion twisted his brow as he pushed off the wall. "Wild, listen to me."

I held up my hands and hated how they shook. "I don't want to hear it, Jaxon. You've said enough." I took a step toward the door and he grabbed my arm.

"Damn it, Wild, just wait a second."

"Let go of me," I demanded, my voice too calm, too low.

A spike of adrenaline coursed through me when he didn't release his grip. The heat of his palm soaked into my skin as he pulled me closer. "You don't understand. It's not like that. Wild, I'm in—"

"You're a fucking liar." I tried to pull away again and failed. "And you used me as some kind of sick confessional…" I tried a different tactic and leaned in, close enough I could feel his breath on my lips. "This past

157

month? Was that my punishment? Or was it the nine goddamn years you left me in the dark, wondering if you were alive or dead, or if you'd done something stupid..." My voice cracked, all of it, every terrible thought, every fear, every worry I'd carried around for so long rushed down my face. "Do you know how many times I thought you might've killed yourself, that maybe you couldn't live with what had happened between us."

Jax dropped his hand, the color in his cheeks drained.

"Stay the fuck away from me, Jaxon. I don't need your kind of punishment. I know who I am."

Chapter 14

JAX

FROM: fool0fatook54@bellinx.mail.com
TO: wildwelleslit@bartpress.com
Date: Aug 11 10:47 PM
SUBJECT: I'm sorry

Wild,

I'm sorry isn't enough for what I've done. I know that. But I am... I'm sorry for cutting you out of my life. I'm sorry for making you worry like you did. I'm sorry for making you feel like you weren't every fucking thing to me. The night my father died, and Jason got hurt, everything that happened was all too big for me. I didn't think about anything except surviving each second, remembering how to breathe. I was young and stupid and blamed myself. And like I told you tonight, I thought God had punished me for loving you. And I've struggled with that every day since.

But you didn't let me finish what I wanted to say before you left. And I probably don't deserve the chance to explain myself. Like I told you before, some things I've done in my life are unforgivable. But what I did to you all this time, treating you the way I did, it will forever be my biggest sin.

I should've called you that night. I should've told you how alone and forsaken I felt. I'm not good with words like you, Wild. Never have been and never will be. But I know that the love I had for you has never faded. Those first few years, when me and my mom were trying to help Jason, trying to pay for everything, and waiting on insurance payments that came months too late, we tried to pick up the pieces. There were times I wanted to die, wished I'd been in that car instead of Jason. I hated myself, and maybe I still do.

When I read your book and read about us, it was like watching my life, but through a different lens. You wrote about me like I was special. Like I was worth something. For the first time in nine years I thought maybe I wasn't this dark and twisted thing. That our love was good. And it was... good. And I reached out to you because I wanted to tell you... you had to know. That your book saved me. Even when I didn't deserve being saved. I never meant to keep writing you. Never meant for it to go beyond that one email. But it was hard to let you go all over again. I should've told you the truth. I should've told you I was a coward. But I guess you know that now. I regret so many things, but hurting you, I'll never forgive myself. I'm sorry for... everything.

Jax~

FROM: fool0fatook54@bellinx.mail.com
TO: wildwelleslit@bartpress.com
Date: Aug 12 12:33 PM
SUBJECT: One last thing

Wild,

I'm not sure if you'll read this or if you even read the other email I sent last night, but Jim's inside the gas station grabbing a drink before we head back to Bell River, and I don't have a lot of time. I wanted to make sure you understood me last night. Everything we've talked about this past month was real. Everything. I want to be comfortable in my own skin. Be out and happy and live like you do. And maybe if I hadn't been so damn confused and scared all those years ago, I might've had a chance at a life. I'd like to think my life would've been with you, but now I'll never know.

I guess what I'm trying to say is, I've already said sorry, and I know that doesn't change anything, but I think I wanted to say thank you, too. You've helped me, these past few weeks, more than you'll ever know or probably care to.

Seeing you last night, seeing what I missed out on, seeing what could have been, that was my real punishment.

Take care,
Jax~

The sun was close to setting by the time I pulled into the gravel drive in front of my house. Lightning ignited the darkening sky as I turned off the engine. I grabbed my duffel from the back seat and headed inside. It smelled like celery and carrots as I walked in, every light in the house was on and I could hear my mom singing to herself in the kitchen.

"I'm home," I hollered, dropping my bag by the couch.

I'd half expected Jason to tackle me to the ground before I even made it into the house.

"Hey, Momma." I leaned against the door frame.

"Jaxon," she squealed, turning away from the stove. "You scared me."

I chuckled and met her halfway across the kitchen. When she pulled me into one of her big hugs, I wanted to break down, give in and let it all go, but I couldn't. I was trapped, and the pain in my chest nearly split me in two. The past twenty-four hours had finally started to sink in. Wild never answered the emails I'd sent after the shitshow that was last night. And why would he? He hated me, and rightly so. I'd messed up and there was nothing I could do to fix it.

Mom squeezed me one last time before pulling away. "Glad you got home safe and in one piece."

I nodded, unable to speak past the tightening of my throat.

"I made chicken noodle soup. It's supposed to rain tonight, figured you and Jason both could use a little warmth when you got home."

"Jason isn't here?" I asked, looking around as if he'd magically appear. "Is he alright?"

Mom patted my bicep. "He's fine. Stop worrying so much. Your hair will go gray before you're forty, and then you'll never find a woman." She lifted the ladle from the counter and pointed it at me. "And I want grandbabies while I can still enjoy 'em."

I wish I had the guts to tell her that gray hair would have no bearing on my ability to produce a grandchild.

"Where is he?"

"Fishing with that nice boy Ethan."

"Ethan?" Shoving my hands in my pockets, my stomach flipped as images of him, shirtless and sun-soaked, paraded through my brain. "This late?"

She glanced at the clock right as a boom of thunder shook the windows. She gave me a nervous smile. "I'm sure they'll be back any minute. You should invite that

163

Ethan to stay for dinner. He's been hanging around here all weekend with Jason. Took him to the pier yesterday."

"He did?"

Ethan and Jason weren't exactly friends in high school, but they knew each other. I was curious why Ethan had spiked a sudden interest in hanging around with my brother.

"Sure did. Said he saw how nervous Jay was when y'all went fishing before you left on Friday. Said he wanted to try and keep Jay's mind in a good place while you were gone." Another flash of lightning, and the sky opened up and pounded onto the roof. My mother's face went pale. "Maybe you should—"

"I'll drive down to the river, make sure they're okay."

"Be careful," I heard her say as I opened the front door.

I ran to my car, but before I even got to the driver-side door, headlights flooded the driveway. Ethan's Toyota pulled up next to me, and before it came to a full stop Jason hopped out of the car.

"You're home!"

He barreled into me and I laughed. "I am, buddy."

"Did you miss me?" he asked, pulling away and holding his hand over his head as if that would keep the deluge from his face.

"Why don't we talk inside about how much I missed you. Mom made soup."

He clapped his hands and raced to the house as Ethan rolled down his window a few inches. I peered inside, the dashboard lights casting him in a blue glow. His hair was wet, and his t-shirt clung to his broad chest.

"Got caught in the rain," he said with a shy smile. "Probably should've headed in earlier."

"Wanna come in for dinner?" I found myself asking. My mom had suggested it, but I hadn't actually planned to do it. "My mom made chicken noodle soup."

The rain saturated me from head to toe as I stood there hoping he'd say no and yes at the same time. I liked Ethan, and I appreciated him helping my brother, but after the weekend I had, I didn't necessarily feel like pretending over a bowl of soup that I wasn't attracted to him.

"Sure," he said, and cut the engine.

We both ran to the front door, and by the time we got inside, my mother was waiting with her signature, we-have-guests-don't-embarrass-me-smile and two towels. "Oh, look at you boys." She fretted over us. "You'll get pneumonia," she said, handing us the towels and waving us off toward my room. "Jaxon, get something for Ethan to wear."

Ethan's smile stretched into dimples, "That's alright, Mrs. Stettler. This towel should do the trick. These swim trunks will be dry in no time."

I waited, wishing my mom would leave well enough alone, and knowing I wasn't lucky enough for that to happen.

"Please, call me Barb. And I insist, Jax don't mind. Do you, darling?"

"No, ma'am." I worked down a swallow. "Come, on. I'm sure I got some sweats or something."

Ethan hesitated, uncomfortable. He'd helped my brother while I was away, the least I could do was give the guy something dry to wear while my mom cross-examined him. I clipped him on the shoulder and gave him a crooked grin. "Trust me, she won't stop pestering you until you put something else on. And when she sets herself to pestering..." He nodded, an all-knowing smile warming his brown eyes.

"I'll see you boys in the kitchen. Jason, you too. Wash up and I'll get everything ready."

My annoyance at my mom's persistence faded when I saw the excitement in her eyes. She rarely had guests. Her life had been altered just as much as mine or Jason's had. Who the hell was I to keep her from feeding the neighborhood?

I grabbed the bag I'd left by the couch earlier and headed for my room with Ethan in tow. I opened the door, embarrassed by some of the shit I still had laying around. Ethan walked toward the small trophy shelf my mom had insisted I keep. All my awards from high school, and some from college. I turned away, leaving my bag on the bed, feeling exposed. That was my old life. Those trophies meant nothing to me now.

I opened up one of my dresser drawers and grabbed a pair of old gray sweats and t-shirt I figured he'd fit into.

"These might be too big," I said, catching him flipping through a copy of *The Two Towers* I'd left on my desk.

"Thanks," he said, taking the pants and shirt from my hand. "You honestly didn't have to—"

"If it makes you feel better, consider it repayment for that time I had to borrow your shirt. Besides, it's the least I can do." I gathered my courage and looked him in the eye. "Thanks... for helping with Jay while I was gone."

"Anytime. I like having someone to fish with. He's good company."

"He is," I said. The silence stretched between us and my face heated. "If you want, I can throw your wet stuff into the dryer."

"That'd be great, thanks."

I opened up my dresser again, and grabbed some shorts, boxers, and an old Eastchester hoodie. When I turned around Ethan had already pulled off his shirt. His golden skin had a hint of pink at the shoulders, and I wondered how long he and Jason had been out fishing today.

"Be right back," I said, as he slipped on the t-shirt I'd given him.

I changed in the bathroom as fast as possible, leaving my wet clothes in the laundry basket, and headed back to my room. Ethan sat on the edge of my bed, and as I walked in, he stood. He ran his hand through his hair, another shy smile curling at the corner of his lips.

"Fit okay?" I asked when I realized I'd been staring at his mouth.

"Great, actually."

The sweats were a little long, and I attempted to focus on that and not on the outline of his dick that was visible through the cotton material.

"Great," I repeated, feeling like a pervert.

Ethan glanced around the room, eyeing the old angler-themed wallpaper and hunter green quilt. All things my parents had gotten for me as an early teen. All things I hated, but kept because if I was that son, the one who loved fishing and playing basketball, and dated girls, then maybe they'd never figure out I was gay.

I wanted to tell him this wasn't me, that this room belonged to a man who didn't exist, and that as much as I didn't want to be, I was attracted to men, and that I liked the way he looked in those sweats.

Of course, I didn't say any of those things.

Awkwardly rubbing at the back of my neck, I asked, "Ready for the best fucking chicken soup you'll ever eat?"

● ● ●

I glanced at Ethan over my shoulder as I opened the refrigerator door. "Want a drink?"

"Nah, gotta drive home."

I grabbed two cans of soda and handed him one with a chuckle. "I think you can handle one drink."

He laughed as he set down the dish towel and took the soda from my hand.

"You didn't have to clean up." I popped open the can, the crisp sound echoing in the kitchen. "I would've done it after you left."

"It's the polite thing to do. Well, at least, that's what my mom always says."

"And she's right," my mom confirmed, her carefree tone making me smile. "Jason's in the shower, and Ethan, sweetie, your clothes still have about twenty minutes in the dryer. I think it might be time to trade the old girl in. She don't work like she used to." Mom glanced at the back door. "Why don't y'all go sit on the porch and watch the lightning."

I huffed out a laugh and shook my head. "What she means to say is, get out of my kitchen so I can clean it the way I want to."

"Jaxon Stettler, I mean no such thing."

"Mm-hm."

She waved her hands at us, basically shooing us toward the door like two toddlers.

Outside, the rain had settled down to a drizzle, the thunder a distant roll as we stepped out onto the back porch. It was covered, but the air was muggy and thick.

"I think our mommas would get along great," Ethan teased.

He leaned against the railing next to me. Not too close, but close enough I could smell the faint scent of sunscreen and sweat.

"Probably." I took a sip of my soda and set it on the wood rail. "My mom is... set in her ways."

"Whose isn't?" he asked, and I thought I might've heard a hint of irritation.

The shadow of the kitchen window disappeared as the light went out.

"Guess you did a good job. She's usually up cleaning until after Jay has fallen asleep."

"My momma would be proud." He smirked and took a swig from his can.

"Do you live at home?"

"Moved out a few months ago. I got my own place down on Deer Pond Road. It's not much, but it's mine." He set his drink down, and rested his elbows on the wood, staring straight out into the black void of my backyard. "It was time."

"I know what you mean."

He looked at me then. "Do you ever think of moving out?"

"Sometimes," I admitted. "But I can't leave them. It'd feel wrong."

"Have you ever talked to your mom about it?"

"Why would I? I'd never want her to feel guilty."

"Guilty?"

"Yeah, if I talked to her about the possibility of me moving out? She might think I feel trapped."

"Do you... feel trapped?"

Ethan's direct questions should've made me uneasy, poking around in the personal space I'd closed off to the rest of the world.

It was a lonely place.

I wanted to talk to someone, just one damn person, about real shit for once, and I'd gone and screwed everything up with Wild. The memory of him in that bathroom. His cheeks wet with tears, his eyes rimmed in red and smeared with black. I'd done that. I'd broken him again. I was tired of ruining everything I loved, tired of telling lies all the time.

"Sometimes," I whispered, more to myself than to Ethan. "It's difficult..." I swallowed, aware of his body heat, of how he leaned in a little to hear me speak, of the way his eyes had dropped to my mouth. "I want things for myself and it makes me feel selfish."

"There's nothing selfish about wanting to live a life that's yours."

It could have been unconscious or intentional, I had no way to gauge it as Ethan's fingers brushed my hand.

"Ethan—"

His lips pressed against mine and I forgot what I was about to say. His lips were softer than I thought they'd be, and I was starving for something, for touch, anything to make me feel human, if only for a second. His hand slid into my hair, my heart pounded in my chest, feeling light and then heavy as I cupped the back of his neck, pulling him closer. My fingertips were numb as his tongue swept over my bottom lip and I opened for him, tasting him. I forgot I was supposed to be playing the role of the straight son. I forgot we were standing on my mother's porch and not hiding in a dorm. I stopped thinking about the guilt and the shame, and how I'd ruined everything with Wild. I disconnected as he backed me into the railing, and aligned our bodies. He rutted against me, the friction making him moan. The sound of it was a cold wash of reality and I gasped for air, pushing him away.

"Oh fuck," I breathed and took a step back. "I'm sorry," I mumbled and wiped at my mouth, wiped away his taste. It didn't belong on my lips.

"Jax." He reached for my hand, his fingers grazing my arm, "Don't be sorry."

I shook my head over and over, backing myself toward the door.

"It's okay," he said in a calm whisper, like I was a wild horse about to run.

His hair was a mess from my hands, his lips swollen, his chin red. My throat narrowed and I reached for the door. "I'm sorry," I said again, this time on the verge of a full-on panic attack.

Ethan placed a steady hand on my shoulder. "I'm the one who should be sorry, alright. I shouldn't have kissed you."

"Kissed you back," I managed to say through the chattering of my teeth. I was shaking from the inside out. I'd given him too much.

"Jax... I thought..." He swore and ran his hands through his hair. "I shouldn't have done that. No matter how much I wanted to." He stared at me, waiting for me to fall apart. "And God, I've wanted to do that for forever."

Confused, I took a few deep breaths. "You have?"

"I wasn't joking when I said you were my first crush. I always thought you were straight, though."

"I am," I argued, hearing how ridiculous I sounded even to my own ears.

"Jax..." He let my name hang in the air and it pissed me off.

I didn't owe him an explanation.

"I can't do this," I said, my tone final as I pushed open the door.

"Don't do that."

"What?"

"Act like that wasn't fucking amazing." He spoke, his anger heavy in his whisper.

The house was too quiet, the fear strangling me. Had my mom heard what he'd just said? Had she seen us kiss.

"It's..." I stammered. "I'm not ready."

Ethan's shoulders relaxed.

"You don't have to be. I can be here for you. If that's what you want."

I wanted Wild.

I wanted to reverse time and fix every stupid mistake I'd made.

"I think you should go."

Hurt flashed across eyes, and he nodded, his jaw tight. "Yeah... I guess I should."

"I'll bring your things by the store tomorrow," I said as he stepped off the porch.

Ethan paused, looking right through me with a confidence I'd never be able to wield. "A year ago, I was in the exact same situation as you. I went through a lot of it on my own and it sucked. When you're ready, Jax. You know where to find me."

Chapter 15

WILDER

The bed shifted but I didn't move. With my head buried under blankets and a pillow, I had no idea what time it was. My hair was matted against my forehead with sweat, and if I hadn't already grown accustomed to it, my stench alone would have driven me out of hiding. But it was the light jingle of the bell that hung from Gandalf's collar that finally pulled my head from the darkness. He hopped onto my chest with a soft meow.

"Go away," I said, but lacked the energy to mean it.

He started to knead his little paws into my skin like he was making biscuits, purring loud enough that if I hadn't already had a headache I would now.

"What?" I sat up onto my elbows. "Are you hungry?"

He curled into a ball on my lap, staring at me. I glanced into the bathroom and I could see he hadn't eaten everything I'd given him the night before. Feeling less guilty, I lay back down and covered my eyes with my arm. It had been five days since Jax showed up with a grenade and destroyed the carefully constructed walls I'd built for myself.

"I'm fine." Apparently, I'd moved on to the talking-to-your-pet phase of my depression. "My life is just fine."

A total lie, but it didn't matter. I was happy enough. I was successful. I had friends and lovers if I wanted. I didn't need anything else. Love and all that other shit caused drama. Drama I didn't want or need. I was perfectly dramatic on my own.

Gandalf stood and slinked his way along my side, into the crook of my arm. "I wouldn't stay there if I were you," I warned him. "We both know it's been days since I showered."

"Are you talking to yourself now?" Anders's voice echoed in my aching head.

I sat up too quickly and black spots burst in my peripheral. Gandalf scampered away, and I rested my face in the palms of my hands. "How did you get in here?"

"June let me borrow her key. She told me I had one hour to drag your, and I quote, 'skinny, drama queen ass out of bed.'" He chuckled and I raised my gaze.

"I'm such a joke."

His smile faltered. "No... Wilder, I—"

"You shouldn't have come here. Leave the key on the kitchen counter and get out."

I pulled the sheets back with a force I didn't think I'd have after not eating for—God, how long had it been? I didn't care that I was naked. The pity in Anders's eyes only served to infuriate me more, and as I stood on weak and unstable legs, I stumbled right into his arms.

I shoved my palms into his chest, pushing him away. But he had always been stronger than me. He wrapped his arms around my torso without a fight and pulled me closer. I couldn't hold it in anymore. I'd tried to keep myself in check these past few days. Choosing sleep over reality. But I grabbed his shoulders, clinging to that familiar heat, and cried into the cotton of his shirt. In five or ten minutes, my embarrassment would be paralyzing, but right now I needed this. Needed something solid.

"You're not a joke, Wilder." He lifted my chin.

Anders wiped the tears from my cheek with his thumb, and I panicked, worried he would kiss me. I couldn't handle another complication. But I knew I wouldn't stop him if he tried. I'd do anything to feel something other than this gaping emptiness. I think he saw it then, that black hole I'd hidden so well, and drew back.

"June told me what happened." His expression was too careful.

"Everything?"

"Yeah." He tried to hide it, but I could hear the pain of my lie in his tone.

"I should've told you... the ending of my book wasn't the truth. I didn't know... if he was alive or dead, all I knew was that he left and never came back."

"It doesn't matter." Anders brushed a knuckle along my jaw.

"It's pathetic. I'm pathetic."

"It doesn't matter how he left, Wilder. He hurt you."

My breath caught in my throat, expanding until I couldn't speak without lifting another floodgate. I wanted Anders's anger. This tenderness made me feel worse.

"What can I do?" he whispered.

Kiss me. Fuck me. Let me sleep.

I shrugged my shoulders. "Nothing."

"Nothing isn't an option." He took my hand and I let him walk me to the bathroom. "Let's start with a shower."

I nodded as he let go of my hand and turned on the water. The room filled with steam as he stripped out of his clothes. I didn't turn away or avert my eyes. I watched him with a blank expression, seeing him like this, naked, like we hadn't broken things off, it was wrong. This constant cycle, where we both used each other for whatever reason, loneliness, release. I couldn't do it again. Jax had made sure of that when he bulldozed his way back into my life. I couldn't fake it anymore, all my cracks had been exposed. Still, I allowed Anders to take my hand, and stood with him, skin to skin, under the hot water. Let him wash my hair, my body, numb to the touch of his fingers. I was stuck inside my head, thinking about Saturday night, seeing Jax, his green eyes, his regret so fucking honest on his face. What had his life been like all this time? He'd said everything he'd told me in those emails had been real. If that was true? All that sorrow, it was debilitating. I was grateful for the water trickling down my face. It hid the new wave of tears spilling over my cheeks.

I didn't want to cry for Jax anymore. I had every right to be angry. I'd already given him too much of my time and my heart. But all the words he'd given me, they swam inside my head, and I hated him for making me feel guilty.

"Hey." Anders ran his fingers up my arm. "Feeling better?"

"Yeah."

My stomach dropped as he leaned down and kissed me once, twice, and when I didn't respond, he pulled away.

"June will be here soon." He spoke without emotion and stepped out of the shower.

I shut off the water and he handed me a towel. We got dressed in a weighted silence, but even so, I did feel better.

"Thank you," I said, but he didn't look up from where he sat on the edge of my bed, tying his shoes. "For being here."

A spark of irritation furrowed his brow. "I'll *always* be here, Wilder. Whenever you need it." He stood, shoving his hands into his pockets. "That's what I do for the people I love. I show up." The alarm his words conjured inside me must have been written across my face. He laughed. "Calm down. It wasn't a declaration." Anders crossed the room. Standing in front of me, he brushed a curl of hair from my eyes. "I do... love you. How could I not?"

"I love you too, you know that."

He kissed my forehead. "Too bad it's not enough."

"You're too good for me." I tugged on the hem of his shirt.

"I am." His bravado brought a smile to my lips. "Will you be okay?"

"It might take me a minute."

He briefly took my hand in his, and with a gentle squeeze he let go. "Take all the time you need."

About twenty minutes later June showed up at my front door. We had originally planned to go out for my birthday today, but as much as I loved Gwen, I needed some one-on-one time with my best friend without her too-adorable-for-words relationship being paraded for my misery.

"Has he tried to contact you?" June asked, sitting next to me on a stool. She poured an obscene amount of vodka into a glass half filled with tonic.

I pulled my phone from the back pocket of my jeans and handed it to her. "He emailed me. Twice."

"Asshole."

June entered in my password and tapped away on the screen. Once her fingers stopped moving, her lips whispered Jax's words as she read. I stole the vodka from the counter and drank straight from the bottle. I coughed, the burn of the alcohol singeing my throat.

"Whoa... slow down. You're not allowed to get wasted in your apartment on your birthday. Heartbreak or not, today is your thirtieth, and you *will* celebrate out in the real world, like an adult. You hearing me?"

I lifted my hand, mimicking a puppet talking and she smacked it.

"I am not in a celebratory mood," I whined, taking another fiery gulp of alcohol.

She ignored me and finished reading Jax's emails. "Jesus, this guy."

"I know."

"How sad."

"I *know*."

"Are you going to text him?"

"What?" The room was too warm. "Hell, no. I deleted his number."

"You could just email him, then." June took the bottle from my hand. "What he did, lying to you about his name, it's messed up."

"But..."

"But nothing. It's messed up. He should have manned up and told you who he was from the get-go."

"*But...*" I prompted.

June was predictably empathetic.

"But..." She winced when I kicked her foot. "He's been through the wringer. His dad, his poor, sweet brother. He was young when this all went down."

The ache in my chest spread through my limbs. I was dangerously close to crawling back into bed. My anger had been my anchor. But this guilt, it came at me in waves, shaking me loose from the justifications I'd used to hold me ashore all these years.

"He could have at least called. Something..." A sharp spike of pain cracked through my chest. "I understand, June. I can't imagine what he went through. How alone he must have been. But at some point... he should have contacted me. Even if it was to say, 'fuck off, you made me queer and now my dad is dead. P.S. I hate you.'"

"He obviously loved you... loves you. I'm not saying you should call him up and pretend it's all just water under the bridge. But sometimes people do crazy shit to cope. Jax cut you out of his life, and you push everyone else out of yours."

"You're defending him?" I asked, incredulous.

Furious, I stood, putting some distance between us.

"I'm not defending him, I—"

"And what the hell does that mean? I haven't pushed anyone out of my life?" My restless fury bubbled underneath my skin.

"Wilder," she whispered my name, her sad eyes fixing on mine. "Jax abandoned you, and then your parents go and do the same thing... maybe you don't push people away, but you sure as hell don't let anyone in. Not really."

Close to tears again, I took a deep breath. "I let you in."

"I'm one person. Anders... that man loves you, and you don't even care." She held up her hand, silencing my retort. "I shouldn't have said that. I know you care, and that's why it makes me so damn mad. You have people in your life who want to be there for you. And you refuse to let them."

I sagged against the back of my couch, exhaustion pulling me under. "I don't love Anders like—"

"Like you love Jax." She handed me my phone. "He made a big time, catastrophic, life-altering mistake. But the truth is... you love him, you always have.

"Whether I love him or not is irrelevant. How can I forgive him when I can't figure out how to forgive myself?"

She leaned into me, her shoulder pressing against mine as she sat on the back of the couch. "Forgive yourself? What for?"

"I pushed him that night. Before he left campus. I wanted him to come out, I was tired of hiding all the time. He wasn't ready and I pushed him. What if..." The room was too bright, the light from the kitchen cut through my head like a blade. "What if he wasn't ready for any of it? June, he was so disgusted by our relationship that he convinced himself his father's death was a punishment from God. If we never got together in the first place, he wouldn't have that guilt."

She shook her head, unwavering. "Nope, no way. If it wasn't you then it would've been some other guy. Or maybe he'd blame it all on his *impure thoughts*. He's gay. And not because of you. It's not a choice, Wilder, and you know it."

"Seeing him again... it's like I'm back at Eastchester waiting for him in my room, wondering if tonight will be the night he decides he can't do it anymore. I think not knowing what happened to him was the easier option."

"Or... I know this might sound left field..." She smirked and I rolled my eyes. "You get the closure you desperately need and respond to him."

"I don't think I can. At least not right now. I'm too... raw. I don't think I'd be receptive to anything he had to say."

"That's fair."

All it would take was a few clicks and a couple of words for Jax Stettler to be back in my life. And that thought was terrifying.

Gandalf jumped up onto the counter, distracting me from my melodrama, and sniffed the untouched vodka tonic. He wiggled his head and sneezed.

"Gross. That one's yours."

"Since it's your birthday... sure." June walked to the counter and scratched Gandalf's head. Picking up the drink, she asked, "Where do you want to go after dinner?"

I gave her the best puppy dog eyes I could muster. "Can we please do take out?"

"Absolutely not. Go make yourself pretty. We have a reservation at seven."

Sulking, but secretly thankful for her nagging, I said, "Fine, but I refuse to be happy about it."

"Sometimes I wonder if you ever hit puberty." She smacked my ass as I walked away.

The weight on my shoulders had eased some as I got ready. I brushed my teeth, changed into my favorite pair of skinny jeans, and decided to wear the oversized, sheer white t-shirt June had given me for Christmas last year. I was applying liner when my phone vibrated on the countertop.

Unknown number: Happy Birthday, Wild.

My hands trembled as three dots appeared, and then disappeared, on the bottom of the screen. I waited a full minute for those damn dots to reappear, but they never did. I typed out three separate messages and deleted each one. *Thank you. Fuck you. Lose my number.*

I stared at Jax's message, reading it over and over again, trying to imagine the sound of his husky voice saying the words.

Happy Birthday, Wild.

I'm sorry for making you feel like you weren't every fucking thing to me.

Happy Birthday, Wild.

The love I had for you has never faded.

Happy Birthday, Wild.

I'd like to think my life would've been with you, but now I'll never know.

"Ready?" June asked, startling me.

My pulse flaying, I exited out of my messages.

"As I'll ever be."

Chapter 16

JAX

August was by far the hottest month in Florida, the humidity almost unbearable as I dug into the heavy dirt. Laying down a sprinkler system wasn't easy, and when I was stuck doing it by myself, it was damn near impossible. Chuck and Jim had left about an hour ago to help out another crew with a plumbing issue, and Hudson had called in sick. Though, I figured he was probably hung over. When he wasn't working, he was drinking. I wondered how he had any money at all to pay for rent when most of his nights were spent at the bar. I wiped the sweat from my brow with the back of my arm, internally cursing Hudson's shitty work ethic. He had me second-guessing my choice to go to Marietta with him and Jim next month.

I set the shovel down and picked up my bottle of water. I sprayed a bit over my head before taking a long swig. The water had warmed under the sun and made my stomach feel queasy. I pulled my phone out of the back pocket of my shorts, hoping to have a text from Jim letting me know they were on their way back. It was almost lunch time, and I was stuck here without a ride. Every day I drove to the JW Construction offices and then hitched a ride in one of the company trucks. We all did. Stinking to high heaven and almost out of water, I regretted not driving myself today.

I typed out a quick message to Jim.

> **Me:** How long till you get back?
> **Jim:** Not sure, waiting on the plumber to get here.
> **Jim:** Right now, we're ripping down all the fucking drywall we hung last week.

I cringed. Materials were expensive, but time, to Jim, was priceless. He owned one of the largest construction companies in Destin. If it wasn't for his son's help, the business might've gone under a few years ago. Derrick wasn't into hard labor, but the kid could run numbers. And he budgeted time like it was made out of gold. And with Jim taking the Marietta job, there wasn't time for pipes to burst.

> **Me:** Take your time.
> **Me:** Everything will be dug up when you get back.
> **Jim:** Don't forget to take a break. I don't need you getting sick too.

I sighed and scrolled through my contacts, hesitating at Ethan's name. After that embarrassing kiss, I almost skipped going into Harley's that next morning to give him the clothes he'd left behind to dry. Horrified at myself for losing control like I had, I was grateful when he'd acted like nothing had happened. Smiling at me like always, he hadn't mentioned a thing. But after Hudson and Chuck left the store, he'd handed me a slip of paper with his number on it. Told me to call him when I was ready, or if I just needed to "work shit out." Which, after his cheeks had flamed, I'd realized he didn't mean talking about my feelings. I hadn't ever planned to call or text him, but Jason had kept asking when we could go fishing with Ethan again. Eventually, I'd given in and told myself I was capable of having a friendship with a man I was attracted to.

Since then we'd gone fishing with Jason a couple of times. And if we did text it was mostly about Jay, and how Ethan said he would help out if I decided to go to Georgia. If my head wasn't so far up my ass, and my heart in Wild's hands, I could easily see myself with a guy like Ethan. He was good to Jay, and I liked that he was rough around the edges in ways Wilder wasn't. But I'd meant it when I told him I wasn't ready. I could want someone like him, want Wild, but it didn't change the fact that I wasn't able to give up my closet—my life with my family.

I wet my sun-cracked lips and called him.

"Hi," he said, and I could hear the surprise in his tone. "What's up?"

"You at Harley's?" I asked, rubbing the back of my sweaty neck.

"I'm off today. Everything okay?" he asked, and I appreciated the concern in his voice.

"Jim had to run off to another property, left me here without a truck and I'm running low on water."

"Ahh. You need a ride?" he asked.

I couldn't tell if he was annoyed or genuinely asking.

"Kind of. But if you're busy, I—"

"I'm not busy," he said and chuckled. "God, I sound too eager, huh?"

I smiled and huffed out a laugh. It was nice to know I wasn't the only one who was nervous all the damn time.

"Nah, I feel like a dick. I'm always asking you for favors."

"Then ask me out for lunch and it won't be a favor."

I glanced around the empty street like an idiot. No one could hear or care what the hell we were talking about. And asking him to lunch didn't have to be a date. He was a friend. Friends were allowed to eat lunch together.

"Lunch sounds good right about now. Air conditioning too."

He laughed. "Are you out at Mrs. Hornsby's place?"

"Yeah."

"Give me about fifteen minutes?"

"I really appreciate this," I said.

"See you in a few."

When I ended the call, I saw an email notification. My stomach dropped and the ground became unsteady beneath my feet. It had been a week since I'd texted Wild. I'd promised myself I'd leave him alone, but when I realized it was his birthday, I couldn't *not* text him. And like I'd assumed, he'd never responded. The excitement that rolled through me quickly turned into a sigh of disappointment. The email was from the property manager in Marietta letting me know the two-bedroom

I'd reserved online for me and Hudson had been confirmed. I forwarded it to Jim, but before closing out of the app, I opened up the email chain I should've deleted weeks ago. I reread the last email Wilder had sent to me, and read the last two I'd sent him, guilt pinching at my ribs every time I took a breath. My remorse had morphed into something bigger, something I couldn't contain as I opened up a new message and started typing.

FROM: fool0fatook54@bellinx.mail.com
TO: wildwelleslit@bartpress.com
Date: Aug 23 1:06 PM
SUBJECT: Pushing my luck

Wild,

I'm leaving for Georgia on the 30th. I'll only be there for a couple of months. Well, that's if everything goes like it should. Which it won't, so I'm betting I'll be in Marietta longer. I shouldn't be writing to you like this anymore, but I can't stop thinking about you all the time. I wish I could go back and change everything. But no matter how hard I wish for what I want, there are some things in life that aren't meant to be. You've already moved on, living your life. It's going to be hard, knowing you're only a thirty-minute drive away. Don't worry, I won't come to you, not until you ask me to. And I hope you will.

I know it's been said, but I'll say it one more time.

I'm sorry.

Jax~

I pressed send before I could talk myself out of it, and as I slipped my phone back into my pocket, Ethan showed up.

"Hey," he said, smiling as I slid into the passenger seat.

Ethan had on board shorts and a tight gray tank top that stretched across his chest. His hair looked damp, and as I shut the door, the smell of chlorine stung my nose.

"Were you swimming?" I asked, a fresh wave of guilt pulling me under.

He bit his bottom lip and shrugged. "Not really. My apartment complex has a pool. But there's always a million kids." He gave me another one of his crooked smiles. "I'd rather have lunch with you."

"Okay." I didn't want to read too much into what he'd said. "Where do you want to go." Ethan glanced at my dirty fingers, and my sweat-stained shirt. Insecurity rippled through me. "I'm not fit for more than a drive-thru."

He laughed as he pulled onto the main road. "I'm kind of liking the whole sweaty-working-man thing."

"I don't think you'd like it if you got much closer. Nothing good about the stench I've got going on."

He leaned over and wrinkled his nose with a laugh. "Maybe you're right."

My face heated, but I laughed too. "Sorry. I've been digging up Mrs. Hornsby's yard all morning. August heat is no joke."

"Don't apologize for being a hard worker, Jax." The car slowed, approaching a stop light. "I think it's sexy... a man who can take care of things. Fix shit."

I didn't know how to respond. He was always casual about his sexuality, where I hadn't even said the words, *I'm gay*, to anyone except Wild. But I guess sticking your tongue down a guy's throat with a raging hard-on was enough of an admission.

"I'm really good at freaking you out," he said, his lips pressed together suppressing a growing grin. "I should work on that."

My hands fidgeted in my lap. "It's just..." I turned and watched the buildings pass by, not truly focusing on anything. My mouth was dry, my stomach turning inside out as I said, "I've only been open with one other person about... this thing inside me. And he's... it was a long time ago. I guess it's weird to talk about it when I've been silent for as long as I have."

Ethan turned into the parking lot of Billy's, a burger place south of Bell River. Instead of pulling into the drive-thru, he parked the car.

He left the engine running as he stared at me. "You don't have to tell me anything, Jaxon." I studied his chest as it moved. I counted five breaths before he spoke again. "When I came out to my parents last year, I thought I was gonna die. I can't even describe to you how hard it was for me to open my mouth and say the words. My dad threw me out, and I slept on a friend's couch for two weeks. That's when I got the job at Harley's. But I didn't die. And me and my folks, we're working it out. I moved back in for a while, but it isn't the same. I know they love me, but they don't accept me as I am. Maybe one day I'll go over there, and I won't notice how my dad keeps a few feet between us, or how my momma always looks like she wants to cry. I can't take it back... coming out, and I don't want to. But I forget sometimes, what it was like to hide who you are all the time. All the little things we have to sacrifice. I'm sorry if I've made you feel like you owe me some sort of explanation."

He didn't have to tell me how hard it was to speak the truth. I could feel it in my chest. Like an anvil. I picked at a thread near the pocket of my shorts to keep my hands busy. "You didn't make me feel that way." I lifted my gaze and sucked down a ragged breath. "I've known I was... gay since I was a kid. Nothing you've said is wrong. If anything, I wish I could be as open as you."

"I'm not as open as you think... I mean, I don't deny that I like men, but I have to be careful." Ethan hesitated. "I want to ask you something, but I'm afraid it's too personal."

"Ask me."

"The guy you mentioned before... how long ago—"

"A little over nine years."

His eyes widened. "Was he a boyfriend?"

He was more.

"Yeah. When I was at Eastchester. No one at school knew, though, and then everything happened here. The relationship ended."

"Shit, Jax... all this time you've been dealing with this on your own?"

"It's not as hard as it sounds. Jason became my world. And I'm grateful for every second I have with him and my mom."

He opened his mouth to speak but stopped himself. Shaking his head, he said, "Jason is a good kid."

"What were you really going to say?"

His face flushed as he tapped his fingers against the steering wheel. "What about..." He looked at me, waiting, and when I furrowed my brow, he blew out a breath. "Sex, Jax... haven't you missed it?"

"I have sex," I said, hating how defensive I sounded. I knew what he was getting at. The physical connection I'd had with Wild was something I'd never been able to recreate with any of the women I'd slept with.

Confused, he asked, "You have?"

"I was with Mary for a year and dated a few other women before her."

Understanding dawned in his caramel eyes. "I dated women for a while, until I couldn't. It wasn't the same. And I hated feeling like I was using them."

"I know what you mean." I could feel him watching me as I stared through the windshield. "I don't think I can do it anymore. But I have no idea how to move forward. I don't want to lose my family."

"I wish I could promise you everything will be good, and that your mom will be okay with having a gay son, but you know as well as I do, that's a promise I can't keep."

"I'll be in Marietta for a few months… Maybe while I'm there I can figure out a way to do this."

"You decided to go, then?" I didn't miss the disappointment in his voice.

"I did. But only if you're still okay to help out with Jay?"

"Help? I *get* to hang out with Jason."

"Are you sure, I don't like asking you for favors all the time?"

His smile flattened. "Would you quit it? I said I would. I *like* being around Jay. He's fun… I don't know… he makes me realize how much I take for granted. Life shouldn't be as hard as we make it."

I probably should've kept the thought to myself, but I wanted his smile back where it belonged. "You're kind of cute when you're pissed off."

"Don't even look at me like that and start something you have no intention of finishing."

I held up my hands in surrender, my grin sneaking its way across my lips. "What?"

He cut the engine, laughing as he opened the door. "Come on, you owe me a burger."

Billy's had a takeout window on the other side of the building, and I followed behind Ethan, feeling more like myself than I had in weeks. We ordered a couple of burger combos and took a seat at one of the tables while we waited for them to call out our order number. The red and white umbrella covered us from the sun, but not the heat.

Ethan ran a hand through his hair and caught me staring. "We should go to the beach together... with Jason, before I leave."

"Yeah?"

"If you want?" I asked.

"Absolutely."

"Order number seventy-five," a shrill voice echoed over the intercom.

Ethan and I stood at the same time. "I got it," he said.

"Thanks."

As he walked away, my phone chimed in my pocket. I figured it was Jim telling me he was on his way back. But when I unlocked the screen, I had an email waiting. I tried to tamp down any sort of expectation that it might be Wild and was completely blindsided when it was actually him. I shot a quick glance at Ethan waiting in line to pick up our order before I opened the message.

FROM: wildwelleslit@bartpress.com
TO: fool0fatook54@bellinx.mail.com
Date: Aug 23 1:34 PM
SUBJECT: RE: Pushing my luck

Jax,

I read your emails, and I got your apology. What happened to your family, it's awful, and my heart hurts for you, for your mom, and Jason. I wish I could've been there for you. But you never gave me the chance. I wish you could've seen how much it hurt me when you disappeared. It was like you died. And for all intents and purposes, you had died.

I don't know what to say to a ghost. And I can't help with your guilt or your regrets. Regrets are for cowards. It has always been my belief you should chase after the things you want with actions, not words. There is no such thing as never meant to be.

So, this apology... not accepted...

Love always,
Wild~

My pulse raced as I read between the lines he'd written.

Love always, Wild.

This apology.

Chase after the things you want.

Did he want me to fight for him?

No such thing as never meant to be.

"You okay?" Ethan asked, setting our tray on the table.

I wanted to separate the love I had for Wild from all the terrible shit that had happened to me. I wanted to stop the growing attraction I had for Ethan. I wanted to fight for Wild. I wanted to fight for myself. And most of all, I wanted to stop feeling so goddamn selfish for wanting any of those things in the first place.

"Yeah," I held up my phone. "Just an update on the Georgia trip."

He handed me my drink. "I think it will be good for you... to get away. Take some time for yourself and figure out what you want."

"I think so too."

Except I already knew what I wanted. And this time I'd make sure I didn't mess it up.

Chapter 17

JAX

The Saturday sun low in the sky didn't quite touch the horizon, reminding me I couldn't stay like this, floating in the ocean, forever. I could hear Jason chatting away with Ethan on the shoreline. I'd left them to their three-story sandcastle and took a moment to center myself. I would miss these lazy moments with my brother, the saltwater on my skin, and the way an afternoon could fade without it feeling like any time had passed at all. With my eyes closed and the water holding me steady, I could pretend like my life here was as it should be. But then I thought about Marietta, and Wild, and the peaceful calm I'd created washed out with the seaweed. I hadn't emailed Wilder back, unsure of what to say. I wanted to wait until I was there to contact him again, but I worried if I put too much distance between us, the sliver of a chance I thought he'd given me could disappear. But if I pushed too hard, he might pull away again. The sudden quiet distracted me from my thoughts. I opened my eyes to find Jason, alone, hovered over his masterpiece, adding pieces of shells to his castle. My feet touched the sandy bottom of the Gulf, the water only up to my shoulders, and I scanned the beach for Ethan. I never let myself drift too far from shore, wanting my brother in my line of sight at all times. Pissed Ethan had left him while I wasn't paying attention, I started toward the shore when Ethan surfaced a few feet in front of me.

"Shit," I said, my earlier aggravation apparent in my tone. "I thought you left Jay alone, I was pissed for a second."

He pushed his wet hair from his face, slicking it back with his fingers. "Sorry about that."

Droplets of water clung to his lips as he smiled. I liked that his right front tooth overlapped the left. If I was being real with myself, I liked a lot of things about Ethan. But none of it mattered. I had too much shit going on to lend out anymore pieces of myself to anyone other than Wild. I had to leave in less than a week, and all I could think about was the possibility of seeing him again.

"We should head home soon," I said. "It'll be dark before you know it."

He waded toward me, leaving little space between us. "The best time to swim is at night."

"If you wanna get eaten by a shark."

"You're afraid of sharks?" He laughed, and his fingers grazed my hip under the water.

I rubbed away the goosebumps on my arm. "Not really, just getting bit by one."

"That's the same thing," he said, and I couldn't help the laugh that bubbled up in my chest.

I shook my head, trying to contain my smile. "Everybody knows you shouldn't go in the water at night."

He pointed toward the pink and orange horizon. "Dusk is more dangerous."

I didn't know if that was true or not, but it freaked me out anyway. "Are you messing with me?"

His smile grew and I realized I'd unconsciously moved closer to him. "Unfortunately, it's true. Early morning isn't safe either."

Ethan reached up and brushed a wet strand of hair from my forehead, letting the tips of his fingers linger on my cheek. My breath hitched as I pulled back, looking toward the shore. Jason stood with his feet in the water, watching us. Pressure lodged itself inside my chest.

"We better go," I said, and ignored the way Ethan's smile fell as I swam back to the beach.

With the sun setting, the air had cooled enough I got goosebumps as I stepped out of the water. I could hear Ethan behind me, but I didn't look at him or Jason. Afraid of what my eyes might reveal. I grabbed my towel and dried myself off in silence, annoyed at Ethan for thinking he could touch me like that. Especially in front of the whole goddamn world, but mostly I was irritated with myself. My body betrayed me when I was around him. He pushed my boundaries, but I needed him to be a friend, a space where I could be myself without overthinking it.

"I got the buckets," Jason said, and I turned to look at him.

Jay stared at me, no judgment in his eyes, and I wondered if he even realized what he'd seen. "I'll get the blanket," I said. "Ethan, do you mind grabbing the shovels?"

"Sure thing," he said, not meeting my eyes.

I'd made it weird, and the uneasy silence followed us all the way back to my house. When we pulled up, Ethan was the first to get out of the car, slamming the door behind him.

"Jay, why don't you head on inside, alright. I'll be right in."

"Is Ethan mad?"

"Nah. Just head on in, buddy. I'll get everything."

I cut the engine as Jason made his way to the front door. He waved at Ethan, and I was glad he gave my brother a smile. Jay didn't deserve to get caught up in my business. With Jason inside, I walked over to Ethan's Toyota. His shoulders were hard set, his arms crossed over his chest.

Before I could say anything, he said, "You run hot and cold, you know that?"

"I'm sorry... I got spooked. Jason was watching us."

"He was?"

"That's the thing, Ethan. Anyone could've been watching us. Friends don't touch each other like that." I lowered my voice. "At least not around here they don't."

Frustrated, he cut a hand through his damp hair. "Shit... I shouldn't have done that... I shouldn't have touched you... I'm sorry." His shoulders relaxed. "I like you, Jax... I like being around you."

He took a step toward me, glancing at the front door, he stopped, leaving a few feet between us. I liked him too, but it wasn't enough to pull me out of the closet, and it sure as hell wasn't enough to pull me away from Wild. I didn't want to lead him on or give him anymore mixed signals. I'd trusted him with the truth about who I was, but he didn't know about Wild, maybe if he did, he'd understand my hesitancy had nothing to do with him.

"There's something I didn't tell you the other day... that guy I mentioned—"

"The one from Eastchester?"

"Yeah... he lives in Atlanta."

"Oh." His posture deflated.

"I messed up. Did some things I need to make up for. This trip to Marietta... if I have a chance to set things right—"

"You should take it." A small smile lifted his lips. "If it's what you want, Jax, you should do it."

"I don't know if he'll even want to talk to me, but I gotta try. I think this is the last thing I've been holding on to."

He furrowed his brow. "You think setting things right with this guy will make it easier for you to come out?"

"I don't know. Maybe?" I could tell Ethan wanted to say something but held it back. "What? You don't think it will?"

"I think you had a panic attack today because you thought I'd accidentally outed you when I touched you. I think you're putting a lot of weight on this guy's shoulders." He sighed and lowered his gaze. "You're the only one who will know when you're ready, Jax. If you want things to work out with this guy, you'll have to trust yourself."

"I'm working on it," I said. "Having you to talk to has helped a lot. Knowing you went through this too, and came out unscathed..."

"I definitely have some bumps and bruises." He gave me a lopsided grin. "But yeah, I survived, and I know you will too."

"I'm sorry if I led you on."

He held up his hands. "I might've been hoping for more... but that's on me."

The front door opened, and my mom stepped out onto the porch. "You boys gonna stay out here all night?"

"No, ma'am," Ethan said with a chuckle.

"Good. I got a pot of dumplings waiting on you. Hurry up, before Jason eats them all."

"I guess I'm staying for dinner," Ethan said as my mom shut the door. "That alright with you?" I nodded and he bumped his shoulder into mine. "Good, I was gonna stay whether you liked it or not."

"We're good, then?"

"Yeah." He glanced at the door before tugging at my hand with his. "We're good."

🖊 🖊 🖊

My eight-o'clock alarm went off, the annoying buzzer piercing through my sleep-addled brain. I sat up and rubbed my eyes. I'd never considered myself a morning person, always reluctant to get out of bed, wishing for fifteen more minutes. I worked hard every day, and it didn't matter what time I went to bed, it was never early enough. But Sunday mornings, I hated those the most. Every Sunday I had to fight myself to get dressed, to put on a tie, to smile like I didn't think I was going to hell the minute I stepped into Bell River Church. Some Sundays I'd skip it, but today was the last Sunday before I left for Georgia, if I didn't attend, my momma would be madder than a wet hen. I'd never hear the end of it.

I could smell bacon cooking as I made my way to the bathroom for a shower. I went through my morning routine on autopilot. My head already in Georgia. After talking with Ethan last night, what he'd said about me depending on Wild, I was nervous all over again. Nervous I'd put too much hope in the idea of Wild. It'd been nine years. How much had he changed? What if he didn't want me like that anymore? It had been almost a month since we'd been on good terms. A lot could happen in a month. I thought about the kiss I shared with Ethan and regretted it instantly. What if Wild had found somebody else?

"Hurry up, eggs are getting cold," Jason yelled from the other side of the bathroom door.

I shut off the shower faucet and grabbed a towel. "Give me five minutes," I hollered when he started knocking again.

Living in this house, sometimes it was like I was sixteen all over again. Even though I had to share a place with Hudson in Marietta, I looked forward to the privacy. I ran the towel through my hair and wrapped it around my waist. Once I was in my room, I dug through my closet, looking for the least wrinkled long sleeve I could find. I settled on a dark blue button-up. Finishing up, I straightened my tie as Jason pushed open my bedroom door.

"Geez, Jay, what've I told you about knocking first? What if I wasn't dressed?"

He plopped down on my bed. "You lock the door when you don't want me to see what you're doing. The door wasn't locked."

I laughed, watching him in the mirror as I adjusted the knot of my tie again for the third time. "It's called privacy, Jay. I'm not hiding anything."

He shrugged. "Then why lock the door?"

The knot was crooked, but I decided that was as good as it was going to get. I sat next to him on the bed. "Sometimes people need some time to themselves, that's all."

He lowered his head, his nostrils flaring. "I don't want you to go."

Pulling him into a hug, his shoulders shook. "I'll come home as much as I can."

"I'll be alone," he said, the sound of his voice muffled in my shoulder.

"Ethan's gonna be here all the time. He told me he wants to take you fishing and to the beach."

Jason leaned back and wiped at his eyes. "Ethan isn't you."

My throat ached as I tried to keep my shit together. I couldn't break or I'd never leave. I cleared my throat twice, finding my voice. "Two months... Jay. If the job runs over, I won't stay. I'll tell Jim he only has me for two months."

"Two months is forever. Why do you want to leave me and Mom at all?"

A few tears found their way down my cheek. The way his brain worked, betraying him every day, stealing away the earned years of his life, keeping him trapped as a child, he didn't understand. And watching him, a grown man, falling apart like this, it was too much to take.

"I don't want to leave. I told you that. It's a work thing." I held his face between the palms of my hands. "People travel for work all the time. I'm not leaving forever."

"It'll feel like forever," he said. "You promise you'll come home?"

"I swear it, Jay."

We sat on the edge of my bed for a few minutes, giving each other time to breathe. If we walked into the kitchen a crying mess, Mom would want to know what happened. I had a feeling she'd start crying too, and I wasn't prepared for her tears this early in the morning. After a while, Jason stood up and I followed his lead.

"Your eggs are probably cold," he said.

"That's okay, I'm not that hungry, besides we gotta leave for church anyhow."

My mom had finished covering a large tray of biscuits with plastic wrap when we walked into the kitchen. "Jaxon, baby, will you get the honey from the pantry? I promised Pastor Thomas I'd bring something for the luncheon after the service."

"Yes, ma'am."

"And, Jay, grab a few of those paper fans I keep in the junk drawer. The A/C went out in the meeting house again."

I grabbed the honey and set it on the counter. Rolling up my sleeves, I said, "Nothing better than sweating to death."

Mom swatted my shoulder. "Jaxon... sweating is the least you can do for your Lord and Savior." She tried to hide her smirk and failed.

"I think God would want us to be comfortable," I teased.

"Hm-mm. You're lucky I love you so much, joking about the Lord like that..." She wrapped her arm around my waist, and I pulled her into a hug.

"Sorry, Momma, I'm just playing."

She patted my chest. "I know you hate mornings as much as I hate Ms. Arlene's mustard greens. I'll give you a pass this one time. Now hurry up, or we're gonna be late."

I took the tray of biscuits and honey out to the car and set them in the back seat next to Jason. Mom handed me the keys as I shut the door. "You drive, you're faster. But not too fast, I don't wanna have a heart attack."

"Fast, but not too fast. Got it." Grinning at her scowl, I slid into the driver seat.

We kept the radio off on Sundays. Mom used to say too much noise made it hard to hear the Lord's voice. I cranked up the A/C instead as I pulled onto the main highway, hoping to absorb some of the cold air before we got to the meeting house.

Mom made a show of shivering. "You're gonna freeze me out."

"You'll thank me for it later."

She hummed again under her breath as she dug through her purse for something. She pulled out a tissue, lowered the visor mirror, and wiped away the pink lipstick she had on.

"What are you doing?" I asked.

"I hate this color on me, it makes me look old."

"You look nice," I said, and she lifted the visor, ignoring me.

After a minute, she said out of nowhere, "I invited Ethan to the service today."

"Why?"

"Why not?"

"Ethan doesn't like church," Jason said.

I flicked my gaze to the rearview mirror.

"I'm sure that's not true," Mom said, twisting in her seat to look at Jason. "What would make you say such a thing?"

He shrugged. "Just something he said, I guess."

I clutched the steering wheel. Did Jason know about Ethan?

"What did he say?" Mom pressed.

"Nothing really." He squirmed, and I could tell he was worried he'd said something wrong.

"Momma, leave it, it isn't our business," I said.

"Isn't it? If he's hanging around my sons."

"He didn't say nothing bad, Momma," Jason said. "When we were fishing, I told him I thought it was smart that God made fish with gills so they don't drown, and he said he thought God had made him wrong."

"He said that?" I asked, the ache in my chest unbearable.

"Yeah."

Mom finally turned back into her seat. "It makes me sad he feels that way. God made each of his children just as they should be."

"You mean that?" I asked, trying not to hope too much.

"Yes." She looked at me like I'd lost my mind. "Of course, I do."

Everything I'd been afraid of all these years raced through my mind. Did she even know what she'd said? Our church taught us that being gay was a choice—a sin. I wanted to ask her if God had given us that choice, if my love for Wild had been a part of His plan? Or was it my suffering He wanted?

"Jaxon, slow down or you're gonna miss the turn."

I let my foot off the gas, feeling heavy as we rounded the corner and pulled into the parking lot.

"Well, look who's here," she said with a hint of I-told-you-so.

Ethan leaned against the hood of his car in gray slacks and a pale blue button-down that fit like he'd had it tailored. I might not have recognized him if Mom hadn't pointed him out. I parked in the spot next to his and he smiled at me as we all got out of the car.

"Morning," he said, and I swear to God my mom blushed.

She patted him on the shoulder. "Glad you could make it."

"It's been awhile," he admitted.

"That's okay... isn't it, Jax?"

"I'm not the best about my attendance either," I said.

Jason handed my mom the fans she'd wanted him to bring.

"Thanks, honey."

"What about the biscuits?" I asked.

"Just leave them in the car, we can get them after the service." She laced her fingers through Jason's. "Let's head in before there's no seats left."

Ethan and I followed behind, until Mom and Jason disappeared behind the church doors.

"You didn't have to come today," I said.

"She asked... I showed up. It would've been disrespectful not to."

We stopped outside the church door as the organ started to play.

"You're a good friend," I said.

He pressed his fist softly into my shoulder, and with a lopsided smile, he nodded at the doors. "Do you think I'll catch fire when I go in?"

I laughed. "Nah, but if you do, we'll burn together."

Chapter 18

WILDER

Shitty pop music played over the loudspeaker while I waited on a posh, white, oversized couch inside the women's dressing room at Baileys, this new hipster boutique Gwen had insisted we check out. I tried desperately to ignore the lyrics about love and soulmates. It was one of those places that catered to the tone deaf, alt-left, intellectual, vegan type, who posted on every platform possible, pretending to be activists for the marginalized as they dropped two-hundred dollars on a pair of overly distressed jeans. Not that I was judging, I liked to spend money on clothes just as much as the next girl, but I didn't do it to fit into some neat little stereotype. I winced at my mood and tipped my head back to stare at the ceiling. My bitterness left a bad taste in my mouth. I needed to get out of this depressed headspace. And I hated that I'd let Jax in, only for him to ghost me again. I hadn't heard back from him since I'd sent him my sorry-not-sorry-come-fight-for-what-you-want-hopefully-it's-me email. It took a lot of convincing from June, and two bottles of merlot for me to send it in the first place. According to June, I was a miserable mess to be around.

She'd told me I would never move on with my life if I didn't at least try to patch things up with Jax.

"I'm not telling you to invite the guy over for make-up blow jobs, for Christ's sake," she'd said. "But he's coming to Georgia whether you like it or not. You might as well get some closure."

Closure.

I thought knowing he was alive and why he'd stayed away would be enough. Enough for me to move on. I thought I'd break down, cry until I couldn't move, and sleep until it didn't hurt. But the days came and went, and yep, it still hurt. Hurt to think. Hurt to smile. Hurt to breathe. I couldn't stop thinking about the way he looked at me that night at the coffee shop. He'd looked at me like I was his saving grace, like I was the last thread holding him together. It wasn't healthy to be needed like that. Jax Stettler wasn't my responsibility.

You love him.

Loved. I tried to convince myself, and then pulled my phone from my pocket and opened up my email again for the billionth time.

Nothing.

Zero. New. Messages.

Fuck you, Jaxon.

I was a walking catastrophe.

In his email he'd said he'd be in Marietta this past Thursday. It was Monday and not a word from him. I scrolled through all of our emails, ending on the last one I'd sent. I reread it. Maybe I'd been too harsh. Jax definitely held the first-place prize for self-loathing.

He'd probably thought I'd told him to fuck off. Which I guessed I kind of had. But I'd dropped several, well-placed hints, thanks to June, that I wanted him to prove to me his words actually meant something this time. Had he truly never stopped loving me, or was it all a lie? Was everything he'd said a bunch of bullshit? Undone deeds he had to get off his chest to clear his conscience?

"Would you stop looking at your phone for five minutes," Gwen said, and I lifted my head. "Ahh, so that's what you look like?"

"I was answering an email, so sue me," I lied.

She pulled back the dressing room curtain and narrowed her eyes. "Please tell me he finally emailed you back?"

I sank like a sulky teenager into the cushions of the couch. "No... he hasn't."

"He will," she said, and gave me the most pitiful expression.

I couldn't stand it, all the worry inside her eyes. Like an immature man-child, I threw one of the decorative pillows at her and she caught it.

"Nice catch," I said, laughing at the shock on her face.

She threw it back at me, and the corner of it hit me right in the balls.

"Christ," I rasped, leaning over to catch my breath. After a few immensely painful seconds, I sat up. "You are the absolute worst."

"It's not my fault you have zero pain tolerance," she said, her hands on her hips.

I glared at her.

"Email him again."

"Who?" I asked just to irritate her.

She exhaled, exasperated. "Jax."

"Uh... no. I'm not that desperate." I cringed as I tugged my jeans down, relieving some pressure.

"Then can I ask you a favor?"

"It depends on what it is," I said.

"Can you please find a way to curb your crabby attitude, at least for tonight. This is a big night for June, and..."

"Got it," I said, holding up my hands in surrender. "As much as I'd like to think the world revolves around me, it doesn't."

"I want tonight to be perfect."

"It will be," I said, taking her hand and spinning her in a slow circle.

The red dress twirled around her knees. "What do you think?" she asked.

"You look stunning."

And she did. The red silky fabric hugged her curves and made her skin look like porcelain.

"Do you think it's too much?" Gwen adjusted her cleavage as she stared at herself in the full-length mirror, and I had to hide my smile.

"You know me... there's no such thing as too much."

She puffed out a laugh. "I mean for the club. Do you think a dress is too fancy?"

Last week June had been promoted to the labor and delivery nurse educator position she'd applied for but had refused to do anything to celebrate. Gwen, being the best girlfriend on the planet, had planned for us to go to one of June's favorite clubs tonight after dinner.

"Maybe... but so what? No one at Underground will care when they see your tits in that dress." She smacked my arm and I chuckled. "I'm serious, Gwen... like I could go full-on straight for you tonight."

Her face flushed as she shook her head. "I'm wearing jeans."

"Oh my God," I whined as she stepped back into the dressing room and snapped the curtain shut. "Wear the damn dress, Gwen. June will die."

She poked her head out from behind the curtain. "I'll buy it, but I'm not making any promises that I'll wear it."

An older woman, and who I assumed was her teenage daughter, walked in with an armful of clothes, giving me a dirty as hell look. I smiled, wide, baring all my teeth, and the younger girl rolled her eyes.

"I'm going to check out a couple of those shirts I saw when we walked in," I said.

"Okay, I'll hurry."

As I walked out, I waved over my shoulder. "Take your time, Gwen. I'm in no rush."

I sifted through the rack, finally settling on two mesh tops. A red short-sleeve and a black long-sleeve. I brought them up to the register and was finished paying by the time Gwen had resurfaced.

"Are you hungry?" I asked as we stepped outside.

It must have rained while we were in the store. The city sidewalk was wet, and steam hovered over the street, the asphalt soaking up the late summer heat.

"I could eat."

I checked my watch, my meeting with my PA, Andrew, wasn't until later this afternoon. I had a couple of hours to burn. Not that I looked forward to being trapped in a room with him. In a weak moment, I'd told him everything about Jax, and now he hounded me about him all the time.

"I'm dying for a burger," she said. Gwen wrinkled her nose. "Can we go to McDonald's?"

"Ew, no."

"Please," she said, and stuck out her bottom lip. "They have the best fries."

I laughed. "Should I get you a Happy Meal? Because the look you're giving me reminds me of Anders's five-year-old niece who eats paste."

"Has anyone ever told you you're a bully?" She smirked when I held my hand to my chest in mock horror.

"Moi? A bully..."

Laughing, she shoved my shoulder. "Fine. No McDonald's..."

"Now I feel bad."

"You should," she said.

"What about pizza?"

Her face lit up. "*Tratoria*?"

"You read my mind."

◊ ◊ ◊

Even though I'd checked my inbox less than fifteen minutes ago, I couldn't stop myself from opening up the app one last time before I got in the shower.

Empty.

The rest of my day had deteriorated after my meeting with Andrew had run late. I'd had to haul my ass to the bakery down the street from the publishing offices to pick up the cupcakes I'd ordered for June. They'd lost my order, and I might've had a bitch fit and gotten a dozen eclairs for free. Feeling like a total dick, I'd purchased a half-dozen cookies that I would no doubt eat all by myself when I came home drunk tonight, feeling morose and dramatic over the fact I'd most likely made a huge mistake sending Jax that fucking email. Before I could let the sinking feeling in my gut ruin my night, I tossed my phone onto the bathroom counter, and stepped into the shower. I turned on the faucet to the hottest setting I could stand. My skin was red, but I didn't care. The muscles in my shoulders ached with the realization of how much I still loved Jax, how much he affected me, how much hope I'd allowed to linger. In my head I'd kept these snapshots of him. His head rested on my dorm room pillow with the sunlight on his face, his lids heavy and hooded, sleepy and fucked out. In those moments, with the world asleep, oblivious to the two boys lying next to each other, with nothing but love in their eyes, Jax could be who he'd wanted to be, do what he'd wanted to do. But last month, when he'd shown up and tipped my world upside down, I'd witnessed with my own eyes how the years, how that ever-present world, had changed him. He had this hard edge now. Time had made him rough and solid and heartbreaking. I clenched my fists as rivulets of water dripped down my face and let the image of him blur into the anger that fed my pulse. It wasn't enough, I still burned for him. My cock heavy between my legs, I turned the faucet all the way to cold. Like needles, I closed my eyes, allowing the frigid water to infiltrate my skin until I was numb.

When I finally stepped out of the shower, freezing and shivering, I toweled off as fast as I could. Gandalf was perched on the counter, his tail swishing back and forth watching me. I scratched the top of his head and he stood, arching his back until I scratched him there too.

"Why are you so needy?" I asked and he purred with appreciation.

I imagined if he could talk, he'd tell me I was the needy one.

I wrapped my towel around my waist and picked up his food bowl from the floor. He jumped down from the counter, and I laughed as he purred and roped himself through my legs. "You eat like a hobbit. I swear I fill this bowl at least five times a day."

As I scooped some food into the bowl, my phone chirped. I tried to be calm, but I almost tripped over the damn cat to get to it. It was an email notification. I opened the app.

"*Holy shit.*"

It was from Jax.

Gandalf looked up from his bowl of food unimpressed.

I tapped on the message, the words swimming on the page. Why the hell I was crying, I had no clue. It was a blatant overreaction most likely brought on by a combination of low blood sugar and days of anxiety. I could have used one of those cookies right about now.

FROM: fool0fatook54@bellinx.mail.com
TO: wildwelleslit@bartpress.com
Date: Sept 3 06:38 PM
SUBJECT: RE: Pushing my luck

Wild,

I didn't know if you'd want me to reply to your last message. But the way I see it, it wouldn't hurt any if I did. You'll either contact me or you won't. I wanted to wait until I was in Georgia though, make sure I had everything settled and right in my head. I can't be sure, but your email made me think you might be reaching out, and if it's a chance you're giving me, I don't want to mess it up. I'd like to try my best to set everything right with you.

Remember Ethan? We're sort of friends now. I told him about you, about me, and it's weird, being out to someone other than you. But it felt good to tell someone. Felt like I might be on the right track. Anyway, the reason I'm even bringing him up is because he told me I had to start doing what I wanted and quit worrying about everyone else and what they think. I don't know if I'm ready to quit worrying, but I know I want you. At least a chance at making things right between us.

Like your email said, I want to show you with actions, not words, how sorry I am. How much

I've missed you, and how all I ever think about is you. I see you, Wild. Every night when I close my eyes. I remember everything. Feel everything. Feel you.

I don't know if you'll forgive me, or if you'll ever want to see me again. But I'm here. Waiting.

Jax~

I brushed my fingers over my wet cheeks. "Well, shit."

Reading over his words again, I wished June was here. She'd know exactly what I should say. No doubt a perfect mix of take-me-I'm-yours and not-in-this-lifetime-asshole. I almost called her, but remembered I wasn't supposed to make this night about me. I walked into my room and plopped down onto my bed. The chill from the shower completely gone. My day had put me totally behind, but I couldn't leave this house without responding to him. Otherwise, I'd inevitably end up brooding in a corner all night, effectively stealing my best friend's thunder.

I know I want you.

"*Why did it take you so long to figure that out?*" I asked a little too loud and scared Gandalf.

He scampered under my bed as my fingers tapped across the touchscreen.

FROM: wildwelleslit@bartpress.com
TO: fool0fatook54@bellinx.mail.com
Date: Sept 3 6:53 PM
SUBJECT: Sorry not Sorry

Jax,

You barged your way back into my life, fucking me up all over again, and I want to hate you. I should hate you. In fact, I shouldn't even be writing this email. Yet, here I sit, typing away, wondering what the hell I'm doing. I don't know if you can make things right. Too much time has passed. But that's the shit of it, isn't it? Nine years, Jax, and goddammit, I see you, too.

I can't deny I haven't thought about what it would be like to know you again, but my life is different now. Who I used to be back at Eastchester, that Wilder, doesn't exist anymore. But there are parts of me that haven't changed at all. I can hate you as much as I want, but those parts will always belong to you.

I don't think I'm ready to see you yet. But I'm not saying no.

Love always,
Wild~

P.S. I feel you, too.

Chapter 19

JAX

"I think it's working, Momma." Jason's face filled the screen of the laptop I'd purchased before I'd left for Georgia. It cost way more than I had any right to spend, but if it gave my little brother peace, knowing he could see my face as often as possible, and not just on the small screen of a phone, I'd buy a hundred laptops. "*Jax, I can see you.*"

I huffed out a laugh and leaned back against the headboard, propping the small computer on my thighs. "Hey, buddy. I can see you, too. Where's Mom?"

"She's in the kitchen, want me to get her?"

"That's okay. I want to talk to you first." I made a show of squinting into the camera. "Did you get a sunburn today?"

Jay touched his cheeks, grinning, he said, "I did. Went fishing with Ethan when he got off work."

"Yeah?" I asked.

"Nothing was biting, though."

I chuckled at the deep crease between his brow. "Maybe next time."

His eyes lit up. "We might go camping this weekend, though." Jason glanced over his shoulder, then leaned in and whispered, "I haven't asked Momma yet."

"Oh?" I asked, feeling uneasy. Ethan taking Jay fishing was one thing. But a whole night out in the woods? "You think you'd be able to sleep in the wilderness, buddy?"

He grit his teeth, and his face transformed into that man I'd see every now and then. "I'm not afraid, Jax."

"I know that." I sighed. "But what if it rains?"

"Ethan said his tent was waterproof."

"Tents don't have a lot of space. What about—"

"I'm not scared of small spaces anymore." He lowered his eyes. "Ethan said his tent fits like ten people or something,"

Resigned to the idea, I said, "Looks like Ethan has everything figured out."

He sat up and smiled. "I think it'll be fun."

"What will be fun?" my mom asked as she sat down next to Jason.

"Um..." Jason's blue eyes widened. "Ethan... well... Ethan asked if—"

"Ethan wants to take Jason camping this weekend," I interrupted.

"Is that so?" Momma raised her brows.

"I think it's a great idea, don't you?" I asked.

"Ethan talked to you about this?" she asked me.

"Yeah, and I told him just one night shouldn't hurt anything. As long as the weather looked alright," I lied.

Jason couldn't contain his laugh and slapped his hand over his mouth. Mom stared at him hiding his smile, and a small smile of her own lifted at the corner of her mouth.

"You're really excited about this?" she asked.

Jay nodded and dropped his hand. "Can I go, Momma? Please?"

"As long as Ethan doesn't go somewhere that doesn't get service on his phone, I suppose you can go camping for one night."

Jason almost knocked Mom over as he hugged her. Laughing, she patted his back, and I was homesick for the first time since I'd left.

Mom smoothed her fingers under her eyes and looked into the camera. "Is the apartment nice?"

"It is. Fully furnished and everything. I don't think I'd have picked these floral sheets. But they're fine for now."

"Floral?" she snorted. "Are you pulling my leg?"

I lifted the computer to show her the comforter covered in what looked like giant, pink and red roses. "Right out of the eighties."

She hadn't stopped laughing when I placed the laptop down again. "And what about Hudson's room?"

"Exactly the same as mine. I'll probably go to the store tonight or tomorrow and grab a new set."

"Good idea," she said. "Heaven knows who's been rolling round in those sheets anyhow."

"Gross, Momma. Now I'm definitely going tonight."

She shrugged. "Just being honest is all." The familiar sound of the oven timer chimed in the background. "Sounds like dinner's ready."

"I won't keep you then."

"Call tomorrow?" Jason asked and I nodded.

"As soon as I get home from work, promise."

"You better take care of yourself. Cook something once in a while, don't be eating from the microwave every night. You'll lose all that muscle and won't be able build a thing for Jim."

"Yes, ma'am."

"Miss you, Jax." Jason waved into the camera with big, sad blue eyes.

"Miss you, too."

I waited until Jason ended the call, laughing while he and Momma argued about which button to push. Eventually the screen went black. It was weird, not being there with them every day, but as the silence of my room surrounded me, I had to admit it was nice to be on my own. And Jason having Ethan around made it a lot easier to feel at ease here. I grabbed my phone off the nightstand to text Ethan and noticed I had an email notification. My heart rallied as I opened it and saw it was from Wild. I wanted to read it right then and there, but I worried my mom might call Ethan before I had a chance to warn him. I closed the email app and typed out a quick text.

Me: Heads up. I lied and told my mom you asked me first about taking Jason camping.

Three dots appeared immediately, and I tapped my fingers on the back of my phone, eager to read the email waiting in my inbox.

Ethan: Did your mom say it was okay?

Me: Yeah, but you should have asked me first. You can't get his hopes up like that.

My cell vibrated in my palm as Ethan's name and number lit up the screen.

"I'm sorry," he said. I was an asshole for making him feel bad. "I didn't think, it just slipped out. He looked sad today because he didn't catch anything, and I suggested camping to make him feel better. I should've asked you first."

"I'm a dick. I shouldn't have—"

"He's your brother. I should have asked."

"Yeah… alright." I chuckled. "My mom said just one night, though. And I think that's probably all he'd handle anyway."

"The weather looks good this Friday," he said.

"He told me you have a huge tent?"

He laughed. "It can fit ten grown ass men."

"Good, since the accident, he hates small spaces."

"He mentioned that."

"I'm glad he talks to you." I cleared my throat. "Thanks for being there for him when I can't."

"You know I don't mind it, Jax."

"I know," I said. "You're a good friend."

"You say that a lot." I could hear the smile in his voice. "Maybe on one of your weekend visits we could go camping?"

"Yeah… Jason would love that," I said, knowing damn well his invite had only been for me.

"Sure." If he was disappointed, I couldn't tell. "Just tell me when."

I could almost see it, though. Long weekends at the river, and nights with just him and me and the black night sky. It was easy enough to picture, but this pain in my chest, that email waiting for me, made it impossible for me to want it.

"I will."

"Listen, I gotta get going, but thanks for covering my ass with your mom."

"Of course."

"Have a good night, Jax."

"You too," I said, and ended the call.

Trying not to overthink that entire conversation, I set my phone down, opened my laptop, and read Wild's email as slow as I could.

I feel you, too.

Those four words took the breath right out of my lungs. I read his words again, tripping over *always belong to you* and *I'm not saying no*. Wild had opened a door for me. I hadn't completely fucked it up. He was right, so much time had passed, but my feelings for him had never changed. He could be a different man now, but I wanted to meet him.

My fingers numb, fumbled across the keyboard, leaving all caution behind. I had one chance and I was done holding myself back.

FROM: fool0fatook54@bellinx.mail.com

TO: wildwelleslit@bartpress.com

Date: Sept 3 8:05 PM

SUBJECT: RE: Sorry not Sorry

Wild,

You said you're not the same person I knew back at school, well, neither am I. But there are some things that never change. I know what it's like to kiss you, and how you wouldn't close your eyes until I did. I never wanted to stop looking at you. I shouldn't be writing any of this, but I want you to know it doesn't matter how much time has passed. I know you. I know how your skin feels, and how you sound when I'm inside you. I can hear your laugh, and your smart-ass mouth when you're pissed about something. It's on this constant loop in my head. And it's my fault that it's all just a memory now. Sometimes I feel like I made it all up in my head, what we were like when we were together. But I know I could never create something that good out of nothing. You're the storyteller, not me.

I wish I'd never walked away from you.

I hate myself for everything, so it makes sense that you'd hate me too. You're right, it's been too long and there's no way I can fix the shit I've done. But maybe we can start over? I want to meet the man you've become, whenever you're ready.

Jax~

P.S. Remember that night when Eastchester choked against Southern Cross?

My hands were clammy by the time I hit send. Before I had a chance to regret some of the things I'd said in the letter, Hudson knocked on my bedroom door.

"You decent?" he asked.

"Yeah, come on in."

Hudson opened the door. "I'm gonna order a pizza, you want anything?"

"Pizza sounds good."

He eyed my laptop with a smirk. "Watching porn?"

"If I was, do you think I would have invited you in?"

"I don't know, probably. You're always hanging out with that hardware store kid."

"Ethan," I reminded him, the muscles in my shoulders stiffened.

"You know he's into dudes, right?"

I debated how to answer, and decided indifference was my best option. I had to live with this dickhead for the next two months.

"And?"

"*And...*" Hudson's face contorted. Half disgust. Half shock. "The guy sucks dick, Jax. Probably takes it up the ass, too."

"Why are you so interested in his sex life?"

His face flushed, and he shoved his hands into his pockets. "I'm not. But you should be."

My stomach bottomed out. "Why should I care?"

"I heard he's hanging around your little brother. Doesn't that freak you out? What if he tries something? Jason won't know it's wrong."

"First of all, my brother isn't stupid." Anger flared as I pushed my laptop onto the mattress and stood. "He knows right from wrong."

Hudson backed up.

"It's not my business, or anyone else's who Ethan sleeps with. And if he's into men, it doesn't mean he wants every guy in a twenty-mile radius. He's not a fucking predator, Hudson. And I trust him with my brother more than I'd trust your sorry ass, alright?"

"Okay, man." He held up his hands. "Chill out. I was trying to help."

"Thanks, but I'm good. I don't need your help."

I sat on the edge of my bed, willing myself to calm the hell down. The last thing I needed was to punch this bigot and get fired.

"Does your mom know he's gay?" he asked.

"Hand to God, Hudson... I am asking you to shut your fucking mouth."

"Listen," he said. His voice was low and easy. "I didn't mean nothing by it. I didn't know if you knew, or if you'd care. Obviously, you don't, so forget I said anything."

I looked him square in the eyes. "Done."

"You still want pizza?" he asked.

"Get whatever you want."

He shut the door on his way out and I fell backward onto the bed, bumping my head on the corner of my laptop. I stared at the ceiling, wondering if I'd ever get to be an out gay man in Bell River. That nagging, persistent voice inside my head, the same one I'd tried to ignore more and more every day, broke through. How could I do that to my mom, to Jason? How could I rip apart our family? My thoughts didn't get a chance to spiral too far down the rabbit hole when an email alert sounded on my phone. I sat up and grabbed my computer.

FROM: wildwelleslit@bartpress.com
TO: fool0fatook54@bellinx.mail.com
Date: Sept 3 8:28 PM
SUBJECT: RE: Sorry not Sorry

Jax,

For the record, you're so lucky I've had a few drinks already, because wow… you don't play fair.

And without a bit of liquid courage I might've told you not to say those kinds of things to me. That you don't have the right to open up all my old wounds. But I'm at a club, sitting in a dark corner, instead of celebrating my best friend's success, thinking about all the things I've never been able to forget. Things I didn't put in the book.

Do you still like Hershey Kisses?

I remember, Jax, and all the things you know about me are yours to keep. But I know you, too. I know that you used to taste like chocolate, and when you were frustrated, you'd chew on your bottom lip. I liked watching you sleep and watching you come. Maybe it was the vulnerability of them both. Or perhaps, it seemed like the only time you were ever at peace with yourself.

I don't even know what I'm saying. I blame the gin.

Love always,
Wild~

P.S. Speaking of not playing fair, or dirty, in this regard. Gin-addled brain or not, how could I forget that night? I don't remember anything about the stupid game, except that you got ejected. I don't think I'd ever seen you so... angry... unhinged I think is a better word.

FROM: fool0fatook54@bellinx.mail.com
TO: wildwelleslit@bartpress.com
Date: Sept 3 8:40 PM
SUBJECT: RE: Sorry not Sorry

Wild,

I know I'm not playing fair, but I figured I'd throw myself into the fire and see what happens. And to be honest, I can't remember the last time I ate a Hershey's Kiss. But I should let you get back to your friends. I hope you don't wake up tomorrow regretting anything you've told me tonight. I think if we ever want to move forward, we have to open up some of our old wounds.

Being with you was the only thing that ever brought me peace.

Jax~

P.S. I was a mess that night, but you knew what I needed before I ever did.

FROM: wildwelleslit@bartpress.com
TO: fool0fatook54@bellinx.mail.com
Date: Sept 3 8:57 PM
SUBJECT: How very Aragorn of you

Jax,

No need to sacrifice yourself. I'm still open to negotiations. And how tragic that you've forsaken your love for tiny, bite-sized pieces of chocolate. I demand you buy a bag and eat until you puke. That way I won't be the only one hugging the toilet tonight. I'm really not that drunk. Not yet, at least.

But all humor aside. I can't be the one to bring you peace. You have to find that for yourself.

P.S. The way I remember it, I was the one who needed something that night. I've never felt so fragile.

The memory of that night flooded through me, and heat pricked at the back of my neck as I palmed the bulge in my shorts. That night I'd been furious at myself, at my coach, the entire fucking world. After that game, I couldn't stop the anger from building. Looking back, I realized it was a culmination of everything. Getting ejected for swearing at the ref, then Carson had made some homophobic joke in the locker room, and I couldn't say shit about it without revealing my sexuality to the whole team. By the time I'd made my way to Wild's dorm room, I'd been itching for him. Needing his hands, his mouth. Anything to sate the anger. But like always, he'd given me more than I'd ever been worthy of. That night, Wild had given me his trust and his body for the first time. I wanted to earn back that trust, not because I wanted to fuck him again, but because I wanted to be worthy of it, of him. I wanted to be his.

I started to type out another email when a text came through on my phone. Thinking it was probably Jim wanting to go over the plan for tomorrow, I closed out of my email.

> Wild: This is June, Wilder's friend.
> Me: Hey?
> Wild: Listen, I have to be quick. He'll be back from the bar any second.
> Wild: I need you to do me a favor.
> Me: Okay?

Feeling confused as hell, I waited.

> Wild: I need you to either shit or get off the pot because I CANNOT deal with his mopey ass one more minute.
> Wild: You fucked up, but I'm going to tell you how to fix it.
> Me: How?
> Wild: We're at this club, just outside of Atlanta, called The Underground. You have GPS?

Me: Yeah

Wild: Then use it.

Me: You think I should just show up? That didn't work last time.

Wild: Believe me, I know.

Wild: Shit, he's coming over here.

Wild: He needs this. You both do. Don't be a fucking coward.

Me: Hello?

How did I know this was actually June? And not another one of his friends fucking with me? Or worse, if it was Wild fucking with me.

Me: Wild?

I waited for Wild to email me, to text me and tell me if I stepped foot in that club tonight, he'd never speak to me again. I waited for a full twenty minutes, debating if I should text him back, call him, or like June had said, if it was really June at all, just show up. My stomach was sick and empty when Hudson called out to tell me the pizza had arrived. Dropping my phone on my bed, I stood and rummaged through the closet. I didn't bring much, and I had no idea what to wear to a club. The nicest thing I had with me was a pale gray t-shirt that was too tight to wear to work, and a pair of jeans. I settled on those, snagged my towel from the back of the desk chair, and I almost ran into Hudson when I opened the bedroom door.

"Pizza is on the stove."

"Thanks," I said. "But I'm going out."

Chapter 20

WILDER

Tonight, I was supposed to be the best friend for once. Shelve all my dramatic bullshit, but that hadn't lasted more than a few hours thanks to Jax and his goddamn perfect emails. I was irritable and moody and not drunk enough to deal with some of the grenades he'd thrown at me tonight. I could see June eyeing me from the dance floor, but I refused to let her worry. I tried on my best smile and waved. She frowned and headed toward our table.

"Nope," I said under my breath and hopped down from the stool I'd permanently attached to my ass since we'd been here.

I weaved through a sea of sweat and skin, realizing too late that the line at the bar was inconveniently long. Telling myself I needed a distraction, and by no means was worried whether Jax had emailed me back yet, I reached into my back pocket for my phone. When I found it empty, I had a moment of panic. The gin I'd already consumed made everything more heightened than it needed to be. I'd most likely left my cell on the table, which could be problematic if someone stole it but, at this point, I'd consider that an intervention planned by the universe. It was stupid and definitely damaging to want Jax's attention. What good could come from any of this, from that fleeting feeling building in my stomach. It was like the day before I released my book, or that second before a kiss, that hesitation, it's the highest peak before a huge drop. That heart in the throat, everything clicking into place kind of feeling where everything was scary but right and good. Jax was the only man capable of making me feel this way. And his emails tonight, it was like he reached into my brain and said everything I'd ever wanted to hear from him.

"'About time," I mumbled.

The guy in front of me turned and gave me a dirty look. Luckily, the line moved, sparing me an awkward conversation.

I stepped up to the bar and smiled at the cute bartender. He had a lip ring and lots of tattoos. Not usually my type, but maybe that was my problem. I had to get over this whole clean-cut, All-American-boy bullshit.

He smiled as he wiped down the counter. "What can I get for you?"

I thought about flirting, but everything I wanted to say sounded ridiculous in my head. I wasn't in tip-top form tonight and should probably focus on getting as drunk as humanly possible.

"Hendrick's with tonic, please. Actually, can you make that a double?"

"Having a bad night?" he asked, grabbing a glass and scooping ice into it.

"Possibly. I haven't decided yet."

He laughed and set the glass on the counter. I smiled as he filled it mostly with gin.

"Hopefully, this will help," he said.

"I have no doubt it will."

His tongue toyed with the silver loop pinned through his bottom lip as he poured the rest of the drink, plopping a lime on the rim of the glass. I was curious what it would be like to kiss a guy with a piercing, would it be fun or more of a hindrance.

He noticed me staring as he set the drink in front of me, and I swear he licked the ring on purpose.

"You have a tab?" he asked, and I nodded.

"Wilder Welles."

He smirked. "That's a great name."

His cheesy line fell flat, but I smiled for his effort. "Thanks..." I leaned forward and read his name tag. "Mike."

"Not so great name," he said and gave me another smile as I took a sip from the drink.

"Whoa, did you put any tonic in this?"

He winked, and any attraction I had for him dissipated. "Hope your night gets better."

I walked back through the crowd, a little let down by bad boy Mike, and was almost to the table when I saw June texting someone. As I got closer, I realized it was my phone in her hand.

What the hell?

"What are you doing?" I asked as she set it on the table.

"Might I remind you tonight is my night," she said, blocking me as I attempted to reach behind her. "I'm gonna need you to take a few sips of that drink and have a listen, alright?"

"June..." I tried to get to my phone again and she slapped my hand. "Are you serious right now?"

"Drink up," she said with a grim smile that told me she wasn't messing around.

Rolling my eyes, I drank half of the glass. "Why won't you let me have my phone?"

"My night... I'll ask the questions."

"Fine," I said, sounding more like a teenager than a grown man.

The gin had started to work its way through my system, warming my limbs and stomach. The music was loud, and the bass had my heart thumping in an uneven rhythm.

"Why were you over here looking like you were about to cry earlier?" she asked.

"I wasn't about to cry."

"Wilder... I'm not doing this with you tonight. Do you think I'm stupid?" she asked, raising her voice.

"Jesus, June."

"Answer the question."

Exhaling, I said, "No, you're not stupid."

"Everything okay?" Gwen asked, handing June her drink. "Things looked a little tense from the dance floor, I figured I better make sure you two don't kill each other."

"June has my phone and is holding it hostage."

Gwen raised her eyebrows. "Interesting."

"Do you know how hard I worked for this educator position?" June asked.

Guilt sobered me up. "I do. And you deserve it."

"I know you're not trying to be selfish. And I know you can't just drop everything that's going on in your life, but I asked for one night. And you're sitting over here, staring at that damn phone, looking like the saddest asshole in the room."

"I'm sorry, I shouldn't have even opened my emails."

"Did Jax finally respond?" Gwen asked, her excitement making me even more uncomfortable.

"He did, but who cares." Careful not to spill my drink down the back of her silk blouse, I pulled June into a hug, "I'm sorry I stole your thunder. I definitely should be awarded the most selfish asshole award."

She squeezed me and I laughed through a cough as she let me go. "I forgive you."

Skeptical, I said, "You never let me off the hook this easy."

She shrugged with a secret smile playing at the corner of her lips.

"Uh-oh..." Gwen giggled. "What did you do, June Gailey?"

"I need you to remember I did this for your own good, Wilder." June reached for my phone and handed it to me.

"Did what?" I asked, my heart more unsteady than before.

"You and Jax are never gonna make things right, pussyfooting around each other like scared little kids. It's time for one of you to take a leap. You've been in your head for a month... longer than that, if you want me to be honest. Jax did what he did, now let's move on already. Haven't you given him enough of your life?"

The music in the club, June's voice, it all went quiet in my head as I read the texts she'd sent him.

"Why would you do this?" I gripped my phone to stop my hand from shaking.

June took my drink from me and set it on the table. "Because I love you, and I want you to be happy."

The anger drained from my limbs, replacing itself with anxiety. "I'm not ready."

"You're never ready, Wilder. And you sure as hell are never gonna be happy. Not with Anders, not with anyone. You have to do this. You both need it. Take the leap."

"What if he doesn't show up?" I asked, hating how much I wanted him to show up and how much I feared it.

"Then you know... that he'll never show up for you. And maybe then you can find someone who will."

"Wait..." Gwen's eyes were wide. "Jax is coming here?"

"I sure as hell hope so," June said, pulling me in for another hug.

"This is exciting." Gwen clapped, her red curls bouncing against her bare shoulders.

"Holy shit," I said, numb all the way down to my toes.

June grinned. "You're welcome."

"I still don't know if I hate you or love you right now."

"You managed to turn my night into your one-man drama show and I forgave you..."

"I need another drink," I said and sat down on the stool.

"On it." Gwen leaned into June and kissed her. "Want one too?" she asked, and I turned my eyes to the dance floor as June cupped her ass.

"No, I'm good, baby."

"I told her you'd love that dress," I said as Gwen headed to the bar.

"I give you my permission to take her shopping anytime you like." June sat next to me. "Honestly, how much do you hate me right now?"

I finished off my gin and tonic, hoping it would revive the buzz I had earlier. "I couldn't hate you if I tried. I know why you did it. I just wish you hadn't."

"Do you think he'll come?" she asked.

"To a gay club, on a Monday night, his first week in Georgia? Let me grab my Magic 8-Ball..."

"It is certain?"

"More like, don't count on it," I said.

"I bet he shows up and sweeps you and your skinny ass off your feet."

"I'm anxious as fuck right now, June. Don't make fun of me." I picked up my phone. "I'm going to email him and tell him my friend was drunk and lost her mind, and that he should no way in hell drive all this way."

She snatched the phone out of my hand. "You will do no such thing."

"Oh God... I can't do this." Panic surfaced. I held on to the table and took a deep breath. "I think I hate you now. How far away is Marietta?"

"Maybe thirty minutes. If the traffic is good, less than that."

"And how long ago did you text him?" I asked, nausea working its way to the top of the shitty-things-about-this-night list.

She swiped her thumb over the screen of my phone. "Twenty minutes ago."

"Christ, that means he'll be here soon."

Her shoulders shook as she laughed. "You're a mess."

"Your fault."

She hummed. "He probably had to get ready, right? I bet you still have plenty of time to Calm. The. Hell. Down."

"There is no way I'm going to be calm about this, June. The last time I saw him I broke down into tears and destroyed a fucking coffee mug."

"You were caught off guard. Now you're prepared." I glared at her. "What? You know he's coming, right?"

"I have like forty minutes until he gets here. That isn't even an adequate amount of time to prepare for a blind date, let alone the guy who ruined you for all other men, and who I am hopelessly and pathetically still in love with."

"At least you look hot."

"Yeah?" I asked, tugging at the hem of my red mesh top.

She smiled and shook her head. "Yeah... I think he'll have a hard time keeping his hands off of you."

"Stop. Not happening."

She narrowed her eyes. "We'll see."

"We haven't seen each other in over nine years, except for that whole coffee shop debacle. I think talking is more appropriate."

"Since when have you ever been appropriate?"

"I'm so nervous right now that I might actually throw up. Sex is the last fucking thing on my mind, okay."

"Okay." Her smile was soft. "I'm sorry... I was trying to distract you from losing your shit, I guess."

Gwen showed up with a drink like the goddess she was, and I might've finished mine in one gulp. She laughed and handed me hers. "Figured you'd do that, so I ordered one for myself just in case."

"Are you sure?" I asked.

"You're gonna need that more than I will."

"Don't get too wasted," June cautioned. "You want to be able to have a coherent conversation, right?"

"Coherency is overrated." I took a small sip from my glass to make her happy. "But... I think if I'm going to make it until he gets here, we should probably go join your co-workers on the dance floor."

I tucked my phone into my back pocket and followed my friends, letting the sea of people envelop me, letting the music move me. As much as I wanted to be pissed at June for inviting Jax, she was right. I wasn't ever going to let him go. We were inevitable, like a storm surge during a hurricane, there was nothing to stop the flood from devouring everything in its path. I had nothing left to give anyone because I'd already given all of myself to Jax.

"You okay?" June asked.

I finished my drink, letting it burn its way down to my stomach. "I will be."

We danced and I promised myself I wouldn't worry about the time or look over my shoulder at the door every five minutes. And for the most part, I held up my end of the bargain. But as more songs played, and more time passed, I found myself checking the door and scanning the crowd. What if he came and didn't see me? What if he showed up and realized it was a gay bar and ran home with his tail between his legs?

"Stop looking at the door," June said, offering me a pink and green shot.

I ran my fingers through my hair, letting the unruly waves fall across my forehead. "I'm not."

"You're a terrible liar."

"What is this?" I asked.

She shrugged. "I don't know. I just told the bartender to make me some shots."

I sniffed it and it smelled like cotton candy. "Are you *trying* to make me sick?"

She tapped her glass against mine. "To best friends."

We both swallowed the overly sweet drink at the same time.

"That wasn't too bad," she said.

"It was terrible." Laughing, I turned to set my shot glass on one of the tables near the edge of the dance floor and froze. "Oh, shit."

"What?" June turned toward the door. "Is that him?"

Jax moved through the crowd, his six-foot-four frame towering over everyone. The gray shirt he had on hugged his shoulders and biceps, and Jesus Christ, I didn't know if I wanted to run away or hop right into those big arms. Arms that, I was sure, felt as safe as they had nine years ago.

"I'm so screwed."

"Wow." June took my hand and I held on for dear life as his eyes landed on mine. "Yeah, you are."

He stopped, and even from across the dance floor, I could feel him.

"You sick yet?" June asked and I shook my head. "Good, because he's headed this way."

"Remind me again why I shouldn't hate you for this?"

She didn't get to answer.

"Hey." His deep voice resonated through me.

June tugged at my hand when I didn't respond.

"I... I didn't think you'd actually come," I managed to say.

His face flushed. "I wasn't sure you'd want me to. But I figured I don't have much to lose."

June's lips spread into a smile and she let go of my hand. "I'm June, by the way."

He shook her hand, and for a moment I was jealous that she got to touch him. "Jax, thanks for inviting me."

"Want a drink?" she asked, but his green eyes stayed fixed on me.

"Probably shouldn't... I've gotta drive myself home."

"I think you'd be alright if you had one. Might help you relax a little," she said and when he laughed, I wanted to melt into the floor.

What the hell was wrong with me? I should hate him. But I saw the way his hands were clenched tight at his

247

sides, and how the muscle in his jaw pulsed, the worry in his eyes. He was just as nervous as I was.

"Wilder? Do you want another drink?" June asked.

"Maybe some water."

"I'll tell Gwen." She smiled up at Jax. "It's nice to finally have a face to put with the name. Don't run away before I get back."

If I could, I'd stab her.

"We'll meet you over at the table," I said and nodded toward the back of the room where we'd sat earlier.

"Alright," she said, and left to find Gwen.

He followed me to the back of the club, and without Jax's eyes on my face, I was able to breathe and remember I wasn't some love-struck kid in college. We had a lot of history between us. He showed up here looking like he ate men's hearts for the thrill of it, but that didn't mean I was ready to hand him mine on a platter. Heat radiated off his body behind me as we navigated the room, and despite everything, it steadied me. I kept my eyes on the tabletop as we sat down and was grateful he took the seat across from me.

"Are you sure this is okay? If you don't want me here—"

"If you would've asked me that an hour ago, I would have said no." I exhaled and willed myself to look him in the eyes. "The truth is, I was pissed at June for inviting you. But I think her motivations were right."

"Her motivations?" he asked, leaning in over the table.

"She wants us to rip off the Band-Aid. It's like you said in your email..." My face heated and I stared at my hand on the table. "I think we both need it, a chance to start over."

Jax reached across the table, and on instinct I wanted to pull away. He hesitated, and I wondered if he'd sensed the overwhelming fear swallowing me whole. Maybe he was sinking, too. When I didn't move my hand to my lap, he brushed the back of his finger against my skin. An electric pulse ran up my arm as he exhaled a shaky breath.

"Does that mean... you're gonna give me a second chance?"

There was a lot of shit we had to get over, a mountain of time we had to sift through. But he had changed. His eyes were softer than I remembered, his skin worn by the sun. It suited him. His demeanor was quiet, the confident kid I knew at Eastchester was gone. I didn't know this man sitting in front of me, with his heart on his sleeve, but he was just as beautiful, if not more than the boy I'd once known. As much as it scared me, I wanted to know this man. The man who couldn't bear to leave his mother and disabled brother behind. The man who sacrificed himself day in and day out. The man I'd thought I couldn't forgive. I hadn't understood. Not until he was here, in front of me, on the verge of breaking down right alongside me.

I linked my finger around his thumb, memorizing the new and unfamiliar roughness of his skin. "I think it does."

Chapter 21

JAX

Wild's skin was as soft as I remembered. The heat from his touch spread up my arm, and I liked the way his finger curled around my thumb. I hoped he meant it when he'd said he'd give me a second chance. I lifted my gaze and found him watching me. Wild's brown eyes were dark in the low light, ringed with black eyeliner. The red shirt he had on was see-through, and I couldn't stop myself from staring. He had more muscle now but was still lean with long arms and a delicate neck I used to love to kiss. The smooth skin of his chest was visible, pale with perfect nipples. My throat went dry as all the memories of us surfaced. Wild sweaty beneath me, those nipples under my tongue.

Shit.

I forced myself to turn away, my cheeks hot as my gaze landed on two guys dry humping in the corner. *What the hell?* I scanned the room, taking it in for the first time. The dance floor was filled with couples, mostly men, grinding on each other and kissing. The few women I saw were dancing close too, hands on hips, eyes locked. I noticed a small rainbow-colored flag hanging above the exit door and I started to sweat.

"You look nervous," Wild said, pulling me back from my impending anxiety attack.

"This is a gay club?"

He slid into the chair next to me, lacing our hands together. Leaning in, he said, "Aww, is this your first time, Precious?"

I laughed, trying not to let the fear win. Hearing him call me Precious in his over-the-top southern accent made me smile. "Not too many gay bars in Bell River."

I had no reason to freak out being this far from home. Hudson and Jim were in Marietta, and even if they did come to Atlanta, I seriously doubted they'd be in this particular club.

"By not too many, I'm assuming you mean none?" he asked.

"I don't think there's a gay bar within fifty miles of Bell River, if you want the truth."

"That's a shame."

Looking out into the club, I was envious. What would my life be like if I lived in a place that was more open-minded? Filled with acceptance instead of hate.

"Don't let it spook you," he said, and I met his eyes.

"I'm here, Wild, I'm not going nowhere."

He let go of my hand and swallowed. "Last time you said that, you disappeared for nine years."

"I can't go back, but if I could I'd change what I did. I want to try again, Wild. I want that second chance." He averted his gaze to the bar. "Hey..." He wouldn't look at me, and my heart sank heavy in my chest. I had no right to, but I placed my thumb and finger under his chin, turning him toward me. He kept his head down, his long, black lashes hiding his eyes. "Wild, I've never stopped loving you."

He lifted his head, his eyes threatening to spill over with tears.

"I want you to trust me again," I said and took his hand in mine.

"I have a hard time trusting you... but I want to," he said. "I want to, Jax, but I might trip up sometimes. When you left... I didn't know what to do with myself. I was in a bad place. It's not easy to file all of that away."

"I know, but—"

He chuckled. "Let me finish what I want to say."

I pressed my lips together and nodded. "Go ahead."

He bit his bottom lip, taking a few seconds to regather his thoughts.

"You've changed. And I can see that your life has reshaped you, and I want to know how. I want to know you now, Jax. I can't expect you to feel sorry for everything all the time. We'll never move forward if you're always feeling bad for what happened. But I can't promise I won't take a few steps backward every now and then."

The tension in my shoulders relaxed. He wanted this. He wanted me.

"I can handle a few steps," I said.

Wild trailed his thumb along my finger and I shivered. With the heat of his hand in mine, I was home.

"You two look cozy," June said with a smirk.

I expected Wild to pull away, but he leaned in, resting his shoulder against me. "Are you jealous?" he asked, and June laughed.

"Not even a little a bit."

A pretty girl with the curliest red hair I'd ever seen placed a bottle of beer in front of me. "I'm Gwen, June's girlfriend. Nice to meet you."

I shouldn't drink with work tomorrow, and the thirty-minute drive home, but I didn't want to piss off Wilder's friends. I'd make a bet they held some type of veto card where I was concerned, and they were still collecting evidence. One beer wouldn't put me over the limit, or give me a buzz, for that matter.

I held up the bottle. "Jax... nice to meet you, too. And thanks for the beer."

She watched me as I took a swig. "So, you're the guy who broke our baby's heart?"

Caught off guard by her remark, I inhaled the beer and started coughing.

"I told her to be nice." June laughed.

Wilder narrowed his eyes at his best friend as he sipped from the glass of water Gwen had brought him. "I doubt that," he said.

"I'm not being mean. I'm simply stating a fact. And I hope he's here to set it right," she said. "You are... gonna set it right, aren't you?"

"I sure hope so."

"Good."

Wilder's laugh almost sounded like a nervous giggle and it made me smile.

"You're kind of scary when you want to be, Gwen," he said.

"I taught her everything she knows." June kissed her girlfriend on the cheek, and she blushed.

"Well, have a seat, but don't grill him too hard." Wilder waved his free hand at the two open seats.

My stomach flipped when they sat down, and I mentally prepared myself for an interrogation. My pulse slowed though as he whispered, "Meet my family... I swear they're harmless."

His family.

The ache in my throat grew as I thought about how Wild's parents had abandoned him. How sometimes you had to make your own family. Anything these ladies had to say to me, I most likely deserved, and they were here for him. For Wild. His protection. The love they had for him was unconditional. After everything he'd gone through, I was thankful he had that.

"What part of Florida are you from?" June asked.

"Bell River, near Destin."

"Destin is nice." Gwen brought a pink drink to her lips.

I exhaled, trying not to feel awkward and exposed.

"How did you two meet?" I asked.

"We work at the same hospital. Gwen works in maternity, and I work in labor and delivery." June, all smiles, looked at Gwen.

"Nurses," Wild said. "We're actually here tonight celebrating June's promotion. She's the new educator for her unit."

"It's not a big deal." June gave Wilder a dismissive wave.

He let go of my hand and smacked the table. "It's a huge deal, June."

"I wouldn't have graduated nursing school if Wilder hadn't tutored me." June raised her brow. "He's one hell of a tutor... wouldn't you agree, Jax?"

"June," Gwen's face was pale. "Don't."

"It's okay," I stammered. Without Wild's hand in mine, I drifted. "I had that coming."

Wild was silent by my side, and I wanted to take his hand, pull him back to the here and now, away from his memories at Eastchester. I couldn't read his eyes as he stared down at the table.

"Damn straight." June looked over at Wild. "I love this guy like he was my own brother." Wild lifted his eyes to hers, his lips slowly spreading into a grin. "This world has dealt us both a shitty hand, and we sure as shit don't need any more of it. Let yourself be loved, Wilder, and you..." She pointed her finger at me, and I stopped breathing. "You let yourself be happy."

Wilder practically fell out of his chair hugging June to his chest. Her dark hair spilled over his shoulder as she winked at me, and I exhaled a sigh of relief.

"Love you, asshole," he said to her as he sat back into his chair.

Gwen laughed. "Can we dance now? I don't want to lose my buzz."

June stood, taking Gwen in hand. "I think it's safe to leave these two alone for a little while. Unless you guys wanna dance?"

"I'm not much of a dancer," I said.

Wild stood and tugged at my arm. "Come on, it'll be fun."

The dance floor was packed, the bright lights flashing, illuminating all the bodies pressed together in a wave of color. Their skin glittered with sweat as they moved, and as much as I wanted to be out there with Wild, to be that open, the thought made me sick to my stomach.

"I'm okay. I gotta finish my beer anyway."

His smile dimmed enough, I noticed, as he took a seat.

"Well, if y'all change your mind, we'll be right over there having *fun*." Gwen grinned at me as June pulled her away from the table.

"Go dance," I said, and Wild shook his head.

"It's your first time in a gay bar. If I leave you alone, the vultures will swoop in and try to get you to blow them in the bathroom."

"*What?*"

He laughed, and the sound of it warmed me from the inside out. "I'm joking... kind of."

"Kind of?"

The song changed, and Wild's eyes went wide. "Holy shit, I love this song. Come on, stop being lame and dance with me," he whined.

I'd always loved the way his bottom lip stuck out when he pouted.

"I'm good. Go hang out with your friends. I'll be fine."

He pulled that tempting bottom lip through his teeth. My dick twitched and my eyes fell to his mouth again.

"Just this song and I'll be right back."

I drank my beer, finishing faster than I should have, and watched him move to the music. At school I'd never had the chance to see this side of him. The Wild I'd known was reduced to the confines of a dorm room and the library. I'd missed out. His body was fluid, and sexy as hell, as he found his rhythm. His black jeans were tight, and hung low on his narrow hips, hugging his ass. Every time Wild raised his arms, his shirt lifted, exposing the well-defined muscles of his stomach, and the sharp curve of his hip bone. Jesus Christ, I needed another beer. Pulling my phone out to check if I had enough time for another drink, I swiped my thumb across the screen and found a few missed texts from Jim.

> **Jim: Contractor couldn't get the lumber. We might have to drive to the lumber yard bright and early.**
> **Jim: Never mind. Looks like we'll have to wait till Wednesday. The shipment was delayed.**

Did that mean we weren't working on the house tomorrow? Confused, I typed out a message hoping he was still awake.

> **Me: Are we working on something else then?**

I glanced up and my jaw tightened. Some guy, who looked like he lived in the gym, inched in next to Wild and started to dance with him. It reminded me of the thing Wilder had said about bathroom blow jobs and I stood, fighting myself. This dormant, yet loud, part of me wanted to haul my ass out there and tell that guy to back off. But I didn't own Wild, and I didn't want to mess up and ruin any of the progress we'd made tonight.

My phone vibrated in my fist.

Jim: Nah. Take the day to get settled in. See you on site at seven on Wednesday.

I had tomorrow off.

I looked up just as the guy ran his hand up Wild's arm. I slipped my phone in my pocket and before I could stop myself, I found my way to the dance floor.

"Changed your mind?" he asked.

I took his hand in mine, casually dismissing the asshole staring at me like I stole something from him. "Like you said earlier, we wouldn't want one of the vultures to swoop in."

He grinned as he rested his hand on my hip. "Jealousy looks good on you."

I chuckled. "You like that?"

He let go of my hand and closed his arms around my neck. Even though Wild had gotten taller since college, I still had a few inches on him. I leaned down as he lifted his lips to my ear. "I like it when you take what you want, Jax. I always have."

Blood pumped through my veins, lighting me on fire as Wild started to move against me to the beat of the music. Not knowing what the fuck to do or how to dance, shocked by his words, being this close to another man in public, I didn't move.

"In order to dance, you have to actually move your legs, Jax."

Wild stepped back and took the heat of his body with him.

"I told you I don't know how to dance."

"I can help with that," he said. "Just listen to the song, don't think so much."

He started to jump in place, waving his arms like a maniac and I laughed. "What the hell are you doing."

He held his hand to his chest, his offense all for display. "Having fun. You should try it."

"I might need more alcohol."

Wilder's smile turned smug as he stared over my shoulder. "Well, lucky for you Gwen and June are here to save the day."

"I got you another beer, I hope that's okay?" Gwen asked.

I took the bottle from her hand. "Thank you."

June handed Wild a shot and he shook his head. "I think I've had enough."

She looked at me and handed me the small tumbler filled with clear liquid. "You have some catching up to do."

"He has to work tomorrow," Wild shouted.

The room got louder as the song changed, and the crowd reacted with whoops of appreciation. Someone bumped into me and I almost dropped the glass.

"I'm off tomorrow," I said. "There was a delay."

"You're off tomorrow?" Wild shouted over the noise and stepped into my space.

"Yeah... I can stay longer. If that's okay?"

"Stay as long as you like, especially if you plan on drinking that shot."

"I'll pay for his Uber," June said.

I swallowed the fiery liquid and whistled. "Shit, what the hell was that?"

"I never ask," she said. "I just get what I get and I'm good."

The alcohol had singed my tongue, and I chugged my entire beer to get rid of the medicinal taste.

Gwen clapped. "Now that's how it's done," she said, taking the empty bottle from my hand. "Should I get you another one?"

My shirt was tight against my skin, my head foggy as the shot made its way through my system. Lightheaded and relaxed, I said, "I don't drink that often, I think I should probably stop while I'm ahead."

"That's a good idea." Wild took my hand and pulled me deeper into the crowd. "How do you feel?" he asked, bouncing to the music.

"Buzzed."

His smile stretched wide across his face. "Think you can let go a little now? Look around, Jax, no one gives a shit here."

Maybe it was the alcohol, or maybe it was the giant smile on Wild's face that had me bouncing with him. The room lived and breathed as bodies swayed, and I wanted to breathe with it. I danced, feeling ridiculous and uncoordinated as each song changed to the next. As time went on, the alcohol wore off, but I didn't need it anymore. I was free for the first time ever in my fucking life, I wanted to be here with Wild, smiling and laughing. Stay in this bubble where I could be myself. Where I was confident again. Where I knew who I was, and I didn't care what anyone thought about it. But the crowd started to thin, and I couldn't stay here forever.

The upbeat electronic music turned over to a lower rhythm that made me think of sex as smokey vocals filled the room. The couple next to us started to kiss and Wild laced our fingers together. The quick ebb and flow of his breath made me wonder if he was just as keyed up as I was. He looped his finger under my belt, pulling me close, his hands found my hips. Soft black curls fell across his forehead, and I brushed them back, removing the shadow from his eyes.

"This okay?" he asked, and I nodded.

The tip of his thumb grazed against the skin of my hip and my heart hammered as I slid my hands under his shirt, placing them on the hot skin above the curve of his ass. His eyes were hazy with lust as I pulled him against me, both of us hard and needing friction. Wild moved with me to the beat and I followed his lead. He turned, brushing against the bulge in my jeans and I grasped his hips. For a few seconds there was no music, no loud chatter, no lights, just us. His back to my chest, his ass grinding into me, I was drifting as he rested his hands over mine. I didn't think about the consequences as I brought my lips to the curve of his neck and tasted the salt of his skin.

He stopped breathing, and I let go of his hips as he turned to face me. "I'm sorry," I said. "I shouldn't have—"

Wild pushed his hands into my hair as his mouth captured mine in a rough collision. My hand covered the back of his head and I dragged him closer. He dropped a hand, his fingers curled into the cotton fabric of my shirt, as the other held the nape of my neck. His thumb pressed into my jaw, and I opened for him, tasting his tongue as it dipped into my mouth. He groaned and our hips, seeking release, impulsively pressed together. I bit his bottom lip as his hands found their way under my shirt, his nails digging into my back. I held his face in my hands, tipping my head to the side, deepening the kiss. He tasted like lime and alcohol, and as he licked my upper lip, I cupped his ass with my other hand. He whimpered and I grinned against his mouth. Nine years, and our bodies hadn't forgotten a thing.

"Last call," June said, her voice filled with humor.

"Fuck," Wild was out of breath, and I rested my forehead against his.

"You boys want a drink to cool down before they close up shop?" she asked.

Wild pulled away first but kept the bottom hem of my shirt in his fist. His cheeks were bright red, his chin pink from the day's growth of scruff on my chin. I looked around the room, filled with people, and waited for the panic to set in.

"Give us a minute?" he asked June.

"I'll be at the table with Gwen when you're ready to head out."

"You're shaking," he said once she was out of ear shot.

"So are you."

He reached up, pushing a wayward strand of hair off my forehead. "Are you upset?"

"Why would I be upset?"

"Because I kissed you, in the middle of a room with a shit ton of people."

I leaned down and pressed my lips to his, and the panic I'd been waiting for never surfaced.

I was safe here.

I was safe with him.

Chapter 22

WILDER

Jax was kissing me. In public. Caught up in the way he tasted, different but the same, I let his hands lift my shirt, letting the coarse pads of his fingers scrape along the lines of my ribs.

Breathless, he rested his lips against my cheek. "I don't want this night to be over."

"Who said it has to be?" I asked.

He leaned back, looking around the room. Most of the people on the dance floor had wandered toward the door, others lingered, chatting now that the music was low, and the lights had turned on. "They're closing."

"Doesn't mean the night is over," I said, afraid to ask him outright to come home with me, worried I was thinking more with my dick than my brain.

His green eyes searched my face as he swallowed, and I wanted to kiss his throat.

"Are you—"

"Our ride is about a mile away. We better head out," June said, interrupting whatever Jax was about to ask me.

Irritated that the night had come to an end faster than I had prepared for, I snapped at her. "Can you give me a second?"

She raised a brow. "Who pissed in your Cheerios? Next time you can call for your own ride if you're gonna be like that."

"I'm sorry," I said. "I didn't mean for that to sound as rude as it did."

June hummed under her breath. This was her night, and I was a selfish prick. Even Gwen glared at me.

I leaned in and kissed June on the cheek. "I'm an asshole."

"Tell me something I don't know," she said with a smile that hopefully meant I was forgiven.

Jax took my hand in his. "I can give y'all a ride."

"The driver is out front," Gwen said, looking at her phone.

Shit.

Adrenaline coursed through me, my heart running a marathon in my chest. I wasn't ready to let him go. I'd just gotten him back. What if this was it? What if he went to Marietta and I never saw him again? I despised the overdramatic bullshit spinning in my head, fueled by gin and kisses.

"I'm going to have Jax give me a ride," I blurted, my last-second decision earning me an amused look from my best friend.

"You okay to drive then?" June asked.

"I wouldn't drive if I wasn't," Jax said.

June hesitated, staring at me, probably wondering what the hell I was doing. I wondered the same thing. This would either be the best or worst decision I'd ever made. I needed to trust my gut. I couldn't let him walk out that door alone.

"We gotta go, babe," Gwen said, giving me and Jax a small smile.

"You be careful." June pointed at Jax.

"Yes, ma'am." He laughed, and the deep and easy sound of it was something I wished I could have on repeat for the rest of my life.

We followed the girls toward the exit, Jax holding my hand the entire time. I worried what would happen once we were removed from the safety net of the club. I thought for sure once we'd stepped back into reality, he'd realize that our hands were still linked and would let go. The closer we got to the door, the harder my heart pounded. I wanted him to not give a shit about the world, about what he thought was expected of him. These were all the things I used to hope for when we were back at Eastchester, but tonight, more than anything, I wanted him to choose me. To choose us. The late-night air surrounded me as we stepped outside, and I almost dropped his hand, not wanting to feel his rejection of the truth. Most of the people from the club had left already, leaving only a few stragglers on the sidewalk, smoking cigarettes and waiting for rides. Jax's grip tightened around my hand, and the brutal beat of my heart slowed.

"Over there," Gwen said, waving at what I assumed was the Uber driver.

I reluctantly let go of Jax's hand to hug my best friend. "Thank you for inviting him, for doing what I don't think I ever would have on my own."

"You seem... happy?" she whispered before pulling away.

"I am."

She kissed my cheek. "Coffee tomorrow?"

"Of course," I said. "Love you."

We all said our goodbyes, June giving Jax another motherly warning about getting me home in one piece. It scared me, watching Jax hug June and Gwen, and how easy it would be if this was something permanent. All I'd wanted was closure, but somehow I found myself at the beginning of something new.

"You ready?" he asked, taking my hand.

I loved, way too much, how simple and effortless it was for him to take my hand in his, even though I knew Jax had to be fighting himself.

"Yeah."

"I'm parked around the corner."

We walked in silence, the humidity and my nerves making my palm clammy in his.

"This is me," he said, rubbing the back of his neck, he let go of my hand. "Sorry about the car, it's not much, and I haven't had a chance to clean out the back seat."

Sure, his car had probably seen better days, but I didn't care about stuff like that. His car could've been missing a door and it wouldn't have mattered to me. Jax was here. He'd chosen us.

"Jax..." I placed my hands on his hips. When he didn't freak out, I leaned against him. "I don't give a shit about your messy car."

His smile was lopsided. "No?"

I shook my head. "Not one fucking bit."

His arms snaked around my waist, and as his tongue slid into my mouth, my hands found their way to his ass.

The fact that we were making out, on the corner of a main road, did not escape me. If anything, it made me want him even more. Jax from nine years ago would have dropped dead before he'd touch me outside of the dorm. Tonight was more than an apology. This was what I wanted. This kiss, this public display, was Jax's way of showing me he meant every word he'd said in his email. And fuck, I was here for it.

A car horn blared, and I laughed, pressing a chaste kiss to his wet lips. "Should we go?"

"Probably," he said, his smile more nervous than shy.

Jax's car smelled like sand and soap. I had no idea what he'd been worried about. His car was cleaner than mine. He had a few towels in the back seat, folded, and CD cases strewn across the floor.

"You still listen to CDs?" I asked, trying not to laugh.

He shoved his key into the ignition and started the engine. "Sometimes. On long drives. I don't have a hook up for my phone. This piece of shit's too old." Changing the subject, he asked, "Where am I headed?"

"Head north for a few miles, until you see Monroe Drive. Then take a right."

As he pulled onto the road, I pressed the play button on his stereo, curious to what he'd been listening to. I didn't recognize the slow and sad song.

"What is this?" I asked.

Jax kept his eyes on the road and exhaled a hesitant breath. "Amber Run."

"It's beautiful."

He blushed. "It helps me remember, I guess."

"Remember what?"

"You."

"Me?" I asked, letting my smile spread.

He glanced at me, the dimple in his cheek popping as he laughed. "I don't know... It's stupid, but I forget sometimes that it's okay to feel shit."

"It's not stupid," I said without any humor in my tone. "The world tells us, as men, we have to be hard, and that crying is for pussies, and if you're not strong, then you're weak. It's bullshit. You're allowed to fucking feel however the hell you want."

"I'm figuring that out." The muscle in his jaw pulsed as he turned onto Monroe Drive.

I waved my hand down my body. "This is who I am. I like to fuck guys, and I'll never apologize for it. You shouldn't either."

The car slowed to a stop at a red light, and he stared through the windshield, his knuckles white against the steering wheel.

"I'm afraid to lose Jason more than anything." Jax spoke as if it hurt to say the words. His voice strained. He finally looked at me, and the defeat on his face crushed me. "I think I could get over it if my mom never wanted to talk to me again. I'd understand. I know how she thinks, what she believes, and I can't hate her for it. But Jason..." He let out a stuttered breath. "He don't know any better. If I was gone for good, he'd be confused and scared, and it hurts, Wild. It hurts to think of him not being in my life."

I reached across the console and placed my hand above his knee.

"Jaxon..." I whispered his name, wishing I could crawl into his seat and wrap my arms around him. But the light turned green, stealing the moment. "My life was the complete opposite of yours. My parents weren't exactly the warmest people, and I was an only child. I've never had any attachments that ever made me feel so anchored to something I couldn't be who I wanted to be."

"I'm tired of living a lie. But I don't know how to hold on to all the pieces anymore without losing one of them."

"You don't have to make any life decisions tonight, Jax." I squeezed his leg. "Baby steps, remember?"

"And that's another thing I feel guilty as fuck about. I should have never emailed you like that. I should have told you it was me from the get-go."

"Who knows what would have happened if I'd known it was you? Listen, it's over and done with. You're here now."

"I am," he said with resolve. The permanence of those two words quieted the last shred of doubt I'd been holding on to. He took hold of my hand and didn't let go until we were parked outside my condo.

Leaving the car running, Jax picked at a crack in the vinyl near the gear shift.

"Did you want to come inside?" I asked.

He glanced at the clock. "You sure?"

I opened the door, gathering all my confidence, and smirked. "I wouldn't have asked if I didn't want you to."

He killed the engine as I got out of the car.

"This is a nice place," he said as I unlocked the front door.

"Thanks."

Once inside, I switched on the lights. Gandalf jumped off the kitchen counter, and Jaxon kneeled down to pet him.

"Hey, cutie," he said, picking up the small ball of fur.

"Jesus, I can hear him purring all the way over here."

Jax chuckled, nuzzling his nose against the cat's head as I shut the front door "This is Gandalf, I'm guessing?"

I dropped my keys on the coffee table. "The one and only."

"I should get Jason a pet. I bet he'd love having a dog or something."

"You want the cat?"

"Are you serious?" he asked, looking at me like I just killed his favorite puppy. "You can't just give him away."

"I'm joking," I said and took Gandalf from his arms. I placed a kiss on his nose and set him down. "Go play. Daddy has a guest."

The bell on his collar jingled as he weaved himself around Jax's legs a few times and then trotted off, most likely to his bed in my office.

I grabbed a couple bottles of water from my fridge, watching as Jax looked around. He stared at the pictures on the wall, stopping in front of one with me and Anders from last year. It was a snapshot of us, smiling at each other during one of our "on again" moments.

I handed him one of the bottles of water. "That's my agent."

His eyes met mine. "Is he the one you—"

"Slept with? Yeah." I took a long drink from my bottle as he turned to look at the picture again. "He's just a friend now. It wasn't smart mixing work with my personal life."

Jax didn't say anything and I followed him in an anxious silence as he moved through the room. He took in every detail, his fingers running along the spines of the books sitting on the shelf.

"Come on, I'll give you the grand tour."

He set his water on the table and followed me down the hall. "This is my office."

Gandalf was curled up inside his bed and lifted his head, giving us both an annoyed look.

"It used to be the guest room," I said. "And there's a bathroom across the hall."

"Is your room upstairs?" he asked.

My blood heated as I took his hand. "It is."

For every step we took up the stairs, a question or doubt popped into my head. Was this too much, too soon? Was I rushing him? Was I rushing myself? When it came to sex I didn't usually second-guess myself, at least not in the moment. But this was Jax. He was the first guy I'd ever been with. The first and only guy I'd ever loved.

The door to my room was open, and I was grateful I'd actually made my bed this morning.

Jax released my hand and walked to the sliding glass doors, pulling back the curtain, he asked, "You have your own deck?"

I kicked off my shoes and set my water on the nightstand. "Yup. It's too hot though. I usually only go out there during the winter."

"You've made a good life for yourself, Wild. It makes me realize how far I am from having one of my own."

"My life is messier than it appears. Don't let all of this neatly placed décor fool you. I'm still figuring shit out, too."

With his back to me, I could admire the muscles in his wide shoulders, and the way his jeans hugged his ass. He was built in college, but not like this. The sleeves of his shirt hugged his biceps as he turned to look at me. His dark blond hair was messy and in need of a cut, but it looked good on him. His jaw was strong and defined, his lips soft and full. And fuck, those hands. The rough skin of his palms. I'd gotten hard just thinking about how they'd feel wrapped around my dick.

"It's late," he said. "I should head home."

"Sleep over." I patted the bed. "For old times' sake."

His laugh nervous, he asked, "Is that a good idea?"

"Probably not," I said. "But I think you driving home this late is worse."

"I can sleep on the couch?" he offered.

"You're not sleeping on the couch." I headed toward the bathroom and turned on the light. "I have an extra toothbrush, it'll be fine. Nothing has to happen, Jax. Unless you want it to."

Without waiting for his answer, I stripped out of my shirt and threw it into the hamper. I pulled the extra toothbrush out of my drawer and set it on the counter.

Jax made his way in as I started to brush my teeth. The weight of his gaze on my bare skin caused goosebumps to prick at the back of my neck.

He picked up the toothbrush, and I handed him the toothpaste. "You're welcome," I said with a smirk, trying to hide how fucking anxious I was.

"Thanks."

I was in my dorm room again, wishing for something I'd never have as I watched him in the mirror. I wondered when I would wake up and realize this whole night had been a figment of my overactive imagination. A chapter I'd written in a book.

We finished up in the bathroom, and I almost had a heart attack when Jax pulled his shirt over his head, revealing miles of muscle and tan skin. All the blood in my body drained to my groin, and I clenched my jaw, trying not to stare as he got ready for bed. He was oblivious to how sexy he was. When he raised his head, I dropped my eyes and unbuckled my belt. The room was too quiet, my breathing too loud as I pushed off my jeans. There was no way I could hide that my dick was up for anything, and in the end, I decided I didn't care. When I lifted my head, I caught Jax staring at me. His neck and chest were red, his green eyes dark as they trailed over my body. He was just as hard as I was, standing in only his boxer briefs. I rubbed a hand over my dick, trying to relieve the ache, and his lips parted. I took that as an invitation.

Heat poured from his skin as I placed my hands against his chest, my fingers mapped the lines of muscles all the way down to his stomach, gliding under the elastic of his underwear. His head tipped forward as I palmed the firm, round globes of his ass, and he grabbed my hips, rutting his dick against mine. His eyes half closed, he kissed me. His tongue diving into my mouth, he moaned as I dragged his bottom lip through my teeth. I bit his jaw and nipped at his neck. Trailing wet kisses down the perfect plane of his stomach, I took the head of his cock into my mouth through the black cotton of his briefs.

He gripped my chin with his hand, pulling me back up to his lips. "You don't have to do that."

"I want to, Jax." My hand dipped under his waistband. "I want to touch you."

"Fuck," he groaned through gritted teeth as I stroked my palm down the smooth, hot skin of his shaft.

"Take these off," I said, tugging down his underwear.

He did what I asked, his teeth sinking into my bottom lip, and as I worked him with my hand, he pushed my underwear down too. Taking a step back, Jax sat on the bed, his fingers digging into my hips.

"Come here," he said, pulling me close, and I straddled his legs.

He wrapped his rough fingers around my cock, and I grasped the back of his neck, kissing him, whimpering into his mouth as I fucked his hand. Heat gathered, collecting over my skin, and I reached down, his dick heavy in my hand, trying to match his rhythm. With his forehead resting against my brow, his lips barely touching mine, we breathed each other in. I wanted more time, but my control failed as Jax shoved his fingers into my hair. Pulling my head back, he licked the line of my throat before sliding his tongue back into my mouth. His lips commanded mine, growling my name as the sticky heat of his orgasm coated my skin. His hand tightened around my shaft, pumping hard and fast, dragging me over the edge with him, until I came on his chest.

Panting and messy, he kissed my shoulder, shuddering as I gave him one more lazy stroke.

I shivered as his tongue tasted my skin. "You alright?" I asked.

He lifted his head, his green eyes bright. "I'm better than alright."

Jax looked at me like I was the only person on this Earth who mattered. I'd forgotten how much I missed that look. The smile growing across his lips, the I-just-got-fucked pink in his cheeks, these were the things I'd locked away, making it easier to survive each day. Feeling more exposed than I liked, I stood and grabbed a couple of towels from the back of the bathroom door.

I was silent as we cleaned up, the worry in Jax's eyes growing as I held on to my words.

"Hey..." He draped his arm over my hip as I lay next to him in bed. Pulling my back to his chest, he asked, "Are *you* alright?"

"This reminds me of the first time you slept over at Eastchester."

He kissed my neck and then my shoulder. "I'm not gonna run away as soon as the sun comes up, Wild."

"You're not?"

"I know I gotta earn back your trust," he said. "But I promise you, I'm done running away."

He rested his hand against my chest, tucking me as close to him as he possibly could.

"I believe you."

If I wanted this to work, I had to believe him.

Jax's breathing fell into an even, calm, quiet rhythm, and I yawned. "I always liked falling asleep next to you," he said. "Made me less restless."

"I think it's the sex, not me."

He chuckled, his hot breath tickling my skin. "Maybe."

If I wanted this to work, I had to let go of the past for good.

Chapter 23

JAX

The sun lit the room, spilling in from the sliding glass doors. Groggy, I turned to my side and found him asleep, stretched out on his stomach with the sheet pushed down. The curve of his bare ass was exposed, and my morning semi turned into a full-fledged hard-on. The images of what we'd done last night fresh in my mind. His lips on my skin, his hand on my cock, the heat of his come on my chest. I reached over and trailed a finger down his spine, watching as his skin pebbled beneath my touch.

Half awake, he shifted closer to me. "Do that again," he said, and I smiled at the sleepy command of his voice.

I leaned over, kissing my way down his back. Softly biting the cheek of his ass, he groaned and rolled over, the pink head of his cock perfect against his pale skin. It had been too long since I had him in my mouth, and with Wild this close, with his dark eyes barely opened, I didn't stop myself from tasting him. Wild's fingers twisted into my hair, his breath a sharp hiss as I licked the tip of his dick. He swore as I took him into my mouth, and I gagged as he lifted his hips. Taking a breath, I stroked him, my face hot as he watched me kneel between his legs. I placed my hand on his knee, gently pushing it back, resting his foot on my thigh. This time he let me set the pace, his bottom lip pinned between his teeth, he ran his fingers through my hair as he fucked my mouth. He moaned as I cupped his balls. The grip he had on the back of my head almost painful as my finger teased the tight ring of his ass. I moved my mouth faster, my eyes watering as I tried to take him deeper. My dick throbbed for release. I wanted to sink into him, lose myself inside his body and forget about everything waiting for me in Bell River.

"Jax..." He breathed my name and sat up, pulling my face to his lips with his hands.

His tongue dipped into my mouth, and I loved the raw taste of him. He teased the tip of my erection with his fingers as he spoke against my lips. "Give me a second."

He wiped his thumb over my wet lips as he leaned over, reaching for the bedside table drawer. Reading me like he always had, he set a condom and a bottle of lube onto the mattress.

My pulse punched inside my chest as I kissed him. Wild's lips never left mine as he grabbed the condom. He tore it open and covered my cock, grinning against my mouth when I groaned.

"You make me crazy," he said and nipped my chin. "You always have."

He leaned back, his head hitting the pillow and my mouth crashed into his. I kissed him with everything I'd held in for the past decade, with every second that should've been his. He rocked his hips, desperate, rubbing his cock against my hip. I moved my mouth down his body, tasting his jaw, his chin, lingering on his throat. I loved the long lines of his neck, loved the soft hollow below his Adam's apple. I reached for the lube as I moved onto my knees, spreading his legs, I opened the bottle and soaked my fingers. Finding my confidence, I bent and swallowed his dick. He gripped the sheets, his delicate neck straining as I took him to the back of my throat. I knew his body. It didn't matter how many years had gone by. I slipped a finger inside of him, relishing in the familiar flush of his cheeks, loving the splotches of pink that colored his chest as I rubbed at the spot that made him whimper.

"More..." Wild's eyes clouded, his brows pinching with need as I pushed another finger inside him. His fist twisted in my hair, pulling until I lifted my head. Panting, he said, "I want you inside me."

I slid a third finger in, stretching him, making sure he was ready. He kept his eyes on me as I picked up the bottle. Pouring more lube in my hand, I rubbed it down the length of my shaft, my eyes partly closing with the contact. Wild spread his legs a little wider for me, and I settled my hips between his thighs.

His lips parted on a groan as I eased the head of my cock into the tight heat of his body. My breath hitched as I slid all the way in, my hips meeting his ass. He held onto my shoulders as I pulled out a few inches, thrusting into him slow and easy at first, trying not to ruin it by finishing in ten seconds. He urged me with quiet pleas to move faster, fuck him harder. Our skin slapped together as our bodies collided, my orgasm building, I reached for his cock, stroking him as fast and frantic as I took his body. Wild's eyes slammed shut, arching his neck, his head tipped back as he came all over his stomach. He held my gaze as I took his body and made it mine again.

"Oh, fuck..." I grabbed his hips, burying myself as deep as I could go, my fingers bruising his flesh as I came.

"Kiss me," he said, out of breath and I leaned down, letting our lips move together, slow and wet, as his shaking fingers rested on the side of my face.

I sat up, bringing him with me, keeping my mouth on his, I stole another taste of his lips before he pulled away.

"I'll be right back," I said and pressed a kiss to his forehead.

I headed to the bathroom to wash my hands and throw the condom in the trash. When I walked back into the room, Wild was on his side, his head propped in his hand.

"Jesus Christ, you're beautiful, Jax." Kneeling onto the bed, his eyes trailed up my body. I never thought I was special in any way, but he looked at me like I was something to behold, and I almost believed him. "It's not fair, if I'm being honest. How will any other guy ever compare?"

I huffed out a laugh as I lay down beside him. "Any other guy?" I asked.

Pulling his bottom lip from between his teeth with my thumb, I kissed him until he was out of breath again.

"It doesn't seem normal, being stuck on one person your whole life," he said. "But I think I always knew there'd never be anyone else."

"Do..." I took a deep breath, holding his gaze, letting the fear go, I asked, "Do you think you could love me again?"

He wrapped his arm over my waist, and when our chests came together, the rapid beat of his heart echoed against mine. "I never stopped."

Relief and guilt warred inside me, heavy with all the time I'd stolen from him.

He still loved me.

I loved this man, and his trust in me, even if I wasn't worthy of it.

"It's always been you, Wild. I never wanted anything else but you. I keep thinking... what our lives would've been like if my dad hadn't crashed his car into that damn river."

"You can't think like that, Jax. It'll drive you nuts." He kissed my collarbone. "Everything that happened was supposed to happen. There are no what-ifs. If you start down that rabbit hole, you'll never get out."

"And I'm here now."

"Precisely." He smiled, dropping his lips to mine.

I wanted to stay in this bed all day. Kissing him, fucking him until neither of us could move. We were both hard again, our hips grinding together, our kiss less coordinated as our breathing intensified. Wild's hand found its way between our bodies stroking us both at the same time. We groaned against each other's lips, close to letting go, when his phone rang.

"Shit, don't stop," I said, reaching down I covered his hand, working to keep his rhythm. "Gonna come."

My climax covered our fingers, his following not too far behind as his phone stopped ringing. Gasping, he fell back onto the mattress. I reached over him and grabbed the towel off the floor from last night. I wiped our hands first and then his chest.

"We should shower," he said, kissing me one last time before climbing out of bed.

"Aren't you gonna see who called?" I asked.

Reluctant, I got out of bed and stood on unsteady legs.

"Nah. It's probably June. I'm supposed to meet her for coffee if you want to go with me?"

I only had the clothes I'd worn last night, and I promised Jason I'd video call him today. I wanted to spend every second I could with Wild while I had the chance, but the real world wasn't something I could put off for much longer.

"I want to," I said. "But I should probably head back. I have to get stuff for the apartment, and I promised Jason I'd call him."

Wild looked at me over his shoulder as he turned on the water in the shower. "Busy day," he said with a smile. But I could hear the disappointment in his voice.

I stepped into the shower, the hot water covering me as I folded my arms around his waist. His back to my chest, he rested his head against my shoulder.

"I don't want to leave."

"I know," he said. "I'm being greedy." I kissed his neck, letting my fingers follow the small stream of water as it ran down the muscles of his stomach. "Do you have plans this weekend?"

"No. I work Friday, but after that I'm done till Monday."

"You should stay with me this weekend. I could show you around Atlanta."

"Go on a real date," I said.

"Gasp... Jaxon Stettler out in Atlanta. Should I order the dragon dildos today, or are you still thinking about it?" I pinched his hip, and he laughed, turning his body in my arms. Chest to chest, he reached up and combed his fingers through my wet hair, settling them at the back of my neck. "Seriously, though. Last night when you kissed me out in the open like that. It meant a lot to me. I know how hard this is for you."

I framed his face with my hands, wiping the water from his cheeks with my thumbs. "I don't know what will happen when I go home, but I know I can't stay in the closet. Not anymore."

"Don't blow up your life for me. Coming out to your mom is a big deal. Make sure you know what you want, Jax. For you, and not for anyone else."

"I want this." I kissed his lips. "I want you... I want a life that's my own."

"What about your brother?" he asked.

My mom couldn't keep Jason from me. I was his family. She could hate me all she wanted to, but there was no way she could deny I loved my brother more than anything.

"Let me worry about that, alright. I'll figure it out. Right now, the only thing I want to think about is the hot as hell guy I have naked in my arms."

Wild grinned as he ran his fingers down my stomach. "I think I can help with that."

◆ ◆ ◆

Hudson was in the kitchen when I got home, cooking something that actually smelled decent. My stomach growled, reminding me I hadn't had breakfast, and it was almost eleven-thirty. I set my keys on the hook by the door and tried, unsuccessfully, to walk past the kitchen without being noticed.

"Are you just getting home?" he asked, a shit-eating grin on his face.

"What are you? My mother?"

"Would your mother high-five you for getting some pussy last night?" He held up his hand and I shook my head.

"You're a fucking idiot."

He dropped his hand, laughing. I had the best night and morning of my life, and I wasn't going to let him ruin it.

"What are you making?" I asked, trying to take the attention off me.

"Grilled ham and cheese, want one?"

"Sure, I'm gonna change real quick."

He smiled like he was in on the secret. He'd probably try and beat the shit out of me if he knew what I'd been up to all night and this morning. Maybe it was a good thing he thought I'd hooked up with a chick.

Once I was in my room, I shut the door. It didn't take me long to change. I'd contemplated taking another shower since I'd dressed in dirty clothes for my ride home, but I liked smelling like Wild's soap. I plugged my charger into my phone and sat down on my bed as it powered on. I didn't have any missed texts from home, and I exhaled, relieved. Thinking about everything last night, I wanted to text Ethan, tell him about Wild. It was obvious he was kind of into me, and I didn't want to lead him on. Maybe if I told him about last night, he'd understand that friends were all we would ever be. And I think he'd be happy that I'd allowed myself to be out, even if it was only one night. *The first night.* I reminded myself. I had work to do at home, and I wasn't totally out of the closet yet, but I would be soon.

I picked up my phone and typed out a message.

Me: Hey.

As I waited for him to respond, I called my mom. The phone rang twice before she answered.

"Hey there, sweetheart." My mom's voice rang through the phone, and that homesickness returned with a vengeance. "Missing home yet?"

Did she love me enough she'd accept me like she'd said that day at church?

"Nah..." I coughed, trying to speak past the lump in my throat. "Not any more than yesterday."

She laughed and it made me smile.

"Listen, I'm about to head next door, did you need something?"

"What do you think about getting Jason a dog?" I asked, hoping she'd be okay with it. "I think it'd be good for him, having something to look after. Make him proud."

"I think that sounds like a great idea, honey."

"Really?"

"If you'll help house train 'em. Why not."

"I was thinking of getting one while I'm here. Training it a little before I brought him home with me when I come to visit."

"Do you want to tell Jay, or let it be a surprise?"

"A surprise," I said.

"Sounds good, Jax. I gotta run."

"Tell Jay I'll video call him later."

"Will do, sweetheart. Love you."

"Love you too, Momma."

I ended the call and opened up the text I'd gotten from Ethan while I was on the phone.

Ethan: What's up?

Me: Any news on camping?

Ethan: I checked out a few camp sites online last night.

Ethan: I think I'll show them to your mom and let her decide.

Me: She'll like that.

Ethan: Are you working?

Me: No. There was a delay with the lumber shipment. But it should be here by tomorrow.

Ethan: Cool.

Ethan: Did you and Hudson do anything fun for your night off? LOL.

I laughed as I tapped out a message.

Me: Hell, no. Living with him is hard enough.
Me: Actually, I saw Wild last night.

The three dots at the bottom of my screen appeared and reappeared four times before a text finally came through.

Ethan: Did it go okay?
Me: It did.
Me: We met up at a club in Atlanta.
Ethan: Was it a ... gay club?

Smiling, I replied.

Me: It was.
Ethan: Shocker.
Ethan: How did you handle it?
Me: I actually danced.
Ethan: Damn... I wish I could've seen that.

Awkward again, I hesitated. When I didn't reply fast enough, he sent me another message.

Ethan: So... you and Wild...
Me: We're gonna try and make it work.
Ethan: Good.
Ethan: Like I said before. You should get to do what you want.

Ethan: Your mom just texted me and said you're getting a dog!!!

I laughed, that woman couldn't keep a secret if she tried.

Me: Yes! I'm going to bring him home when I come to visit in a couple of weeks.
Ethan: It's a boy! Send me a picture!
Me: LOL. I haven't gotten him yet. But I think I'm gonna go look today.
Ethan: Go. Find. Dog. Now.
Me: Talk to you later.
Ethan: Send me a picture if you find one.
Me: I will.

I left my phone on my nightstand to charge and headed to the kitchen. Hudson sat at the breakfast bar staring at his phone with a half-eaten sandwich in his hand. Without looking up he said, "Your food is in the microwave."

"Thanks."

I set the dish on the kitchen counter, standing opposite of Hudson, I asked, "I think I'm gonna get a dog for Jason."

He looked up from his phone. "You are?"

I nodded as I took a bite of the grilled ham and cheese.

"When?" he asked.

"Today. Want to go with me?"

His smile was disarming when it was real.

"Fuck, yeah," he said. Holding his fist up, I rolled my eyes and knocked my knuckles into his. "We're getting a dog."

Chapter 24

WILD

"Wilder." Kris's familiar smile lifted to her dark brown eyes as she looked up from her computer. "It's good to see you."

Standing up, she leaned over her desk to kiss my cheek.

"You, too. It's been a little while. Is this new?" I asked, fiddling with the small family photo she had displayed.

"It is." Her nose crinkled. "I hate that dress."

"You do?" I picked up the picture, pretending to scrutinize it, and lifted a brow. "I think you look gorgeous... if only I wasn't so attracted to your husband though..."

"Oh my God, stop." She laughed, snatching the frame from my hand. "Every time I tell Cesar you think he's hot, he blushes."

My head tipped back as I laughed. "Really? Maybe I have a chance after all."

"You'll have to fight me for him."

I held my hands up in surrender. "I'd never."

"You'd never what?" Anders asked as he opened his office door.

"Steal her husband."

"Wilder is in love with Cesar." She giggled as I lifted my hand to my heart.

"You definitely married up," Anders teased.

"You guys are both terrible," she said, her smile widening as she handed Anders a red folder.

He laughed and nodded his head toward his office. "Come on, I have a few things to go over with you."

Insecure, I stared at the red folder in his hand and wondered if it had the unfinished manuscript I'd sent him on Wednesday. I followed behind him, giving Kris a small wave before I shut his office door. Anders looked good in his charcoal gray slacks, the maroon button-down he wore was open at the collar revealing a small V of smooth, tan skin. The room was filled with the scent of his cologne, and as I took a seat, it was difficult not to notice the way his eyes picked me apart.

"How are you doing?" he asked, leaning back in his chair.

"I'd feel a lot better if you told me the book isn't shit."

"It isn't shit."

"But..."

He opened the folder and started flipping through the pages. The red marks on the white paper were like a knife against my skin.

"You changed the story?" he asked, his tone absentminded and disinterested. "The street vendor's son... he forgives Abel?"

I sat up straight in the chair, the leather making me sweat through my t-shirt. "I trashed chapters five through fifteen and started over."

He lifted his eyes. "Why?"

"Because Abel deserves a happy ending."

Because I deserved a happy ending.

He exhaled and shut the folder. "The original outline was unique, rich... layered. This is naïve and impractical."

"Why is it naïve? Because in the end love conquers all?" I asked, hating the impetuous tone of my voice.

"This is only my critique, Wilder." He sighed. "I don't know... I liked the idea of Abel finding a new path and not getting bogged down by his past. It's more realistic, isn't it? First love never lasts."

"Is this about the book or about us?"

Anders clenched his jaw. "I think Rohen should shop this story instead of me. He's new to the agency and could use some experience dealing with publishers."

"What? Why?" Panic and irritation rooted inside my stomach.

"You know why." Anders scrubbed his palm down his face. "When we talked on Tuesday, and you told me you were giving Jax another chance... knowing the truth of what happened with you two... as a friend who loves the hell out of you, I can't sit back and watch him hurt you again."

"What if I don't get hurt? What if I actually get to be happy?"

He cringed. "I never made you happy?"

"That's not what I meant." I met his eyes. "How many times since we started playing this game have *you* been the one to break things off?"

"That's not the point."

I laughed and he smiled. "Five times..."

"I actually think it was six."

"That's right... when you dated that girl from New York. I always forget about her. It's like I've tried to repress a bad memory or something?" I smirked. "See, this proves my point though. I'm your consolation prize and you're mine. That's not fair to either of us."

"And you trust him?" he asked.

"I do, and maybe I'll regret those words, but I have to at least try." I took a deep breath. "Please don't let this Rohen guy, who knows dick about me or this industry, shop this book."

"Wouldn't it be easier if—"

"I don't want easy, Anders. I want my best friend to shop my goddamn book."

His smile was gradual as he stared at me. "On two conditions..."

"I'm listening."

"One... you don't have a meltdown when I tell you Bartley wants you to pick up extra spots on your book tour."

"When would I have to leave?"

"You'd have to be in Miami on October ninth," he said.

"That's only a month away." The walls seemed to narrow in around me. The heat stifling. A month. I thought I'd have Jax until November. "What if I say no?"

"You can't," he said. "It's in your contract."

"Fuck. I hate Miami."

"Well, they love you." He chuckled. "You sold more print there than any other city nationwide."

I didn't have it in me to care. I'd be bouncing around from city to city, while Jax was here, and by the time the tour was over he'd be gone. My hands were sweaty in my lap. He lived in Bell River. His life was in Bell River. A month wasn't enough time for us to figure out what we wanted, or how this thing we'd impulsively started would work.

Oblivious to my sinking mood, Anders opened his drawer and set a new folder on the table. "Speaking of contracts, I have something for you to consider. It's a foreign rights' proposal."

"What does that mean?" I asked, my head filled with Jax and the sound of a ticking clock.

"I can go over it with you if you want." He checked his watch. "Let's meet for dinner in an hour?"

"I can't," I said. "I have plans with Jax."

"I see..." Anders handed me the folder, slipping into his flat, professional, I-don't-have-time-for-feelings façade he wore so well. "Look over it, let me know if you have any questions."

I stood, tucking the folder under my arm. "I'll call you on Monday."

"Have a good weekend," he said, his eyes busy with the papers strewn out in front of him.

"You too." As I opened the door to leave, I paused. "Wait. You said you had two conditions. What was the second one?"

Tapping his finger against the desk, he stared at me. "If he hurts you again and you write about it..." He swallowed, his voice hoarse when he spoke. "Don't ask me to read it."

"If that's what you want."

"It is." He exhaled and gave me a small smile. "I'll talk to you Monday."

● ● ●

I'd checked the clock about a thousand times since I'd gotten home from my meeting with Anders. Jax had texted me thirty minutes ago to tell me he was on his way over. I figured with rush-hour traffic it would take him longer to get into the city and had made our reservation for dinner accordingly. Tugging on the hem of my shirt, I looked at myself in the mirror one more time.

"What do you think, Gandalf?"

My cat sat on the counter, observing me, his gray tail swishing back and forth. I took that as a sign of approval. I'd chosen to forgo the liner tonight, sticking to a more casual look. The place I'd picked was a laid-back brew pub I'd hoped Jaxon would like. The crowd was chill and progressive and wouldn't give a shit if two guys were there on a date. At least I hoped they didn't. I wanted everything to be as smooth and perfect as possible. With my tour dates getting moved up, the time I had with Jax was limited, and I didn't want to spook him so far back into the closet he'd never come out.

Gandalf stretched and arched his back as I scratched his head. "You get to meet Jax's new dog tonight. Her name's Rosie." I picked up my toothbrush. "Are you excited?" Gandalf hopped off the counter and started eating his food. "I'll take that as a no..." I laughed. "Hopefully, Rosie doesn't eat you."

Right as I finished brushing my teeth the doorbell rang. The butterflies in my stomach stirred as I quickly wiped my mouth, my nerves jittery as I made my way down the stairs. It was absolutely laughable that I was nervous about a date. He'd been in my bed, inside of me, for fuck's sake, only a few days ago. I crossed the living room, the bell on Gandalf's collar jingled behind me as I unlatched the lock. When I opened the door, I was hit by his citrus scent.

The familiar smell drew me in, and his smile split across his face, a dimple popping in his cheek as he spoke. "Hey."

Jax had cut his hair, the blond waves trimmed, and less unruly, fell over his forehead. He had on a nice pair of jeans and a long sleeve, fitted navy blue t-shirt that looked like it had never been worn. It hugged his chest in all the right places, and if I wasn't starving, I might've let him fuck me before we left. The possibility wasn't totally off the table. Stunned by how absolutely beautiful he was, and with the dirty thoughts running around my head, I hadn't noticed his duffel bag and the medium-sized dog crate sitting on the porch next to him.

"Is that Rosie?" I asked, excited, my voice an octave higher than I would have preferred.

"It is." His laugh was warm. "Is it okay if I bring her inside?"

"Of course." I stepped to the side, opening the door wide for him.

"Is Gandalf gonna freak out?"

"Probably." I shrugged as he set the crate and his bag down in the middle of my living room. "He has no right to bitch, though, since he commandeered my condo without my permission."

As he turned to look at me, I wrapped my arms around his waist. "Hey."

He ran his hands up my arms, pressing into the skin with his fingertips. The heat of his body covered me as he leaned down to kiss me. Soft at first, Jax took his time. His lips explored mine, tasting, until his tongue dipped into my mouth, and his hands pushed into my hair. I hooked my fingers into the belt loops of his jeans, pulling his hips against me. With rough hands, he tipped my head back, his kiss greedy and deep. He was hard for me, and when I palmed the bulge in his jeans, he groaned.

"We have an hour before we have to leave," I whispered.

He reached for my belt, his fingers working open the buckle, he said, "I can make an hour work." Jax flipped the button on my jeans as he bit my bottom lip. His hand slipped into my briefs and I hissed as his hot fingers grasped my cock with a firm grip. "All damn week, Wild. I couldn't get your taste out of my head."

I gripped his chin and kissed him with aggressive lips. But as my fingers fumbled with his belt, the dog whimpered and barked, sending Gandalf into a fit. He jumped off the kitchen counter with a high-pitched cry that killed the mood and my hard-on, running faster than I'd ever seen a cat move.

Laughing into my neck, Jax released me and pressed his lips to my heated skin. "Shit, I'm sorry."

Aching and breathless, I laughed too. "It's okay... we have all weekend, right?"

"Rosie probably needs to pee."

"She can go out back." I offered. "It's fenced."

He leaned back, his green eyes assessing me. "I was hoping Hudson would watch her. But he went home for the weekend."

"I told you on the phone it was okay."

"I think you'll love her," Jax said. "She's so damn cute."

When he pulled away, I reluctantly put myself back together. It was actually painful to watch him turn away. Each minute we had together was weighted. I had to fill every second I had with Jax, with us, and I hoped when I told him about Miami, it didn't ruin our entire weekend together.

"Hey, girl... it's okay." He bent down and unlocked the crate. "Come on, Rosie."

He stood and took a step back as Rosie peeked her head out of the cage. She was all golden and white curls, with one dark spot that covered her right eye. She tripped over her paws as she made her way out of the crate.

"She's big for a puppy," I said.

"They told me she was about a year old. Not sure what kind of dog she is either." Jax scratched behind her floppy ears and grinned like a little kid when she licked his cheek. "She's sweet as hell. Come say hi."

I kneeled down onto the carpet, and she warily made her way over to my lap. Her fur was soft and wiry at the same time. I thought she might have been a mix of some type of doodle.

She sniffed my hand as I held it out. "I bet she smells the cat."

"I better take her outside before she meets him, I don't wanna her to piss on your carpet when he scares the daylights out of her."

I laughed. "Thanks for that."

Rosie followed after Jax to my patio door, and when he opened it, she trotted outside with her shaggy tail wagging.

He slid the door shut. "She can stay out there if you want, but the shelter told me she was crate trained too. She's been good at our place. Hasn't had more than one accident, and that was the first day we brought her home."

"She doesn't have to stay outside." I slid my hands up his chest. "It will be fine. Stop worrying." I ran my fingers through his hair. "You look nice."

"I got it cut yesterday after work," he said, his cheeks tinged with pink. "Got some clothes for this weekend, too. Figured you wouldn't want to go to dinner with a guy in Carhartts and sleeveless t-shirts."

"I don't know what a Carhartt is, but it sounds sexy."

"Maybe I'll wear it next time."

Next time.

"I have to tell you something," I said, and his smile fell. "I don't want to ruin our night, okay?"

"Alright." He was tentative. "What's going on?"

I exhaled, tightening the grip I had on his waist. "They bumped up my book tour. I leave the first week of October."

"That's only a month away."

"I know." I lifted my eyes to his, holding his stare. "I just got you back."

"When is it over?"

"Late November. After Thanksgiving, the publishing world sort of shuts down until after the holidays. But if the tickets sell, I could be out until the first week in December."

"I told Jay I would only be gone for two months." He tried to hide it, but the panic in his voice mirrored mine. "We'll make it work."

"How?"

"I have no clue, but what's a few months compared to nine years. I'll wait forever for you, Wild."

"But your life is in Bell River, Jax. We jumped into this... we didn't think—"

"We'll figure it out."

He cradled the back of my head with his big hands, dropping his lips to mine. In less than a minute he had me worked up again. His lips made it impossible for me to think straight as blood rushed to my groin.

"I don't want to leave this condo," I said, Jax's gaze lingering on my mouth. "I only get one month, and I want to be naked the entire time."

His lips broke into a wide smile, stealing away the sad edge that had been there a second before.

"I wanna go out... hold your hand in a room full of people." He brushed his thumb over my bottom lip. "You deserve to be loved out loud, in the open, in front of the world. Let me give that to you."

Warmth radiated through my body, gathering inside my chest as my pulse quickened. I nodded, all the words I had stuck in my throat. Jax was purposefully making himself vulnerable for me. Laying himself bare for me. Exposing everything he'd always feared about himself for me.

Nine years or one month, time didn't matter.

I would make this work.

For him.

Chapter 25

JAX

Tables lined the sidewalk as we walked up to the busy restaurant hand in hand. The patio of the brewery Wild had chosen was filled with people. Some of them looked like they'd come straight from the office, dressed in button-downs and loose ties. The rest of the crowd looked more like college-aged kids. A group of guys sitting on the patio stared at us as we approached the door. They were watching, judging us. On instinct, my hand twitched in Wild's palm. My spine straightened as I fought myself, hoping Wild hadn't noticed that my fingers had started to sweat. A few people were lined up in front of the door, blocking the entrance, and we were forced to stand there as my heart raced in my dry throat.

"It's okay, Jax," Wild curled his arm around mine, pulling me to his side. All my insecurities, those whispered slurs I'd heard rattling around inside my head, the voice, it was my own. "Just breathe," he said, and when I looked into his eyes, the voice disappeared.

I pulled Wild close and leaned into him. Glancing over to that table of guys, I refused to back down as they glared, and pressed a kiss to Wild's lips.

"I'm breathing," I said, and he smiled against my cheek.

That smile made it easier to ignore how my pulse rioted, reminded me that the disgust I'd seen on those strangers' faces had nothing to do with me, and everything to do with the thing they feared inside themselves. If I ever wanted to live, if I ever wanted to be happy, I had to start living for myself, and not those assholes. They knew nothing about me or my life.

"You okay?" Wild asked, taking my hand in his again.

"Yeah, I'm good."

I raised our locked fingers and kissed his knuckles as the line moved into the pub. It was dark inside, the only light came from the small candle-lit lanterns on each table. The music wasn't so loud that I couldn't hear myself think, but it made the room buzz. The hostess smiled at us from behind the raised desk, and I admired the intricate-looking Celtic knot that had been carved into the wood paneling on the wall behind her.

"We have a reservation," Wild said, raising his voice so that she could hear him. "Welles, party of two."

She lowered her eyes to what looked like a list of names and nodded. Grabbing two menus, she motioned for us to follow her. I held on to his hand as she brought us to a small table in the back of the room. Wild sat across from me as she placed the menus down, and I scanned the restaurant, the sea of faces a blur. Instead of giving into the bullshit inside my head again, I confronted it. Nothing I had in my heart for this man was wrong. There was no way our love was a sin. Instead of panic, for once I had pride. The hostess's voice drew my attention back to our table, but I was too wrapped up in Wild to care what she had to say. His eyes were almost black, his pale skin glowing in the low light. He ran his long fingers through his curls and gave her a smile as he listened. Wild was beautiful and graceful and unapologetically himself, and I would give anything for the chance to have him in my life for good.

Once she left, Wild reached across the table, his hand sliding into my palm, and for most of the night that's where it stayed. We found ways to touch each other. My hand seeking his, his foot resting against mine under the table. We ordered beer and burgers and talked about Eastchester. I asked him about his last year, and he didn't sugarcoat how shitty it had been for him. I was grateful for his honesty. I needed to know how hard it had been for him to truly understand how fucking lucky I was to be at this table. He'd told me how he'd almost quit but realized living at home with his parents would have been much worse. I think I apologized about fifty times until he kicked me under the table and asked me to never say the word sorry again. Wild made me less anxious as he changed the subject to his writing and how hard it had been for him to get his book read by the right people.

"I queried I think thirty agencies before Anders picked me up," he said, lifting his pint glass to his mouth.

"Queried?" I asked. "What does that mean?"

He waved his hand and rolled his eyes. "It's a letter you send out to literary agencies to try and get them to represent you. It's the fucking worst."

"You wrote thirty agencies?"

"I did. And I'm very fortunate that I got picked up at all," he said.

"I read that book, Wild, and it was phenomenal. Those other agencies missed out."

"It was self-indulgent. But I needed to write it. It was cathartic." He held up his hand as I opened my mouth to speak. "Do *not* say you're sorry..." He grinned as I pressed my lips together. "Thank you."

I took a pull from my bottle of beer as the waiter stopped at our table. "Did you want another round?"

"I'm good. How about you?" I asked Wild, and he shook his head. "I think we're ready for the check."

After the waiter brought back my card, we walked out to the curb to wait for our Uber. The air was cooler than usual, and Wild shivered beside me.

"Are you cold?" I asked.

He hugged himself. "A little."

I stepped behind him. Pulling his back to my chest, my arms draped around his waist. He leaned in, his head resting against my shoulder. There were a few people lingering on the patio of the pub, but for the most part it was quiet. I focused on Wild's breathing, the heat of his body as it soaked through my shirt. Kissing his temple, I breathed in the smell of his shampoo, letting it fill my lungs. I wanted to stay in the moment as I long as I could, dreaming about a life where every Friday night was just like this. But our ride pulled up to the curb, and I unwillingly let Wild go.

"You're quiet," he said as the driver pulled on to the main road. "Everything all right in that beautiful head of yours?"

"Just thinking."

"Okay..." He smiled as he searched my face. "Feel like elaborating?"

"It's..." I hesitated as the driver looked at us through his rear-view mirror. "I... I want this life with you. I used to feel guilty for wanting a future, when Jason couldn't have the one he deserved. If our lives had been reversed, I'd want Jason to have a good life, and I think he'd want that for me too."

Wild unbuckled his seatbelt and moved closer to me. "You can have both, Jax. You don't have to give up your family."

"Do you miss your parents?"

His eyes fell to our hands, his fingers toying with mine as he cleared his throat. "I want to tell you I don't. But yeah... sometimes I do."

I lifted one of my hands and raised his chin with my thumb. Brushing my knuckles across his cheek, I asked, "Do you think you'll ever talk to them again?"

"No." He pressed his back against the seat. "I figured they loved me, and they'd get over the disappointment of not being able to live out the heteronormative fantasy they'd planned for me." His jaw pulsed as his grip on my hand tightened. "But when my book went public, and my sexuality was written for the whole world to see, I became an embarrassment instead of a son."

"You're not an embarrassment."

"I know that." His dark eyes found mine. "And neither are you."

The car stopped in front of the condo, his words spinning in my head. As we made our way to his front door, he stopped me on the porch.

"On a scale of one to ten," he said. "How freaked out were you tonight?"

"At first... probably an eight."

"Those guys on the patio?"

"Yeah," I said.

"You kissed me though..." He folded his arms around my waist. "You didn't have to do that. You could have ignored them."

"I wanted to kiss you. Fuck those guys."

His lips spread into a wide smile. "Do you want to kiss me now?"

"I always want to kiss you, Wild." I grazed my lips over his. "Right now, I can think of a few other things I'd like to do, though."

"Oh yeah?" He grabbed my ass as I pressed my lips to the soft skin of his neck.

"But you have to open the door first."

* * *

Half asleep, I rolled over, my hand reaching for Wild, but he wasn't there. I sat up, pulling the twisted sheet from between my legs. My eyes adjusted to the dark room, the clock on the nightstand my only light. It was a little after three in the morning, and I'd been asleep barely two hours. Running a hand over my face, I yawned, groggy from being at work all day, then staying up late with Wild. The staying up late was worth it though. Falling asleep with Wild in my arms, totally fucked out of his senses, was something I could get used to. Wondering where he was, I got out of bed, almost tripping over my jeans. I switched on the bedside lamp, and found Rosie and Gandalf curled up in a ball together at the foot of the bed. How or when they both got in here, I had no idea, but it was sweet as hell.

"Wanna go outside?" I asked but Rosie didn't budge.

Gandalf just eyed me as I walked naked across the room to grab a pair of sweats from my bag. Once I was decent, I headed down the stairs and followed the sound of fingers clacking on a keyboard. Wild was in his office, wearing nothing but his underwear, typing away on his computer. He didn't notice me leaning on the door frame, watching him as he chewed his bottom lip. His hands hovered over the keyboard, and he whispered to himself as he read whatever he had written on the screen. After a minute, I stepped into the room and he jumped.

"Shit," he said, and leaned back in his chair. "You can't sneak up on me like that."

His eyes raked over my bare chest.

"Sorry," I said, leaning down, I kissed his lips.

"You're forgiven."

"How long have you been awake?" I asked as he yawned.

"Never went to sleep."

I scanned the two large bookshelves against the other wall. "What are you writing?"

"It's a story I've been working on..." His voice trailed off as I picked up one of those Funko things he'd told me about. I stared at the miniature version of Frodo and smiled. "Do you really want to know?"

"Yes." I laughed, turning to give him my attention. "Unless you don't want to tell me."

"It's about this guy... Abel. He fell in love with his best friend, but it didn't work out."

"Sounds sad."

"It is... but Abel gives him another chance."

"Do they end up together in the end?" I asked.

"They do."

It was just a story, and maybe it was ego that had me wondering if it had anything to do with me. Either way, his answer gave me hope.

"Can I read it... when it's done, I mean?"

"I'd love that." He smiled and pointed at the toy in my hand. "I told you I had a problem."

"It's cute," I said.

Setting it down, I walked over to his desk.

"The tiny baby Frodo is cute? Or are you talking about my addiction for Tolkien?"

"Both."

Looking up at me from his desk chair, he reached for my shoulder, pressing his fingers against the purple bruise on my skin. "Sorry about that."

"I'm not."

Thinking about Wild riding me again, his teeth on my skin, his hand in my hair, had me hard and ready for another round. His eyes fell to the growing bulge in my pants as I cupped his chin in the palm of my hand. I trailed the pad of my thumb over his parted lips, his hot breath on my skin made my balls tighten with need.

"I liked watching you lose control like that," I whispered.

"I can tell."

Wild stood, backing me against the desk as he kissed me. With his hands flat against my chest, he dragged them down my overheated skin. He pressed his lips to the mark he'd given me earlier, placing open-mouth kisses over my collarbone and down my chest. My fingers combed through his hair as he lowered himself into the chair, his lips licking and tasting the ridges of my abs, the tip of his nose tracing a line along the V of my hip bone. It didn't matter how many times we fell into each other like this, each kiss he gave me, each touch, was like a fresh start, a brand new damn day, where everything I'd ever wanted was right at the tip of my fingers.

My skin puckered with goosebumps as his thumbs hooked into the band of my sweats. Too slow, he pulled them down, his lips following the trail of blond hair to the base of my dick. He grinned and I gripped the desk as his mouth surrounded the head of my cock. The wet warmth of his tongue slipped over my sensitive skin, and my eyes slammed shut as his eager lips moved along my shaft. My head tipped forward and he pushed a hand into his underwear. He stroked himself, his dark eyes heavy, and the sight of him, all wound up, cheeks flushed, was almost enough to make me come.

"Wild..."

He stood and I framed his face in my hands. Our kiss uncoordinated as I stepped out of my sweats and he shoved down his briefs. With our clothes on the floor, our bodies came together. Muscle and skin and hands and teeth. His entire body trembled as I ran my palm down his back and gripped his ass, my fingers digging into the flesh as I lifted his body. Wild's legs wrapped around my hips as I pushed off the desk. Our lips met, rushed and hungry, his arms hugging my neck. I loved having him in my arms. Loved the weight of him, the way he fit, snug and perfect, against me.

"Couch," was all he managed to say before his tongue slid into my mouth.

He straddled my thighs, his knees pinned against my hips as I sat us down onto the cushions of the small couch. My teeth scraped the delicate skin of his chin, his jaw. My lips finding a home just below his ear. I licked my tongue along the curve of his neck, sucking on the smooth skin until he moaned, until he was marked like me. I pulled back and kissed the bruise.

"Don't be too proud of yourself," he said, his lips breaking into a stunning smile.

I pinched his ass, and he squirmed in my lap.

"God, I want you again," he said, both of us groaning as our dicks rubbed together. "No one makes me feel like you do, Jax."

"Should we go upstairs?"

"No," he panted. "I think I have a condom in my laptop bag."

Wild kissed me as he shifted his weight and moved off my lap. I tracked him as he walked across the room, loving his long legs and the muscle of his thighs. He bent down, rummaging through his bag, and I enjoyed the front-seat view I had of his ass. When he turned around, he caught me staring. I didn't look away, my appreciation for his body visible in the way my dick twitched as he walked toward me with a condom in his hand.

He straddled me again, my hands resting on his thighs as he positioned himself. My fingers curled around his shaft, my thumb circling the head of his cock as he opened the condom and rolled it down the length of my dick. He rocked against me as I kneaded the muscle of his ass with my hands. Spreading his cheeks, I teased him with my finger, pushing just the tip of it inside him.

"Do we need—"

"I'm good," he said, bearing down onto my finger.

A wash of red colored his neck and chest.

"I don't want to hurt you," I whispered.

"Condom has… lube," he said between fevered kisses. "Fuck me," he begged, his eyes clouded with desire as the pad of my finger found his prostate.

Wild lifted up onto his knees, his nails digging into my shoulders as he sank down onto my dick. I didn't move, waiting him out, breathing through the urge to push all the way in. I'd never get used to the way his body swallowed me whole, the trust he gave each time he let me in.

He eased himself down until his ass met my thighs and a hiss escaped my lips. "Fuck, you feel good."

Raising to his knees, he found his rhythm, and I let him ride me until he shook with the need to come. Sitting up as much as I could, I brought our chests together. Wild's arms draped over my shoulders, his hands twisted in my hair as he pulled me closer. My lips against his throat, a flood of heat poured down my spine. I leaned back and he watched as our skin slapped together with each pulse of my hips. I took his dick in my hand, jerking him until we were both grunting.

Wild came hard with a strangled cry, his head thrown back as the heat of his release covered my chest. I pounded into him, filling him over and over, chasing my orgasm until I was spent and sweaty and he fell into my arms. I didn't care about the mess we'd made as I kissed his shoulder and held him against me. My heart a drum in my chest, Wild whispered a breathless "I love you..." against my ear.

I held his face in my palms, tasting those three words on his tongue as I kissed him.

"I love you too, Wild, so damn much."

Having him like this, all to myself, his scent on my skin, his body wrapped tight inside my arms, I had no idea how I'd ever go back to my old life, or how the hell I planned to survive his absence come October.

Chapter 26

WILDER

Whoever coined the phrase "time flies when you're having fun" never accounted for what happened to time when a person was in love. Time was sand through my fingers, or worse, like rain drops during mid-summer, evaporating before they even hit the hot, black asphalt. One second, I had a month, and then the next it was the last Saturday in September. I had a little over a week before I left for Miami, and after Jaxon went back to Marietta tomorrow, I only had one weekend left with him. I had no idea how I would get through this fucking week, all those days wasted, without him. I tried to remember that I'd been lucky enough to get a few extra days here and there this past month when the house he'd been working on had delays. But my melodramatic heart wanted to shout into the void, *who cares, those days are gone now.* I wanted him to stay with me this week. I wanted to be independently wealthy and pay off all the bills he had, make his mother love me, and then take him on tour with me.

Sulking, I observed him from behind the book I was supposed to be reading. Jax was spread out on my living room couch, all rumpled and sex tousled from the blow job I'd given him twenty minutes ago. His legs covered in the soft cotton of his sweats, draped over my lap. I stared at him, committing the image to memory as he scrolled through his phone with one hand, his other dangling off the couch, absently scratching the top of Rosie's head.

Completely unaware of my mental meltdown, his eyes glued to his phone, he said, "Ethan and Jason are headed back from Henderson State Park."

I hummed, pretending to be engrossed in a book I'd read way too many times. Usually Tolkien was enough to quell my anxiety, today though, not so much.

He laughed and his eyes filled with light humor as he lifted his head. "Ethan's been good for him. I never thought Jay would take to camping like he has. Maybe I needed to cut the cord sooner. Apparently, Jason told Ethan that I was free to stay in Georgia as long as I wanted."

I sighed and let my head fall back against the couch.

"What's the matter?" he asked, setting his phone on his chest.

I shut my eyes as I attempted to channel his cheerful mood and pull my shit together.

"Nothing," I said, and he laughed.

I filed the rich sound of it away with the way he looked at me when he said *I love you.*

"I don't believe that for a second." He sat up, and without the weight of his legs to ground me I almost lost it.

"Can you call in sick on Monday... maybe Tuesday too?"

He pulled me into his lap, my book falling to the floor.

"I wish I could, but if I can get this job done sooner, maybe I can come see you at one of your Florida signings."

He'd already given up this weekend with his brother to be with me. Guilt sat sour in my stomach. "I'm being needy."

"I like you needy." He nuzzled his nose into the crook of my neck. "Besides, it's not needy to want to be with your boyfriend, Wild."

The word boyfriend got tucked into the file with the way his lips curled up on one side when he thought I was being funny.

"You could commute for the week?" I tried, but he shook his head.

"I'd never make it to the site on time. Plus, Hudson is already asking about the *chick* I've been shacking up with every weekend. I'm surprised my mom hasn't asked me about it with how much he runs his mouth to anyone who will listen to him in Bell River."

The mention of Hudson, his mom, his closet, grated on me. He said he would tell them once he was back home. But why not tell them now? Why wait? Give them time to reconcile it before he moved back. My old ghosts had started to push through the door I'd sealed shut since Jax had come back into my life.

He tilted my chin with his finger, looking into my eyes, he said, "I don't want to go back to Marietta tomorrow, and I sure as hell don't want you to go to Miami. But this is what we have to do. I'm yours. No amount of time is ever gonna change that."

317

He kissed me, and I memorized the mint taste of his mouth, stashing it next to the way he groaned when I bit his lip. I'd take all these little pieces of him with me and keep them safe. Hoping that when I came home, he'd be here, and all the memories I'd held onto would be something to cherish instead of grieve.

Rosie jumped onto the couch and Jax laughed against my lips as she pushed her way onto our laps.

"Someone's jealous," he said in that sweet, adorable dog voice. He kissed the top of her head before ordering her off the couch. "Get down, baby."

She hopped down and stalked off to the sliding glass door, Gandalf on her tail. They both stood and stared through the glass, Rosie growling at birds while Gandalf weaved through her legs.

"I think Gandalf likes Rosie better than me."

Jaxon's head tipped back as he laughed. "You are definitely feeling needy today."

He grabbed my waist and lifted me until I straddled his thighs. His biceps bunched as he pulled me toward his chest. I loved the way he manhandled me, his firm touch another thing I didn't want to forget. His hands snaked under my shirt, the calluses on his palms dragging across my skin.

"I'm going to miss these hands," I said. "Among other things."

He grinned as he lifted my shirt over my head. "Oh yeah, like what?"

A weird knot of nostalgia stuck in my throat as his fingertips painted goosebumps along my ribs. When

I didn't answer him, his smile fell. Always attuned to my mood, he kissed me like I was this delicate, perfect, creature, like all those pieces of him I'd clutched to my chest were about to scatter in the wind.

"Hey," he said, brushing a thumb over my cheek. "Today is not goodbye, alright?"

"Alright." The word was a thick whisper.

"And next weekend won't be either," he promised. "This trip is not the end of us. It's just a bump in the road."

I didn't want to ruin the last few days I had with him by focusing on how much I would miss him when I was gone, or on the left-over baggage I had from his disappearance back in college.

"Just a bump," I said and kissed him back.

The soft curve of his top lip, the burn of his stubble, the quiet breath he took every time our mouths parted, these were all the things I'd miss, all the things I'd package and put away for when the miles between us began to overwhelm me.

"We could skip lunch with June and Gwen," he said, pressing his mouth to the hollow of my throat.

"Because that wouldn't piss them off at all."

"I think they'd understand." Jax drifted his nails down my back. "Tell them the truth. We only have so much time together and we want to spend it... here."

Smirking, I shook my head. "I'll call her, and you can tell her."

His eyes widened. "Me?"

"Sure... just tell her sorry, we're skipping lunch today because I want to fuck my boyfriend while I still have a chance. And maybe I'll let him fuck me if he's lucky."

He barked out a laugh and squeezed my ass in his hands. "I think that's exactly what I'm gonna say. Grab your phone."

As I reached for it, he tackled me, pinning my back to the couch, and crawled over my body. A breathless laugh escaped me as his green eyes turned dark.

"You could if you wanted to," he said.

"Wanted to what?"

It was clear to me what he meant, but I wanted him to ask for it.

He lowered his lips to my neck, kissing his way along my jaw to my ear and whispered, "To fuck me... if that's what you want."

I'd only had Jax like that once while we were at school, and never with anyone else. I wanted to be with Jax in every possible way if he'd let me.

"I don't want to make you do something you're not comfortable with."

He rolled his hips, his cock hard and ready, showing me just how comfortable he was with the whole idea.

"I want to."

I raked my fingers through his hair as I sat up. The heat between us had always burned quick, igniting with only a hint of spark. Both of us kneeled on the couch, our lips finding each other again. Consumed with the thought of being inside of him, of him giving me his body, his trust, I didn't care if we'd probably be late for lunch, or if we made it at all, or if June hated me for life. All I wanted was him.

Jax pulled his shirt off, the movement making our bodies wobble on the overly soft cushions.

"Should we take this upstairs?" I asked and laughed against his lips.

He nodded and laced his fingers through mine as we made our way up to my room. Rosie padded behind us and gave me a dirty look as I shut the door in her furry little face. When I turned around, Jax lifted his eyebrow.

"What?" I asked, feigning innocence. "It weirds me out when she's in here. It's like she's watching us."

Jax pulled me into his chest. "She probably just thinks we're wrestling."

"Hmm-mm," I hummed as his nose tickled the curve of my neck.

With everything outside the door forgotten, I licked his lips, teasing them with my teeth until he opened for me. Kissing like it was the only language we knew, I backed him into the mattress. We shed our clothes without ceremony, clumsy and inelegant with tension, muscle against muscle, we fell into each other on the bed. Jax sat back, resting his head on a pillow, and I kneeled between his legs. His body was stretched out, every perfect, sculpted edge of him on display. He watched me, with his pupils blown wide, as I stroked his dick. Thick and long, the soft skin was hot in my hand. I took my time, exploring, licking, and sucking his cock as Jax sifted his fingers through my hair, whispering dirty encouragements. His confidence had grown over the past few weeks, and I loved how he'd learned what he wanted and asked for it without hesitation.

I left wet kisses down his shaft and his inner thigh as I spread his legs. His breath hitched, a choked gasp catching in his throat as my tongue licked and teased his ass. My cock ached as Jax begged me for relief. Leaking onto the sheet, desperate for friction, I reached over to grab the lube and condom from the drawer. I squeezed a good amount of the liquid onto my fingers. He hadn't done anything like this in over nine years, and I didn't want to hurt him. Bringing my lips to the head of his dick, my hand rested between his legs, and as the tip of my finger breached that tight ring of muscle, he swore.

"You okay?" I asked, and he leaned up onto his elbows.

"Yeah."

He didn't take his eyes off me as I pushed my finger deeper. His hands clenched into fists at his side as his head fell back.

"I can stop, Jax... if you need me to."

"Feels... good."

His head hit the pillow as I worked a second finger inside of him.

"Oh fuck... God... Wild, I need..." he mumbled, his words disjointed as my fingers brushed his prostate.

"What do you need?" I asked before I took his cock into my mouth again.

A string of incoherent syllables poured past his lips until he uttered one word. "You."

Adding more lube to my fingers I slipped in a third, pushing his limits. Pressing a soft kiss on his thigh, to the patch of pale hair just above his shaft, I stroked him, matching the slow, even rhythm of my fingers, and his cock swelled in my hand. His eyes were closed, his lips open, inviting me to taste them. Leaning over his chest, I dusted my mouth over his. Jax cupped the back of my neck. His tongue warm on my lips as my fingers slipped from between his legs, and I drowned in the tortured, heavy way he kissed me.

Rising back onto my knees, I opened the condom. Overstimulated and sensitive, I grit my teeth as I rolled it on. Jax spread his legs wide for me, his eyes locking on mine as I stroked myself, my fingers slippery with lube.

"Tell me to stop if it hurts."

He nodded as I pressed against his entrance. Breathing hard, dying a little for every second that passed as the head of my cock pushed inside him. He was so fucking tight. I held my body still, not trusting myself to hold off, craving more, and wondering how I'd let myself forget this, forget how amazing he felt.

"Can you take more?"

"Yes..." he panted, his fingers digging into my hips.

I eased in gradually at first, until I couldn't take it anymore, and sank as deep as his body would allow.

"Jesus..." I groaned, bending down, I held the weight of my body with my forearms and kissed him.

Jax placed his heated palms on my waist, and I rolled my hips with lazy thrusts, drawing out each second, until his teeth were at my lips, growling for me to move faster. I pushed his knees back with my hands, earning another inch inside him. I pulled out and he dropped his eyes, watching as I slammed back into him.

The room filled with the scent of him, and I was captivated by the sight of him underneath me, taut muscles flexed and strung out as he beared down on my dick.

"Wild... I..." he stammered as I stroked my fingers down his shaft. "Fuck, yes... like that..."

He thrust into my hand as I pushed into him, each of us racing after our own heart beats. He came with my name on his lips, his climax taking me with him as I swore through my release. Jax sucked in a breath as I pulled out, and I fell on top of him, out of breath, sticky and covered with sweat. We lay like that, my cheek against the damp skin of his shoulder, his hand in my hair, his finger twisted around my curls as his breath steadied beneath me.

"I think you have what it takes to be a power bottom," I said and he laughed.

Lifting my head, I was greeted with an easy smile.

"Was that okay for you?" I asked.

"Judging by the size of the mess you're lying in, I'd say I enjoyed myself."

"That's kind of hot... I feel proud."

His chuckle rumbled in his chest. "I love how humble you are."

"And I love you," I said, and Jax brought his hands to my face, kissing me with soft and tender lips. "I don't want to move... But we should probably get in the shower."

When I didn't budge, Jax pressed a quick kiss to my lips and smacked my ass. "Tell you what... If you get up now, I'll call in sick on Monday."

"Really?"

"I want another day with you," he said, and I could see my smile mirrored in his eyes.

*   *   *

We'd arrived ten minutes late at the small creperie June wanted to try, and according to Gwen, still rocking the post-coital glow. Starving, I'd ordered enough food for all four of us, and was grateful Jax helped me finish the majority of it.

Jax had just popped a strawberry in his mouth when Gwen said, "June never gave me many details about how y'all met. You were his tutor, right?"

"For chemistry, our sophomore and junior year," I said.

"Come on, Wilder..." June took a sip of her mimosa. "You know you crushed on him longer than that... First semester of your freshman year is what you told me, if I remember correctly."

Jax met my gaze. "You never told me that."

Fucking June.

Grinning, she raised her eyebrows. "He didn't know?"

I picked up a blueberry and threw it at her. "I hate you."

Gwen's face was lit with a wide smile. "Wait... wait... wait," she said, waving her hands. "I want the whole story."

"Imagine if you will... a little baby Wilder sitting in a library—"

Laughing, I kicked June under the chair. "I can tell my own story. *I* am the writer, after all."

Jax gave me my favorite crooked smile. "You saw me in the library?"

"I did," I said, my face heating. "It was my first semester at Eastchester. I saw you at the reference desk." I shrugged. "You're kind of hard to miss."

"Aw…" Gwen beamed. "I can feel the swoon all the way over here."

June pointed her fork at Jax. "He used to go to your games."

"I am not above murdering you in public," I said, but my tone lacked any real ire.

"You did?" he asked.

"Only a few," I lied.

"So how did you end up tutoring him?" Gwen asked.

"We shared a chemistry class," Jax said, his eyes still on mine. "He was always answering all the teacher's questions."

"Of course, he was." June smirked, and I rolled my eyes.

Gwen leaned her elbows on the table. "Were you questioning your sexuality back then? Or did you know you were gay?"

"You don't have to answer that," I said.

I glared at Gwen and her eyes widened. "Shit. Sorry I didn't mean to—"

"It's okay." Jax took my hand in his. "I knew I was gay, but I'd never acted on it. I was messed up over it… if I'm being honest, but being around Wild made it easier sometimes."

"How?" I asked and ignored the prying eyes of my friends.

"You were confident all the time, and I admired that. I looked up to you," he said. "It wasn't always easy though... you were so damn cute... I think I almost failed that first chemistry class because I couldn't concentrate with you sitting next to me."

"The first class?" I asked. "That was sophomore year... we didn't hook up until junior year."

He laughed and rubbed the back of his neck. "I know."

Shocked, I stared at him. "I wish I would have known."

"What was the tipping point?" June asked.

"I'm not sure what you mean," he said.

"What made you finally give in to your feelings for Wilder?"

"It got too hard... fighting it all the time," he said. "We fell asleep studying one night, and when I woke up his head was on my chest."

"You ran your fingers through my hair," I said, the memory as vivid as it had always been.

"You guys are killing me right now." June stared at her girlfriend who looked like she was about to cry. "Look... she's crying."

"It's so sweet, though," Gwen said, wiping at her cheeks. "Look how far y'all have come."

"All thanks to me," June said, patting herself on the shoulder. "Anytime y'all wanna thank me, I'm here for it."

"Thank you," Jax said in earnest, and I squeezed his hand under the table.

"Sorry about that," I whispered to Jax as Gwen asked June something about work.

"I don't mind it," he said as his phone vibrated on the table.

He turned it over and his brother's name flashed across the screen. He rejected the call, but before he could set it down, his phone vibrated again.

"It's Ethan," he said, a crease forming between his brow.

"Answer it. It might be important."

The call went to voicemail before he had a chance to answer it. Jax pressed his finger against the screen, lifted his phone to his ear, and his face paled.

"What's wrong?" June asked and I shook my head.

After several long seconds, he lowered his phone. Refusing to meet my eyes, he said, "I have to go."

"Go where?" I asked but he didn't answer. "Jax... go where?"

"Home."

He stood abruptly, and in his panic, dropped my hand.

"To Marietta?" I asked.

"No... Bell River."

Chapter 27

JAX

"Jaxon," Wild said my name and it cut through the noise in my head as I stormed out of the restaurant. He grabbed my wrist, his eyes wide and worried. "What the fuck's happening right now?"

"I'm sorry..." I pressed the heel of my hands against my forehead... Overwhelmed, I didn't know what to do. "Shit."

"Is everything okay?"

My nostrils flared as I swallowed through the burn in my throat. "I... I don't know. Jason was hysterical. I couldn't understand what the hell he was saying."

"Did Ethan leave a message too?"

Wild held my hand, his thumb rubbing small circles into my palm. I needed his touch more than ever as everything, my life, started to fall down around me.

"All he said was my mom found out he's gay and that some shit went down, and I needed to call him as soon as fucking possible." Wild's thumb froze against my skin. "Can we go... I need to call my brother."

"Give me a second," he said, and brushed his lips against mine. "Let me pay our bill."

Wild let go of my hand and walked back into the restaurant, and even with the sun high in the sky, I was cold. I didn't have enough space in my head right now to worry about what June or Gwen thought about me, or how I'd acted like I'd lost my mind. All I wanted to do was call Jason, but not here on the sidewalk where everyone who passed by could watch as my world was decimated. How did my mom find out about Ethan? Did she know about me? How upset was she? Why was Jason crying like someone had died? These questions looped around my neck and strangled me as I waited for Wild. After a few minutes he was back by my side. His hand in mine made the panic in my chest less painful as we walked to the car.

"At least call Ethan," he said as we backed out of the parking stall. "That way you know the whole story before you talk to Jason."

"That's a good idea."

I opened up my recent calls and pressed my thumb on Ethan's name. The phone rang almost four times before he picked up.

"Jax... Shit... I'm sorry, man."

"Sorry for what?" I couldn't breathe. "Did she find out that I'm..."

"No... just me."

Relief exhaled from my lungs. I still had a chance to tell her myself.

"Jason left me a message, crying, but I couldn't understand him. What the hell happened?"

"Listen..." He sighed. "Your mom... I don't think she's a bad person, alright?"

"Tell me what that means, Ethan."

Wild placed a comforting hand on my leg as my body started to shake.

"I went on a date with this guy I met online Thursday. I guess someone saw us kissing. They recognized me because of all the time I've been spending with Jay. They told your mom while we were on our way back from camping this morning. I'm so sorry, Jaxon. I should've been more careful."

"Don't be sorry." I sank back into the passenger seat and pinched the bridge of my nose. Wild gave me an anxious look as we pulled into his driveway. "Who you kiss is your own damn business."

"Not according to your mom," he said, the underlying anger in his voice rising to the surface. "When we got back today... it was bad, Jax. Your momma was fit to be tied. I don't think I can repeat some of the things she said to me, but it's safe to say I'm no longer welcome in your life or Jason's."

"What?"

All the things I'd hope for shattered.

"It is what it is," he said. "I don't know if you can, but I think you need to come home. Jason is a mess, and he doesn't understand what's going on."

"I'll head back today." I wiped my palm over my face. "I'll tell Jim I have a family emergency. He'll understand."

"The way she feels about me has nothing to do with you. I'm not her son... she has no reason not to hate me. But she loves you, Jax."

"Yeah." The ache in my throat was unbearable. "I need to call Jason."

"Let me know when you're back?" he asked.

"I'll text you when I get into town. And I'm sorry she treated you like that."

"Like I said… it is what it is. I just want to make sure Jason's alright."

I ended the call after I promised to give him an update on Jason as soon as I had one. With the phone in my lap, I dropped my face into my hands and broke down. These past few weeks I'd allowed myself to hope. Allowed myself to imagine a life with Wild and my family. Together. I didn't want to choose between living a life with the man I loved or living a lie with my family alone.

Happiness or guilt.

Love or obligation.

I was torn down and suffocating.

Wild whispered my name, the weight of his palm on my back a reminder of how much I had to lose.

"Tell me what to do for you." I lifted my head, and the fear in his eyes almost crippled me. "What can I do?"

He brushed a thumb over my cheek, and I leaned into his hand. "My mom told Ethan he's no longer welcome in our lives because he's gay."

"Jax…"

"I have to go home, Wild. I have to try and fix this."

He lowered his hand to his lap and stared out the driver-side window. "How do you think you're going to fix it?"

"I don't know… maybe I can talk some sense into her."

He didn't look at me. "Maybe."

"Wild..." I lifted his hand from his lap. "This doesn't change anything." Once I'd said it, I could feel the truth in the words.

This wasn't the way I wanted to come out to my family, but maybe with some time, while Wild was on his book tour, I could figure out a way to get through to her, help her see that Ethan hadn't changed just because he was gay. He was the same great guy who loved Jason like his own brother. If she could see that, then maybe she'd accept me too. Maybe she'd look at me and see her son and not a stranger.

"Let's go inside." Wild let go of my hand and opened his door. "You should call your brother, let him know you're coming home."

We made our way up the walkway and into the house, Wild's silence a wall between us. He was in his head. I wanted to know what he was thinking, if he was here in the present, worried like me about what to do next, or was he back in Eastchester, worried about whether or not I would hurt him again. He set the keys on the coffee table as I let Rosie out back. When I turned around, his back was to me, his hands gripping the kitchen counter, his shoulders tight.

"You have every reason not to believe me... but I promise you, Wild." I slid my arms around his waist, and he leaned into me. "I'm not gonna vanish when I go back to Bell River."

"Okay," he said, but the doubt was there in the way his heart raced under my hand as I placed it on his chest. "It's not ideal, but maybe this is the thing you needed... to force you to tell her who you really are."

"I'm gonna tell her... I just need to see what kind of mess I'm walking into first."

Wild faced me, chest to chest, his eyes met mine. "And if she throws you out? What then?"

The thought turned my veins to ice. The terror in Jason's voice as he'd left me that message, he'd come to depend on Ethan, losing me would destroy him.

"I wish I had an answer, but I don't." He pulled away and my arms fell to my sides. "Maybe if I give her time to calm down... I don't want to rush it and have it blow up in my face."

"Rush it?" He laughed without humor.

Anger rolled off his shoulders as he paced the living room. The trust he'd gifted to me faded with each step he took.

"I just need you to give me some time."

"All I have ever given you is time, Jax."

"I told you this morning that today wasn't a goodbye and I meant it. Whether I leave now, or you leave next week. We knew this wasn't gonna be easy."

"How much longer do you need before it's the right moment to tell her? A month? A year... or maybe nine." His eyes glassy, he said, "You know what... take all the time you need, but I'm taking my time back. I can't do it, Jax. I can't watch you leave again. Because I know what's going to happen."

"You don't know..." I said, raising my voice.

Wild crossed his arms over his chest, closing himself up, and shutting me out as I walked toward him.

"You're not giving me a chance."

"I thought I already did." Wild turned away from me as my phone rang in my pocket. "You better answer that."

He picked up his car keys from the table.

"Where are you going?"

He was slipping away.

"I need some air." His bright eyes flat, he turned to open the front door. "I assume you'll be gone by the time I get back?"

"Wild... wait." My voice cracked, and he stopped inside the doorway. "I love you."

"I love you, too." His words trembled as he turned to look at me with tears running down his cheeks. "It'll never be enough though."

"I know you think I'm lying..." I said, my entire body shaking with the urge to reach out and pull him into my arms. I couldn't lose him again. "You think I'm gonna go back to Bell River and forget the promises I made to you. To myself. You can walk out that door, Wild... But it doesn't mean I'm not gonna come back for you."

"I'll believe it when I see it," he said, and shut the door, leaving me behind like I'd left him nine years ago.

* * *

The weather was shit on my way back to Bell River, adding another hour to my drive. It had taken me a solid thirty minutes to calm Jason down once I'd had a chance to call him. And by the time I spoke with Jim, packed my shit, and got Rosie ready, the afternoon was half gone. The sun had set about two hours ago, and as I pulled up the gravel driveway to my house, I was surprised all the lights were on. I figured my mom would have told Jason to go to bed early, hoping to avoid a fight with me, but as my headlights lit up the front door, it opened. Jason peeked his head out, and when he realized it was me, he came running.

I put the car in park and left the engine on as I got out. Jason slammed into me, breathing hard, his arms cinched around me like a vise. He shuddered as I squeezed him back. I hadn't been away from my brother for this long since before the accident, and having him in my arms, seeing him cry like this, it sent me over the edge. A sob wrenched past my lips, and I held him tighter, afraid to let go, afraid of what would happen when I walked through that front door. Everything poured out of me, the fight I had with Wild, the uncertainty of what would happen between us, and the hope I had that maybe it would all be okay.

"I missed you so much, Jax."

Taking a ragged breath, I found my voice. "God, buddy, I missed you, too."

Rosie barked from the back seat, and Jason's head shot up, rubbing at his nose with the back of his hand. His eyes were swollen from crying, but as he got a better look into the car, a smile burst across his cheeks.

"You got a dog?" he hollered and ran for the car.

Rosie jumped out as he opened the back door and took off running. She wheeled around when I whistled, and almost took Jason out at the knees.

"I got her for you," I said.

"No way." He scratched her behind the ears, and as he bent down, she licked his face. "What's her name."

"Rosie."

He wrinkled his nose. "That's a dumb name, Jax."

Laughing, I asked, "You know how much you like the *Goonies*?"

"Yeah, it's the best movie ever."

"That's how I feel about *Lord of the Rings*."

"That's the really long movie you watch sometimes?"

"Yeah, a good friend of mine made me watch it and I loved it. I even read all the books. Rosie's named for one of the characters."

"Cool," he said unimpressed, and she licked his face again. "Do you think Mom will let us keep her?"

"I already got her permission."

He stood up and glanced back at the house. "She might not let me have Rosie now."

"Why do you say that? Because of what happened today?"

He pushed his hands into the pockets of his gym shorts. "Yeah."

I pulled him into a hug. "That's got nothing to do with you, alright?"

"Jaxon?" My mom called from the porch and Rosie ran toward her.

"Hey, Momma. Let me grab my stuff. I'll come inside in a minute." Jason turned in on himself, his mood shifting. "Would you look after Rosie while I talk to Mom? There's food for her in the back seat. I bet she's hungry."

"Can I show her my room?"

"You better, that's where she'll sleep."

His smile returned as he called her name. I handed him the food from the back, and when he headed inside, I shut off the engine and grabbed my things. I left the crate, folded up in the trunk for now, figuring Jason would benefit from having Rosie by his side as much as possible.

Being away hadn't changed anything, not that I thought it would, but as I walked into the house, it no longer felt like my home.

"She sure is cute," Mom said from the kitchen as Rosie trotted around her legs. "Jason loves her already."

"She's easy to love."

Jason patted his leg and Rosie followed him toward his bedroom.

"How was the drive? I heard it was raining cats and dogs along I-85." Mom moved around the kitchen, trying to make herself look busy. Fussing over nothing, she kept her eyes on the counter as she wiped it.

"What happened today, Momma?"

She raised her eyebrows, her lips pinched tight. "Well, I'm sure that ... *friend* of yours told you everything you need to know. It's embarrassing, having Jason running around with that boy."

"I want to hear it from you." She didn't answer, avoiding me, she kept cleaning. "Momma, stop, you're gonna wear a hole in the damn counter."

"Did you know, Jax... that he was a homosexual?" she whispered the last word.

The guilt I'd once harbored bled into rage. "What if I did? Ethan's a good man. He's good for Jason."

Her tone was quiet and clipped. "Whether or not he's a good man is for God to decide, but he is not *good* for Jason. What if he'd try something, Jaxon?"

It was like Hudson all over again. But this time the hate spewed from the woman who'd raised me to believe it was my life goal to be Christ-like. She wasn't being very Christian right now.

"Please tell me you're not that ignorant, Momma? What about all that shit you preach about God loving us as we are, as he made us?"

"Jaxon Stettler, do not swear in this house."

"But it's okay for you to hate? God made Ethan that way."

"It's a choice, Jaxon... He chooses to live in sin."

"It's not a choice," I shouted, and she stepped back toward the sink and away from me.

"What would you know about it?" she whispered, her hands trembling.

My tongue was fat in my mouth, the words pushing at my lips. The past few weeks with Wild, every smile, every touch, the happiness he'd given me, I was stronger for it. I was tired of lying. I didn't need time. I needed to tell my truths. My heart was spinning inside my chest, but I held onto the confidence I'd gained and said what I should've said years ago.

"The night Dad died... we prayed, remember?"

"I do." Tears welled in her eyes as she stared at me.

"I wanted to swap places with Dad, with Jason. I would have too... There were so many times, after

339

that night, that I wished I was dead. Wished that I was anybody else but me." She used the towel she had clutched in her hands to wipe at her eyes, her tears falling fast and furious as I spoke. "I promised God that night, if he let Jason live, I'd change. I'd be the good son you needed me to be. But the thing is, Mom... I can't change. I'm gay. I didn't choose this, this is who I am. This is how He made me."

"It's a sin, Jax." She shook her head, the disappointment on her face cut me open.

"Love is not a sin."

She didn't reach out to me or hug me like I'd hoped. She just stood there, silent, as I let myself cry.

"You're in love with Ethan?" she asked.

"No."

"Oh..." she said, relieved.

"I have a boyfriend."

Mom lifted her hand to her chest and rubbed her knuckles into the bone.

"Here...in Bell River?"

"He lives in Atlanta. We used to go to school together back at Eastchester." She wrung the towel in her hands, her eyes anywhere but on her son. "I love him, Momma."

"Jaxon, I... I don't know what to say. I raised you one way, and now..."

"I'm not any different than I was yesterday. And neither is Ethan," I said. "Deep down you know that. And you know that God would want you to accept us as we are. What are you gonna do? Throw me out? Keep *me* from seeing Jason?"

"Jaxon," she gasped. "I'd never do such a thing. You're my blood."

"And what? Ethan is trash?" I asked.

I was relieved, knowing I wouldn't lose Jason, and it made it easier for me to call her on her bullshit.

She tried to walk past me, but I blocked her. "I don't wanna talk about this anymore. I'm tired."

"Look at me..." The stern lines in her face relaxed as she met my eyes. "I'm still me. I'm still your son."

"I know that," she said, another round of tears falling. "I love you... no matter what. But I don't know what to think about... any of it."

"Love the sinner, hate the sin?"

"I have no hate in my heart for you," she said, and I pulled her into a hug.

Mom kept her hands by her side at first, exhaling into my chest, she wrapped them around me.

"Why's everyone crying?" Jason asked as he walked into the kitchen with Rosie at his side. "Is it because of Ethan? Can he still be my friend?"

"It's late, Jay," Mom said, pulling back from my embrace. "We can talk about it in the morning."

"I don't care if he likes to kiss boys, he's good at fishing and can start a fire in less than twenty seconds."

Despite the heavy mood, my mom smiled as I laughed.

"Come on, Jay... let's get ready for bed," I said. "You can tell me about camping."

"I think Rosie has to pee." Jason opened the back door and Rosie ran outside.

"Head on into your room." I rumpled his hair with my hand, and he cringed. "I'll let her in when she's finished."

Pouting like no one else could, Jason kissed Mom on the cheek and went to his room. I expected my mom to follow behind him, but she lingered in the kitchen. Exhausted, I didn't know what else to say, and when Rosie scratched on the back door, I let her in.

"I'm gonna get ready for bed." I grabbed a bowl from the cabinet to fill with water for the dog. "I'll see you in the morning."

"What's his name?" she asked. "Your… boyfriend."

The lump in my throat swelled. "Wilder."

She nodded her head, chewing at the corner of her lip.

"And he's good to you?"

"He's the best thing that's ever happened to me."

She squeezed my arm. "Good night, son."

"'Night, Momma," I said, holding on to hope.

Chapter 28

WILDER

Thunder clapped outside the sliding glass door at the same time a bright burst of lightning lit up the sky. Gandalf jumped and skittered across my bedroom, diving under the bed like he was down to the last of his nine lives. Of course, the minute I decided to leave early, adding Ft. Lauderdale to my tour, a hurricane would show up. It was off the coast but had spawned some of the worst weather I'd seen all year. I didn't mind flying. But flying during a monsoon on steroids was not something my depressed ass wanted to deal with. I wanted to get on the plane tomorrow, drink myself sick with cheap wine, and fall into my hotel room. Pass out until I forgot how much I missed Jaxon. As if he could sense I'd been thinking about him, my phone chirped on the nightstand. I'd given him his own notification sound. I didn't want to take a chance and accidentally open one of his texts and start the entire grieving process all over again. He hadn't sent any emails yet, which I was grateful for. It wasn't like I could ignore my business messages because I broke up with my boyfriend.

I shut my suitcase and stared at the bed. The silence too heavy, his presence here had started to haunt me. I could see his head on my pillow, his smile in the morning. Hear his voice laughing at something I'd said. My entire house reminded me of him. I'd washed my sheets, scrubbed my shower, vacuumed the couches, and opened the widows in my office every day, but I couldn't get rid of his scent. It was in my head, suffocating me. This wasn't a break-up. It was worse. Because even though I didn't believe a word Jax had said, I'd somehow allowed myself to hope. It was precisely this reason why I didn't read his text messages or answer his calls. I didn't want to hear any more of his lip service or his bullshit promises. It'd been five days since he'd left, and if he really meant what he'd said, wouldn't he have come back by now? Those messages were nothing more than his way of stringing me along, and just like nine years ago, I'd be discarded while he lived his great and terrible straight life. Jax had used me again. He used me to play out a fantasy of a life he'd never intended to live.

The phone rang, and sure enough, his name flashed on the screen like a punch to the gut. My hand hovered over the phone, my fingers unsteady as my heart warned me with a pulse that stuttered and jumped. Tears gathered along my lashes, and as I blinked, they escaped down my cheeks. When the phone went silent, I exhaled, and tried to rub away the tingling sensation in my palms on my jeans.

"Shit," I shouted, irritated with myself.

Gandalf crawled out from under the bed, most likely to see what the hell I was going on about. He hopped onto the mattress, sat on top of my suitcase, and butted his head into my hand until I scratched him under his chin. Purring, he stalked over to Jax's pillow and made himself comfortable. But it wasn't Jax's pillow, not anymore. I picked up my phone with the intention of deleting his text like I had at least hundred times this week, but that feeling in my fingertips returned. Sharp, like when I'd slept on my arm, or sat funny for too long, and all the blood rushed to the nerve endings. The text was a bomb. Cut the blue wire and delete it or cut the red wire and destroy my heart again. The doorbell rang and I didn't get a chance to decide.

June had persuaded me to let her come over tonight. She said she would help me pack, and that she wanted to hang out one last time before I left. But I figured this little visit was more of a welfare check than a friendly farewell. By the time I made it downstairs, she'd started to knock. The woman had zero patience.

"Why are you so annoying?" I asked as I opened the door.

She gave me a saccharine grin.

"Well, hello to you, too," she said, pushing her way past me. "It's nice of you to come check on me, June."

"Thank you for coming over," I said in the most robotic voice I could muster. "I don't know how I would have ever survived without your immense greatness."

She shoved my shoulder and tossed her purse onto my couch. "I mean... it's true though."

"Want a glass of wine?" I asked. "I'm having two."

"So it's gonna be that kind of night..." she said. "In that case, don't be stingy, make it a big glass."

"White or red?"

"Red."

I grabbed the largest wine goblets I could find and filled them almost to the top. June laughed as I handed her a glass.

"You weren't playing," she said and carefully brought it to her lips.

Curling a leg underneath me, I sat on the other side of the couch. "You're late... I finished packing already."

"That was fast," she said. "How many suitcases?"

"Three."

She stared at me like I had two heads.

"Wow... how minimalist of you."

"I know... I figured I couldn't shove Gandalf in there, so why bother taking much of anything else. Thanks for watching him while I'm gone."

"He's basically mine anyway."

I took a large gulp of wine, draining half the glass.

"Are you nervous about the flight? Or are you trying to get alcohol poisoning."

"This weather isn't exactly the best for air travel."

"They said it's supposed to let up some by morning... They take off during storms all the time." I avoided her eyes and took another long sip. "It's gonna be fine."

"I'm nervous about a lot of things, I guess."

She waited for me to elaborate, and when I didn't, she asked, "Are you still avoiding him?"

"If deleting all of his texts and not answering any of his calls means I'm avoiding him... then yes, definitely."

"Wilder," she said in a tone that made me feel like I was five years old. "You just love to create your own drama, don't you?"

"Excuse me? I'm not the one who left... again."

"What if he told his mom and he wanted you to know? What if something bad has happened? What if he wants to tell you he's sorry, that he wants to come back, but won't because he doesn't know how *you* feel."

I barked out an annoyed laugh. "He knows how I feel."

She narrowed her eyes. "He does? How? You won't talk to the man. He told you he was coming back, didn't he?"

"That's what he said last time."

"This isn't like the last time. He's *trying* to talk to you, he's not MIA."

Angry, I stood and grabbed my glass, finishing it in one swallow.

"Sit down, Wilder, I didn't come over here to argue."

I sat down, setting the empty glass on the table.

"Why can't you stay out of my business?"

June's face fell.

"Because you can't seem to get out of your own goddamn way. I know you have trust issues and abandonment triggers. Your parents, for example... people who were supposed to love you unconditionally, abandoned you. You act like it didn't affect you when they cut you off, and that's bullshit." Truth infiltrated the air, stealing my breath. "This isn't just about Jax. That man loves you and you know it. It's all over his face when he looks at you."

"He loved me back at Eastchester too," I said, an attempt to protect the fragile shield I walked around with every day.

I wouldn't let my parents' choice define me.

"I'd like to remind you that you said you'd forgiven him for that."

"I have."

June hummed as she took a drink.

"Maybe I haven't entirely forgiven him but—"

"You didn't give him a chance to prove you wrong... You're protecting your fragile, dark, little heart. Hurt him before he hurts you." She shrugged her shoulders. "I get it. It's called self-preservation."

"Did you get a therapy degree in the time since I saw you last?" I asked, unable to contain my smirk. "Or is the hospital practicing mindfulness again?"

"You're an asshole, I don't know why I even bother," she said, but I saw the smile in her eyes.

I pulled my phone from my pocket, and without thinking about it too much I threw it into her lap. Anxious, I said, "You think you know him so well, read the text he sent me tonight. I haven't opened it yet. Maybe with you here I won't have a nervous breakdown when he tells me we're over for good."

She picked up the phone and rolled her eyes. "You're dramatic as hell."

"Tell me something I don't know."

She ignored me, her attention on the screen of the phone. I watched her face for some kind of hint, my stomach and heart fighting their way up my throat. But her expression gave away nothing.

"It doesn't say much," she said and dropped it into her lap.

I stared at her. "What the hell did it say?"

"Read it yourself, Wilder."

Groaning, I snatched the phone from her lap.

Jax: Wanted to tell you good night.

Jesus Christ.

I heard his voice in my head, saw his green eyes watching me, nose to nose, with our heads on those damn bedroom pillows, and like someone had opened up a flood gate, I started to cry. Soundlessly, June moved across the couch and pulled me into a hug.

"Just call him."

"I can't." I pulled away and wiped the back of my hand across my face. "If he tells me it's over for real, June, I'll never be able to get on that plane tomorrow."

"You don't text a person to say good night if you're about to break their heart," she said.

"Jax would. He's polite like that." We both laughed, the giant glass of wine I'd downed started to make my head dizzy.

"Just sleep on it, call him in the morning."

"Maybe I will," I said, knowing damn well it was a lie.

❋ ❋ ❋

Rain poured down the windows of the airport. Every seat at the gate appeared to be taken, the room crammed with travelers and kids screaming. It smelled like stale hot dogs, the air overly warm and sticky with humidity. Instead of trying to find a seat, I leaned against the wall.

Thanks to the bottle of wine I'd finished off with June last night, my head pounded. I shifted my bag and rummaged through it, checking for the tenth time that I had my wallet and ticket. I don't know why I thought I'd lost it on the way from security to the gate, but the Atlanta airport had a funny way of turning even the calmest person into a total nervous wreck. A toddler bumped into my leg, and his mother gave me a tired smile that made me feel less stressed than I had a few seconds before.

My assistant had made sure everything was in order. I had a first-class ticket. My books had been shipped to all the stores. He'd updated my calendar with my Ft. Lauderdale signing. There shouldn't be anything for me to worry about. All I had to do was show up. I should be excited, this was what I'd always dreamed about. But instead, like the sky outside, the storm inside me raged on. I hadn't received any correspondence from Jax this morning. He usually texted me around eight every day, but it was after ten and nothing had come through. I could hear June's voice in my head, chastising me. Telling me I'd better call him before he gave up on us. The logical side of my brain said she was right. I should call him, hash things out. If it was over, then at least I had closure. And if it wasn't over—I couldn't let the idea take root. I'd learned from Jaxon himself how dangerous it was to hope for shit.

Wanting to be numb, I pulled my phone from my pocket, and launched a gaming app. I'm not sure how long I zoned out, but eventually the intercom overhead snapped on and they announced that boarding would begin in fifteen minutes. When I shut the app, I saw I had an email notification. Not thinking about it, I opened the email and almost dropped my phone when I read the subject line.

FROM: fool0fatook54@bellinx.mail.com
TO: wildwelleslit@bartpress.com
Date: Oct 4 11:06 AM
SUBJECT: I told my mom

Wild,

I told my mom. I told her the day I got home. She knows about you, knows I'm in love with you. Coming out didn't go as terrible as I thought it would, but it isn't perfect. She's not ready for pride parades or anything like that. To be honest, she hasn't said much to me. It's different now. The space she's put up between us, maybe she needs it. I feel like a stranger in my own house. But I guess this isn't my house anymore. My home is with you, Wild. I want to talk to you, hear your voice. I didn't want to tell you like this, but since you won't answer your phone, I wanted to make sure you knew what happened. I kept my promise. I'm coming back to you. I can't leave today, there's still too much going on. But I might be able to come up on Monday. See you before you leave for Miami.

I love you,
Jax~

I read the message through bleary eyes, sobbing in the middle of the airport terminal. He'd done this big, amazingly brave thing and had gone through it all alone.

I feel like a stranger in my own house.

I'd abandoned him.

I was too worried about protecting myself and I turned my back on him when he needed me the most.

A couple of flight attendants, and who I assumed was the pilot, walked past me and through the gate door. I swore, hating myself enough for both me and Jax. One, for booking another tour date, and two, for being a stubborn, selfish asshole who couldn't pick up a fucking phone. With shaky hands, I scrolled through my contacts and called him. The phone rang a few times, and when he didn't pick up right away, my stomach tied into a million knots.

It rang and rang until finally he answered, "I didn't think you'd call."

His voice was honey. Warm and thick.

"I'm sorry," I said through a gulp of air. "I'm such an idiot."

"I know why you shut me out, doesn't mean it didn't hurt." He sighed. "I want to be mad at you, Wild. I want to call you out for not trusting me like you said you would. I can't keep trying to atone for the past."

"You should be furious with me."

"My whole life has been a fight. I'm tired of it. I just want to be happy."

"You deserve all the happiness, Jax. All of it."

An announcement aired over the intercom, the lady's voice too mumbled to understand.

"Where are you?"

"The airport," I said, wishing I was home, waiting for him.

"I thought you didn't leave till Wednesday,"

"Anders asked me if I'd go to Ft. Lauderdale and I agreed. I didn't know—"

"You're going to Ft. Lauderdale with Anders?" he asked, his voice rough and worn.

"No... Jesus... for a signing, he's not with me." I heard him exhale through the phone. "I swapped my Tallahassee stop with Ft. Lauderdale. I missed you so much, Jax. I couldn't sit around that condo anymore."

"I miss you more than you'll ever know."

"Are you okay..." I asked. "With everything... with your mom, I mean?"

"It's rocky... but I think she's gonna be okay. She's got a lot to figure out," he said. "At least she's letting Jason hang out with Ethan again."

"That's a good sign."

"Yeah... he's way more forgiving than I would've been."

I wanted to ask him what had happened, and if she'd said anything to hurt him. I wanted to know how it all transpired, how he'd finally come out to his family and changed his life. I wanted to know if we were okay, but just like always, time was not on my side.

"They're going to board the plane soon," I said. "Will you go back to Marietta?"

"Jim had to replace me, couldn't have me out this long without screwing up the schedule. I'm gonna start on a new project here until I can find a job in Marietta or Atlanta. Jim said he'd put in a good word for me if I found something. I've been looking every day."

"You have?"

"When are you gonna start believing me?" he asked. "I'm done waiting, Wild. I'm coming home as soon as I can."

"You're my home, too," I said, the rasp in my voice gave away how close I was to breaking down. "I wish I didn't have to leave. I'm pissed that I wasted time being an asshole."

"We've both wasted a lot of time. Maybe if we stop keeping track, time won't matter anymore."

An infinite number of days sprawled out before me. Early mornings, maple donuts, and sex before noon. Coffee and messy hair and sleep swollen lips.

"I like that," I said. "Just us, no more past or present."

"Me and you... Wild... it's all I want."

Chapter 29

JAX

"It's a day program." Ethan reached across the table and grabbed the ketchup.

"Is it... like a school or something?" Jason asked, his expression pinched and uncomfortable.

"Yeah.... You go in the mornings. Plus, it's by the beach. It's supposed to be an amazing program."

"How did you hear about it?" I asked.

"You know the new guy at Harley's?"

"Chance."

"His sister goes four days a week. She loves Benchmark. He said she works one on one with an occupational therapist who specializes in TBI rehabilitation. And, there's the whole social aspect... he has the opportunity to make some friends."

"Friends?" Jason stared at his burger, twisting his napkin in his hands.

"Don't you get tired of sitting 'round the house with Momma all the time?" I asked. "This could be good for you, buddy."

"What if no one there likes to fish?" Jason raised his eyes.

"I'm sure someone might." I placed my hand on his arm and he relaxed. "Tell you what... why don't you, Momma, and I check it out, and if you hate it, we'll never talk about it again."

"And if I think it's stupid I don't have to go?"

"I promise."

His apprehension fading, he agreed. "Okay... I like that it's by the beach."

I wished they would have had something like this nearby when he'd had his accident. Who knew what possibilities he missed out on because we lived in the sticks? He'd work so hard on his physical therapy, but the doctors had made it seem like he'd always be stuck developmentally. It wasn't good to dwell on what could have been, medical stuff changed all the time, and if this school could help him, then I'd do everything I could to pay for it.

"I'll ask Chance to email me the info tomorrow at work and send it to you."

"Thanks. I really appreciate it."

I was afraid to even think about it, for fear that I might jinx myself, but everything had begun to click into place. Two weeks ago, when I'd left Georgia, I had no idea how I would get through it all. I had no idea if Wild would let me back in, or if my mom would throw me out. I could've lost everyone I cared about. But I was glad Wild had taught me to be brave. My life wasn't perfect by any means. Mom was distant, but every day she made some progress. This morning she'd asked me where Wild's next tour stop was. I'd tried not to look too surprised, afraid I'd make her change her mind about asking me things. It was one question, but it was a big step. I could see her changing. She'd stopped talking to Ms. Arlene. That old bat had the nerve to tell Mom she was going to hell for allowing Jason to hang out with Ethan. I don't doubt that my mom might've agreed with her, but she hadn't allowed it to alter her decision. It made me hope she'd taken what I'd said to heart the night I'd come out to her. No, things definitely were not perfect, but the possibilities I had now felt endless.

"What's going on with that job you applied for in Atlanta?" Ethan asked.

"They scheduled an interview two weeks out," I said. "The pay is better than what Jim ever gave me, and when I get my contracting license I'll be set."

"That's awesome." Ethan laughed when Jason grumbled. "Or maybe it's not..."

"I'd get Fridays off, Jay. I could come home for long visits sometimes... and if you do end up liking that school, you'll forget about me anyway." I smiled around a bite of cheeseburger when he scowled.

"I would not," he said, adamant.

"I'm just joking, bud."

His eyes widened and his face brightened. "Could I come visit you and your boyfriend?" he asked, too loud, and I swear to God the whole diner went quiet.

Ethan snickered and I coughed, choking on the burger I'd just swallowed.

"Sure, Jay," I said once I could breathe again. "I don't see why not. Wild isn't much into fishing, but we could teach him."

Just the idea of Wild sitting on a riverbank sweating and swatting at bugs made me smile. I could hear him bitching already. But having him interact with my brother, having the people I loved the most with me, was worth all the complaining.

"I could drive him up if you wanted," Ethan offered. "Even your mom if she could sit next to me that long."

"She could," Jason assured him, eager as hell. "I've never been to Atlanta."

He had but didn't remember, and I wasn't about to tell him.

"We'll see... Wild has to come home first though."

The waitress came by and filled our waters, not so subtly staring at Ethan, her eyes darting between us. The whole damn town knew he was gay now, not that he cared. But every time someone looked at him like he had some kind of disease I wanted to punch them.

"Wilder's in Birmingham, right?" Ethan asked.

"Yeah..." He was too damn far away, if you asked me. "I miss him... I wish the last time we saw each other hadn't been a fight."

"You should go see him." Ethan leaned back in his chair. "Surprise him at his next stop."

"You think?" I asked. "He's busy, might not have a lot of time—"

"Trust me... he'd make time," Ethan waggled his brows. "Don't tell him you're coming and show up at the signing. He'll flip his shit."

"That's a bad word," Jason reminded him for the tenth time today.

Ethan held his hand over his mouth.

"I'm sorry," he said, muffled. And when he pulled his hand from his lips, my brother grinned.

"I shouldn't spend that much money..."

"Says who?" Ethan asked, looking at me like I had a screw loose.

"My paycheck."

"Excuse... go see your boyfriend," he whispered.

The more I thought about it, the more I wanted to make it happen. I pulled out my phone and opened up the calendar Wild had emailed me. He left Birmingham early tomorrow morning for Nashville where he would be for two days before heading to North Carolina.

"How much do you think a ticket to Nashville would cost with this short of notice?" I asked.

"Probably a million dollars," Jason said.

"Probably." Ethan chuckled. "But that's what credit cards are for, right, Jax?"

I had some money in savings, and it was reckless to spend it, especially if Jason liked that school. An image of Wild's dark eyes, his delicate neck, his skin under my fingertips flashed through my head. Christ, I could practically taste him. I needed to feel him again, stay up all night and listen to his voice as he told me about his trip. I loved the way he explained things. Everything was a story. Wild liked actions over words, he liked big fucking gestures. Spending God knows what on a plane ticket wouldn't seem so bad when I got to see the look on his face, and if I left early enough, I could make it to the signing.

"Do you think Jim will kill me if I tell him I need the next few days off?"

Ethan shrugged. "He hasn't fired Chuck or Hudson yet. I think you'll be fine…"

"You have a point," I said and opened the web browser on my phone to look for the earliest flight possible.

● ● ●

I checked my duffel a few times, making sure I had everything ready. My flight left at seven in the morning, and I didn't want to take a chance and forget something because I was tired. The ticket hadn't been as expensive as I thought it would be, but it still took a chunk out of my savings. Wild was more than worth it. Hell, I was worth it. I never did much for myself, and I figured it wasn't going to kill anybody if I did something just for me. Jim didn't fire me, didn't even seem pissed if I was being honest. I suppose he figured he would lose me soon anyway when I moved to Atlanta.

I zipped up the bag and set it on the floor. Momma's voice floated in through the open bedroom door. I strained to hear her and smiled when I realized she was singing. As quiet as I could, I walked past Jason's room. His light was off. He had already fallen asleep about an hour ago. Mom was in the kitchen, listening to the radio while she played Solitaire. She usually played Bridge with some of the ladies in town on Wednesday nights, but she hadn't been keeping up with her friends like she used to lately.

"Want some company?" I asked, as I pulled out a chair and sat down.

"You all packed up?" She placed a card on the table, her attention on the game and not me.

"Just finished..." It was quiet enough between us, I could hear the crickets outside.

"Made some iced tea today while you boys were out."

Iced tea. Small talk. No eye contact.

This was us now.

We danced around the elephant in the room about as well as a cow in heels.

"Why didn't you go out tonight?" I asked.

That got her to look at me. The circles under her eyes made her seem older than she was.

"Didn't feel much like going out." She let out a long sigh and set down the deck of cards in her hand with a slap. "This isn't easy for me, Jaxon... but I'm trying. I don't need those women telling me how to think or feel about my own damn son."

"You told them?" I asked, not knowing if I should be angry or happy that she wasn't as embarrassed by me as I'd thought.

"I told Clarice yesterday. She's never been a gossip." She spun the ring on her finger. "Guess this was even too juicy for her to keep quiet about."

I picked at a scratch in the wood of the table. "The whole town knows then?"

"Not the whole town..." She looked at me. "I shouldn't have said nothing."

A spark of resentment simmered in my gut. She'd outed me. With the way this town worked, even with Jim in Georgia, he'd find out. Maybe he already had. Probably why he didn't give a shit that I'd asked for a few days off. When Hudson and Chuck found out, there'd be hell to pay. I was glad I had a ticket out of here tomorrow.

"It's my business... you had no right." The flame in my stomach burned out when her chin started to tremor. "Please don't cry... I didn't mean to raise my voice."

She waved me off. "You can raise your voice when it counts, son. I should've known better. But that's the thing... I don't have anyone in this town to talk to about all of this who won't have something hateful to say to me."

"You can talk to me," I said, my voice wavering. "I know I've caused trouble for you, but I'm here. Even if what you've got to say might hurt. I'd rather be hurting than have you ignore me all the time."

"You didn't cause me trouble, Jax." She wiped her cheeks. "I just had this vision in my head for my boys... but nothing turned out the way I was hoping. For either of you."

"Jason might go to that school we talked about... maybe they can help him be more independent. And it might not be who you wanted me to be with, but I'm in love with Wild. I'm happy. Jason is too. Isn't that enough for you?"

"It's enough." She took my hand, her skin soft and thin and the familiar touch settled in my shoulders.

After a few seconds she let go and I couldn't hear those crickets outside anymore.

"Wanna play Rummy?" she asked.

"I get to deal?"

She started to pick up the cards. "Have I ever told you no?"

I laughed, ready to argue, when my phone rang. "It's Wild... can I..."

"Go on... I'll deal the cards while I wait."

"Thanks..." I stepped into the living room and answered the call. "Hey."

"God... keep talking... I miss your voice."

"What do you want me to say?" I asked, smiling like an idiot as I sat on the couch.

I couldn't wait to have him in my arms tomorrow.

"Anything..." Wild's voice was muffled.

"What are you doing?"

"Getting into bed, I'm fucking exhausted, and my hand hurts from signing my stupid name.... I need to rethink my signature."

My shoulders shook as I laughed. "That's a good thing though... your hand hurting. It means lots of people came to see you."

The sheets rustled on the other side of the phone, conjuring up thoughts of pale skin and sleepy brown eyes.

"My flight leaves at an ungodly hour tomorrow," he said.

"Sleep on the plane."

"I wish... it's too short of a flight. But it's first class, I'll make them bring me a gallon of coffee before we take off."

"A gallon?" I asked, my smile spreading to my ears at his theatrics.

"Maybe two," he said as he yawned. "Any news on that job yet?"

"I have an interview in two weeks."

"Shut up... really?"

"Really... You ready for a permanent roommate?" I asked.

I wanted to get my own place at first, but he refused. Said it would be a waste of money since I'd be in *his* bed every night anyway. I liked it when he put his foot down and took control.

"No... but I'm ready for my sexy-as-fuck boyfriend to move in with me."

"What if you can't write because I'm in your space?"

"Then I'll go to the coffee shop. I swear I lived there when I wrote *Love Always, Wild*. I should have had a cot in the back to sleep on, I was there so much. You should be warned... my life is a bit of a hamster wheel... I like small groups of friends and familiar places. According to my therapist, June, it's because I have abandonment issues and have to have a routine that feels safe."

"She's your therapist now?"

"Apparently."

"Well, lucky for you, I like guys who like small groups of friends and familiar places."

"I wish you were here," he said, yawning again. "How many weeks till Thanksgiving?"

I counted in my head. "Six or seven, I think. Wait... Will you be home by Thanksgiving?"

"Surprise," he said, sounding half asleep. "Bartley decided it would be a waste of money to have any events after Thanksgiving."

In less than forty-nine days he'd be home with me where he belonged.

"Is it Thanksgiving yet?" I asked.

A chuckle rumbled in my chest when I heard clear, even breathing through the phone. I closed my eyes and listened.

After a minute he whispered, "I think I fell asleep."

"Get some rest," I said, wishing it was tomorrow already.

"Hmmm. Okay."

"Love you, Wild."

"Love you, too."

Chapter 30

WILDER

This shop was the smallest on the tour so far and I loved it. From the outside it looked like a small brick cottage. The architecture like something out of a fairytale. It had this hobbit-hole-esque vibe to it, with earth tones and mossy-looking plants adorning the porch. When I'd walked in, I'd admired the rows and rows of books, and how close they'd been stacked together. Almost too close. But it was cozy and friendly, and I liked the way it smelled like pine and old paper. If time had a scent, it would be this bookshop. Ameren, the owner, had set up a large table in the back of the store and covered it with a green velvet cloth. Everything here was magical, including Ameren's beard. He looked like he'd stepped out of a fantasy novel. I half expected him to pop on a wizard's cape before the day was over.

I stretched my fingers before picking up the cup of coffee Andrew had set down only a moment ago. Having Andrew at the last stop had been helpful. I'm not sure why Bartley hadn't sent me with an assistant to begin with. I was helpless and unorganized and traveling alone wasn't in my top five favorite things. Moving through each city, by myself, had made me miss Jax even more.

Not that Andrew was any type of replacement for my boyfriend, or even that interesting to talk to, but at least he was here. I was curious if the tone of my emails and texts to Anders had clued him into my depression, and he'd packed Andrew up himself and sent him like a gift via overnight delivery.

"Thanks for the coffee," I said, tipping the cup.

"No thanks needed. It's my job." Andrew gave me a smile, and I didn't think he hated being here.

"Did Anders or Bartley send you?"

He cringed and I smiled.

"I knew it." Smug, I shook my head. "Anders is such a mother hen."

"Well, technically, it was Anders and Bartley. He just politely reminded your very generous publishing company that in the contract, they were to offer you an assistant for any business-related travel." He shrugged. "And I don't mind... I've never been to Nashville."

"Me either. But I don't think it gets better than this book shop." I glanced at the staff running back and forth through the tight spaces between the racks like hurried little mice.

I had the sudden urge to read *The Tale of Despereaux*.

"The crowd outside looks pretty decent." He sipped his coffee, hiding what looked like a mischievous grin.

"Oh no." He blinked at me with big, innocent eyes. "You know I hate surprises." Nervous, I stood, trying to peek at the front door. "Is the crowd big?"

"I'd say it is considering you're a debut. Some of the more seasoned authors I've worked for haven't drawn that big of a crowd."

"Shit, I knew I should've had you spike this latte with Sambuca."

One thing I'd learned about being on tour was I did not like large gatherings, or long lines of people staring at me. I had no idea what to say to them when they came to my table. I got anxious and shut down, and they probably thought I was an asshole or a snob. I did much better at the venues that allowed me to have a glass of wine.

"You'll be fine," he said. "I ran into one of the fans when I left to get coffee. Seems like a really nice guy."

I glared at him. "Nice guy?"

Andrew's laugh, for some ungodly reason, calmed me down.

"Jesus Christ, I don't think I'll make it past the end of the week."

"I don't know..." he said in a sing-song voice. "Something tells me today is going to be a great day."

"We're opening the doors, Mr. Welles," Ameren warned me.

"Thank you... and please... call me Wilder."

He nodded and scratched at his beard. "Will do."

One of the staff members brought me a bag of Sharpies, and I exhaled as much nervous energy as I could. I ran my fingers through my hair and shifted in my seat trying to find a comfortable position. Legs crossed? Uncrossed? I tapped my fingers on the table and chewed my lip as I heard the owner talking to the people outside.

"Stop fidgeting," Andrew said, and chuckled when I flipped him off. "That's the spirit."

I didn't think this anxiety would go away, regardless of how many of these signings I did. I was an introvert by nature, only extroverted with the people who knew me or when plied with alcohol.

"Do I look nervous?" I asked.

"Not at all."

"Liar."

"I like your outfit," he said, distracting me as a few people walked in.

I looked down at my white skinny jeans and pale-blue shirt. I didn't think I looked fantastic by any means, but I was comfortable.

"Stop trying to flatter me." I grinned. "But for real, don't stop."

"I'm not trying to flatter you. The eyeliner looks good with the light blue. I couldn't have dressed you better myself."

I looked at him and my mouth popped open. "Did Anders tell you I needed help with my wardrobe?"

He looked out toward the door. "Look, here they come."

Fucking Anders. I could dress myself, thank you very much. A few people trickled in and I plastered on a smile as they approached the table.

Through gritted teeth, I mumbled, "You tell Anders to fuck off."

"Noted." Andrew laughed as he took the book from the reader, opened it to the title page, and handed it to me.

Uncapping a Sharpie, I looked at the yellow sticky note with the girl's name on it.

Becky.

"Thank you for coming out today, Becky."

Her hands shook as she took the signed novel from my hand.

"This is one of my favorite books of all time," she said, her smile wobbling.

She looked about eighteen, or maybe even younger. I couldn't be sure. She was short, and pixie-like, and fit in with the whole theme of the bookshop.

"Thank you," I said, self-conscious. I was terrible at compliments from strangers. "Seriously, thank you, I'm really glad you liked it.

Ugh.

I sounded like a moron.

Becky gave me another excited smile, hugging the book to her chest as she walked away. Once she was out of my line of sight, the room unveiled itself, wall to wall with people. Maybe I was overwhelmed because the store was small, but the collar of my shirt suddenly felt too tight, and as I pulled on it, several people filed in along the table. Andrew did his best, opening up as many books as he could, marching people through the line in a quick and orderly fashion. His ability to keep things organized made me less frazzled, and with the speed people were ushered through, I barely had time for more than a quick smile and a thank you for each guest. My hand had started to cramp after the first hour, and I was grateful I only had thirty more minutes to go. But like Jax had reminded me last night, I was privileged to have people care about my book at all. How incredible was it that my hand had a fucking cramp because I'd just signed a mazillion books?

I took a second to crack my knuckles, and Andrew looked at me totally repulsed.

"Gross... will you grab me a soda out of the cooler?" he asked.

"Sure."

Ameren had set a cooler with an assortment of drinks next to my chair earlier. I reached down and opened the lid, grabbing myself a water as well as his soda.

"Thanks." Andrew took the can from my hand and set it on the table by a new stack of books.

I swallowed a fast gulp of water before he slid another book in my direction. With a fresh Sharpie in my hand, I glanced at the Post-it note, and my heart hiccupped.

Jax.

My eyes snapped up and landed on a familiar, gorgeous, green gaze. I dropped my marker, and I swear to God, an actual fucking squeal lodged itself in my throat, and if it wasn't for the room full of people, I probably would have knocked the table over and tackled him. Speechless, I stared up at him. He was poured into a gray cotton t-shirt, his skin newly sun-kissed. I bet he smelled like soap and sand and coconuts. Jax's biceps flexed as he rubbed the back of his neck, his lip curling up at the corner.

My skin pebbled as he spoke. "You okay?"

I raised my hand to my chest, thinking this might somehow slow my pulse. I shook my head, my throat thickening. "No..." I laughed, or maybe it was more like a choked sob. Andrew handed me a tissue and I swatted it away. Did he know about this?

Reading my mind, he held up his hands. "I had nothing to do with him showing up here, but I did see him outside when I left for the coffee shop."

Jax had been here this whole time. I had to remind myself later, when I wasn't so ecstatic, to yell at Andrew for letting Jax wait in line. I stood, my legs like Jell-O as I rounded the table, desperate to be in his orbit. The room full of people disappeared as Jax's arms engulfed me. He was warm, his muscles caging me in, and fuck my life, I might've cried a little into his t-shirt. He cupped my face, his thumbs skating across my cheeks, and kissed my forehead. The public display of affection shot straight to my heart.

"What are you doing here?" I asked through a watery laugh but kissed him before he could answer.

Jax dipped his head, parting his lips, and the room erupted with hoots and whistles. Jax smiled and ducked his head into my shoulder. I looked out at the crowd, my cheeks heating as everyone stared at us while they clapped.

Jax lifted his head, a sheepish look on his face. "I had to see you..."

"I can't believe you're here," I said my fingers clinging to the cotton of his t-shirt.

"I bought the ticket yesterday... hope it's okay I'm—"

I pressed another fast kiss to his lips, earning us another round of applause.

"I don't think I can sneak out of here," I said, and he chuckled.

"I don't suppose you could... that's alright. Finish up, I can look through all these books while I wait."

"Screw that... you're sitting with me. You just got here." I laced my fingers through his. "I'm not letting you go until I have to board another plane."

● ● ●

Jax flipped on the light and the hotel room door clicked shut behind me. Exhausted, all I wanted to do was take a shower and indulge in my boyfriend. The signing had run later than it was supposed to, but that was kind of Jax's fault. Everyone who came up to the table had something to say about our kiss. How cute we were, and how long had we been together? As uncomfortable as I'd been earlier, with Jax by my side, I could be myself. It had been a different experience, and I wished I could get Bartley to pay for Jax to come with me instead of Andrew. When I'd suggested it earlier, Andrew just laughed.

"Wow..." he said, taking in the large suite, he set down the duffel we'd picked up from the concierge after Jax had canceled his reservation. "This is the nicest place I'll ever sleep."

Behind him, I set my chin on his shoulder, my arms draping around his waist. "Who said anything about sleeping."

His laugh was grumbled and warm as he turned in my arms. "I guess sleep is overrated."

"Mm-hmm."

He leaned in and tasted my mouth with soft lips. I tucked my fingers under the waistline of his jeans, the swell of his ass hot under my touch as I pulled him against me. He bit my lip, both of us hard and trapped under denim and zippers.

"We should shower," I whispered.

"You don't want to get room service first?"

"Not unless you do?" My stomach was tangled in glorious knots having him this close. "Sex first... food later. It's the natural order of things, if you ask me."

Jax lifted me at the waist, and I clutched my legs around his hips. "I'm not gonna argue," he said as he walked us toward the bathroom.

When we walked in, the light automatically came on. The room was covered in bright white marble, almost too bright if it wasn't for the black countertop. I hadn't had a chance to clean-up before I'd left for the signing, and all my stuff was spread out in a messy disarray.

"This is bigger than my kitchen back in Bell River," he said and set me down on my feet.

The shower was huge, with two heads on either side.

"When I'm ridiculously rich we can have a bathroom like this," I said.

"You don't have to be rich... I'll build it for you."

"For us."

Jax smiled and lifted his shirt over his head. Under the shock of white light his tan skin stood out, each ridge of abs defined. He reached into the shower and turned on both faucets, testing the water with his hand until steam billowed around him. The last time I'd seen Jax I'd been angry, but he was here, and it was impossible that we'd gone through all of this in such a short time. There'd never been anyone else for me. It's always been Jaxon. It was clear to me now. I was done pushing away the people I loved.

I wet my lips as he moved toward me, each step a spike in my already-ragged pulse. He kissed me before lifting my shirt over my head. His fingertips ran down the center of my chest, his eyes cast down, watching as goosebumps lifted under his touch. I raised his chin and took his lips with a hungry kiss. His tongue danced with mine as we unbuttoned and unzipped each other. We discarded our clothes until we were skin to skin, the hot water and steam enveloping us as we stepped into the shower. Jax backed me into the wall, his skin damp as I licked the line of his jaw. Every touch I'd give him would add up to the miles we'd had between us, every taste he'd take of me, for the hours we'd been apart. I owed him that. My lips stinging from his five-o'clock shadow, I reveled in the burn of him. He gasped as I grazed the crown of his cock with my thumb. With slippery hands, I jacked us both. Jax wrapped his fingers in my hair, his mouth open as water dripped over his lips. And when I couldn't take it anymore, I kissed him, sucking on his bottom lip until he groaned.

Panting, Jax grasped my wrist. "Wanna come inside you."

"What?" I asked, wanting that more than anything.

"I got tested, I'm good."

He laid soft kisses on my chin, my cheek.

"When?"

"Last week... When you told me you'd gotten tested, before everything blew up, I'd planned on it anyway."

He stroked my cock in his hand. "I don't want nothing between us anymore."

Jax captured my lips as I exhaled into him. His hands, slick with water, covered every surface of my body until my muscles were pliant. Every time I tried to touch him, he'd move my hand, and with lips and teeth, he marked my skin. My shoulder, my hip, my thigh. Jax slid his tongue up my shaft once, and I shook with restraint as he stood. I was too close to the edge, and I needed him inside of me, raw and bare. I turned and faced the wall with the small marble bench as Jax's arms found their way around me. He was hard as stone behind me, his dick teasing the crease of my ass. He rubbed my shoulders, his touch smooth as his palm ran down my spine. I bent over, bracing myself on the bench, offering myself up to him. Jax held my hips as I looked over my shoulder. His lip pinned between his teeth, his eyes on my ass he lowered one hand. He worked me open with his fingers, my head falling forward, I breathed through the quick, sharp pain. It stung as he pushed in past the ring of muscle, but it wasn't anything I couldn't handle.

The water trickled over my skin, over my cock, every nerve ending on fire as he aligned his body with mine. I stole a glance over my shoulder again as he pressed inside me. He kept his eyes on me as inch by inch, flesh against flesh, we became one. I'd never been with anyone like this. No barriers. His heat was my heat. This was our truth, and as he moved, thrusting into me, I cried out his name. My hands slipped with each pump of his hips, a delicious scramble as his body smacked against my ass.

Jax whispered through heated grunts, his dirty prayers just for me. He told me he loved me, that my body was his, that he would never let me go again. I lifted my hips as much as I could, his hands holding me steady, the angle changed.

"God, Jax..." My entire body buzzed as the head of his dick pounded against my prostate.

Once, twice, and I was coming, moaning louder than I had any control over as it echoed through the room. My body spasmed around his cock, pulling him deeper. Jax swore, and he let go inside me, filling me with his heat. His nails dug into my skin as he caught his breath.

Overheated, my legs trembled as he pulled out. Jax lifted my body and I turned, pushing my fingers into his wet hair. He held me up, my legs weak and wobbly as his tongue slid into my mouth. Lazy kisses turned into quiet touches. Taking his time, Jax washed my hair and my body, taking inventory of every freckle, adding a few more to the list since the last time he'd seen me. I returned the favor, knowing and loving that he'd smell like me when we were done. Eventually, we got out of the shower and dried off when his stomach had growled, and the tips of my fingers had wrinkled.

I ordered room service naked, and Jax gave me a salacious grin as he pulled on a pair of blue boxer briefs. He was rocking a semi that I had plans for, but I decided food would be needed for strength.

When I hung up the phone, he sat on the bed. "I ordered burgers and fries, hope that's ok?"

"I'll never say no to a burger." He patted the bed. "Come here."

"Let me at least get pants on, we don't want to freak out the room service guy." I smiled as I dug through my suitcase and pulled out a pair of sweats.

I slipped them on without worrying about underwear and sidled up to Jax on the bed. I rested my head on his shoulder, his arm cradled around me. My fingers splayed over his stomach, my thumb drew small circles against his skin.

Hesitant, I asked, "What did your mom say... when you said you were coming to see me?"

He kissed the top of my head. "She was excited for me."

I sat up, tucking my legs underneath me. "She was?"

"It's getting better. She said all she wants is for me to be happy." He reached out and rubbed his hand over my knee. "I told her I'm happy... with you."

"And Jason... he's okay with you moving out?"

Jax sat up, a crooked smile on his lips. "I don't think he'll ever be okay... but we're looking into this rehabilitation school that has a day program. They can help him, Wild. Help him more than I ever could."

"Don't do that... don't downplay what you do for him. You're more than a brother, Jax." He took my hand in his and I tangled our fingers in my lap. "You're like a father to him."

Jax took a moment, gathering himself before he spoke again. His smile trembling, he said, "Jay wants to come up to Atlanta... I thought maybe when you got back, we could have him and my mom up for Thanksgiving."

I hadn't had a Thanksgiving since my parents cut me out of their life. June always worked and I was always alone. I tried to picture his brother and his mom sitting at my small dining table, eating turkey that I would probably have to have delivered because I was a terrible cook. It would be awkward and weird, and everything a holiday that involved a family should be, and as I twisted the image around in my head, the more I wanted it. The expectation in his eyes as he waited me out thrilled me. He wanted his family to be a part of us, and I hadn't known how much I wanted that until it became a possibility. He wanted to lay down roots, and I wanted to be the soil he'd forever call home.

"I'd love that," I said, and his entire soul illuminated around me.

"Yeah?" he asked, leaning over, he cupped my face between his strong hands.

"I just hope your family doesn't hate me."

"They're gonna love you... even my mom," he said. "When she sees how happy you make me, I gotta feeling we'll never get rid of her."

"I hope you're right."

"I should warn you though... Jay's gonna make you go fishing."

"Like... with worms and shit."

He kissed me and I gave into his willing lips.

"Don't worry," he said. "I'll bait your hook."

Epilogue

JAX

Two Years Later

"I can't believe it's almost finished," June said, her hands on her swollen belly. She walked up the driveway and kissed my sweaty cheek. "This is pure talent, Jaxon. This house is amazing."

I bent down and whispered at the bump in her belly. "Your momma is the nicest lady I know. You better be good to her."

June smacked my bare shoulder and her face crumpled as she wiped her hand on her jeans. "You and Wilder are gonna spoil this kid rotten. Gwen too."

"Isn't that what uncles are supposed to do?" I argued.

"You better rein in Wilder," she hissed. "He cannot be buying this girl all the shit she wants."

I chuckled as I set the shovel against the porch. It was almost a hundred degrees today, and not a rain cloud in sight. Which worked for me. I didn't have time to waste getting this sprinkler system installed.

"I can't make any promises. What he wants he gets. You know that man owns me."

She rolled her eyes as she stalked past me. "I assume he's inside. Heaven forbid he gets his hands dirty."

I wanted to tell June he was pretty good at getting dirty when he wanted to, but I figured she wouldn't appreciate that kind of crude humor.

"Yeah, he's inside with Jason and my mom. She's teaching him how to make apple cobbler." I smirked. "You might wanna go in and save him for a spell."

"Oh hell, this should be good."

I followed June inside, the smell of cinnamon masked the layer of fresh paint I'd thrown up in the guest bathroom last night.

"You've done a lot," June said as we walked into the living room.

I'd built this house from the foundation up. I had help from a few of the guys I had working for me. My old boss drafted the design exactly how I wanted it. I was glad Jim hadn't given a shit about my sexuality, as for Hudson and Chuck, I didn't mind that I'd never have to see them again in my life. It had taken me six months to get the house to a place where we could move in. Two bedrooms all on the bottom floor. The main bedroom was upstairs, with a shower almost exactly like the one at that hotel we'd stayed at in Nashville during Wild's first book tour. I'd sanded the wood floors myself, laid the stone for the fireplace. With just starting my own contracting business, I had to pinch pennies when I could.

June stopped in her tracks, her laugh filling the room. "Oh my God, I don't think I've ever seen you look so miserable."

Momma covered her grin with her hand as Wild

wiped flour off his face with his fingers. "Not in the mood for your bullshit... June"

"Mind your language, son, there are women present." Mom clicked her tongue and Wild gave me a pointed look. "How are you feeling, honey," she asked June.

"Fat," June said and sank down onto a bar stool. Rosie nudged at her hand until she gave in and pet her.

"You're glowing. How many more weeks?" Momma asked, shooing Gandalf off the counter.

"Two... But I'm thinking with this heat I might go early. Last time I worked, the charge nurse said I was dilated to a three."

"Wait?" Wild wrinkled his nose. "Your charge nurse put her hand up your va—"

"I almost got the sprinklers in," I said, smiling when my mom blushed.

Jason came out of the guest bathroom, his eyes wide when he saw June. "I didn't know you were here. Where's Gwen?"

"Picked up an extra shift at the hospital," she said as he gave her a hug.

"I'm thinking of going to the park tonight to shoot some hoops," I said. "If you and Momma don't have anything planned, you wanna come with me, Jay?"

"I'm not very good." He stared at the mess on Wild's face.

"Remember what Ms. Wilson said, you have to keep trying, even if it's hard." Wild bumped his shoulder into Jason's. "I think you're better than you think."

"What happened to your face?" Jason wiped a patch

of flour from Wild's nose.

"Your mom is torturing me again," he said. "I don't know what's worse... Cooking or fishing."

"Cooking," Jason and I said in unison.

"See... I told you, Barb, cooking is the *absolute* worst."

"When you're done whining," she said, "Would you hand me that."

My husband, looking completely disheveled and cute as hell, handed her the cobbler he'd been working on.

Jason snickered as she shoved it in the oven. "Hopefully all your hard work will be worth it when it's finished."

"Or poison us all," he grumbled under his breath.

I placed my hand at the nape of his neck. Not caring that I had dirt under my nails, or that I probably stunk to high heaven, I pulled him in for a kiss.

"It'll be delicious," I said, and kissed him one more time for good measure.

"I like when you smell like you've been rolling in dirt all day," Wild said, smiling against my lips.

"We don't need to know about any of that," June said, and my mom laughed.

"I better head home or I won't have time to stop at the supermarket," Mom said. "Remember what I told you, if the crust isn't golden, leave it in a little while longer."

"Yes, ma'am." Wild pulled her into a side hug. "I'm sorry I'm such a disappointing student."

She patted his chest, the interaction making my cheeks hurt as I smiled. She'd come such a long way since that first Thanksgiving, and like I'd told Wild, once she'd seen how happy he'd made me, she'd fallen in love with him too. Mom and Jason had moved up to Atlanta about three months ago. The resources here for Jason were much better, and honestly, I hated having him and my mom so far away. When Ethan moved to Colorado with his boyfriend Chance, they'd lost their last tie to Bell River. Mom had said she didn't fit in much there anymore anyway. She'd left her old church for one of those new, all-accepting-non-denominational-type churches. She'd sold the house and got a condo about twenty minutes from us. It felt right, having them here, leaving behind that old river that had tried so hard to keep us under water. And, I figured Jason would have to stay with us permanently one day, when Momma couldn't tend to him on her own anymore. It's why I'd built this house as big as I did. I wanted him to have his own space, and I wanted a space just for me and my husband. When Wild married me in January, I made it my goal to make us a home worth all the love he'd given me. There was work to be done, little things here and there, but every day it looked and felt more like how I'd imagined.

Momma kissed me on the cheek. "I'll bring him 'round later if he wants to come over. He might be tired."

"Just give me a call," I said.

Jason and my mom got another round of hugs from Wild and June before I walked them out.

The sun made the gray in my mom's hair shine as I opened the front door, and for some reason, it'd knocked the wind out of me, tying a knot in my chest.

"What's the matter, honey?"

I pulled her into my chest, ignoring her when she

fussed about the dirt on my hands. After a second, she leaned into me, her arms hugging me tight.

"Thank you for coming over today," I said, reluctant to let her go. "He may fight you on it, but this means a lot to him... you teaching him my favorite recipes."

"That man looks at you like you've bottled the sun just for him... I'll teach him anything he wants to know as long as he keeps loving you like that."

"You can't bottle the sun," Jason said. "It's too hot."

Laughing, I hugged him too, and he groaned when I messed up his hair. I couldn't make myself shut the door until they pulled away.

June and Wild were talking when I walked through the living room. Wild rolled his eyes, dramatic as ever, as June barked at him about something. His eyes met mine as I entered the kitchen, the smile he had for me, reeled me in. I draped my arms around his waist, and he snuggled his back against me.

He lifted my hand to his lips and kissed my knuckles, unraveling that knot in my chest.

I never thought I'd have this.

A life with love and family and pride.

Wild was too animated, jumping on whatever June had tried to say. I didn't think he'd hear it, but in this moment, when everything was good and whole, it had to be said.

I kissed the soft curve of his neck, and he shivered as I whispered, "Love you, Wild... Always."

THE END

https://spoti.fi/32SzfnB

Playlist

What a crazy ride this last year has been, am I right? *Wild* will be the first book I've published in over a year, and there is no way I could have done it without some awesome people by my side.

First of all, I have to thank my freaking fantastic readers. Y'all stuck by me while I bounced around from book to book, while I cried about my stress, and gave me strength when I needed it most. Thank you so much from the bottom of my heart for holding out!!!!

Thank you to Gwen and Amanda: "The Pretty" for helping me flesh out the idea in my head and helping me finally plot a goddamn story worth writing. And Braxton, thank you for enlightening me on so many things. I solemnly swear I'll never stroke a length ever again. I feel like I've finally earned my wings. To Beth and Jodi, I promise Anders will get a hot enemies-to-lovers book, just not with Ethan. Thank you for all the support y'all have given me. I don't deserve you. To my beta team, Elle, Ari, Cornelia, Alissa, Sarah, Anna, Taylor, Sheila, Sammie, Braxton, Kristy and Lucy, y'all are my rock. To Marley Valentine, my therapist... I owe you. And Linda at Foreword for believing in *Wild*. And Murphy and Ashley for this gorgeous damn cover.

Acknowledgements

To all my friends, you know who you are. I love you so damn much it hurts. Thank you for the daily conversations, the tears and the love. I feel you too.

To my editors Elaine and Kathleen, my books would not be books without you. And thank God y'all know about commas and keep my plots as perfect as possible!

To Ari... I can't say much without crying, but you stepped in when I needed you most and picked up the pieces left behind, and without you I would have probably drowned. Thank you for running all the magic behind the scenes. Thank you for running my amazing ST. Biscuits, I love you!!! Ari, you are truly a miracle, even with the plague.

To my family, thank for dealing with the late nights, the pizza, the McDonald's, and zombie Mom. To my babies who will probably never read this, you are the reason I exist.

Last, but certainly not least, to 2020, thank you for showing me the world and it's true colors, thank you for ripping away the falsehoods and the lies and exposing the truth.

Here's hoping 2021 will be the beginning of something great.

Black Lives Matter and Love is Love. Remember

that. <3

Much love and side hugs,
Amanda Johnson

Other Books

Forever Still Series:

Still Life

Still Water

Still Surviving

Avenues Ink Series:

Possession

Kingdom

Poet

Twin Hearts Series:

Let There Be Light

Seven Shades of You

Made in the USA
Monee, IL
14 March 2022